THE CHOCOLATE LOVERS' DIET

Also by Carole Matthews

THE CHOCOLATE LOVERS' DIET

Carole Matthews

headline
review

First published in 2007 by HEADLINE REVIEW
An imprint of HEADLINE PUBLISHING GROUP

Apart fron this publication may o ny form, or by any m ublishers or, in the with the term g Agency.

All chai resemblance t lental.

Cataloguing in Publication Data is available from the British Library

978 0 7553 3585 5 (hardback)
978 0 7553 3586 2 (trade paperback)

Typeset in Bembo by Palimpsest Book Production Limited,
Grangemouth, Stirlingshire

Printed and bound in Great Britain by
Mackays of Chatham plc, Chatham, Kent

Headline's policy is to use papers that are natural, renewable and
recyclable products and made from wood grown in sustainable forests.
The logging and manufacturing processes are expected to conform
to the environmental regulations of the country of origin.

HEADLINE PUBLISHING GROUP
A division of Hachette Livre UK Ltd
338 Euston Road
London NW1 3BH

www.reviewbooks.co.uk
www.headline.co.uk

It's about time that I gave a big-up to some of our friends who help to keep me relatively sane and grounded – mainly by constantly reminding me that I haven't got a real job – and who don't mind being subjected on a regular basis to my experimental chocolate desserts, particularly in the name of research.

In no particular order – I don't want to be accused of favouritism or the invites to the barbecues will dry up – this book is for:

The Tattenhoe Posse – Lee and Marcia, Albert and Ayesha, Gavin and Angela, Paul and Alison, Martin and Lyn next door, Barry and Ruth.

The Old Timers (in terms of length of friendship, not age) – Sue and Roger, Martin and Sally, Donna and Malcolm, Chris and Jim, Mad Mike Bentham and Tina 'Donks'. Dave 'The Rave' Sivers and Chris. Paul and Paula. Vivien and John Garner. Tom and Julie 'Bling, Bling' Reid. Tony 'Captain Baldy' Kirkby and Cindy. Adrian and Amanda. Marjorie and Norman Peebles – my unofficial Northern PR team. Jeremy, Suzannah and girls. Hazel 'Careless Whisper' Ketley, hubby Dennis and their lovely family who have been such staunch supporters over the years.

The Ladies Who Lunch – Lynne, Lesley and Heather. And to the ladies at The Boot who treat us so nicely and never mind us shrieking with laughter. (Or if they do they don't tell us . . .)

Sorry if I've forgotten anyone, but that's what comes of having a sieve for a brain. Lovely Kev and I love you all. Thanks for being our friends.

Chapter One

There are two types of women, I've found. There are those who are addicted to chocolate and there are bitches. Bitches are the sort of women who say, 'Oh, I couldn't possibly eat a *whole* Mars Bar, they're *so* sickly!' Or, 'I find *one* square of dark chocolate is *more* than enough, don't you?' Or, even worse, 'I'm not really that *keen* on chocolate. I'm more of a savoury person.' All said whilst nibbling conservatively on a Twiglet as if it's a sufficient substitute for sheer pleasure. What's all that about?

We, the members of The Chocolate Lovers' Club, are out-and-out addicts. We love the world's finest foodstuff in all its varied forms. No shame in that.

Today, my good friends and I are assembled at our club headquarters, a cosy haven in one of London's more salubrious back streets. It's called Chocolate Heaven – and chocolate heaven it is.

It's also a week before Christmas and I'd like to describe an outdoor scene of Dickensian snowiness and charm, but I can't because this is London in the era of global warming and, as such, the sky is school-skirt grey, it's sheeting down with rain and there's a gale blowing. We care not. Despite the elements raging around us we're out in force. Chantal, Autumn, Nadia and I, Lucy Lombard – chocoholic supreme and founder member of the club – are hunkered down on the sofa in front of the fire. It might not be a roaring log fire, but it's the modern gas equivalent and works just as well for us, as we're dug in for the duration. Frankly, no one else is going to get anywhere near our prime space this side of closing time. We have a plate of chocolate fancies in front of us – featherlight sponge topped with a swirl of cappuccino icing – and some delectable fudge brownies. There's also a selection of

1

the finest truffles known to man made with fresh cream and Madagascar chocolate – a personal favourite. Because they're made of fresh cream they only last for a couple of days – as if that's ever going to be a problem! Believe me, this is the closest you can get to an orgasm in a public place. A little appreciative moan escapes my lips.

The owners of Chocolate Heaven, Clive and Tristan, are gloriously gay men – you're not going to get straight guys running a chocolate shop, right? – who indulge us as we're their best customers by far. If they'd let us rope off this area and have a *VIPS ONLY* sign put up just for us then we would, but they churlishly insist on having other customers in this place even though they don't eat nearly as much chocolate as we do.

Our damp coats are steaming gently in a heap next to us. My youthful blond bob, styled into a wondrous arrangement with a pair of straightening irons and pound of Frizz-ease, is now clamped flat to my head. Still, things are looking up. We all have glasses of hot chocolate, spiked with the intense flavour of red chilli and topped with a veritable excess of whipped cream. My taste buds don't know whether to swoon or set on fire. Contentment is but a hair's breadth away. Well, it would be, except for one slight snag.

On the wall of Chocolate Heaven there is a cheery, pottery plaque. Clive, in festive mood, has covered it with a swathe of silver tinsel. It reads:

Survival tips for times of stress

1. Take deep breaths
2. Count to ten
3. Eat chocolate

This is our policy statement. Our solemn edict for the way we live our lives. I take a deep breath, get as far as three, then I push in another truffle. A deep sigh of relief escapes before I can edit it out. This is a time of *great* stress. I'm wearing my knickers that bear the legend FORGET FALLING IN LOVE, I WANT TO FALL IN CHOCOLATE – which might give you some hint as to the nature of my predicament.

'Haven't you heard from Crush yet?' Nadia wants to know from beneath her frothy, cream moustache.

And that's the slight snag. I shake my head. My current boyfriend, Mr Aiden Holby – aka Crush – is presently Missing In Action. In Australia.

Somehow, being MIA in Australia, on the other side of the globe, makes it worse. If he was MIA in, say, Belsize Park, then I could go round there on the bus or Tube and bang on his door at regular intervals until I could find out exactly what was happening. As it is, I'm a bit stuck. My fervent emails to him have remained unanswered. My calm but concerned phone calls to him all trip straight to voicemail and, even though his computer tells mine that he's online, there's no response. I know not why. We were having long, transcontinental calls via our respective webcams – some of which were getting rather pleasantly steamy. Long live modern technology! Then nothing. Absolutely nothing.

'I can't understand it,' I say. 'It's not like him.'

Chantal snorts, loudly. It's a snort that says, 'He's a bloke, what do you expect?'

'Really,' I insist. 'He's not like other guys.' For 'other guys' read he's not like Marcus, my bastard, bollocky, recently ex-fiancé, who was the most unfaithful man on the planet. Even if you count Bill Clinton, Tom Jones and Darren Day.

My American friend with the perfect hair and the overflowing bank account snorts again. I try to bite my lip. Even though she's one of my very best mates in the world, relations between Chantal and me are still a little strained at the moment. This is due to the fact that she dated my ex-boyfriend – not Marcus, but another, much nicer one called Jacob. It's a very confusing time for me right now. My love-life has been the romantic equivalent of a major pile-up on the M1. Tangled metal, sirens wailing, total grid-lock, destruction, bodies everywhere. Excuse me, but I'll have to ingest some more chocolate simply to keep my system going . . .

Let me fill you in while my chocolate hit kicks in. Jacob and I enjoyed a brief but mutually satisfying fling, despite never having got down and really dirty, through a combination of very unfortunate circumstances. He was, unlike Marcus, a very lovely guy. Although the shine did rather go off the relationship when I discovered his chosen method of earning a living. Jacob told me he worked in the leisure industry, which wasn't strictly a lie. It was just that he turned out to be a male prostitute. Why do I always find out that the men in my life have hidden depths way, way too late? My dear friend, Chantal, *did* know about Jacob's choice of employment, however. And, I suppose, all things considered, that she didn't really date him, she simply rented him by the hour. The knowledge that she slept with Jacob, even in a professional capacity – while I didn't get anywhere near his underwear despite wanting to – has, as you can imagine, left things somewhat scratchy between us. Then I got back with Marcus which was a Big Mistake to end all Big Mistakes. He just proved to me that, basically, he cannot be trusted as far as I can throw him. He will never change his philandering ways and I will never again believe that he will. That phase of my life is now over. The debris has been cleared, the motorway of my life is flowing smoothly once more. I've matured emotionally and have moved on. Thankfully, I'm now in a loving relationship with my old boss, Aiden 'Crush' Holby. Except that he seems to be temporarily misplaced. Maybe it's nothing more than a pesky traffic cone in the way.

'Aiden will turn up,' Autumn says, as if she's talking about some slippers that I've recently lost. She twines a finger round one of her crazy, red curls and gazes earnestly at me. I'd love to be like Autumn, whose glass is perpetually more than half-full. I mainly have one solitary drip left lurking miserably at the bottom. 'There'll be a perfectly plausible explanation,' she continues. 'You just wait and see.'

'I'll try him again later,' I tell them. Then I stuff in a few truffles in a desperate manner and my aloof façade is completely blown.

Keeping a relationship going over such differing time zones

was, I guess, always going to be a trial, but – believe me – Crush is worth it. He's lovely, lovely, lovely. By far and away the best boyfriend I've ever had, and while it may not be an extensive list, there have been a few.

Aiden Holby and I both work for Targa, a data recovery company that, well, recover data. Don't ask me anything more technical than that. As I've said, Aiden was my boss, which is where my little 'crush' on him began – hence the nickname foisted upon him by The Chocolate Lovers' Club. Now Crush has been promoted to Head of International Something-or-another, terribly important, and that's why he's in The Land Down Under while I'm stuck in London in the Sales Department in a temporary and unspecified role and pretty much pass the time trying to avoid doing anything too taxing. I may be the most permanent temp that Targa has ever had, but I don't intend spending the rest of my days there. Oh no. I'm waiting to find my pre-destined role in life, you could say. Which, of course, is currently eluding me.

I was supposed to be joining Crush in Sydney to start a new life of fun and frolics as a bona fide, signed-up, full-time girl-friend. We were going to live together and everything. The whole Happy Ever After. But, as luck would have it, I broke my leg falling downstairs when some of the practice frolicking got a bit out of hand. Then, to add insult to injury, I was banned from flying for weeks due to my cumbersome plaster cast.

Crush had to zoom off to Australia without me – an import-ant job waits for no man. But he was supposed to be getting things ready so that I could join him as soon as possible. However, now that my fractured limb is mended and the plaster has come off, I can't afford the air fare out there at this time of goodwill and extortionately jacked-up prices. And, in the meantime, lovely overseas boyfriend Crush, it seems, has vanished from the face of the earth.

'You don't know if he's coming home for Christmas then?' Nadia says.

'No. He did talk about it, but . . .' But he hasn't been returning my bloody phone messages, emails or anything. Instead of checking out the beer, barbecues and Bondi Beach, aforementioned boyfriend has gone walkabout. This definitely calls for more chocolate and a reinforcement of our policy statement. A bit of that fudge brownie looks as if it will just do the job.

Breathe. Count. Eat. Mmm. Ah, that's better . . .

Chapter Two

Whoever said money couldn't buy you happiness clearly didn't spend their cash on chocolate. After a lazy few hours with my friends consuming our favourite food – the fancies, truffles and fudge brownies are long gone – there's a rosy glow to my cheeks and a warm fullness in my tummy. I'm feeling very mellow and am finally starting to allow in something of the Christmas spirit. Am I the only person who thinks Christmas should come along only once every five years? That would be great. Once a year is far too often. I've barely put my decorations away when, lo and behold, it's deemed time to dust them off again. The only thing I'd miss are all the lovely special Christmas chocolates – selection boxes, chocolate coins, two-pound boxes of Milk Tray with snowflaked cellophane wrapping which it is technically possible to eat in one sitting.

Every year, despite vowing not to, I've somehow mega-maxed my credit card to buy Marcus my ex-fiancé something wildly extravagant that he probably didn't need and, most certainly, never appreciated. It's not much fun being in debt well into June just so that my once dearly-beloved could go racing round a track in an Aston Martin DB9, experience the joy of hang-gliding or float serenely across the sky in a hot air balloon, glass of champagne in hand. But then he always bought me such wonderful Christmas presents that I felt as if I had to reciprocate, sometimes even compete. When he was buying me a day out at a fabulous health spa or a gargantuan box of Belgian delights, I couldn't just wrap him a Greatest Hits CD and some cheap smellies, could I? Crush is a much more down-to-earth kind of guy and I'm sure that he will be more than happy with a small token of my love. Another great reason to be rid of Marcus.

Flopping down on my sofa, I undo the top button on my jeans and let my stomach sag comfortably. Controlling my chocolate consumption is a nightmare at this time of year; the temptation of all those tins of Quality Street, Celebrations, chocolate-covered brazil nuts and Terry's Chocolate Orange by the ton, is more than one woman should have to bear. And what about the metre-long boxes of Cadbury's Chocolate Fingers that you *have* to eat to be polite because someone in the office thought it would be fun to buy you one? Mmm. One of those little suckers is never enough, is it? I bet I could get into the *Guinness Book of Records* with the world's fastest consumption of a metre of Chocolate Fingers. Think of all the training I could do. My outlook suddenly brightens. Yes, maybe Christmas isn't so bad after all.

For reasons best known to myself, I've made a bit of an effort to spruce up my rather shabby lounge. Perhaps it was because I hoped that Crush might be coming home for a Yuletide visit. I've bought a real tree from Camden Market – not too much effort as the market is directly opposite my flat and the bloke, in a rush of unexpected seasonal goodwill, even carried it here for me. Though it did set me back nearly twenty quid. And I did give him a big tip. Now it's draped with red chilli-pepper lights which are winking on and off festively and not a little soporifically. It's supposed to be some indestructible strain of blue spruce or something, but already there's a growing pile of pine needles on my carpet. At this rate, it will be bald as a coot before Boxing Day. Maybe I've been sold a pup. No wonder the guy was in a hurry to get rid of it. So much for goodwill to men – or women – and all that.

I watch the lights on the tree some more and start to send myself into a trance. Before my eyes close completely, I decide to phone Crush again.

It's late afternoon here which makes it – oh, I don't know, probably some completely unsociable hour in Crush's world. It's virtually impossible to find a time to call him when we're both supposed to be awake and not at work. Australia, I'm sure, is a great country; I just wish it were a little nearer. Like just beyond Ireland, so that easyJet could get me there for less than the price of this rapidly moulting Christmas tree.

What will we do if Crush does manage to come home over the holidays, I wonder. I can see us taking long walks on Hampstead Heath, both wrapped up in soft, stylish woollies in primary colours – possibly from Gap – against the crisp, white frost. I can see us toasting marshmallows in front of an open fire, even though I don't actually possess an open fire and generally eschew marshmallows as inferior confectionery due to the absence of chocolate content. I can see us doing all kinds of furtively festive things on the floor beneath my fading fir tree and flashing chilli lights.

I nip into the bathroom to give my hair a quick rake with a brush. Let's face it, webcams don't generally show you in the best of lights and I want to give the air of not having tried too hard, but not looking too scruffy either. Casual glamour is a very hard look to achieve. Slicking on some lip gloss, I decide that I'm ready to meet in cyberspace with my loved one.

I log on to my computer and wait to see if my boyfriend is there waiting at the other end. But instead of Crush's lovely face looming large in front of me on the webcam, there's suddenly a very pretty woman on the screen.

'Hi,' she says at me, rather sleepily.

I can't speak. I'm too busy staring at the slutty underwear she's got on. It's black and very lacy with bright pink embroidery on it. The sort of underwear you wouldn't want to be caught wearing in the Accident and Emergency Department of your local hospital. The sort of underwear that doesn't look good on women with cellulite.

She whacks the computer on the top of its head. 'I can't hear anything,' she complains. 'Hello? Hello?' Then the woman turns and speaks over her shoulder. 'Did you leave this thing on? I think someone's trying to get through.' Whack. Whack.

Still my voice won't come.

'Ugg.' She purses her lips. 'All I have is the view of the inside of someone's nose.'

I back away from the camera.

'Here,' she says. 'See if you can make it work.' Then she moves her wondrously trim figure out of the way and, frankly, the inside of my nose is nothing compared to the view that *I* now have.

Lying on the bed behind this . . . this *tart* . . . is a naked man. A very naked man. Bottom in the air. Not even a sheet covering his modesty. I must at this point mention that Crush and I have never been involved in an intimate situation of this nature, so I don't instantly recognise the bare bottom. But who else's bottom could it possibly be? I wonder if I've somehow managed to hook up with the wrong computer. Can I possibly have contacted the wrong person in cyberspace and this lovely, if rather underdressed, woman is not really in my boyfriend's bedroom? Unfortunately, I somehow don't think so. I'm sure this is Aiden's computer. And those are definitely his curtains and his wallpaper. Which means they are actually in Crush's bed. Her with her little matching bra and briefs and him and his buck-naked arse.

It's a very fine bottom, I have to say. But I don't really want to make acquaintance with it in this context. I'm blinking rapidly, as if one of the blinks will change the frame and will come up with a different and less disturbing image.

'Maybe it's for you,' Miss Skanky Pants says over her shoulder. 'Who would be calling at this hour?'

'Here, let me look.' The voice doesn't sound an awful lot like Crush, but then again that could be distortion due to the length of the airwaves or microwaves or something.

It's definitely an English accent. No doubt about that. The naked man starts to move and I decide that I don't want to see any more, that I've already seen enough. This is *such* a familiar scenario for me. I've been the victim of this kind of betrayal more times than I care to remember. Marcus was the past master at it. Now it seems that Aiden Holby has taken over the baton from him.

I don't want Crush to see me, mouth gaping open, brain frozen, fatter and more frumpy than the woman he's with, so I quickly log off. Then I sit staring at the computer, not knowing what to do. My palms are sweaty and my eyes are burning hot with tears. I dig my fingernails into my palms. I will not cry over this. I *will not* cry over this. I will calmly, and with a supreme degree of control that I never knew possible, carry on with my life as if this had never happened. I will not entertain any further thoughts of a lovely new life in Australia with a hunky man. I will leave him to get on with his new, ridiculously slim girlfriend without me. I will stop phoning or bothering Mr Aiden Holby in any way and he will simply cease to exist in my world. That's what I'll do.

Taking a Mars Bar from my emergency stash next to my computer, I sit and stare at it blankly. This is such a shame because Crush was really, really nice and I really, really liked him and I did so hope that things would be different this time. What's so wrong with me that no one can remain faithful to me for more than ten minutes? Fuck the flipping deep breath. And the poxy counting. I unwrap the Mars Bar and take a big bite from it. A humungously big bite. Then I think, Sod it, and I cry too.

Chapter Three

'Does this mean that Crush won't be coming home for Christmas?' Autumn is wide-eyed with shock. But then Autumn is often wide-eyed with things.

What would we all have to talk about, I wonder, if my love-life wasn't such a disaster zone? I stare morosely at my cup. 'I guess not.'

Barely twenty-fours hours have passed since our last meeting and already I've had to text my best girls with a CHOCOLATE EMERGENCY. As always, they came running as fast as they could to my aid.

It's still effectively brunch, so Clive has served us with some warm, homemade *pain au chocolat* and some necessarily strong coffee. A selection of festive hits are playing on the stereo and, to be honest, I'd like to smash the speakers. Bing and his flipping 'White Christmas' is currently doing my head in. I'm not dreaming of a white Christmas, I'm dreaming of a very drunken one. And I'd like it to start as soon as possible.

'Do you think Crush realised that it was you on the other end of the webcam?' Nadia wants to know.

'If he did, then he hasn't tried to contact me.' Which is a good job for Aiden 'Bare-Bum' Holby. There are approximately seven thousand swear words in the English language and I know virtually all of them. I would have shared that knowledge with him. Very loudly.

'You're not going to be alone over the holidays?' Chantal asks.

'No. No.' I shake my head vehemently. 'No, no, no.' Actually, I am.

The thing with expecting Aiden Holby to come home and

sweep me into his arms beneath the mistletoe is that I've turned down all manner of exciting invitations simply to keep my time free to be with him. Well, I turned down an invitation from my dear mother to go to Spain to stay with her and her ageing, balding man, The Millionaire, and watch them cooing over each other like teenagers. Particularly horny teenagers. And one from my dad to go to the South Coast to spend my time watching him and his peroxide paramour, The Hairdresser, press themselves up against each other at inopportune moments. Frankly, with those choices I'd rather it was just me, bad telly and a family-size tin of Cadbury's Roses. And it looks as if that's exactly what I'm going to get.

'Hey, maybe you could come over and have your Christmas lunch with me and Ted?'

'I'll be fine. Really.' Chantal and Ted are still on very shaky ground after their recent acrimonious split. He wants kids – she doesn't. She wants loads of sex – he doesn't. Not sure how the possibility of procreation is going to fit in with that scenario – which is, I guess, the crux of the matter.

Chantal, as a sort of empty revenge for her husband's lack of libido, has been extensively continuing her sex-life with all comers. It's led her into some very tricky situations, I can tell you. Frankly, Ted doesn't know the half of it. He has no idea about Jacob The Male Escort or, even worse, Mr Smith The Gentleman Thief who had a one-night stand with our libidinous friend and then relieved her of thirty grand's worth of jewellery. Who says that the sex-life of a married woman can't be exciting, eh? Unfortunately, the only person it seems that Chantal *wasn't* sleeping with was her dear husband. But that's all in the past. Sort of. Now they're trying to make a go of their relationship, but Ted is blowing very hot and cold. One minute he thinks that they can repair their marriage, the next he's not answering Chantal's calls. I'd imagine that when your husband has found out that you've been indiscriminately sleeping with all and sundry – including one of my boyfriends – it's not going to be an easy wound to heal.

Chantal is still living separately from Ted, but they've agreed to spend the time together over Christmas. Which has to be good, right? But I *so* don't want to be a gooseberry in between those two. No way, Jose. Can you imagine it?

'Are you going to see Addison over the holidays?' Nadia asks Autumn.

'Yes,' Autumn responds, but she does it in such a distracted way that we decide not to pursue the subject.

Addison is Autumn's new boyfriend and they're totally loved-up. Which is good, because Addison has been Autumn's only boyfriend since time began as she doesn't have time for men as she's so busy Doing Good. It's really great to see that Autumn is actually doing something that she wants to do rather than propping up her lame, drug-dealing brother and her lame, drug-taking clients at the KICK IT! programme she works on.

Her brother, Richard, is currently still in rehab in California or Arizona or Nevada – one of the American states ending in 'a' – although he absconded out there to escape a posse of thugs who were after his blood rather than through having seen the error of his druggie ways.

'How's Richard doing?' I ask.

'He's okay.' Autumn shrugs. 'His emails are very sporadic. Apparently, the clinic limits his time on the computer.'

Very sensible too. Look at all the trouble computers can get you into if you begin to rely on them. I clench my jaw firmly, so that I won't be tempted to cry again.

'He's not coming home?' I squeak.

'No,' she says. 'Thankfully, my parents have very deep pockets. I'm sure Rich will stay away for as long as they continue to fund him.'

'I'm dreading it,' Nadia pipes up. 'I'm dreading the whole bloody thing. The last thing I need is any more expense.'

Nadia's a beautiful, British Asian woman and, if I were her, I'd dredge up something from my cultural background – or, frankly, make it up – so that I'd got a perfect excuse for having absolutely nothing whatsoever to do with Christmas. There's got to be something, right?

'I used to love it when I was a kid.' She shakes her head. 'Now it's so horribly commercial. Why on earth do we do it?'

Nadia and her husband, Toby, are also recently estranged. Which, on the positive side, means that it isn't only my love-life that's a disaster zone. In present company, we'd still have plenty to talk about.

Toby had become seriously addicted to internet gambling and was on the fast-track to ruining their lives with his expensive obsession. They're absolutely up to their eyeballs in debt. But he's supposed to be clean now – if that's the right term for a reformed gambler? Nadia's precarious finances mean that the rest of The Chocolate Lovers' Club bankroll her visits to Chocolate Heaven, but it's a small price to pay to enable our friend to continue to use her sanctuary. Besides, out of all of us, Nadia eats the least chocolate, so her bills are relatively small.

'Toby and I are going to spend the day playing happy families for Lewis's sake,' Nadia continues. 'It's such a farce. I just wish it would all go away.'

Christmas, I suppose, is a great time of year if you're a happy, shiny person with no troubles in the world. For the rest of us, it's the time of year that seems to show up your shitty little life in the worst possible light.

'Blimey,' I say. 'We're all going to be slitting our throats before Christmas Eve. It can't be that bad.'

Chantal and Nadia glare at me. Even Autumn joins in.

'Think of all the special edition chocolates,' I coax them. 'The selection boxes, the chocolate tree decorations. Chocolate advent calendars. What better way to start a day?' I'm on a roll. 'The over-size bars of Galaxy. Whopping great Toblerones.' Four pairs of eyes widen involuntarily at that. Who could resist those triangles of Swiss milk chocolate laced with honey and almond nougat? Not me, for one. Even though it meant the risk of losing a tooth. I look at my friends. 'Surely those will see us through the dark times?'

'Maybe you're right,' Autumn says anxiously. She reaches for the last comforting morsel of *pain au chocolat*. 'Maybe we're panicking unnecessarily.'

Then Clive pops up beside us with more choccy supplies and some fresh coffee which he puts down on the table. He's whistling 'It'll Be Lonely This Christmas' softly to himself. 'How are my darlings today?' he asks chirpily. 'Looking forward to Christmas?'

In unison, we all reach out for a cushion and, with a certain unrestrained venom, throw them at him.

'I was only asking,' he mutters at us as he rearranges his soft furnishings in a more orderly fashion.

My friends, arms folded, fear in their eyes, are still looking too unsettled for my liking.

'We can do it,' I assure them as I hand round the *grand cru* truffles Clive brought for us. 'We can get through this. If we have enough chocolate.'

Chapter Four

This is my cunning diet plan to see me through the Christmas period. I reckon if I work out like a mad thing now, then I can have some extra calories in hand to cope with my annual Christmas greedfest. Like everything in life, it's all a matter of achieving a balance.

The bad thing is that I've left it a little late to start this new regime – like by about six months. So, at the moment, I'm actually ten thousand calories or so down on where I need to be. That's hardly any Toffee Crisps at all. Maybe less than one Terry's Chocolate Orange. No wonder I'm in severe panic mode. Christmas will be utterly miserable if I'm both alone *and* can't gorge myself on chocolate. That is more than one person should be forced to tolerate – although I have vowed not to over-indulge this year. But then I'm working on the premise that I've vowed not to over-indulge for approximately the last fifteen years and I always have.

To combat my current calorie deficit, I'm leaping around my lounge like a woman possessed by something entirely demonic and shaking the floor of my flat. I have Nell McAndrew's *Ultimate Challenge, Ultimate Results* on fast forward and, ultimately, I'm struggling to keep up with it. Oh, to have such toned thighs and such a ping-pong-ball-sized bottom. How does she do it? I bet not so much as a morsel of Twix ever passes her pouting lips. Am I permanently destined to look like the 'before' picture on a 'before and after' comparison? I huff and puff a bit more. I'm going to do this DVD three times more and then I'm going to have a Bounty Bar as a reward – which I will, of course, deduct from the chocolate I'm planning to eat over the next few days.

Christmas Eve is tomorrow and still no call from Crush. To say that I'm devastated is an understatement. I'm well and truly 'crushed'. Maybe a little tear mingles with some sweat as I do my leg curls and knee lifts and thigh-ripping lunges and goodness only knows what else. I was looking forward to a very romantic Christmas for once. It only goes to show what can happen when you get too wrapped up in a lovely, unrealistic dream. At the age of thirty-two, you'd think that I'd be able to spot a bastard a mile away, but somehow I still manage to see the best in everyone – until, inevitably, I'm shown otherwise.

I'm just about to embark on my first coronary, when the phone rings. I can't stop now, I could give myself a hernia or lock-jaw at the very least. Even if I did pick up, I wouldn't actually be able to speak. Gasping for breath is not attractive in a woman of my tender years.

The answerphone kicks in and there's lots of whirring and thunking. There's also a bit of uneven breathing coming down the phone line and I wonder if I've got a pervy phone call until I hear a woefully familiar voice speak out, which stops me dead in mid-lunge.

'Lucy,' Marcus says. And then there's another shuddering breath and a big sigh. 'It's me. Marcus.' As if my ex-fiancé, to whom I dedicated five long and faithful years, needs any introduction. My heart is banging against my chest and not just because I'm terminally unfit.

'I was just calling to see how you are.' Lots more uncomfortable pausing. At this rate the tape on the answerphone machine is going to have run out by the time he gets to the point of his call. Strangely, I find myself urging him to continue, whilst having no similar urge to pick up the phone. 'I feel that we left things on very bad terms last time we met.'

Ah, that'll be the time that he was bonking busty, bouncing Joanne on his kitchen table, and I walked in on them. I very nearly returned my engagement ring to a place where the sun very definitely doesn't shine. Marcus clearly hasn't realised what a narrow escape he had.

'The thing is,' he continues, 'I miss you and I still love you. I'm not with Joanne any more.' Now there's a surprise. I suspect that she was just a little bit pissed off with him too when she found out that the supposed ex-girlfriend was now, in fact, his fiancée. 'I'm having time on my own to reflect on my behaviour. I realise that it's ridiculous. It's ruining my life.'

It didn't do a lot for my life either, I seem to remember.

'But I simply can't seem to stop . . . well,' he says sadly. 'You know only too well what I can't stop doing.'

I certainly do.

'I'm even considering signing up for some sort of sex addicts' course.'

A course to *stop* him being a sex addict rather than one to teach him how to be one, I assume. Marcus has more than enough expertise in that area.

'Well . . .' Lots more sighing and pauses. 'I'd better go. I just wanted to tell you that I'm thinking about you and that I hope you have a great Christmas.' His voice cracks. 'I'll always love you, and if you ever want to give me a call then you know where I am. Be happy, Lucy. Bye.'

And then Marcus hangs up. I stare at the television screen. The demented flashes of Nell's Nike sportswear blur in front of my eyes. There's nothing quite like a call from your ex to bring you down. Sinking to the floor, dazed, I reach for my Bounty Bar. If there was ever a time I deserve to experience the taste of paradise, it's now. Sod the thunder thighs and the rest of this exercise routine. I need the sort of comfort that only chocolate can bring.

Chapter Five

Autumn Fielding glanced at her watch and saw that her next mosaics and stained-glass class at the Stolford Centre was due to start in ten minutes. Or 'doing good for the terminally disaffected' as her brother sneeringly called it. Learning how to make a basic suncatcher might not seem that important in the scheme of things, but if she could teach just one of her students enough to give them a glimmer of enjoyment or relaxation, or even show them that they had an untapped seam of creativity in their abused bodies then it was worth it for her, no matter what anyone else said.

It was rare that any of her students came in early, but she always liked to have the workbenches ready prepared for them with their latest work-in-progress laid out or a selection of brightly coloured sheets of glass for them to choose from. Her clients might all be thieves, drug addicts and down-at-heel, but she cared deeply for them and wanted to make their short time in her classes as enjoyable as possible. And she hoped that what she did might occasionally reach out and touch some of the kids, improving their tough lives.

Most of the students were currently working on seasonal pieces – cheery Santa suncatchers, coloured glass stars with silver thread to hang on the Christmas tree, a festive candle-holder or two – some to brighten up squalid squats, some to go to the dysfunctional homes where the problems so often started, some to be left behind on the workbenches because there was no home for them to go to. It was hard to find a place to hang a suncatcher when your residence was a cardboard box.

Recently, there had been a new intake of clients joining the

KICK IT! programme, but a few of the stalwart drug addicts remained or came back with dismal regularity, unable to KICK IT! for a depressing variety of reasons.

Addison slipped in through the door and wound his arms around her. 'Hi, there.' He kissed her warmly and soundly on the lips, crushing her to his broad chest.

She'd always loved her job, and now she had an extra reason to rush in here every day with a smile on her face. It perhaps wasn't ideal to be having a love affair with one of her colleagues, but it certainly felt very nice. Addison had been the first person that she'd dated in a long, long time who had been on her wavelength. He was socially responsible, Green, kind, caring and not in any way unattractive to look at. Being Green, she'd found in the past, had meant that most men had an excess of facial hair, body odour and a penchant for brown jumpers with holes in them. They didn't generally dress like Addison, in sharp black jackets and crisp shirts. He looked more like a drug dealer than someone from the other side of the fence; perhaps that was what made him so successful with his charges.

His job as the Centre's Enterprise Development Officer involved him in finding gainful employment usually for people who'd never managed to hold down a job in their entire lives. He was exceptionally good at it and, with his easy charm, managed to cultivate and keep a raft of extraordinarily tolerant employers on board – employers who frequently overlooked their troubled employees' tendency to abscond, not appear for work at all or even steal from them more often than not.

Autumn eased away from him, glancing nervously at the door. 'Someone might see us.' She tried to smooth down her mass of burnished ginger curls which had suddenly seemed to bounce madly with excitement. If only she had sleek hair like Chantal's, that didn't mirror her emotions but remained well-behaved on all occasions.

'Don't you think your students would be pleased to see that their tutor's in love?'

'Who said I'm in love?'

His beautiful black face broke into its trademark wide grin. 'I think that was me.'

'That's very presumptuous of you, Mr Addison Deacon,' she said, trying to sound stern.

'Admit it,' he said. 'You're crazy for me.'

'I'd be crazy not to be,' she agreed. 'But my students would all tease me mercilessly and they already make fun of me for my upper-class upbringing and my supposedly posh accent.'

'They love you really,' he said fondly. 'Just as I do.'

She grinned back at him and carried on with the preparations for her lesson while he leaned on the workbench and watched her over his dark glasses.

'Did you decide yet what you want to do for Christmas?' he asked. 'It's only a few days away.'

'Two more shopping days, I think you'll find.'

'Do your parents still want us to go to them for lunch?'

Autumn wrinkled her nose. 'Mmm.'

'You don't sound very keen.'

'Addison,' she said. 'I haven't taken anyone home to meet my parents for many years. With good reason. I'm not feeling very comfortable with this.'

'They'll love me,' he said. 'I'll be the perfect guest. I'll try not to get drunk. I won't tell your mother dirty jokes. I might even help with the washing-up.'

'There are things that I haven't told them about you.'

'Such as?'

'Well . . .' Autumn tucked a recalcitrant curl behind her ear. 'I haven't told my parents that you're—'

'Extremely handsome?'

She smiled. 'Yes, but—'

'That I don't have my own trust fund?'

'Yes, but—'

'That I'm younger than you?'

'Are you?'

'I sneaked into the Human Resources office and checked in your files.'

22

'How much younger?' Autumn asked.

'A measly five years.'

'Wow.'

'Is that a problem?'

'No.'

Then everything will be fine.'

'Yes, but . . . Addison, they don't know that you're . . . black.'

He looked shocked. 'I'm not, am I?' He picked up a mirror from the workbench. It was in the middle of having a fat-bottomed Santa attached to one corner of it. Her boyfriend stared at it in amazement. 'My Lord, I am. When did that happen?'

Autumn burst out laughing.

'So they won't mind that I'm younger than you or poorer than you, but they might object to me being from an ethnic minority.'

'I'm embarrassed to admit this, but they're white, upper-class and very conservative. I'm worried how they're going to react to you. I know that we're supposed to be a fully integrated, multi-cultural society these days, but I don't think anyone has told my parents.'

Addison laughed. 'You mean that they didn't envisage their daughter hooking up with an impoverished black social worker specialising in crack addicts – and a toy boy to boot?'

'I think they were rather hoping that I'd settle down with a middle-aged, spectacle-wearing barrister called Rodney, who would be able to curb the worst of my liberal excesses and intro-duce me to the joys of golf.'

'Then they'll be very disappointed in me.'

Autumn took his hand. 'I'm prepared to risk it, if you are.'

His arm curled round her again. 'I happen to think you're worth a little parental scrutiny,' her boyfriend said. 'Perhaps even a little disapproval. I've spent my whole life having to fight my own corner, so I'm sure I'll be an adequate match for anything white, upper-class Mr and Mrs Fielding can throw at me.'

'Thank you.' Autumn kissed him tenderly. 'I hoped you'd say that.'

Chapter Six

'Hey, Lewis,' Chantal said. 'Pass me over one more of those baubles, please.' Nadia's son's interest had already waned and was drifting towards the *Chicken Little* DVD that was playing on the television. She smiled indulgently at the back of his head and folded her arms. 'I thought you were supposed to be helping me?'

'Sorry, Aunty Chantal.' The child tore his attention away from the TV and dipped his hand into the box of tree decorations that she'd bought from Harrods. They were tin toys – soldiers, trains, trumpets and guitars fashioned in garish colours – all chosen to appeal to the tastes of her new four-year-old best friend rather than her own cream, minimalist leanings. Lewis pulled out a Jack-in-the-box. 'Cool.' He handed it over to her with a smile, handling it as if it were made of glass.

Who could blame him for being a little bored with the build-up to Christmas? She'd had more than enough of it herself, but when you were four years old, the wait must seem interminable.

Chantal had spent the last couple of months doing pieces on festive homes for the magazine that she worked for, *Style USA*. She'd had her fill of fake holly garlands and had seen enough red ribbon to last a lifetime. Her fellow Americans who were living over in Britain still went for dressing their homes for the Christmas period in a big way. If she were simply staying at this apartment by herself then she probably wouldn't have even bothered to pretty the place up – all this was being done for Lewis's sake. Not that her young friend seemed to appreciate her efforts. He was leaning against the sofa absently sucking his thumb and staring into middle distance.

'That looks great,' Nadia said, coming to join them. At least

Lewis's mother was more appreciative. 'Do you do everything so perfectly?' she wanted to know.

'Yes,' Chantal said. 'Everything except relationships.'

'You and me both.' Nadia toyed with a jolly Santa. 'I know that you're only doing this for us.'

'Don't be so sure about that. This is fun – right, Lewis?' Chantal sat back and ran her fingers through her glossy dark hair as she admired her handiwork. 'That doesn't look so bad.' The apartment that they were currently sharing was comfortable, stylish and filled with fun now that Lewis was here. It wasn't home, but it was certainly a close second.

'I don't know how we would have managed without you, Chantal.'

'Now,' Chantal said with a wave of her hand, 'don't start up with all that again. I've loved having you and Lewis stay.'

Nadia and her son had moved in with her when they'd left their home to escape Toby's gambling debts – something else that Chantal had been able to help out with. By giving Nadia an indefinite loan of £30,000, it had got her out of immediate trouble. If she hadn't stepped in, then maybe Nadia would have been looking at Toby facing bankruptcy or having their home repossessed. For her own sanity, Nadia had decided to split from her husband until he could straighten himself out – *if* he could.

The shock of losing his wife and son had, by all accounts, helped Toby to stay away from the glittering lights of the casino websites. Chantal and Nadia's current co-habitation was a temporary arrangement to tide them both over until they could, hopefully, start to repair their marriages – but it was one that Chantal hadn't imagined would suit them both quite so well. Lewis came over and leaned against Chantal, wrapping his small, sturdy arms around her. Chantal squeezed him fiercely. 'I love you so much,' she said.

Lewis giggled. 'I love you too,' he lisped in return and an unexpected surge of joy ran through her.

'Who would have thought that you'd have got on so well with children,' Nadia noted.

'*One* child,' Chantal corrected. It seemed ironic that when her marriage had broken down due to her lack of desire to have children, that she should become so attached to the first kid that she'd really had anything to do with. Maybe she had been missing out here. She ruffled Lewis's hair. 'Let's not get so carried away.'

'Still not inclined to hear the patter of tiny Hamilton feet?'

'It's something that Ted and I are still working on.' Her husband was so keen to have children, yet it was never something that had figured in Chantal's life plans.

When she had asked Nadia to move in here with her after they'd both split with their respective husbands, she had to admit that she'd completely forgotten about Lewis's existence. Even though she'd tried to factor him into her lifestyle, it was still a shock when he'd turned up carrying his appropriately named teddy, Mr Smelly, under his arm. It had taken even longer to get used to the regular addition of chocolate fingerprints on the pristine Kelly Hoppen paintwork. Now she couldn't imagine life without him, for who else would race to the front door and throw himself into her arms the minute she arrived home? But if Nadia was hoping to effect a reconciliation with her husband over the holidays, it was something that Chantal would have to get used to pretty soon. And what of her and Ted? Was her husband ever going to be able to forgive her infidelity and begin to trust her again?

'More toys.' Lewis clapped his hands together. Now *Chicken Little* was the tedious one.

'Okay. Go for it,' Chantal suggested. The boy searched through the reams of tissue paper and, finally, handed her a red and gold trumpet with glee. 'Fabulous. I would have made just that choice. Where should we hang it?' Lewis pointed to a suitable spot. 'Then there it is.' Chantal slipped the bauble onto the selected branch. 'You wanna do the next one?'

Lewis jumped up and down excitedly, his face the picture of ecstasy as he pulled a toy train out of its wrapping. It was a moving sight. Maybe Ted was right when he'd said that their materialistic lifestyle was all pointless without the addition of a family to share it with. It would be nice to see her husband doing this kind of thing with their own son. Chantal smiled to herself. Perhaps, after all, she was going soft in her old age.

She guided Lewis as he hooked the perfectly formed miniature train over a branch, then gave him a squeeze. 'Good work, champ.'

Chantal then turned to her friend. 'We're nearly done here. I'll just tidy the boxes away.' She noticed that Nadia's eyes had filled with tears. 'Then I think you and I should put our feet up, open some festive champagne and some of Clive's finest chocolates, and drink a toast to our future.'

'I'm frightened to think what mine might hold,' Nadia admitted quietly.

'We'll both work something out, I'm sure,' Chantal said, as she took her friend's hand and gave it a reassuring squeeze. But her voice didn't sound convincing, even to herself.

Chapter Seven

Back at The Chocolate Lovers' Club, as it's Christmas Eve, we exchange presents. Autumn gives us all a selection of Fairtrade chocolates. I love the idea of Doing Good while eating chocolate. Frankly, there are cocoa-bean farmers living in tin shacks all around the Equator who rely solely on my emotional crises for their livelihood. I'm already doing my bit for the world economy. If I had a quiet life, they'd all be bankrupt.

Nadia gives me a book of chocolate recipes. Chantal has found us all trendy T-shirts dyed with cocoa beans on one of her trips to America. They smell divine and are a delicious shade of chocolate, and I'd definitely be tempted to eat mine if I was desperate – which I frequently am. I take a moment to wonder what Crush would have bought me if we'd still been a couple this Christmas – something wonderful, I think – and I feel my heart squeeze painfully once more. I try to push the vision of his bare bottom and his comely companion to the back of my mind. I will not waste time fretting over yet another man.

We coo over our respective gifts, much kissing and hugging ensues and then we return to the job in hand. Clive has brought us all a slice of chocolate cheesecake with a sublimely smooth topping of his salted caramel that's just waiting to be devoured. He's already closed Chocolate Heaven for the evening, so now we're his favoured guests. Chantal has paid for a babysitter for Lewis so that Nadia is able to join us. We wouldn't want her missing out on this, our last choc-fest before Christmas. Our host hands round the chocolate vodka and we top up our shot glasses.

'Where's Tristan tonight?' I ask.

Clive looks discomfited. 'He's already left,' he tells us. 'He's spending Christmas with his family.'

We're all taken aback. I stop pouring my vodka mid-flow. 'You're not going to be together?'

'Well,' Clive says with an uncomfortable cough, 'things are a little difficult between us at the moment.'

This is the first we've heard about this. Clive and Tristan seemed to be the only ones around here who'd got their shit together. How depressing to think that relationship difficulties aren't purely down to the battle of the sexes.

'You're not going to be alone?' Although I'm sorry that Clive won't be spending Christmas with his loved one, there is a little glimmer of hope that I might have found another sad sack single to spend my holidays with. It won't just be me and *Chitty Chitty Bang Bang* after all. Hurrah. I could save my Cadbury's Selection Box for a rainy day, as Clive is bound to bring great truffles!

'I've already made alternative arrangements,' Clive tells us mysteriously.

My heart sinks. And then Clive looks all embarrassed, so he disappears off into the back of the shop.

'Lucy?' Chantal is fixing me with a quizzical stare. 'You *have* got plans for tomorrow?'

'Oh, yes,' I say. 'Most definitely. I have plans.'

'Plans that don't involve Marcus?'

I feel myself flush. 'Why on earth would I be seeing Marcus?'

'Because he's always your fall-back guy, Lucy.'

'You haven't called him, have you?' Nadia says, eyeing me suspiciously. 'Tell me you haven't.'

'No,' I say, but even I can spot the hesitancy there. '*I* haven't called *him*.'

They all lean forward, frowns in place. 'But?'

I shift uncomfortably in my seat. 'He called me.'

The girls sigh out loud.

'He only called me a little bit,' I say, somewhat defensively. 'And I didn't even pick up the phone. I just let it go straight to voice-mail. Even though I was there.' I hope they appreciate that this is the equivalent of a snowball remaining frozen in the depths of Hell.

My friends don't look as if they do, so I spell it out for them. 'I've already been hurt by Crush. Very hurt. Do you really think that I'm stupid enough to open myself up to all that stuff again with Marcus?'

My friends look as if they do.

'Give me more credit than that,' I say huffily.

'We're just worried about you,' Autumn tells me. 'Spend the day with one of us. You can come to my parents' house with Addison and me.' But even Autumn doesn't look as if she thinks that's a great idea. 'Don't be alone.'

'Tell us where you're going?'

'Don't worry.' I give a light-hearted laugh. 'I'll be surrounded by people.'

'Lucy Lombard.' Chantal sounds stern. 'I'd break both of your legs if I thought you were going to go *anywhere* near Marcus again.'

'I'd break both of my own,' I tell her, and having recently broken a limb I know how painful that is, so it's not a threat I make lightly. So it looks like my Christmas is going to be spent singing along with Dick Van Dyke and chewing the sleeves of my chocolate-scented T-shirt.

Chapter Eight

Waking up alone on Christmas morning is not a great feeling. This is definitely a time designed for lovey-dovey couples and families – however warring. This is a time for making up, forgetting old hurts, putting feuds aside. This is not a time to be by yourself. Even though I've never actually achieved this scenario with my own family, I can't help imagining everyone else out there having a warm and loving holiday together, gathered round the Christmas tree opening their presents.

I plod into the kitchen and stick two chocolate Pop-Tarts into the toaster. There's a bottle of champagne chilling in the fridge and I suppose that I could start on it now – there's nothing to stop me. I'll be back on my cheap and cheerful wine by tomorrow, so I might as well make the most of it. If you're going to have empty calories, make them expensive ones, that's what I say. So I crack it open, let the cork ricochet off the ceiling and swig heartily from the bottle. The bubbles make me do a little burp. Hmm. Not bad.

I take my breakfast, such as it is, into the lounge and sit in front of my tree. My red chilli lights wink happily at me. Even the sight of me, miserable and alone, can't dismay them. There's no great pile of presents here. In fact, there aren't any at all. My parents both gave me cheques – they know my needs – and I've opened and eaten everything else I was given. Except for Chantal's chocolate T-shirt – but the day is still young.

Staring at the phone, I try to curb my urge to speak to Crush. Would one little call have hurt him so much? I can't believe that he hasn't got in touch with me at all. He could at least have contacted me to say that he was sorry and that he was a low-life and that, frankly, I deserved better than him. I look at the clock. His Christmas Day will nearly be over. He's probably been on the beach, barbecuing succulent prawns with Miss Skanky Pants in a skimpy bikini and simply doesn't care about the broken heart he's left behind. Choking down a bit more of my Pop-Tart, I follow it with a swig of champagne. I wonder if I've even crossed his mind.

Still, I *am* going out today. I wasn't just saying that to appease my lovely mates. I was determined not to sit here at home feeling pathetically sorry for myself. There are people much worse off than I am. I can't actually bring any to mind, at the moment – but I'm sure there are some.

Taking myself into the bathroom, I have a good, vigorous scrub-down under the shower, which instantly makes me feel a lot better. I pick out a smart, but not overtly glamorous outfit, put on some slap, do something wonderful with my hair and then head on out.

I've never been inside a soup kitchen before – I don't even know if that's the correct term any more. They're probably called Eating Venues for the Under-Privileged and are awarded the equivalent of Michelin stars. This is normally more Autumn's bag than mine. And, I suppose that I could have easily asked Autumn for one of her contacts – as undoubtedly she has them – but I didn't want any of the girls to know that I was planning to do this sort of thing, as they would have tried to talk me out of it. All I did was look up 'homeless' on the internet, found out who was running a volunteer programme, then I called these guys and they were more than happy to have me come along to help out. And why wouldn't they be? Any old idiot can dish out a few sprouts.

A three-course traditional Christmas lunch for all-comers is being served in a crumbling church hall not too far from where I live. If they do get stars for this kind of establishment, then it wouldn't get many for décor. Unless, of course, peeling paint becomes *de rigueur*. When I arrive, there's the smell of roasting turkey in the air, but it's overlaid with the rancid hum of unwashed clothes and bodies. Sitting at the rows of makeshift tables are a range of people from under-nourished teenagers with pizza faces to crusty old tramps with potatoes growing under their finger-nails and matted hair. It shocks me that every seat is filled and there are more people waiting in line for spaces to become vacant. I had no idea that there were so many people who were alone at Christmas.

'Here you are, dearie. Good to see you.' Before I can decide that dishing out a few sprouts is, frankly, beyond me and make a run for it, an ample woman hands me a ladle and a red Christmas hat. She's sufficiently jolly to stop me from getting too maudlin. She grins at me and I grin back. I too can do cheerful in the face of minor adversity. I might be miserable and alone, but I have a lot more to be thankful for than these folk. 'Give them a nice big bowl of soup to start with,' she tells me. 'There's plenty to go around.'

Feeling slightly dazed, I find somewhere to put my handbag where it won't be nicked and then I take my place in the soup distribution line. I'm just about to launch into my new role as humbled and selfless volunteer with a cheery disposition when I hear my name being called.

'Lucy!' My head spins round. I hadn't expected to know anyone here. Which, to be truthful, was part of the attraction. Three people along the line, I see Clive, also ladle in hand. 'What are you doing here?'

I shift places, budging a silver-haired, twin-setted woman and man in a corduroy jacket and sandals out of the way, until I'm standing next to my friend. 'The same as you, I guess.'

'I couldn't face being on my own,' Clive admits as we dish out our soup to grateful recipients. 'This seemed like a useful alter-native.'

'Great minds think alike.'

'How did we end up like this?' Clive wants to know. 'We're nice people, aren't we? Why does no one want to be with us?'

'You haven't heard from Tristan?'

He gives me a sad shrug. 'Not a thing.'

'When we're through here, let's spend the rest of the day together,' I suggest. 'I have champagne. I have chocolate. I have a wide range of microwavable food and some really rubbish board games.'

Clive gives me a hug and my spirits lift. 'Sounds perfect.'

When we've finished serving lunch and the washing-up has been done, then the remaining volunteers sit down together. The turkey's looking a little dried up by now and the roast spuds have gone soggy, but there's laughter and camaraderie to help it down and it doesn't taste so bad at all.

As Clive and I are tucking into a tired helping of Christmas pudding and vaguely lumpy custard, his mobile phone rings. 'It's Tristan,' he mouths to me, then moves away from the table and paces the floor anxiously as he talks.

Looking around at my fellow volunteers, I feel the warmth that has formed between us. I came here looking for a way to distract myself from being alone, but I'm surprised at the sense of community that I've found. To be honest, I might even consider coming back here next year. Particularly if I'm still a miserable spinster with no one to love. If my life continues as it is then I might even be standing in the soup line myself, by then.

When Clive comes back to the table, there's a pensive and slightly troubled look on his face.

'Bad news?'

'Tristan's missing me,' he says. 'He wants me to join him at his parents'.'

'That's good news!'

'Yes,' he says. 'But then I'll have to leave you.'

'Oh.' Hadn't thought about that part. 'You must go,' I say. Even though I actually want to beg Clive not to. 'You should be together.'

'What about you?'

'I'll be fine,' I insist bravely. 'I've been fed, and I'm perfectly capable of entertaining myself for the rest of the day.' At least I have a comfy sofa and a telly and don't have to head back out into the cold, hard streets with nothing but a few cardboard boxes for solace.

'If you're sure you don't mind.'

'Clive. Go. I'll push you out of the door if I have to.'

'You're a lovely person, Lucy. Free chocolate for all of next week for this.'

'I can eat a lot,' I threaten. 'And I'll be in every day.'

'You already are and we love you for it.'

Clive gives me a bear hug, plants a kiss on my cheek and then waves over his shoulder as he goes out of the door – leaving me to wonder if it's possible to have a game of Pictionary with just one player.

Chapter Nine

Addison took a step backwards as they approached the front door of the house.

'Your parents own *all* of this place?'

Autumn nodded.

'Not just one floor?'

'All of it,' she confirmed.

Addison pursed his lips and she thought she saw a gulp travel down his throat. Everyone's reaction was the same when they saw where her parents lived. She used to wish fervently that home was a tiny terraced house in some northern industrial town. Their wisteria-covered mansion was very grand and imposing, and was always a great embarrassment to her when taking home impoverished and socially-aware boyfriends. It had ended more than one relationship.

She was sure that it wouldn't come to that with Addison. He wanted her for herself, not for what her parents did or didn't have. Or had too much of. He was cooler, more accepting and, at least he *had* a job, which was an improvement on most of the men she'd been romantically involved with over the years. Autumn didn't think, however, she'd mention to him just yet about the family's other homes in the Bahamas, Gstaad, Nice and various other places around the globe. Or their country 'bolthole' as they called it – a sprawling farmhouse in the Cotswolds surrounded by acres of land.

'You said they were upper-class, Autumn,' he reminded her. 'Not one step down from royalty.'

Wiping her palms on her dress, she chewed nervously at her lip. 'We don't have to do this.'

'We can't do a runner now. What will happen to all the festive delights your mother will have spent hours preparing?' Addison put his arm round her shoulders and squeezed. 'Don't worry,' he said. 'It'll be fine.'

'They can be quite over-bearing,' she warned.

'And I can be quite charming,' Addison countered. 'They'll love me.'

Autumn hoped that he was right. She hadn't really cared that her parents had disproved of every other man she'd ever taken home to meet them, but suddenly, this time it mattered that they should like Addison – and that they should like him a lot.

The door opened and they stepped inside. 'Merry Christmas, Miss Autumn.'

'Thanks, Jenkinson. Merry Christmas to you.' The butler-cum-housekeeper who'd run her parents' London home for many years, took their coats.

'Your parents have a *butler*?' Addison said when the elderly gentleman was out of earshot.

Autumn didn't dare tell her boyfriend that they had a cook and cleaner too. 'Jenkinson isn't really a butler, he's a . . .'

'Faithful retainer?'

'Now you're teasing me.'

'Not really,' Addison said. 'But you might have warned me that this wasn't going to be lunch with your average parents.'

'They're the only ones I've got, Addison.'

'Well, as we've already agreed, it's too late to run away, so you'd better introduce me.'

If her parents were at all shocked by Autumn's choice of boyfriend, then they managed to hide it very well. They sat sipping Kir Royale in the drawing room, making polite conversation, while the final preparations for lunch were made. Addison didn't make any comment about the absence of her mother slaving over a hot stove. Autumn didn't think that her mother ventured into her kitchen very often. Most of their Christmas lunch had probably come directly from Fortnum & Mason.

'You have remembered that I'm vegetarian, Mummy?'

Her mother looked blankly at her. 'I'm sure that Jenkinson has. Besides, we're having goose, darling. That hardly counts as meat.'

Autumn sighed to herself. They should have stayed at her apartment by themselves. Then she could have cooked a nut roast and Addison wouldn't have been subjected to this.

'Do you live near here, Alan?' Her father had decided to hold court.

'Addison,' he corrected patiently. 'No. This is a bit above my price bracket. I have a council flat in Streatham.'

'How lovely,' Autumn's mother piped up, her voice just too shrill to be perceived as sincere.

Her father looked less than impressed. 'What's your line of work?'

'I'm an Enterprise Development Officer,' he said. 'I find jobs for reformed drug addicts.' He shrugged. 'Not all of them reformed. It's very hard for some of these kids to kick the habit.'

Her parents exchanged an anxious glance. 'Perhaps lunch is ready,' her mother said.

Addison looked at Autumn as if to say, 'What have I said wrong?'

Before she could intervene with an explanation, Jenkinson opened the door. 'Master Richard has arrived.'

'*Richard?*' He was the last person Autumn had expected to see.

'He wasn't sure if he'd get back in time to join us,' her mother explained. 'He's come straight from the airport. We wanted it to be a surprise.'

'It's certainly that,' Autumn agreed.

At that moment, Richard swung through the door. 'Sis!' he said, and grabbed Autumn in a rough embrace.

It was the first time in her life that she hadn't felt relieved simply to see Rich in one piece. She had imagined, after his months in rehab in the States, that he'd have looked healthier than he did. She'd envisaged him a few pounds heavier, the shadows gone from beneath his eyes, maybe even the glimmer of a tan, but her brother still looked gaunt, his cheeks sunken. When he pulled away from her she could see that his eyes were unnaturally bright, not quite focused, and she knew instinctively that Rich was still using. All the months that he'd supposedly been in rehab had been completely pointless. Their parents might as well have dug a hole in the ground and buried all their money in it.

'Darling,' their mother said to him as she kissed the air either side of her son's cheek. 'It's so good that you could make it back.'

Richard embraced his mother stiffly. 'Mumsy.' He shook his father's hand, who then attempted to pat him rather uncomfortably on the arm.

'This is Addison,' Autumn said, when it seemed that no one else was going to introduce her boyfriend. Richard looked taken aback. He gave Addison the sort of scrutiny that she'd expected from her parents and made no move to shake his hand. Typical Richard, Autumn bristled. 'We work at the Centre together.'

'Ah,' Rich said. 'Another do-gooder. We're *so* short of those in the world.'

'Perhaps lunch is ready,' her mother repeated anxiously.

The only consolation was that her parents always bought wonderful chocolates for Christmas. Autumn wondered who'd be more desperate for their hit of their chosen drug by the end of lunch – would it be her, or her brother?

As she slipped her arm through Addison's to steer him towards the dining room, Autumn surreptitiously glanced at her watch. All they had to do was get through the next couple of hours without incident, and then they could be out of here. For Autumn it couldn't come soon enough.

Chapter Ten

Ted had tried hard, Chantal thought. He'd booked them into a quiet country hotel on the outskirts of Bath. He'd held her hand on the journey down there. There was an excellent restaurant – Michelin-starred. Their lavish room had a four-poster bed. A superb arrangement of white lilies, from her husband, scented the air. There was an extravagant box of chocolates waiting on the coffee-table, that she simply had to check out at once.

She'd tried hard too. There was a new, filmy nightdress in her overnight bag and she'd gone through the abject pain of having a full Brazilian wax – the ultimate sacrifice in her book. And now she was doing her best to sit quietly in the drawing room and sip her cocktail while all she really wanted to do was go upstairs and make love to her hunky husband.

'Are you happy to be here?' Chantal asked him.

Ted nodded, but there was a ponderous quality to the response which made her think that it wasn't entirely a joyous, spontaneous emotion.

'This is a lovely hotel,' she said. 'Great choice.'

He nodded again and then, just as she thought the whole of the conversation was shaping up to be monosyllabic, her husband said, 'But is a hotel the best place to be spending Christmas?'

'We could have stayed at home.' Though she was fully aware that she wasn't even living at her home at the moment.

'What do you class as home?'

'You don't have to ask that, Ted. I've rented the apartment to give you some space to think about things. That's what you wanted.' Her hand found his thigh. 'What *I* want is to come home. You know that.'

'I couldn't have faced being at home this year.'

He didn't need to tell her why. It was clear that her husband wanted to see their home filled with children and toys and milk spilled down her designer clothes. After the time she'd spent with Nadia's son, Lewis, she could now actually see the attraction of having a family Christmas. Nadia had told her not to, but she'd left a dozen beautifully wrapped and extravagant gifts for the little boy under the Christmas tree – all things that she hadn't been able to resist – and they'd both called her this morning to say thank you. Lewis was completely hyper with excitement. She was missing him desperately, and all these things had left her wondering whether Ted might be right. Would their lives together be better if they had a child?

She looked around at their opulent surroundings. This hotel was beautiful, but it was the sort of place frequented by stuffy, middle-aged couples. Even the great chocolates couldn't compensate for the fact that it was like a museum. No one would dream of bringing children here. Was that what made it seem so sterile in its beauty?

What on earth were they going to do to pass the time until dinner? She'd brought a book, too literary to be an easy read and she couldn't settle into it. Ted seemed reasonably contented to sit and stare into space, but she was getting restless. 'Why don't we go to the spa and take a swim?'

Her husband shrugged. 'Fine.'

A little more enthusiasm would have been nice, but she'd take what she could get.

The small swimming pool was empty apart from Chantal. The area was intimate and lushly decorated like a tropical paradise, secreted away from the main part of the hotel. Large palm trees crowded around the turquoise water, the loungers were made of bamboo. It was an intricate shape, not suited to swimming lengths, but she made a few strokes up and down while she waited for her husband to join her.

When Ted appeared, she called jokingly, 'Come on in. The water's lovely.'

He laughed and jumped in, spraying water all over her.

'Hey! Not fair.' Chantal climbed onto his back and tried to duck him under the surface. They splashed around playfully, having fun as they hadn't done in years. Too many years.

Chantal wound her legs round Ted's waist and twined her arms round his neck. He held her bottom and pulled her to him. Then his mouth found hers and they clung to each other in the water as they kissed. Ted pushed her against the side of the pool and, as he held her up with one arm, his other hand caressed her body, which thrilled to his touch. His fingers found the edge of her swimsuit and teased inside, rubbing over her nipple.

Chantal let her head fall back. She could feel Ted growing hard and wondered whether they'd make it back to the bedroom in time. In years gone by, they used to relish making love in reckless places. Then her husband's fingers strayed to the inside of her thighs, toying with the fabric of her suit and she wondered whether he might still be prepared to risk it.

'There's no one else here,' she whispered huskily. 'Come inside me.'

He looked anxiously over his shoulder. 'Someone might see us.'

'They won't,' she assured him, even as she was slipping down the front of his shorts and urging herself towards him. 'There's no one else here. We're absolutely alone.'

He stilled her hands. 'I can't,' Ted said, his hardness suddenly dissipated. 'I can't do this.'

'We can go back to the room,' Chantal said. 'We **can be** there in minutes.'

'It wouldn't make any difference,' her husband said. He let go of Chantal and slipped away from her. She couldn't read the emotions in his face.

'Talk to me about this, Ted. What's the problem?'

'I think that's abundantly clear,' he said crisply as he hauled himself out of the pool. 'I'm sorry.'

'It doesn't matter,' she called after him, as he headed back to the changing rooms without glancing back in her direction. But she knew it did. It mattered a lot to both of them.

Chapter Eleven

I snuggle down into my sofa, surrounded by a veritable feast of treats to see me through the rest of Christmas Day – a tub of Heroes and a giant bar of Galaxy are nestled next to me within easy reach. Minimum exertion is going to be employed for maximum consumption.

The smart outfit has gone and I'm back in my slob-out gear of faded black T-shirt and combats. The remains of my bottle of champagne – slightly flat – is pressed into service again. Because I don't want to be sober, I slug down half of it in one go, then settle back for my wild night of telly. And then, tragedy ensues! *Chitty Chitty Bang Bang* isn't even on, and it's *always* on television at Christmas. What's the festive season without Dick Van Dyke? It's usually slap bang in there amongst *The Sound of Music* and *The Great Escape*. There surely must be some mistake. Can you rely on nothing in this life?

I throw down the festive TV guide in disgust. What am I going to do now to pass the long, lonely hours until bedtime? Picking up the remote control, I give channel-surfing a cursory go, and just as I realise there's absolutely nothing on worth watching, my doorbell rings. Who the hell could this be? Then my heart quickens. What if it's Crush, come to tell me that this has all been a hideous mistake and that he got the first flight out of Sydney that was humanly possible, to rush to my side? I'm off the sofa and make the door in three strides. When I wrench it open, Marcus is standing there.

'I have chocolates,' he says. 'I have champagne. I have a cuddly toy.'

In fact, he has a large, fluffy polar bear snuggled beneath his arm.

'I couldn't stop thinking about you,' he continues before I have a chance to speak. 'So I dropped by on the off-chance to wish you a Merry Christmas. If you want to tell me to fuck off, then I'll go.'

Marcus looks gorgeous and not a little drunk. His blond hair is all messed up and he's looking very boyish. He makes the polar bear wave a paw at me. It's very cute. Whether it's because I'm experiencing a feeling of goodwill to all mankind after spending the afternoon in the soup kitchen or whether it's because my only other option is a thirty-year-old episode of *The Best of Morecambe and Wise,* I sigh and say, 'How can I tell you to fuck off – it's Christmas?'

I open the door wide and Marcus lurches into the lounge. 'Are you alone?' he says. 'I hoped you would be.'

'I've just got back from seeing friends.' It's not strictly a lie as Clive was at the drop-in centre too.

'Where's Lover Boy then?'

'Lover Boy is in Australia.' Marcus needs to know no more. 'Do you want coffee?' I ask. 'You look like you could do with it.'

'That would be great.' My ex-fiancé sinks onto my sofa and makes himself comfortable.

In the kitchen I bang about with coffee cups and stuff while my mind whirls in turmoil. If I was a hard-hearted and sensible individual, I'd show Marcus the door. But I'm not. I'm a pushover and I'm lonely. Would it be so wrong to spend the rest of the evening with him? I need some company, Marcus is here and available – so who's using who this time round? I'll make him play Pictionary with me and then just when he thinks it's too late to go home and is eyeing my sofa – or my bed – wistfully, I'll call him a cab.

I take the coffee through to the lounge and put the cups on the table. Marcus has slipped off his jacket and his shoes. I'm not sure where to sit. Shall I casually slip down next to Marcus, or plump for the armchair out of harm's way? But while I'm in the process of making this crucial decision, Marcus's arms snake round my thighs and he pulls me down on top of him.

'Marcus!' I thump him in the chest and try to extricate myself from his clutches. His arms are strong and solid around me and, I shouldn't be thinking this, but it feels oh, so good to be locked in his embrace.

He grins at me. 'God, I've missed you.' Then he kisses me deep and hard. His hands are on my face, in my hair, on my breasts, bum, everywhere. I can't breathe, I can't say no. His lips are hot and feverish and it reminds me of the first time Marcus and I ever slept together – it was wild, passionate and I loved him from that very minute. We tumble to the floor, the coffee-table gets knocked over, the cups go for a burton. That's my carpet stained.

'I love you,' Marcus is saying over and over. 'I love you so much.' He tugs my T-shirt off and then makes short work of my trousers. His mouth never leaves mine and, I don't know how it happens, but minutes later we're both naked, a trail of discarded clothes on the floor. We're lying beneath the Christmas tree and I've got carpet burns everywhere. I should say no. I *definitely* should say no. But I can't. I'm alone and Marcus needs me, wants me, loves me. There are pine needles sticking in my bottom, but there's a strange comfort from knowing every inch of this man as he eases himself inside me. Marcus has always been a fantastic lover and sometimes I might hate him for it, but I can never deny it. My ex-fiancé is moving above me. There's love and lust in his eyes. He holds me tight. 'Lucy,' he gasps as he comes inside me. 'I love you.'

'Oh, Marcus,' I say. But I don't know what the emotion is behind it. Is it love, familiarity, contempt or plain old frustration? The red chilli lights are blinking, but there's a new knowingness in their flashes.

Marcus lies next to me and, without thinking, I curl into him. He strokes his fingers lightly over my body, caressing, teasing. I feel his breath on my neck. I've given in to Marcus again. And I know that I could very well hate myself in the morning. But, for now, I just want to be loved.

Chapter Twelve

When Toby opened the door to them, he was wearing an apron. Beads of perspiration peppered his brow and his cheeks showed a flustered glow. There was a tea towel over his shoulder.

'I think I've got the timings all wrong,' he said, a note of panic in his voice. 'We might have to eat the potatoes now and the turkey at ten o'clock tonight.'

Nadia laughed. She was already stripping off Lewis's coat. Her own followed quickly. 'Do you want me to come to the rescue?'

'I'd love it,' Toby said with a relieved sigh. 'I had no idea there was so much to cooking a Christmas dinner.'

'That's because you were always at the pub while I prepared it all,' she teased.

He stopped and kissed her on the cheek. 'It's good to have you both here,' he said.

'Daddy,' Lewis said. 'Aunty Chantal bought me an electric guitar.'

'Really?' He looked at Nadia for confirmation.

'She hasn't got any kids,' Nadia said by way of explanation. Only someone without children would think that it was a great idea to give a small boy a loud present. 'It's a pretend one, but it's certainly noisy enough to make you believe it's the real deal.' It would be the first toy to be hidden as soon as the batteries ran out.

Toby scooped his son into his arms. 'Hiya, champ. Have you got a kiss for your dad?' Lewis giggled as Toby buried his face in the soft skin of his neck. He swung his son back to the floor. 'Look what I've got for you.'

'Toby,' Nadia said quietly. 'You shouldn't have bought him anything, not while we have so many debts outstanding.' She felt terrible that she couldn't even stand her round these days at Chocolate Heaven, but the girls were so understanding. Nadia had no idea what she'd do without them. They were her lifeline.

'It's just a little something,' Toby insisted. 'I couldn't buy him nothing at all. I'm his dad.'

Nadia wished that Toby's paternal instinct had extended to abstaining from gambling their money away on the myriad internet sites that he frequented.

'We're back on the right track now, Nadia,' he told her as if he'd been reading her mind. 'I'm not even buying so much as a lottery ticket. I promise you.'

They both sat and watched Lewis's delighted face as their son opened the gift that no self-respecting kid should be without – a talking workbench and a full range of plastic tools.

'That's a nice present,' Nadia said. Though in truth she thought it had every bit as much potential to be as annoying as the electric guitar and even more potential to be downright dangerous.

'*Are you going to build a space ship today?*' the bench asked in irritatingly perky tones.

Lewis shrieked with delight. She'd have to find a very big cupboard to hide this in.

'*Thanks for putting the hammer away!*'

'Come through to the kitchen,' Toby said.

'Are we safe to leave him?' Nadia whispered. 'Or do you think the hammer will end up through the television screen?'

'I guess the older he gets, the more destruction he's likely to create.'

'Lewis, play nicely,' Nadia instructed. 'Don't break things.' That monkey wrench might be plastic but it still looked lethal to her. 'Daddy and I are going to cook lunch.'

In the kitchen there was steam bubbling from an assortment of pans. The windows were running with condensation. Nadia switched on the extractor fan.

'I'll do everything,' Toby assured her, 'but I need you as the project manager.'

'Give me my apron back and you can put your feet up for a minute while I sort everything out.'

There was a tear in Toby's eye as he said, 'I don't know how I've managed without you.'

Slipping her arms round him, she gave him a hug.

'I've tried to think of everything,' Toby told her. 'I've bought parsnips, bacon rolls, fancy napkins and a box of your favourite chocolates from that place you go to with your friends.'

'You went to Chocolate Heaven?'

Toby nodded.

'You shouldn't have.'

'I wanted it to be perfect.'

'There's only one thing that I want you to do,' she said.

'And I'm doing it. I'm on the straight and narrow now. Honestly.'

'It's good to hear it. I really hope that you mean it.'

'I swear,' he promised. 'You and Lewis mean the world to me. I don't want to see you walk out of my life. I'd rather die than let that happen.'

Putting her fingertip to his lips, she said, 'No more talk of it now. It's Christmas, we should forget about our troubles for today.'

'I agree with that wholeheartedly,' Toby said with a grateful sigh.

'Then let's get this lunch sorted out, shall we? Otherwise we'll be eating it on Boxing Day.'

Nadia set to and was pouring boiling water on the packet of stuffing that Toby had bought when he told her, 'I've invited my parents to come along for lunch. I hope that's okay. They wanted to see Lewis — and you, of course.'

'That's fine.'

'They're really missing him,' Toby told her.

'They can see him any time they want,' Nadia said. 'They know that.'

'But it's not the same, is it?' Her husband gave her a sad, self-conscious smile. 'Anyway, I thought it would be nice for us all to be together. Christmas is a time for family.'

That was true, and all of the celebrations at this time of the year never ceased to make Nadia feel the absence of her own relations even more keenly. There was always the hope in the back of her mind that one day, something might cause them to put their bias against Toby to one side, and take them all back into the fold. Her mother and father hadn't even met their grandson, though she continued to send photographs of him to their home every year on his birthday, but their receipt was never acknowledged. In her culture, family was everything – unless you shunned your parents' choice of husband for you, of course – and it was a continuing sadness in Nadia's life that she was estranged from those she cared for most of all. Now that she was back here with Toby, she realised how much she'd missed the closeness of her own small family unit. It had been especially nice that her husband had put so much effort into making today special – despite the expense. Maybe things really had turned a corner and they could both look forward to a brighter future.

The lunch was wonderful, but it was so late that it was technically dinner and they were all so hungry by then that they'd have eaten whatever was put in front of them. Nadia and Toby were clearing away the dishes while Lewis's grandparents gladly entertained their only grandson. Toby's dad was currently showing Lewis how to drill a pretend hole in the coffee-table. Her son was giving the task his undivided attention, but still the plastic drill-bit slid uncontrollably across the polished surface. Nadia decided not to watch. It looked like this was going to be yet another Christmas present they'd live to regret. Their furniture was shabby enough without it being peppered with inadvertently drilled DIY holes.

The day had been a great success and she was feeling very mellow and uncomfortably full; astonishingly, she'd even had to leave some of her Chocolate Heaven delights for tomorrow. It wasn't often that her capacity to consume chocolate failed her. 'That was a lovely dinner,' she said.

'It's all down to you, Nadia,' her husband said. 'You hold everything together. I'd be lost without you.'

Before she could reply, Lewis came into the kitchen behind them. He was sucking his thumb and tugged at Nadia's skirt. His eyes were heavy with tiredness.

'Looks like it's past your bedtime, young man.' Lewis, for once, didn't protest. She turned to Toby. 'We should go.'

'Can I stay in my own bed tonight?' her son piped up.

'No, darling.'

'Please, Mummy!'

'You don't have to leave,' Toby said. 'You could both stay.'

Nadia smiled. 'Think you can cook me one decent roast dinner and then have your wicked way with me?'

'It's worth a try,' Toby said, grinning back at her. 'I could open another bottle of wine.'

Nadia shrugged. 'Okay.'

'Really?' Toby's grin widened.

It was late, she was pleasantly tired and she'd probably had too much to drink already. Nadia had planned to have no more than one glass and drive home, but getting through the day without a few bolstering drinks had proved more difficult than she'd imagined. Now, she'd have to call a cab and it would be hell trying to get one on Christmas Day. Horribly expensive, too. To be honest, she had no desire to go back to Chantal's apartment knowing that her friend wouldn't be there and that it would just be her and Lewis rattling around by themselves for the next few days. There wasn't any great desire to tear herself away from Toby either and the sleepy, cosy warmth of her own home. 'Yes. We'll stay.'

'Lewis, go into your bedroom and find some pyjamas. Mummy'll be up in a minute.'

As their son ran excitedly out of the room, Toby wrapped his arms round her. 'Come back for good, Nadia. I want you both home.'

Could she trust her husband enough to make a go of their marriage? Would he ever be able to give up gambling, despite his promises? She looked into his eyes and they seemed so sincere, but how could she be sure that he'd changed? Had Toby had enough time alone to reflect on his actions? There was no doubt that she still loved her husband. That had never really been in question. It was only his behaviour, his addiction, she abhorred. After a few glasses of cheap bubbly it would be easy to make a rash decision, based on the emotions she was feeling now, but she'd disrupted Lewis's life enough. It wouldn't do him any good to settle in at home again, only for her to find that things were just the same. She couldn't do that to her son – she had to think of his future stability. But it would be so good to be in Toby's arms again. Despite his faults, he was a handsome, loving man and she'd missed him so much.

Leaning into him, Nadia rested her head on his shoulder, gently kissing his neck. 'We'll stay tonight,' she said, trying to keep a grip on the reality of their situation. 'Let's take it one step at a time.'

Chapter Thirteen

Autumn found herself holding her breath, and already a stress headache was forming behind her eyes from the effort of trying to maintain a veneer of normality. Her brother had downed glass after glass of champagne before Christmas lunch was even served. Now he was waving his arms about animatedly as he talked, his speech babbling and slurred, his movements frantic and uncoordinated.

Richard lurched into the dining room ahead of Addison and her.

'Addison, do sit here beside me,' Mrs Fielding said, as if nothing untoward was happening.

And, if her boyfriend was overawed by the palatial dining room, he too was handling it all very coolly. He turned to Autumn and gave her a reassuring wink.

The glossy mahogany table seated sixteen people and had been laid with the very best of the family china and silver for the occasion. Cut-glass wine goblets glittered in the light from the candelabras. Lavish bowls of seasonal fruits were decorated with sprigs of holly. Mistletoe garlands hung in swathes from the picture rails and the ornate marble fireplace. A fire roared in the grate, bringing a much-needed warmth to the room. It was the sort of scene that would have looked at home on a Christmas card. Idyllic. And that was what her family life had always been like – an utterly perfect surface, masking the myriad tensions that ran barely beneath it.

As her boyfriend left her side, she grabbed her brother by the arm and held him back. 'Rich,' she whispered, 'cool it. You've had enough to drink.'

'A few glasses,' he insisted. 'Loosen up, Autumn. It's Christmas, and the Prodigal Son has returned to great rejoicing. Jealous because the fatted calf is never served up for you?' He took another deep swig from his flûte. 'Oh, you're vegetarian – wouldn't touch it, anyway.'

'You're making a fool of yourself and we have company.'

'Must keep up appearances, mustn't we?'

'It wouldn't hurt,' she said quietly. 'Our parents have just spent an inordinate amount of money on your supposed stay in a rehab clinic. You might make some effort to pretend that you've actually been trying to give up drugs.'

'I could give them up whenever I liked, my darling sister, but I've decided that I rather like a distorted picture of life. So much better than harsh reality, don't you think?'

'Sit down and shut up,' Autumn said. 'Let's just get today over with.'

'You've suddenly come over all assertive,' her brother remarked. 'Have the do-gooders group been sending you on training courses?'

'Have I ever told you that you're a very infuriating person to be around when you're in this mood? Be nice. For me.'

Richard looked at her, very slightly cowed. She just hoped he could stay civil throughout the rest of the day. Now she could see him closer up, Autumn thought he did, in fact, look even worse than he had before he went off to America. His face bore an unhealthy pallor, there was a sheen of sweat on his skin and a discernible shake to his hands.

When they were all seated, Jenkinson brought in a large silver server with the roasted goose sitting proudly on top.

'Fuck,' Richard said loudly. 'Don't they even give you Christmas Day off, Jenks, old boy? What century is this?'

'I won't have that language at the table,' their father said. 'Keep a civil tongue in your head, Richard.'

'You treat people like medieval serfs and you think *I'm* the one with the problem?' Her brother laughed without humour. 'Let me cut up this damn thing.' He lurched unsteadily to his feet and grabbed the carving-knife.

Their father also stood up. 'I think I should do that.'

'No. No. No.' Richard swatted him away and Mr Fielding reluctantly sat down again, glancing worriedly at his wife. Not only the goose, but the atmosphere, could have been cut with a knife.

Jenkinson returned with a tray laden with dishes of steamed vegetables and roast potatoes. There was, thankfully, a nut roast too. 'This is the vegetarian option, Miss Autumn,' he said quietly to her.

'Thank you.' She gave him a grateful look.

Jenkinson placed the dishes on the table and then beat a dignified but hasty retreat back to the kitchen.

With a flourish, Richard speared the goose with the fork and then started to attack the huge bird with the knife.

'Steady on,' their father instructed.

'Do be careful, Richie darling.' Her mother's face was ashen. 'Let Daddy take over.'

Addison looked on, uncomfortably. 'Do you want me to give you a hand, mate?'

'I know what I'm doing.' The knife went slash, slash. It was times like this when Autumn was glad that she didn't eat meat. Greasy lumps of flesh were hacked out of the poor bird. Her stomach churned over. Then the knife slipped, missed the goose completely and skidded across the table. Richard overbalanced and suddenly the goose parted company with its dish and shot into the air taking with it the dishes of vegetables and potatoes. The goose hit the floor with a greasy thud, while the vegetable dish up-ended and a selection of carrot batons, petit pois, Brussels sprouts and roasted parsnips landed squarely in Addison's lap. Her boyfriend jumped up and did a quick tribal dance as the steam threatened to burn through to his skin. Her father, perhaps harking back to his cricketing days, caught the potatoes on the fly.

They all stood and looked at the disarray. Jenkinson, sensibly, didn't come back to see what all the noise was about. Richard, Autumn noted, was shaking violently.

Her parents, it seemed, had gone into a state of catatonic shock. 'Addison,' she said crisply, 'I'm going to take Richard upstairs. Can I leave you to start on this mess?' Her boyfriend nodded to her and she gave him a thankful glance as he immediately set about the task of retrieving root vegetables from the floor.

'Perhaps the champagne didn't agree with his jet lag,' her mother suggested optimistically.

'Yes, yes,' Richard muttered. 'That must be it.'

Jet lag my arse, Autumn thought. She steered Rich up the stairs and into the room that had been his since childhood. Without protest, she took him over to the bed where he lay down on the dated counterpane and rolled himself into a ball as if experiencing severe stomach cramps.

She stroked his damp forehead. 'Are you all right?'

'You know, I don't feel all that well, sis.' He retched dryly.

'What have you been taking this time, Rich?'

'A bit of crack,' he confessed meekly. 'Nothing much.'

So much for rehab. It seemed that his time away had only served to get him into harder drugs. 'Oh, Richard.' She sank down on the bed and lay next to him.

'I don't know how it happened.' He sounded genuinely confused. 'I was *never* addicted to cocaine,' he said, with a bravado that didn't come through in his voice. 'A few grammes, that was all. Maybe a bit more. Then suddenly it wasn't enough. It didn't give me that same feeling.' He sounded frightened for the first time.

'How long can you go on like this, baby brother?'

'I've got it under control,' he insisted, his teeth chattering. 'I *will* get it under control. Can you just help me to the bathroom?'

Autumn helped to haul him to his feet. He felt light, insubstantial, weak. He staggered like an old man to the en-suite bathroom. She stood by him and bathed his forehead with a cool, damp cloth while he emptied the contents of his stomach into the lavatory. That's what you get, Autumn thought bleakly, when you have a Christmas that's just *too* merry.

Their Christmas lunch ordeal had eventually ended, with very little food actually having been eaten and her parents fawning over Addison and begging him to come back another time. Autumn felt she would be very lucky ever to get her boyfriend over their doorstep again.

Now he was driving them back to Autumn's apartment. As he pulled away from the front door and into the light holiday traffic, without turning towards her, Addison said, 'So – how long has your brother been a drug addict?'

Autumn leaned her head back against the seat. 'Is it that obvious?'

'I guess if you're in the record industry, you can spot a good singer a mile away.' Addison shrugged. 'I'm in the drugs business.'

They stopped at traffic-lights and Addison took her hand. 'Do your parents know how bad it is?'

She shook her head. 'I don't think so.'

'Do you?'

'Yes,' she said. 'But I pretend that I don't.'

'You know that you're facilitating his behaviour?'

'I try to protect him,' she protested. 'That's all.'

'And in doing so you cover up for him, provide excuses for him, and that gives him the opportunity not to face up to what he is.'

The lights changed and still they sat there. Thankfully, being Christmas Day, there was no one behind them impatiently tooting their horn.

'How do I help him?'

'Perhaps you can't, Autumn.'

'Well, I can't just stand by and watch him self-destruct.' She wrung at her skirt with her hands. 'He's in deep. He was using a bit of coke – recreational.' She repeated the lie he'd often told her. 'Now it's different. While he's been away he's moved onto heavier stuff. I thought he really wanted to clean his act up this time, yet I realise now that he simply went to America to get away from his problems here. Nothing more. To be honest, I don't even know if he's been to a rehab clinic at all. Some hard men were after him for money. Drugs related, of course. It was bad enough to scare the life out of Richard.'

Addison raised an eyebrow. 'And to think you were worried that your parents would be shocked by me.'

Autumn laughed. 'Thank goodness the nut roast escaped unharmed. What would we have had to eat otherwise? Perhaps for the first time in their lives my parents were grateful that I'm a vegetarian.'

'You don't have to cope with Richard by yourself, Autumn,' Addison told her. 'I can help. Lean on me.'

Autumn felt tears spring to her eyes and Addison pulled her to him. 'Thank you,' she said.

Chapter Fourteen

I wake up next to Marcus and I'm appalled at what I've done. He's lying beside me, arm slung across his pillow, his leg over mine. He's comfortable. So comfortable. And I am not.

I lie stock still, unable to move. Now what? That really wasn't a good idea at all, was it? Even the fluffy polar bear, which is now sitting on top of my cupboard, is staring at me judgementally. Gingerly, I ease myself away from my ex-fiancé. If I wasn't already at my own place, at this point I'd get up and sneak off home.

I sigh at my predicament – a bit too loudly – and Marcus's eyes open, so I make a grab for the sheet. Yeah, where were you last night, modesty, when I needed you?

'Hello,' my unwanted guest says sleepily. Already, he's all smiles and I check for any trace of smugness, but can find none. His fingers lightly caress my arm. My fucking traitorous body gets nice goosebumps all over. Stop it! This is bad, bad news.

Marcus snuggles against me. His skin is searing hot – very good for putting feet on in cold weather, not so good for resisting sexual temptation. I try to push him away.

Summoning up all of my courage, I say, 'I think you should go, Marcus.'

Now he's wide awake. 'Go?'

'Last night was a mistake. I shouldn't have let it happen.'

He pushes himself up onto his elbow and doesn't look at all put out, as he should. His fingers continue a languid journey over my weak, weak, weak and too-bloody-willing-by-half skin. 'You didn't protest too much at the time.'

I know now that I should have stuck to my best friend chocolate for comfort. That's why chocolate is better than sex – you never have to feel guilty after chocolate. Well, not that much. 'I was lonely and vulnerable.'

'You were *very* sexy,' he tells me with a slight raising of his eyebrows. I know Marcus well enough to realise that at any minute, he's going to be making a tent in my duvet. I have to get him out of here now before my resistance is further lowered.

'We've been here too many times before,' I say, gradually pulling more of the sheet around me. 'I can't go through this again.'

Marcus looks unconvinced and I realise that I'm in a poor bargaining position – being naked and in bed with him.

'We don't have to make love again,' he says, tent forming. 'I could stick around and we could go to one of the parks for a long walk.' Huh. Next he'll be offering to wear jumpers from Gap and do the technically impossible toasting marshmallows thing – all of the activities I'd planned with Crush.

'No,' I say firmly. 'Thanks for the offer, but I'd really like you to leave now.'

'Don't I even get breakfast?'

I wonder how to get out of the bed and make it to my dressing-gown without exposing myself. Can't work out how to do it, so stay put, further increasing my discomfort. 'It's better this way.'

'Not for me, it isn't,' Marcus points out. 'I'm starving. And I still love you, Lucy. I know we've had our problems . . .'

I go to speak, but he holds up his hands. 'All of them my fault. But don't harden your heart against me. It isn't like you.'

Then, before I can tell him that this is the new, improved me and that he can no longer mess with my emotions – okay, with one small aberration – the phone rings. Because I still have the dressing-gown dilemma, I stay put in the bed and let it go to answerphone.

'Hi, Gorgeous. It's me.' The sound of Crush's voice causes my jaw to drop open. 'I'm so, so sorry that I haven't been in touch,' he says brightly. 'I hope you haven't been worried about me. You won't believe what happened. I can't wait to make it up to you. Anyway, I'm sorry. Really sorry. Hope you had a great Christmas Day and I love you. We'll speak really soon. I love you, love you, love you. Did I say that already? Love you. Bye, Gorgeous.' Crush hangs up.

This doesn't sound like a man who's been caught waving his willy around on a webcam. He sounds suspiciously like a contrite boyfriend who's had a genuine problem. I've heard enough lame excuses from Marcus to know when I'm being spun a line. So what does this mean? I sit as still as a stone while my brain crashes around inside my skull with all the coordination of a Friday-night drunk. What on earth has really been happening on the other side of the world? I feel as if I'm one piece of a jigsaw missing. One very important piece.

'He loves you,' Marcus says eventually.

Somehow, I find my voice. 'Yes.'

I look at the person sharing my duvet and a whole heap of smugness is evident now. 'Then it seems as if you have some explaining to do.'

Chapter Fifteen

The Chocolate Lovers' Club has reconvened – and not before time, in my opinion. It's fair to say that we're not at our sparkling best. It's January and we're all suffering from that post-Christmas lethargy. I'm back at work but no one – especially me – can be bothered to do anything. It's even quiet in Chocolate Heaven, the atmosphere unusually muted. We're welded to the sofas, trying valiantly to buoy ourselves up with some of Clive's finest delights. We have fresh mango strips coated in rich, dark chocolate – because fruit is good for us. And this counts as one of our five daily portions of good stuff. We have some mocha and pistachio truffles – because we don't want to be sickeningly healthy. We have fudge brownies too – because we're fat pigs who are addicted to chocolate.

'How was Christmas?' Nadia asks.

'Uneventful,' Chantal complains, biting viciously into her brownie. 'Ted took me to a fabulous hotel, the mood was right, it should have been perfect. But it was still *uneventful*.' She shakes her glossy hair. 'I don't know what I have to do to get that man to sleep with me. He says he wants me to have his baby, but he doesn't want to perform the dastardly deed that procreation normally involves. What does he think he's going to do? Send his sperm through the mail to me? Is that what he thinks Special Delivery is for?' She huffs. 'Perhaps my marriage is a lost cause.'

'Don't give up,' Autumn says. 'I'm sure there'll be a break-through just around the corner.'

'Chocolate is a great substitute for sex,' I remind her.

Chantal looks at her half-eaten brownie with disdain. 'Says who?'

'Say people who can't get any sex,' I concede.

'Was your Christmas with Addison perfect?' Chantal asks Autumn.

'My drug addict brother turned up unannounced, drunk and as high as a kite. Christmas lunch ended up on the floor and Addison narrowly avoided third-degree burns of the testicles. But, apart from that, it was wonderful.'

We all laugh. 'That's what being in love does for you,' I tell her. 'Just when you think it's all going swimmingly, along comes the dreaded Family Christmas and messes it all up.'

'Well, my Family Christmas was fabulous,' Nadia says with a contented smile. 'Lewis and I had a great time with Toby. He really tried hard and it was so nice being a family again. I've missed that so much.'

'Will I be looking for a new lodger?' Chantal asks, a little sadly.

'I think we might get back together eventually, but I don't want to rush into anything,' Nadia tells us. 'Toby promises me, faithfully, that his gambling is a thing of the past. But we still have our mountain of debt to tackle. Life isn't a bed of roses just yet.'

Then Clive comes over with some more coffee and chocolate supplies for us. This man really knows how to look after a woman. Shame he's gay. He perches on the arm of the sofa next to me and squeezes my shoulder. 'Sorry I had to abandon you at the soup kitchen,' he says brightly, while I wish that the ground would open up and swallow me whole. He kisses me warmly on the cheek. 'You're a wonderful woman. I'm so proud of you.'

'Ha, ha,' I say.

When he's gone, the girls fix me with a collective stare. 'Soup kitchen?'

I hug my legs to me and avoid their eyes. 'That's where I spent Christmas Day,' I fess up. I feel bad because it sounds as if I would rather have spent the day with a pile of dossers than with my best friends. 'Clive was there too. It was nice. It was fun.' That might be stretching it too far. None of them look as if they believe me – except for Autumn, who seems to be viewing me with a new regard.

'I think that was a lovely thing to do, Lucy,' she tells me earnestly. 'Very selfless.'

'Thanks.' They continue to stare at me and I don't know if they all got X-ray vision as Christmas presents, but I can tell that they know that there's more that I'm hiding. So I might as well fess up the rest as well. I give a shrug that's intended to look casual. 'Then I went home and shagged Marcus.'

Three jaws drop. Three mouths fall open. Three faces look at me, aghast.

'I think that was an unwise thing to do, Lucy,' Autumn tells me earnestly. 'Very silly.'

'I know.' I put my head in my hands. 'I was lonely. I was vulnerable. I was drunk.' They're still staring at me in amazement. 'I was *incredibly* stupid,' I add before anyone else does. None of my friends disagree. But they weren't there and they don't know how miserable I felt. 'That was it. One night. Then I sent him on his way. Without breakfast.'

'Boy,' Chantal remarks. 'You know how to treat your men mean.'

For one who comes from a nation who don't understand irony, she makes a pretty good stab at it.

The excruciating rash on my back from my night of passion under the Christmas tree has very nearly gone and that's the last trace of anything remotely connected to Marcus that I ever want to encounter. I try not to itch. I had no idea that I was allergic to pine needles – or perhaps it's Marcus I'm having a severe reaction to.

'Nothing from Crush, then?' Autumn asks.

'No.' How can I tell them that he's been calling me repeatedly but that I've been steadfastly ignoring my phone and the messages on my computer? I never want to go near that damn and blasted thing again.

Nadia says, 'What was Clive doing at the soup kitchen?'

I lower my voice. 'He and Tristan are having relationship difficulties too. I don't know what the problem is.' Which means that no matter how much I probed Clive, he wasn't dishing the dirt.

'Gay men have trouble with long-term commitment due to their voracious sexual appetites,' Autumn pipes up in the manner of an expert on the dynamics of homosexual relationships.

'Christ,' Chantal says miserably. 'Why couldn't I have been born a gay man? It's been so long since I've had any sex that I'm struggling to get into my own pants.' She holds out the waistband of her trousers and, even though she's joking, it does look as if Chantal's impossibly slender waistline has thickened out slightly. I'm glad to see that I'm not the only one who's pigged out over the holidays. Depressed, I reach out for another brownie. Then, because I decide it's better for my midriff bulge, I switch to the mango and chocolate option. Mango has hardly any calories, right? And I'm thinking skinny, skinny, skinny thoughts.

'I guess this is down to all the great Asian food that Nadia's cooking for me,' Chantal continues. 'Plus we get to keep the fridge stacked with chocolate and blame it on Lewis.'

'We must start the new year in a better, healthier and more wholesome frame of mind,' I observe piously. 'I have no boyfriend. No money. No room in my clothes. This year can only bring about an improvement.'

'We have to do something,' Autumn says. 'Something positive.' With Autumn, that normally involves doing a circle dance or something strange with runes or joss sticks.

'We could go on a detox diet,' Nadia suggests tentatively. 'Give up chocolate and stuff.'

We all breathe in sharply.

'Sorry, that was a very idiotic statement.' She hangs her head in shame.

'I started *Carol Vorderman's 28-Day Detox Diet*,' I admit. 'Well, I watched the DVD, then I lasted twenty-eight minutes before I gave in to a Kit-Kat.' I have no willpower. So sue me.

Perhaps I can get hold of a copy of Victoria Beckham's book – she surely must have some tips on how I can sick-up to a size zero in six days. Not that I don't have some experience in that area myself, but no self-respecting celebrity is without an eating disorder these days. Or so it seems. They set us 'real' women impossibly high standards that anyone with even a vague addiction to Cadbury's Caramel couldn't meet. What's the attraction in a grown woman having the body of a seven-year-old girl? That's so dodgy, it's untrue. Even a modicum of slenderness would do for me.

Tristan comes into the café and leans on the counter. 'How are our best customers today?'

'Depressed,' I answer for us all. 'We're fat. We're broke. We're not getting any action.'

'Speak for yourself,' Nadia corrects me with a wink.

'We need to diet. We need to rejuvenate ourselves,' I tell him. 'Preferably without giving up chocolate. Or cheap wine. Any suggestions?'

Tristan mulls it over. 'Isn't there a spa somewhere that bases all its treatments on chocolate?'

There is much hyperventilating around the table. Could it be that our dreams have all come true?

'Where?' My voice holds a note of disbelief. If Tristan is joking then this is too, too cruel. I could withhold my custom for less than this. Well, not really.

He muses some more, rubbing his chin in a scholarly manner. 'California, I think.'

It had to be.

'I've heard of this place, I'm sure,' Chantal says. 'It's supposed to be great. Why have we not thought of this before now?'

'My goodness.' Nadia has gone all glazed and vague. 'We could spend all day being smothered in chocolate and still lose weight. That's my dream come true.'

We all let out a blissful, 'Ooohhh.'

This makes my tub of Body Shop Cocoa Body Scrub pale into measly insignificance.

'You ladies are *too* sad,' Tristan tells us with an indulgent shake of his head.

'If this doesn't sort out all our problems, then nothing will,' Autumn says with a breathy voice. Even she can see that this would be better than anything to do with chakras or chanting.

'We need to go there,' Chantal states. 'We need to go there now.'

'Oh, we do,' I agree. 'We certainly do.'

I daren't think about the pain that this will cause my credit card. I just have to think how good it will be for my body and soul.

Chapter Sixteen

I'm feeling wretched. Much chocolate has been consumed. I'm busy at work – which is very depressing in itself – and Marcus has already texted me ten times this morning to say that he loves me. Ten times, I've ignored him.

Burying the phone in the depths of my handbag, I gaze into middle distance. Marcus has been calling me every day since our supposed one-night stand to tell me that we should be together. I'm weary with arguing that we shouldn't. What am I going to do about him? This is a decision too big to be made without excessive sugar intake and, besides, I have work to do. Too much of it. I rifle through my chocolate stash and choose a Toffee Crisp for my sugary succour. Even the vanilla vapour from it is making me feel better. I pull a pile of papers towards me. Things must be really bad if I'm using work as an avoidance technique.

Behind me, I hear whistling and cheering. I spin round, unable to imagine what has roused the employees of Targa from their usual lethargy. Ohmigod. My eyes can't believe what they're seeing. They go wider and wider and wider, but still the view is the same. Large as life, Crush is standing there.

The sales team are pumping his hand and patting him on the back, but his dreamy brown eyes lock directly on mine. He looks slightly crumpled, as if he's just come straight from the airport. His face is tanned, the strong Antipodean sun has lightened his hair, and his body is taut and toned. Even though he's only been gone for a short time, he's every bit as handsome as I remember. Despite the fact that I'm wearing mascara that could well smudge, I rub my eyes in case I'm hallucinating due to sugar rush. But I'm not. Aiden Holby is really here.

He strides across the room to me in a very manly way and comes to a halt in front of my desk. 'Hi, Gorgeous,' he says with a big grin.

No one has called me gorgeous since Crush left.

'W . . . w . . . w . . . w . . .'

'What are you doing here?' he guesses when it becomes clear that I'm incapable of coherent speech.

'W . . . w . . . w . . . w . . .'

'Welcome back?' he tries. I don't think he's right, but then I'm not exactly sure what I'm trying to say myself.

'W . . . w . . . w . . . w . . .'

'Where have you been?' He's struggling now. 'What about m . . . m . . . m . . . missed you?'

I nod vehemently.

His smile widens. 'I've missed you too. You don't know how much.' Then, despite the office being busy, he curls his fingers round mine. 'God,' he says, 'I can't wait to get you alone. All I really want to do right now is take you in my arms and do extremely rude things to you on your desk.'

I can feel the heat rise to my face. That sounds like a very nice idea, even though it might get us both sacked. So what? There are other jobs. But then I think of Mr Aiden Holby cavorting on his bed with the woman in the slutty underwear and my head and my heart both start to ache.

'Why didn't you answer my calls?' he continues. 'I was getting frantic with worry – as you must have been about me.' Crush gives me a wry smile. 'So, what have you been up to while I've been away, you saucy minx?' he teases.

Still, my brain and my vocal cords won't hook up.

'I like the strong, silent type,' Crush says patiently, 'and I know that this is something of a surprise, but do you think at some point you might regain the power of speech?'

More nodding.

Crush leans in towards me. 'Look, I'm really sorry about what happened,' he says quietly into my ear. 'It was a complete nightmare. The least they could do was get me straight back on a flight for a bit of rest and recuperation for a couple of weeks.'

Recuperation?

'I guess they've filled you in all about it here.' Aiden inclines his head towards the Human Resources Department. Those bitches wouldn't tell me the time.

'I have no idea what you're talking about,' I finally manage to say.

'Me.' He gestures around him. 'My Outback adventure.'

'No,' I say. 'Still no idea.'

'I was on a team-bonding exercise.' There's something new. Targa employees seem to spend more of their time on team-bonding exercises than they do actually working. Crush looks for some degree of recognition from me. There's none. 'I've been missing in the Outback for two weeks,' he says. 'Unintentional walkabout. Didn't you realise something was wrong when I hadn't called?'

'I . . . I . . . I . . .'

'Don't start that again, Gorgeous,' he begs.

'I just thought you'd gone off me,' I say weakly.

Crush laughs out loud. 'I've been at death's door, wandering around some bloody desert, living only on the enormous stash of chocolate I'd taken with me and you thought I'd gone off you?' He laughs some more. 'They dropped four of us out in the middle of nowhere for a total "wilderness and survival" experience. I told you we were going in one of my emails.'

Did he? Perhaps I skipped that bit to get to the rather more interesting steamy moments.

'It was that, all right,' Crush continues with a hearty laugh. 'We were supposed to be gone for three days. Just a couple of overnighters in the middle of nowhere, that's all.' He chuckles again at the thought of it. 'We got hopelessly lost – not my fault, of course – and failed to make the pick-up destination. Because some bright spark had decided we should truly embrace a "back-to-basics" approach and they'd taken our mobile phones off us, we couldn't get in touch with anyone and they couldn't find us. We walked for days and days, probably going round in circles, until we finally came to a road. One of those enormous road-train lorries stopped and took us back to civilisation.'

I'm obviously looking completely blank, because he says, 'Surely someone told you what was going on?'

'No,' I say, and wonder why not.

'Bloody hell.' Crush sinks into the nearest chair. 'It was only the thought of coming back to you that kept me going. We had some pretty hairy moments out there.' He rakes his hands through his hair. 'And no one told you?'

'No,' I repeat.

'You must have wondered what on earth was going on.'

You could say that. 'Can I just get this straight?' I'm not sure how best to broach this, so I think the best way is just to blurt it out. Which is exactly what I do. 'Does that mean that it wasn't you that I saw on your webcam, naked and with another woman?'

Now Crush looks blank and perhaps he even recoils slightly. Maybe I should have couched this more sensitively.

Then he laughs and slaps his thigh as if I've told him a really great joke. 'My brother and his girlfriend were staying at my apartment for a few days before Christmas. They've recently set off on a world tour.'

'Lovely,' I squeak.

'I forgot to tell them about the webcam.' Then his eyes go round. 'You didn't see them getting down to it?'

My face, which was so flushed, has suddenly drained of all colour. 'Sort of.'

Then Aiden freezes. 'Wait,' he says. 'You didn't think that was me, did you?'

I feel the guilt-ridden gulp travel down my throat. 'Yes,' I tell him. 'I'm afraid I did.'

Chapter Seventeen

We each get a sandwich from the deli down the street and we sit on the low brick wall outside Targa's offices to eat it. I get ham, which was a mistake as it tastes like plastic. Or perhaps it's because my tastebuds feel as numb as the rest of me. The traffic roars past and scruffy streetwise pigeons pick at the crumbs by our feet. Opposite is a big branch of HMV and a Kentucky Fried Chicken place. It's not quite the same view as afforded by the Sydney Harbour Bridge, I'm sure. Crush is quiet and I wonder if he's regretting coming back – but then I remember that he's recently spent a million hours on a plane and is probably just exhausted.

'Sorry I can't take you out to lunch,' Crush says wearily. I feel as if he hasn't stopped apologising to me since he's returned when, quite frankly, it's me who should be doing all the grovelling. 'I have a meeting in fifteen minutes.' He glances at his watch again. 'They want to do a debriefing.'

I'd like to be doing my own kind of debriefing, but I guess that isn't going to be on the cards until we've got things straightened out between us.

'You liked Australia?'

'Loved it. If only you'd have been able to come out with me.'

If only.

'I wonder why no one in Human Resources kept you up to date with what was happening?'

I wonder. Not. Those Human Resources harridans wouldn't cross the street to wee on me if I was on fire. But I will get my revenge. One day.

'You didn't return my calls either,' Crush says, sounding

wounded. 'Or read my mails. That hurt. I couldn't understand it. I thought you'd be delighted to hear from me after my unexpected walkabout. I almost wondered whether you'd gone walkabout too.' He smiles at the thought. 'But I know why that was now.' His smile widens. 'You silly chump.'

How right he is. I cannot disagree. I'm a silly chump.

'I'll probably have to work late too tonight,' Aiden tells me. 'After that, we can start to put all this behind us.' He gives a relieved sigh which puts another knot in my stomach.

'I thought you were here for some rest and recuperation?'

'That comes later.' He wiggles his eyebrows at me in a seductive manner. 'Why don't I come round to your place when I've finished?'

I shrug and try to ignore the increased pitter-pattering of my easily influenced heart. 'You'll have jet lag,' I say. 'Terrible jet lag. Perhaps it would be better if you went straight home and got some sleep.'

Crush looks slightly put out. He shrugs too. 'Maybe.' He puts down his cheese sandwich. Perhaps Aiden's food tastes like plastic too. 'This isn't really the homecoming that I expected. I feel there's still some distance between us. I wanted us to rush into each other's arms and that everything would be the same, but I guess it's not easy when we're at work.' His hand finds mine. 'I want to make it up to you, Gorgeous. I've only got to get through today and tomorrow and then we'll have the weekend to enjoy each other's company.' He kisses me gently on the cheek. 'We can get to know each other all over again.'

'I'd like that,' I say. Tears spring to my eyes. How can I have forgotten how wonderful this man is? 'I'd really like that.' Then something in my sluggish brain clicks slowly into gear. How can I have forgotten that I've booked to go away with The Chocolate Lovers' Club for the weekend? 'Oh.'

'What?' Crush looks concerned. 'What's the matter?'

'I'm going away,' I tell him.

'Away?'

'To California.'

'For how long?'

'A few days.'

'But I've just got back.'

'I'm going to a chocolate spa. I booked it before I knew you were coming.' I sound completely pathetic. The traffic rushes by us and the fumes choke my throat.

Crush looks into my eyes. 'Things are going to be okay between us?'

'Yes. Yes. Of course.'

'You're not avoiding me, Gorgeous?'

'No. No. Absolutely not.' But I know in my heart that I am.

Chapter Eighteen

Crush has come with me to the airport. He takes my face in his hands. 'Come back safely to me.'

'I'm only going to a chocolate spa,' I remind him. 'I think it will be less fraught with danger than your trip.' The only danger is that instead of coming back svelte and lovely, I'll come back fatter than I was before.

'I'll miss you.'

I adore this man and can't believe that I'm going to abandon him as soon as he's returned to me. My dear chocolate addict friends and I had, indeed, rashly booked this long weekend before I knew that Crush would be making an impromptu visit home after his equally impromptu shave with death. While I hate to be leaving Aiden, I feel that I can't let the girls down by cancelling at such short notice. Even though the object of my affection is putting a brave face on this, I can tell that he's less than happy about me deserting him the minute he's back on home turf.

It may be the most cowardly thing to do, but part of me is certainly glad to be getting on a plane heading away from London and my current predicament. What I need now is to be enveloped in my favourite substance to let my cares float away. I can't think of anything finer.

Crush is more than keen to restart our relationship, as I am, and can't understand my reticence. But he might not be quite so enamoured of me when he finds out that I've had a dalliance with my old boyfriend in his absence, however brief. Even though there were extenuating circumstances, it being Christmas and everything being crap. Would it count in my favour that I didn't really enjoy it – well, not much? It was familiarity rather than desire that drove me back into Marcus's arms. Loneliness rather than love. Whatever excuses I can drum up, I still feel mortified that I could have done this. And I got a rash for my pains. But I guess it was only on my back. With Marcus's track record it could have been a lot worse, believe me.

I've kept Aiden at arm's length for the last couple of days while I've tried to decide how to tell him that I've betrayed him. And tell him, I must. I want to fall in love with him all over again and him with me – but we can't have secrets between us, so I know that I must come clean. If I get it right, then I might be surprised about how understanding he is. Would he have wanted me to be alone at Christmas? Perhaps given the alternative, he would have. But then I've had years of being on the receiving end of such treatment and I know exactly how crummy it feels. Still, I've got a lengthy flight ahead of me which should give me plenty of time to consider my options.

I see the other members of The Chocolate Lovers' Club coming towards me, laden down with luggage even though we're only going for four days and for most of that we'll be lying around naked and smothered in chocolate. Nadia has left Lewis with Toby at great emotional cost as she's never left her son behind before. She's, once more, indebted to Chantal who's picking up her bill. They're all in high spirits and I feel my own depleted soul lift in response.

'I should leave you now,' Crush says.

I nod to him. 'I'll be fine.'

'Have a great time. I love you,' he says. 'You know that.'

'Aiden . . .' But before I have a chance to reply, Nadia, Chantal and Autumn descend on me and my chance is lost. They're all smiles and unconcealed excitement.

'This is Aiden,' I say, even though he needs no introduction.

'Ah, so this is the famous Crush,' Chantal says.

Aiden looks to me for an explanation. 'Crush?'

'The girls used to think that I had a bit of a crush on you,' I reluctantly explain.

'Crush.' He laughs, and smiles at me indulgently.

'It's lovely to meet you,' Autumn says. 'I hope we see more of you.'

'We'd better go and check in,' Nadia tells us with a glance at her watch. 'Time's tight.'

Crush kisses me again and my friends, grinning stupidly, look to be one step away from going, 'Aawwhh!'

'See you soon.' He rubs a thumb gently over my cheek, then I watch as he strides away.

'He's fabulous,' Chantal says with an appreciative sigh. 'Don't mess this one up, Lucy.'

And the horrible thing is, I think that I might already have.

Chapter Nineteen

The chocolate spa is fantastic. It's called Melted and is housed in a minimalist white building overlooking the enticing sands of Santa Monica beach. The big yellow California sun is scorching and the sky is impossibly blue.

We're all sitting together on bamboo loungers in one of the airy treatment rooms waiting for our first appointment to begin. We've all booked chocolate facials and, later, massages with cocoa and passion fruit oils. Already, the heady scents of coffee and vanilla have transported me to a state of bliss. The French windows are open and as a background to the soothing music, there's the sound of the surf rolling in. All that's missing is the Beach Boys singing 'Surfin' USA'.

'I can't believe how chubby I'm getting,' Chantal complains to us all as she pinches at her waistline. 'I think I might get a personal trainer.'

'Are you mad?' I say. 'Just think what happened with Jacob. You'd be back to square one again. I thought you were trying not to get involved with *other men*.' I mouth that in order to protect her from the keen ears of any lurking therapists. 'Could you resist that?'

'As Oscar Wilde said, "I can resist everything, except temptation",' she quips.

'If you did get a personal trainer, he'd be turning up twice a week in tight shorts stretched over his firm buttocks, biceps bulging from his muscle top . . .'

'Lucy,' Chantal says, 'is this supposed to be *dissuading* me?'

We all laugh.

'I'm going to skip the facial,' she tells us. 'I've booked an appointment with the nurse instead. I just want to get a few things checked out. There's this weight gain. I've been feeling a little under the weather, a little nauseous.'

'Why didn't you tell us?'

'I'm sure it's nothing. It's probably a hormonal thing. Unfortunately, I'm getting towards that age.' Our friend shrugs. 'Maybe my thyroid's underactive or my oestrogen's on the way out. I'm sure the nurse will be able to put me straight. I'll catch up with you a little later for the massage.'

There's a facial therapist at the head of each of our beds and they've cleansed our faces with tiramisu foam before exfoliating us with cocoa seeds, and now they're smothering us with a chocolate mask. Yum. I think I'm having an out-of-body experience. I'm so delicious, I could eat myself.

'My New Year's resolution is going to be to pamper myself more often,' Nadia informs us. 'This is how my life should be led. I just have to work out how to find the money.'

Despite my own New Year's resolution to try to get my chocolate consumption under control, I have zero willpower. If my tongue was long enough, I'd definitely be licking this stuff off my own face. All the goodies from my festive stash have long since gone – even my Bob the Builder Christmas stocking which I bought for myself and which I was going to save for a rainy day. Actually, it didn't survive beyond Boxing Day – which, in my defence, was quite rainy for a time – but it was very nice. To be honest, I also ate the box of chocolate farm animals that was supposed to be a present for Nadia's son, but all those cute little sheep and pigs just looked so tasty. I'm sure he was just as happy with the Boots voucher I gave him instead.

The therapists cover our eyes with thin slices of cucumber, leaving me feeling even more delectably edible. Then they slip out with murmurings to us to relax. We take no further encouragement. Autumn lets out a contented sigh. But we've no sooner settled into the zone, when the door bursts open and there's an anguished howl. We all shoot up, scattering our cucumber. Chantal comes in, clutching her arms around herself and she's crying.

'What?' I say. 'What's happened?'

Chantal is sobbing too much to speak.

'What's wrong?' Nadia asks soothingly. 'Was it something the nurse said?'

Our friend nods her head miserably. 'I *have* got a hormonal problem,' she tells us, trying to steady her voice.

'A bad one?' I want to know. She's desperately upset.

'I think I'm pregnant.'

There is an amazed silence. We all exchange an anxious look and it's up to me to be spokesperson. 'That sounds pretty serious.'

'Yes,' she gulps. 'Because I've no idea whose baby it might be.'

Chapter Twenty

We get the therapists to come and take off our yummy chocolate masks, abandoning our treatments so that we can comfort our friend. I think of asking can I save mine to eat it later, but good manners get the better of me.

Then the four of us find a quiet spot, sitting on a swing out on the front porch overlooking the beach, giving ourselves succour in the form of ice-cold honey and vanilla milkshakes and hand-made caramel truffles, a speciality of the house. They're helping, but I think we should all eat more. I hand round the plate again, making sure that it stops twice at Chantal. Let's face it, it looks as if she's going to be eating for two now.

Our friend has got her crying under control, but her usual cool assurance has yet to reappear. She shakes her head as if dazed. 'What am I going to do?'

'You're absolutely sure?' I ask.

'I'll have to go out and get a pregnancy test to confirm it, but it looks pretty certain.' She takes a shuddering breath. 'I've missed my period for a couple of months, but I put it down to stress. The same with the nausea. The nurse is absolutely convinced that's what's wrong with me.'

I don't point out to Chantal that pregnancy isn't generally considered an illness – this may not be the moment.

Our friend spreads her hands over her possibly pregnant belly, showing us her burgeoning bump. 'Does that look like a baby?'

Now she comes to mention it, it does. Either that or she's got a Terry's Chocolate Orange in there whole, which isn't beyond the realms of possibility.

'What an idiot,' she spits out with a sigh.

I flick a glance at Nadia and Autumn, asking with my eyes if we should pursue this further, but I guess it's something we can't ignore. They nod their approval.

Resting my hand on Chantal's knee, I ask, 'Whose baby do you think it *might* be?'

Chantal lets her head fall back against the cushion and takes a moment to answer. 'It could be Jacob's,' she admits, giving me a rueful look. This is my ex-boyfriend and male escort with whom Chantal had a brief liaison. Even though I'd only dated him for a few weeks, I really liked him and the thought that he may well be the father of Chantal's child does make me feel a bit weird. 'I thought we were careful with protection, but in the heat of the moment . . .' She leaves the sentence unfinished for us all to draw our own conclusions.

And I thought Jacob was supposed to be a professional.

'Even worse,' she continues, 'it could belong to that smooth bastard who I slept with at the hotel in the Lake District. The one who robbed me of all my jewellery afterwards.'

'And the one who we managed to get it all back from with a superbly executed heist at Trington Manor,' I remind my friends.

We allow ourselves a little giggle at the memory of our victory.

'It could even be Ted's,' she says with a melancholy air. 'We did sleep together once during that time.'

'This isn't the end of the world,' Nadia assures her. 'Look how great you've got on with Lewis while we've been staying with you. I bet you never thought that would happen in a million years. You're wonderful with him. A natural.'

Chantal puts her hands over her eyes as if trying to envisage it. Nadia gives us a nervous glance.

'And Ted would love a baby,' I remind her. 'He's dying to become a father.' ·

'I might be on the verge of motherhood, but Ted may not be about to become a father,' she reminds me.

'There's DNA testing,' I try to reassure her. 'You can find out.'

'But suppose that I don't want to know?' Chantal drains her milkshake and then stands up. 'I should get this over with,' she says, putting a brave smile on her face. 'Anyone want to take a walk with me to the nearest drugstore?'

Chapter Twenty-One

We come back from our all too brief stay at the Melted chocolate spa feeling refreshed and lovely, except for Chantal, who couldn't have any of the treatments because, no surprises, she *is* pregnant. Our friend has come back looking very stressed instead of relaxed. Her delicate features are pinched and drawn, and my heart goes out to her.

On the other hand, I'm pink and glowing and feel as if I've been scrubbed and polished from the inside out. I'm sure I've lost about seven pounds of unwanted skin alone. I also feel very positive about my future, which is good news as I'm meeting Crush for dinner tonight and I'm going to take the bull by the horns and come clean about my ill-advised fling with Marcus. I can only hope that he'll understand.

In an attempt to blind him with my beauty, I've bought a new dress. As my credit-card limit has already gone stellar, a little more will make not the slightest bit of difference. I've chosen a pretty blue silk, girly dress, and to ensure that I'm heading even further towards poverty, I bought some espadrilles to match. Not exactly attire for the full force of the British winter, but I'm still basking in the reflected glow of the California sun and some judiciously applied St Tropez tanning cream. I can only hope that the goosepimples will stay away long enough for me to wow Crush.

My cab pulls up outside Victor's, a trendy restaurant in Charlotte Street that Marcus took me to a couple of times when he was trying to apologise for misdemeanours. How much we have in common now. Who would have thought that the boot would ever have been on my unfaithful foot? It's too mortifying for words. Despite the cold, my palms are clammy. A rush of warm air hits me as I enter the restaurant and then I go all warm inside as I see Crush sitting waiting for me. I quickly strip off my coat, and the maître d' leads me across the crowded room to join him.

Aiden stands up as I approach. 'You look fabulous,' he tells me earnestly, and his voice is filled with affection.

I kiss him and then slide into the seat opposite. He pours me a glass of wine and we chink glasses together. 'To us,' he says.

'To us.'

'Did you have a wonderful time, Gorgeous?'

'It was great,' I say. 'It was the first time that we've all been away together and I hope we'll do it again.' I just feel sorry for Chantal, but I don't want to tell Crush about that just yet. 'The spa was lovely.'

'I liked to think of you naked and smothered in chocolate,' he lets me know, and I blush. I have to confess that when I was naked and smothered in chocolate, I thought of Crush a lot too. 'I've missed you so much.'

'I've missed you too,' I tell him truthfully.

'And I've got some good news for you.' He grins while I wait to hear it. 'I'm not going back to Australia,' he says.

I nearly spit out my wine. 'You're not?'

Crush takes my hand in his. 'I don't want to mess up this relationship,' he says. 'I realise that us being apart was putting a strain on things. This is too important to me.'

Having nearly spat it out, I now glug the rest of my wine down hurriedly.

'Targa have agreed that I can be based in the UK. I've put a great deputy in place in Sydney. I'll have to go out there on a regular basis, but most of the time I'll be here.' He spreads his hands jubilantly.

'Wow,' I say.

Crush frowns – as well he might. 'You don't sound overjoyed,' he notes. 'I thought you'd be pleased.'

'I am,' I say. 'I'm really, really pleased.' This is going a bit quicker than I imagined it and, if I'm honest, I'd quite liked the sound of going to live out in Australia. My heart goes into freefall. Crush, it seems, has given up a great opportunity for me. How am I going to tell him about Marcus now?

'But?'

I sigh heavily. 'There's something I have to tell you. I've done something very bad and it's eating away at me.'

'How bad?' Crush teases. 'This sounds interesting.'

'I don't want us to have any secrets,' I say, with wavering voice. 'I want to be completely honest with you, so that you know even the most terrible things that I've done.'

He still doesn't look convinced that I'm deadly serious. I try to inject an air of solemnity and hang my head. 'It has to do with me seeing you naked on the webcam.'

'Not me,' he corrects with a broad smile. 'My brother. You've not yet had the pleasure of seeing me naked, Gorgeous. Though I hope we can correct that terrible omission very soon.'

'Me too,' I squeak.

'So.' Crush sits back like someone waiting to be told an entertaining story. 'Are you going to confess this heinous crime?'

Clearing my throat, I begin, 'I was alone at Christmas—'

'I know,' Crush says, 'and I feel terrible about that. I'm going to do all I can to make it up to you.'

'—*very* alone,' I reiterate. 'And I thought that you'd found someone else. I had no idea that you were in trouble. No one told me. I just thought . . . I thought you'd forgotten all about me.' I'm on the verge of tears.

'Hey,' Aiden says. 'That's all behind us now. We know that it was a silly mistake.'

'I made one other silly mistake too.' I can feel myself gnawing anxiously at my lip while he waits for me to spill the beans. There's a puzzled frown on his handsome face and I want to reach out and smooth it. Instead, I wring my hands together in the manner of the wretched fool that I am.

'Tell me,' he urges gently. 'Nothing can be that bad.' He even laughs a little.

'I slept with Marcus,' I say.

I see him recoil and blink a lot.

'I slept with Marcus on Christmas Day, because I was alone and feeling sorry for myself.'

Crush's face has turned ashen.

'It was once,' I continue. 'Just the once and I'm deeply, deeply sorry.'

Aiden says nothing, but his jaw has set and his eyes have darkened alarmingly. Around us the jolly, amusing chatter continues unabated while we sit here in our bubble of misery. When Crush eventually finds his voice, he says, 'How could you, Lucy? How could you do that?'

'I was alone . . .'

'And I was in the *fucking* desert,' he snaps. 'Worried sick. Not about myself, but about you and how concerned you'd be.'

'I knew nothing about it.'

'Is that an excuse?' he asks. 'Is that any reason to jump straight back into bed with your ex-boyfriend? Your *bastard* ex-boyfriend as I seem to remember you referring to him on many occasions.'

'I . . .' What can I actually say that will vindicate this?

Crush holds up his hands. 'Does this relationship mean so little to you?' He shakes his head in disbelief. 'I can't believe that you've done this. Have you so little trust in me? Do you have so little self-respect? When Marcus has continually let you down, you still run straight back to him the minute anything goes wrong?'

I can't really argue with that candid assessment of the situation.

'I wish I was getting straight back on a plane to Australia.' He rubs his hand over his forehead. 'Now I'm going to be stuck here, thanks to you.'

'I would never, *ever* have deliberately set out to cheat on you, Aiden,' I plead. 'It was a moment of madness. I know exactly how it feels to be on the receiving end of this. I'd never do it intentionally. I was drunk . . .'

'What a great excuse! Are you going to go out and shag another bloke every time you've had one over the eight? Is that what I have to look forward to?'

'Of course not,' I say quietly.

'How do I know that?' Then the fight goes out of his voice. 'How do I know that now?'

Crush knocks back his wine and then he folds up his napkin.

'Please don't go,' I say. 'Forgive me. I want to give this another try.'

'We spent so long getting together, Lucy, and now you've destroyed it all. I'm just so . . . so . . .' He searches for a word bad enough. 'So *disappointed* in you.'

Disappointed isn't so terrible. Disappointed I could work with. 'We could make it work, couldn't we? If we wanted to.'

Aiden Holby looks at me and all I see is overt dislike in his eyes. Gone is the twinkling mischief that I've secretly loved for so long. Gone is the love that was growing there. 'No. We can't make it work. I don't have the heart for it.' He sighs at me. 'I used to feel sorry for you, Lucy. I hated the way Marcus treated you. Now I pity you.'

I put my hand on his arm. 'Aiden, please . . .'

He shrugs me off. 'Go fuck yourself, Lucy,' he says. 'Better still, go fuck Marcus. You deserve each other.'

I'm shocked at his coldness, but perhaps I shouldn't be. He's hurt and I know exactly how that feels. Aiden marches out of the restaurant and I sit there, face burning with shame, trying not to cry.

The waiter comes over. 'Would madam like to order?'

'Yes,' I say shakily. 'Could you get me a new brain, please? The one I have doesn't seem to function properly.'

Chapter Twenty-Two

Chantal looked at her body in the full-length mirror in the living room. She turned sideways and pulled her shirt tight over her blossoming bump. Currently, her stomach simply looked as if she'd been eating way too much chocolate over Christmas, but she knew it wouldn't stay like that for long.

'Aunty Chantal,' Lewis said. 'You've got a fat tummy.'

Nadia put down her magazine and gave her a wry glance over her shoulder. 'Out of the mouth of babes.'

Chantal knelt down and cuddled Lewis to her. 'Shall I tell you a secret?' Her little friend nodded enthusiastically. 'Aunty Chantal's going to have a baby.'

'Oh.' Lewis wrinkled his nose. 'Will it be my brother?'

'No, honey. But I hope the baby will be your friend.'

'Oh.' He didn't look too impressed at all. 'Will he be able to play football with me?'

'Yes, I'm sure. But the baby might not be another boy, it might be a little girl.'

Lewis looked as if he didn't like the sound of that at all. 'I think I might watch television now,' he said, snaking away from her.

Chantal sighed. She sincerely hoped that she'd get a better reception from her husband when she broke her news to him. Well, she'd know soon enough, as she was due to meet Ted tonight to talk to him about their future. Her hands went to her bump. 'I still can't believe this is real,' she confided to Nadia.

'You'll be a great mum,' her friend reassured her. 'You should try to enjoy your pregnancy, Chantal.'

But how could she, when for the next six months she'd be

wondering who the father was. Would she be able to tell when the baby popped out exactly who it favoured? Would it have Jacob's chiselled good looks? Or her husband's strong, straight nose? She could barely even remember what the other guy she'd slept with looked like. Or would the baby come out looking like all of them did – like red, wrinkled, screwed-up old blokes – lovable only to their parents?

Chantal had been on the internet visiting all the paternity-testing sites, so she knew that she could have a pre-natal DNA test to determine who the daddy was, but there was a risk to the baby going down that route: tests on the foetus were invasive and potentially dangerous. This little tyke might not have been planned and the exact circumstances of the baby's conception might currently be vague, but he, she or it was most certainly wanted, and there was no way that Chantal would consider anything that could possibly harm the child.

An abortion wasn't even an option, even though it might well have solved some of her problems. Now that she was pregnant there was no doubt that she wanted this baby – no matter whose it was. A fierce, protective instinct had already kicked in as soon as her pregnancy had been confirmed. First and foremost, the baby was *hers* – and that was all that she cared about. The DNA test could wait until after the child was born. Then it was simply a matter of taking a hair or saliva sample and sending them off to some anonymous laboratory with the appropriate fee. There was no choice as far as she was concerned. She'd have to wait until after the birth to find out for certain whose genes Baby Hamilton had inherited.

She and Ted had gotten tickets for the theatre tonight – a modern and controversial performance of *Othello* at the South Bank. Chantal couldn't imagine why she'd bought seats for such an emotive play, other than the fact that it was the hot ticket in town. If she'd been thinking straight, she would have gone for something with a more neutral subject-matter. Perhaps it was true that pregnancy reduced your brain cells. Ted loved his Shakespeare, though; he'd been looking forward to the performance for weeks and she didn't want to spoil it for him. She just hoped it wouldn't put any ideas in his mind about killing his unfaithful wife.

Their relationship had been even more strained since they'd been away together at Christmas, but Chantal was determined to make it work. She wondered why they hadn't noticed then the way her 'love handles' were developing. Maybe it was their failure – once again – to get naked with each other. Let's face it, as much as she wanted their marriage to continue – albeit in a stronger form than it currently was – this news could be make or break for them. Could Ted live with the fact that the child could be another man's? What would this do to their already shaky status?

So when to drop her bombshell on him? They were meeting in a bar for a drink – strictly soda for her from now on. Would that be the best place to tell him? Or should she wait until the interval in the show? Or maybe it would be best to broach it when they were enjoying a little late supper afterwards. If the play was as good as they said, Ted would be in a mellow mood. She hoped that the critics could be relied upon. Her marriage might depend on it.

Chantal spent the afternoon window-shopping, browsing mother and baby stores, trying to fix in her mind that this title was about to become appropriate to her. Then she'd taken herself along to her hairdressers for a blow-dry and a manicure to make sure she was looking her best for the evening.

They were meeting at one of Ted's favourite bars near his office. By the time she arrived, the bar was already busy with City types enjoying an after-work drink mixed with a sprinkling of theatre-goers, but Chantal had managed to find a bar stool and perched on it while she sipped slowly from her tumbler of mineral water. She'd always drunk lots of water, but suddenly it didn't seem so great now that it had been foisted on her. Bizarrely, her body was craving a chilled glass of Chardonnay. And a cigarette. Even though she'd never smoked. There was nothing quite like being told that you couldn't have something to make sure that you wanted it.

Chantal glanced at her watch. It was nearly seven o'clock and she was getting worried about Ted's continuing absence. He'd said he'd meet her at six-thirty. They'd need to be leaving for the theatre soon as the play started in half an hour. She'd called his cell phone several times, but it had gone straight to voicemail. Maybe she should call him and tell him that she'd leave his ticket at the box office if he'd been delayed. Punching in his number once again, she was surprised when Ted answered.

'Hi there,' she said brightly. 'I was beginning to worry that I'd been stood up.'

There was an uncomfortable pause at the other end of the phone. 'Chantal,' Ted said. 'Something's come up at the office. I'm not going to make it tonight.'

'Oh.' She couldn't keep the disappointment out of her voice. There was always some impending crisis in his office; she shouldn't be surprised.

'Sorry, honey,' he said. But Chantal thought he said it rather glibly. 'Maybe another time.'

Maybe another time?

'Ted,' she said calmly. 'I have something I need to discuss with you.'

'Can't it wait?'

'It's important. Shall I wait for you and we can have dinner instead of going to the show?'

'No. No,' he said distractedly. 'You go along. I don't know how long this will take. I'll call you.'

'Well, okay,' she said reluctantly.

But Ted had already hung up.

Chantal stared at her cell. That was a little chilly. She finished her glass of tepid water. So what would she do with her tickets now? Sitting alone in a theatre watching a play about love gone wrong suddenly didn't seem so appealing. Flicking through her contacts list, she located another number and pressed to dial. A moment later, the other cell was answered.

'Hi, Chantal. Good to hear from you.' The warmth in his voice was in stark contrast to her husband's cool manner.

'Are you busy tonight?'

'Nothing that I wouldn't drop for you.'

'Could you get to the South Bank in half an hour?'

'Yes.'

'I have tickets for the National Theatre. *Othello*. Are you up for it?'

'Sounds great.'

'I'll see you in the foyer, Jacob,' she said. Then she hung up.

She wasn't about to tell Jacob that she might be carrying his child, but if her husband couldn't make time for an evening out with her then there was no reason for her not to enjoy someone else's company.

Chapter Twenty-Three

Nadia and Autumn were sitting in Chocolate Heaven. 'Are you sure you don't mind?' Nadia asked for the third time.

'I don't mind,' Autumn repeated with a tolerant smile. 'Not at all.'

'I should go,' Nadia said, nibbling at her nails anxiously.

'We'll be fine,' Autumn assured her. 'Won't we, Lewis?'

Nadia's son nodded, licking at the chocolate ring that had already formed around his mouth.

'As soon as we've finished our chocolate milk and cookies we'll go to the park,' Autumn told him. Lewis's cheeky face broke into a grin and he ate his biscuit even quicker.

Nadia frowned. She was unused to leaving Lewis with other people. 'Make sure he keeps his hat and gloves on.'

'Don't worry,' Autumn said. 'It's not that cold today.'

Perhaps it was a chill round her heart that was making Nadia feel cold, rather than the actual temperature. 'I promise that I'll be as quick as possible,' she said.

'There's no rush. Really. I don't have a class to teach until this afternoon.'

Nadia lowered her voice. 'Toby should be out this morning,' she said so that Lewis couldn't hear her. 'I want to be in and out of the house before he comes home.'

Her friend looked at her, frowning her concern. 'I hope you know what you're doing, Nadia.'

'I have to be sure,' Nadia replied. 'This is the only way.' She kissed her son on the cheek. 'Be good for Aunty Autumn,' she warned him. Then she kissed Autumn too. 'Thanks for this. I'll see you later.'

★   ★   ★

Nadia took the Tube to the station at the top of her street. Her heart was pounding as she walked down the road towards her house. This was ridiculous, she told herself. All she was doing was having a look round what was still her own home. The only difficult point was that she didn't want her husband to know that she'd been snooping here while he was out. He wanted her to trust him, but the fact was, she still wasn't fully able to do that. It was concrete proof that she needed.

The estate agent's For Sale sign was still in the garden, but they'd had no interest in the house over the slow Christmas period. Now Nadia wasn't even sure whether she still wanted to sell the house or not. They'd had such a lovely time together over the holidays, was it wise to persist in breaking up the family unit? It would be so much better for everyone if they could make their marriage work again. If Toby really had managed to crack his internet gambling habit, shouldn't she do all she could to support him? Lewis had missed him so much. Though her son was having immense fun at Chantal's apartment because of the novelty value, it wasn't the same as being in his own home. However reluctant an 'aunty' Chantal might have been initially, she'd certainly now embraced Lewis as an important part of her life and was thoroughly spoiling him. Being a typical male, Lewis wasn't objecting to all the attention – or all the chocolate. But it was still no substitute for having a dad around.

Thankfully, Toby's van wasn't parked outside the house. Nadia didn't want it to look as if she didn't trust her husband – but, essentially, that was what today's little escapade was all about. It was much easier too, to do it without the ever-inquisitive Lewis in tow. At four years old, he was also the world's worst keeper of secrets and she didn't want to involve him in her cloak-and-dagger operation.

The house was tidy enough inside. She couldn't fault Toby for his housekeeping skills since she'd been gone. In the kitchen, there was a single cereal bowl and a mug in the sink, and just seeing them sitting there looking so alone made her want to cry. She couldn't bear the picture of Toby that it brought to mind – him sitting here by himself every morning.

On the worktop, the place where they dumped all of their post and their junkmail detritus, there was a pile of opened envelopes awaiting their eventual transport upstairs to the office in their tiny spare bedroom to be dealt with. She slipped each of the contents out and examined them. A lot of bills – as usual – but all legitimate and mainly connected with Toby's plumbing business. Nadia felt a bubble of relief rise within her; nothing untoward there.

Nearly forgetting that she was an intruder here, Nadia almost took the bills upstairs for Toby. Instead, she left the pile as she'd found it and climbed the stairs empty-handed. In the cramped office, she searched Toby's desk and rifled through the drawers. The more she tidily ransacked her own home, the more terrible she felt about having to do this in order to quell her doubts about her husband's sincerity when he told her that he was no longer in the grip of this awful gambling disease that had blighted their marriage. If it wasn't for Chantal's selfless generosity, they'd now be facing bankruptcy, homelessness and who knows what else.

She logged on to Toby's computer. Thankfully, he hadn't changed his password. Was that a good sign? Did it mean that he no longer had anything to hide from her? She still had to look. Scanning Toby's internet history files on the computer, she could see no evidence of the colourful names that caused otherwise sane human beings to part with their hard-earned cash. There was no Virtual Vegas or Cash Casino or Mansion of Millions or any of the other hundreds of sites that he'd been so keen on visiting. It wasn't that he was alone. There was an online gambling epidemic across the globe. These days it was so easy to be ensnared by the promise of huge riches. There was none of the stigma of sleazy gaming clubs, none of the effort of evading the family to visit a casino, no need for late-night poker games – all of your gambling could be done on a credit card and at the click of a mouse. It was a secret, nasty and potentially destructive pastime that could be carried out in the comfort of your own home. Practically every day in the national newspapers there was a story of someone who'd lost thousands of pounds on these treacherous sites. She sincerely hoped that her husband had managed to break free of his demons.

The USA was currently trying to ban its citizens from online gambling. Which on the surface seemed like a great idea, but Nadia wondered how that would succeed. Wouldn't it simply serve to drive it further underground? Would all the people who were currently addicted to the flashing lights and empty promises simply shrug their shoulders and give up? She didn't think so.

Logging off, Nadia went through to their bedroom. Now she was losing heart for her miserable task. This was unfair on Toby. If he said he'd cleaned up his act then she ought to believe him, otherwise there was no future for them. A cursory search of the drawers in the bedside table was also fruitless. As far as she could tell, there was no evidence in the house to show that Toby was still gambling. Was that because he really had quit? Or was it because he'd become more deceitful?

Nadia had left the house and scurried to meet up with Lewis and Autumn in the park. Now her son was currently working himself into a frenzy of excitement as a kind elderly lady had given him a stale crust of bread to throw for the shivering ducks. It was clear that her son had been perfectly happy during her absence and it made Nadia realise how accepting Lewis was to all the changes that were happening in his life. Children were extraordinarily resilient and it made her glow with pride when her son smiled across at her. She and Autumn sat on a bench overlooking the lake watching her son play happily.

'How did it go?' Autumn wanted to know.

'Fine,' Nadia replied. 'I think.' Then she smiled weakly at Autumn. 'There was nothing in the house to suggest that Toby's still gambling. Maybe he's managed to get it under control.'

'That's good,' Autumn said.

Nadia folded her arms across her chest and stared across the lake. 'Yes, it is.'

'Are you going to go back to him?'

'I don't know,' Nadia answered honestly. She turned to her friend. 'What do you think I should do?'

Autumn slipped her arm round her shoulders and smiled at her. 'I think perhaps, for Lewis's sake, that you should give him the benefit of the doubt.'

Nadia let out a sigh which was visible in the cold air. She looked across at her son, running up and down like a mad thing, scattering the quacking ducks. Pursing her lips, she said, 'That's exactly what I was thinking too.'

Chapter Twenty-Four

Autumn was watching two of her favourite clients who were currently working side-by-side on differing projects. Fraser, a teenage heroin addict and occasional dealer, had been coming to the Centre for two years, as had Tasmin who had a lot in common with him in terms of drug usage, but little in terms of talent with stained glass and mosaics.

Seeing Fraser flirting tirelessly, and unsuccessfully, with the disdainful object of his affections was making her smile. Tasmin had attitude to spare, and no callow youth, however streetwise, was going to persuade her to drop that. They say that love is blind and, in Fraser's case, that must certainly be true. There was no doubt that Tasmin was a pretty little thing, but she managed to disguise it quite well with heavy layers of Goth clothing, dyed black hair and a thick coating of eyeliner. They'd make an oddly matched pair – if Fraser ever managed to persuade Tasmin to go out with him – but Autumn hoped that they would one day make a couple.

Fraser was ham-fisted and his work with stained glass had more to do with enthusiasm than skill. Sometimes she wondered why he'd kept coming back for so long; most of their clients were of a much more itinerant nature, sometimes attending just one lesson, never to be seen again. Perhaps this was the only place where Fraser could be certain of kindness and respect. Perhaps it was simply to see his future girlfriend. Whatever it was, Autumn was certain that it wasn't his love of arts and crafts.

Tasmin, however, was a different kettle of fish. She was a budding artist in the making. Eschewing the usual suncatchers or basic candleholders, the girl had very quickly shown that she had an exceptional eye for colour and style. Clinging to the only thing that she'd ever been praised for in a short life that had been full of degradation and destruction, Tasmin had progressed to making highly commercial pieces of jewellery from kiln glass, bound with delicate silver wires. When the budget from the KICK IT! programme threatened to dry up, Autumn often funded the glass and other materials for the kids to continue their projects out of her own pocket. She would love to do more for these two, to try to make sure that they ended up in a safe, secure environment and weren't tempted back to a life of drugs and crime simply because no one cared enough about them.

'That looks great, Tasmin,' she said, always careful to praise the girl. A large glass pendant with a Japanese design lay on the workbench while Tasmin meticulously fashioned a decorative holder from threads of silver.

There was a tentative knock on the workshop door and, as she moved towards it, her brother Richard poked his head inside. Instantly, her heart sank. He was the last person she'd expected to see here, and it must mean that he was in trouble once again.

'Rich,' she said. 'What's happened now?'

As she moved closer to him she could see what the trouble was. He touched the livid bruise on his cheek gingerly. There was a cut across the bridge of his nose and his lip was swollen. 'Slight skirmish,' he said. 'Nothing to worry about.'

Autumn steered them both away from the students so that they could talk more freely. 'Does this mean that the people you were running away from have caught up with you?'

Richard shook his head. 'I wasn't running away, sis. I was merely absenting myself from the scene for a short period.'

Running away couched in another language, Autumn thought with a sigh.

'I came to ask a favour,' Richard said. There was always a catch with her brother. She couldn't remember the last time he'd paid her a purely social visit. 'Any chance in taking up my old bedroom in your flat? Until I get on my feet again.'

Until he'd made enough money from drugs to buy his own place, more likely.

'Are you still with Mummy and Daddy?'

'Yes.' Richard toyed with a shard of glass from the bench. She wanted to warn him not to cut himself, but had to remind herself that he should be more than aware of the dangers of broken glass. 'But I can't stay there,' he said. 'They're killing me.'

'No quicker than your drugs habit is,' she retorted.

'I can't move without them asking where I'm going,' he complained. 'At my age. Can you believe it? They treat me as if I'm fifteen.'

'Perhaps it would help if you didn't behave as if you were,' she suggested.

Her comment fell on deaf ears. 'Can I move my stuff in tonight?'

Autumn felt torn. She'd always been the one to help Richard. Who else could he turn to? He might be infuriating, but he was her brother. Didn't she owe it to him?

Her train of thought was interrupted by Addison coming into the room. As they were at work and there were students present – who were currently taking more interest in her conversation than their creations – he didn't kiss her, but they exchanged a glance that said they would make up for that shortfall later. The look didn't go unnoticed by her brother and his face darkened.

'Richard,' Addison said warmly. 'How's it hanging?' He held out his hand.

Her brother, somewhat reluctantly, took it.

'What happened to the face?'

'A misunderstanding,' Richard said tightly.

'Autumn seems to think you're running with some heavy people.'

Richard glared at her. 'Nothing I can't handle.'

'We can help you,' Addison said gently. 'You don't have to do this alone.'

'I'm not one of your sink-estate druggies,' Rich scoffed. 'Do you think I'm going to come and make pretty things with glass to save my soul?'

'There are other things we can do,' Addison continued calmly. 'Other programmes.'

'Keep your charity for these no-hopers.' He flicked a thumb in the direction of Fraser and Tasmin. Autumn wanted to curl up and die at her brother's bad manners. 'I'll see you later, Autumn,' he said, and went to stride out of the door.

Her heart shot to her mouth and, as he grabbed the handle, a voice from somewhere inside her said, 'No.'

Richard spun round.

'You can't stay with me,' she continued. There was no way that she wanted to go back to sleepless nights, worrying where her brother was or, when he did eventually turn up, wondering who he was going to bring back to the apartment. 'It's too stressful for me.'

Her brother glared at her boyfriend. 'I know what this is about,' he said. 'You're choosing *him* over me.'

'That's not true at all, Richard,' she said. 'What I'm doing is finally giving you back responsibility for your own life.' She thought back to what Addison had said about her own behaviour facilitating her brother's addiction, and prayed that this was the right thing to do. This was the first time that she'd ever said no to Richard and it didn't sit comfortably with her. The words rushed out now that she'd started. 'I can't always be there to pick up the pieces for you.'

Richard's face turned thunderous. 'Right,' he said crisply. 'I know exactly where I stand.' He stormed out of the door and slammed it forcefully behind him. The glass shattered and crashed to the floor.

All eyes in the workroom went to the pile of fallout.

Autumn tried a tired smile. 'Looks like I'm not going to pick up the pieces for Richard by picking up *these* pieces.'

'I'll do it,' Addison said kindly. 'Go to the staff room and I'll join you in a minute. Put the kettle on. You look like you could do with a cup of tea.'

And some recuperative chocolate, Autumn thought.

'We'll help, mate.' Fraser came forward to join Addison in clearing away the broken glass.

'Thank you,' Autumn said tearfully.

Addison took her hand. 'Richard will be all right, you know.' His voice was sure, comforting. 'You did the right thing.'

'Did I?' she said. 'I can only hope so.'

Chapter Twenty-Five

I have to look for another job. As soon as I've got a minute to spare then I'm going to phone up the agency and ask them to move me as soon as possible. Which could be tricky as I think I've been banned from working in a large range of offices throughout London due to my track record as a less than perfect employee.

Targa is, currently, not a healthy place to work. My sometime yoga teacher – Persephone – would tell me that the bad vibes will be messing with my karma or something, and I'm sure she'd be right. You could cut the atmosphere in here with a knife. My stomach is ragged with nerves. I would have to stand on my head for a very long time to counteract the bad effects if Persephone had her way.

Crush has been whisking past my desk all morning at a furious pace, failing to make eye-contact and generally looking as if he'd like to murder me in a slow and very horrible way. I really want to talk to him about what happened last night, but he's clearly not ready yet to open the channels of communication, so I'm sitting here feeling pathetically useless.

To protect myself from his harmful death-ray glances and to pass a certain amount of time, I've constructed a wall between me and the rest of the office with Mars Bars, Snickers and Double Deckers. They let me have two boxes of each at bulk discount price in the canteen here when they heard of my plight. If I hunker down low to my desk, I can remain completely shielded behind my barricade. All I have to do is resist the temptation to eat my way through it. Mmm. Though surely my safety wouldn't be too compromised if one measly Mars Bar went missing? I'm sure it would actually help to strengthen my immune system. A bar of chocolate has more protein than a banana and that has to be good, right? Perhaps some protein would help to build up my courage to tackle Crush head on.

I'm just starting to rip the wrapper off one when I see that Aiden Holby is heading my way. His face is set with grim determination and a black frown is settled on his brow. It's supposed to make him look fierce, but all it does is make him look cute. At this moment, I think I love him more than ever. I slip the chocolate surreptitiously into my desk drawer and try to pretend that I'm working – an art that I have practised extensively and have still failed to master.

Crush stops in front of my desk. His pose is Alpha male aggressive.

'Hi,' I say meekly.

With one sweep of his arm, Crush knocks my carefully constructed chocolate wall to the floor. So, this is war.

'Do you think you could prepare these figures for me, Ms Lombard?' *Ms Lombard?* I think that's taking it a bit far.

'Yes, *Mr Holby*,' I reply. 'When would you like them for?'

'I need them for the sales meeting this afternoon.'

'I'll start them immediately. Once I've picked up all my chocolate off the floor.'

I think I see him flush a bit. But only a little bit.

'You can have one of my Mars Bars,' I tell him with an uncertain smile. 'If you like.'

Crush hesitates slightly.

'As a peace offering,' I say.

He straightens up. 'No, thank you.' Even the offer of a Mars Bar can't break the ice here. That's bad.

'Aiden . . .' I say softly.

'Lucy,' he interjects. 'I think it would be better for everyone concerned if you asked your agency to find you another job.'

'One where you don't have to breathe the same oxygen as me?'

'Preferably.'

104

'I still love you,' I tell him, swallowing the lump that comes to my throat. 'But if you think it's best that I go, then I will.'

'Fine.' He goes to turn on his heel.

'But I just want to say one other thing.'

I see him weaken for a moment and then he says, 'I think we've said enough.' And he walks away from my desk.

'Loving someone doesn't mean that you only care for them when you feel like it,' I shout after him. 'It means that you forgive them when they mess up.'

His stride breaks and, for a brief moment, he stops and my heart has a little flutter of hope. But then, without looking back, he continues towards his office.

'Bugger,' I mutter to myself. Then I notice that everyone in the department has stopped working and is staring at me. 'What?' I shout.

People cower at their desks.

'Just so that you know,' I bellow across the room, 'I've cocked everything up again. Does anyone want to make an issue of it?'

Heads are lowered to paperwork and computer screens. With a sigh, I start the onerous task of picking up the pieces of my scattered chocolate wall which might as well be a metaphor for my life.

Chapter Twenty-Six

Phoning the agency was a complete waste of time. They told me that they have no other jobs for me, but I'm sure they were lying. Perhaps businesses have one of those alerts on me like they do in pubs to prevent undesirables. A Lucy Lombard Alert. All the people whose businesses I've trashed in the past, they've all phoned each other to put my name on a blacklist somewhere. I'm sure of it.

I take the Tube home, heavy of heart, feeling that I'm trapped for ever at Targa like some unfortunate genie in a bottle, unable to escape unless someone gives me a kindly rub. If anyone has inspiration about what I should do with my life, I wish they'd tell me.

It's raining and it's miserable. My ropey old umbrella makes a pitiful shelter and keeps threatening to blow inside out. The greyness of my life is reflected perfectly by the weather. To top it all, Marcus is leaning against the wall in the street opposite my flat when I get home. He doesn't have an umbrella and he's very wet. My ex-fiancé has been stationed out there every night since our Christmas close encounter of the carnal kind and since I've been refusing to answer his phone calls. As he sees me, he raises his hand in a wave and starts to cross the road. 'Lucy,' he calls out. But the traffic thwarts his plan to reach me and I dart inside my front door.

When I'm inside, I shake the rain off my coat and throw my sodden umbrella to the floor. Sneaking up to the window, I check outside and, sure enough, Marcus has returned to his station and is still leaning against the wall. I watch him for a moment, shivering against the cold and I reluctantly admire his staying power.

Would Crush have stood out there in the pouring rain for me night after night? I don't know, if you want the truth.

Running a hot bath, I whack in a ton of vanilla-scented bath soak and lower myself in. My skin is still silky soft from my Melted spa treatments, but I feel that all other benefits have dissipated far too quickly since my return home. I let the scalding water soothe my cold bones. Inhaling the vanilla scent, I try to let my mind go blank. Normally, when I want my mind to do something useful – like thinking – it's steadfastly blank. Now, when I'd welcome a bit of empty space, it's whirring.

I think all is lost with Crush. Look how many times I've taken Marcus back after various misdemeanours. I didn't give up on our relationship after one paltry mistake. Surely that's what love is all about? You take the rough with the smooth. I think of Marcus standing out there in the pouring rain. At what point should forgiveness end and the heart harden so that self-preservation can kick in? Perhaps it's different for everyone.

I towel myself dry and slip on my old tracky bottoms and sweatshirt. Before I head into the kitchen to find something for dinner, I take another peek out of the window. The rain is now horizontal. It's bouncing back off the pavements. The grids are all overflowing and water is running in torrents along the kerbside. Though my window is blurry with raindrops, I can see that Marcus is still outside. How can I let him stay out there in this? Why doesn't he just give up and go home?

Finding my mobile phone, I call Marcus's number.

'Hi,' he says, and his voice doesn't sound weary as I expect it to. It sounds bright and full of hope. I can hear the rain beating down on him.

'Go home,' I say.

'I can't.' The brightness and the hope have gone. 'I love you. I just want to be near you. I'll stay out here as long as it takes.'

What can I say to that? 'You can come in for dinner,' I say. 'But it will be something crap because I haven't been shopping.'

'I don't care,' Marcus says. This time, there's a crack in his voice.

Chapter Twenty-Seven

A moment later, Marcus is at my door. 'Don't drip on my carpet.' I try to sound stern, but how can I? Look at him – he's a complete mess. Is this what I've reduced him to? Rivulets of water are running from his hair and down his face. There's a waterfall at the end of his jacket. He's dripping on my carpet, despite my warning.

'You can go and hop in the bath,' I tell him. 'Try to get warmed up.' I'm hoping that my boiler will just about run to two baths in quick succession. Normally, it has to be given a while to think about it.

'Thanks, Lucy.' He sounds ridiculously grateful even through his chattering teeth.

'There are a few bits of your clothes still in my wardrobe. I'll dig them out for you.'

I help him to ease out of his jacket. His fingers are blue.

'You're lucky you didn't catch your death of cold,' I admonish him. 'What a stupid thing to do on a night like this. I'm not worth it, Marcus.'

He stills my hands and takes them in his. Those baby-blue eyes meet mine. 'I happen to think that you are.'

I pull away from him. 'Get in the bath before hypothermia sets in.'

Obediently, he heads to the bathroom.

In my bedroom, I ferret through the wardrobe. There are some of Marcus's jeans and a couple of T-shirts. I don't know why, but I hold one of the T-shirts to my cheek. It still holds the scent of Marcus's aftershave and my heart contracts painfully – even though the real deal is probably at this very moment getting into my tub.

There's also a sweater that I bought him years ago for Valentine's Day which he's never worn. Well, he can start now.

There are even pants and socks in the back of my drawer and I wonder why I've never summoned up the energy to take them to the charity shop. I leave the clothes out on the bed for him and go through to the kitchen. In the cupboard I find pasta shells and a tin of crushed tomatoes. Italian it is, then. The fridge contains some celery that's not too bendy and a nub of rock-hard Parmesan cheese that's more rind than anything else. It's past its sell-by date, but these things are never accurate, are they? And cheese doesn't go out of date anyway, does it? I'm pleased to see that what I lack in wholesome and nutritious food, I make up for by having a great stash of chocolate. There's a box of Clive's very finest jewels from Chocolate Heaven nestling there, waiting for Mummy. At least I'm always certain of a great dessert. If Marcus is good, I might even share them with him.

I chop up the vaguely floppy celery and fling it into the pan with the tomatoes. The pasta goes on to boil.

My unexpected guest appears at the kitchen door. He's wearing just a towel, slung low on his hips. There's an attractive flush to his face and his hair is washed and tousled rather than plastered flat to his head. It takes me back to the night we spent together and I *so* don't want to go there.

'Something smells good,' he says.

I think Marcus must be desperate.

'Pasta and a tin of tomatoes,' I tell him. 'My speciality.'

He comes towards me. 'I love you, Lucy.' His arms go to slip around my waist, but I neatly sidestep him.

'I've left you some dry clothes on the bed. Dinner will be ready in five.'

I hate to admit this, but Marcus looks quite cute in that sweater, so I try not to look at him. We sit on the sofa and eat our dinner from trays. I've opened a bottle of cheap red, but I'm monitoring very carefully what I drink. I remember only too well what happened last time I was sozzled when Marcus was in the vicinity.

109

There's some rubbish on the telly, and we're both pretending we're glued to it.

Eventually, Marcus having eaten every last morsel of his dinner, he puts down his tray and turns to me. 'Did you tell your boyfriend that we slept together?'

'Yes.' There's no point lying to Marcus.

'Are you still together?'

'What do you think? Not everyone is as forgiving as me.'

His hand inches across the sofa towards mine and he covers it with his fingers. 'I'm glad you've broken up.'

'Well, I'm not,' I tell him crisply, snatching my hand away. 'I'm devastated.'

'I really have changed, Lucy,' he tells me earnestly. 'I've had a lot of time to think about things. I've grown up in the last few months.'

This is from a man who's been standing in the pouring rain outside my flat.

'I'm going to get counselling to help me modify my behaviour,' he continues. 'Just as soon as I don't have to spend every night standing outside your flat.'

'You don't have to stand outside my flat any more,' I promise him. 'We're friends again.'

A smile lights up his handsome face.

'*Just* friends,' I add. 'I never, ever want a relationship again, as long as I live.'

Marcus looks doubtful.

'I mean it.'

He sits quietly while he digests that, along with his pasta. When it's clear that I'm not going to fill the gap, he pipes up again. 'We could watch a romantic film. That will make you feel better.'

'It wouldn't.' Actually, it would. A nice controlled weep at someone else's fucked-up love-life would make me feel great, but I hate to think that Marcus knows me so well.

'*An Officer and a Gentleman*,' he says decisively. 'That never fails.' And before I can do anything about it, he's flicked through the DVDs on my shelf and is slotting in said romantic film.

'Have you got any chocolate?' comes next.

I give him a withering glare. 'Why would I not have choco-late?'

'I'll get it,' he says happily. 'This is turning into a perfect evening.'

On the screen, the delicious – and much younger – Richard Gere is being hotly pursued by Debra Winger. The knowledge of hopeless love is doing nothing to thwart her enthusiasm for the task in hand, I note. Foolish woman. I wriggle uncomfortably on the sofa when they eventually get down to it while she wears Richard Gere's very fetching peaked cap and nothing else. I can barely resist the urge to snatch up the remote and jab it onto fast forward. This scene never used to go on for so long, I'm sure. Marcus grins smugly while on screen, the lovers continue with their artistic groans of ecstasy. I have another chocolate. A rasp-berry and cream truffle.

By the end of the film, we've steadily worked our way through my box of Chocolate Heaven delights. I already know that when the newly graduated and uniformed Officer Mayo whips the girl of his dreams into his arms that I'll cry. I always do. The music builds to a crescendo, the strains of 'Love Lift Us Up Where We Belong' filling my lounge as Richard Gere carries a joyfully weeping Debra Winger off to a better life, and I weep along unashamedly. 'That's so romantic,' I sniff.

Marcus sniffs too.

'And it would only happen in Hollywood,' I add tartly as I remember our circumstances.

Marcus snuggles up next to me. I put a cushion between us. My ex-fiancé knows that this is usually the point where he'd comfort me and then we'd end up having hot sex on the sofa. Those days are gone.

'We've watched the film, now you can have a cup of coffee and then you're going home,' I tell him firmly. 'We do this on my terms from now on.'

'Anything you say, Lucy.' He grins at me and it's clear that he doesn't believe a word of it.

Chapter Twenty-Eight

Nadia had thought about her situation for over a week now and she still wasn't sure that she was doing the right thing. She hadn't even told Toby what she was planning for fear that she might change her mind at the very last minute. Now the decision had been made and there was no going back. Tonight, when her husband got home from work, she and Lewis would be there to surprise him. Home for good. A family once more.

Chantal lifted the last of her bags into the boot of her car. 'That's you all set.'

Nadia finished strapping Lewis into his car seat. 'Thanks, Chantal. I don't know what I'd have done without you.'

'It's been great having you here,' her friend said. 'I'm going to miss this little guy.' They both glanced at Lewis through the car window. He was eating a Chocolate Finger bribe and was oblivious to the emotional turmoil going on around him.

Nadia glanced wryly at Chantal's growing bump. 'You'll soon have one of your own to spoil.'

'Don't remind me,' Chantal said, patting her tummy fondly. 'I'm still in denial. I keep pretending that this is fluid retention.'

They both laughed.

For someone who insisted that she was in denial, Nadia thought Chantal was coping remarkably well with her unexpected pregnancy.

Chantal hugged her tightly. 'If this doesn't work out, you know that there'll always be a place here for the both of you.'

'I hope it won't come to that,' Nadia said.

'You guys will work it out,' her friend said reassuringly. 'You'd better get moving if you're planning to have something hot on the table for your husband when he gets home.' She gave Nadia a wink.

Nadia flicked a worried glance in her direction. 'You will be all right here on your own?'

'Sure.' Chantal nodded. 'Don't you worry about me.'

'I'll help you as much as I can with the baby,' Nadia said. 'We all will.' Nadia was sure that she could speak for the two other members of The Chocolate Lovers' Club.

'Go, before you make me cry!' Chantal wiped a tear from her eye. 'Go and make that husband of yours grateful that you've come back to him.'

It felt strange to be back in her own home. She'd spent the afternoon getting to know her own things again, settling back into her own space. Now Lewis was bathed and in his pyjamas and, as a treat, was watching his favourite *SpongeBob SquarePants* cartoon on the television. She watched her son transfixed by the colourful figures on the screen, sucking his thumb, finger hooked over his nose, engrossed. He looked so angelic, as if he was a graduate of the *Supernanny* school. Nadia hoped it would last until Toby arrived home. Glancing at the clock, she nibbled anxiously at her lip. She would have expected him to be home by now.

The latter part of the day had been spent unpacking their clothes, returning them to their rightful place in their own wardrobes. Already her time at Chantal's swish apartment felt a lifetime away. This place might not be anywhere near as plush, but it was still home to her. She belonged here.

Dinner was bubbling away on the hob – the scent of spices wafting through to the living room. Maybe Toby had popped into the pub on his way home for a quick pint. After all, he had no idea that she'd be here waiting for him. Now nerves gripped her stomach. Should she have called him? Perhaps he'd made other plans for tonight and she'd be waiting alone while their delicious dinner turned into a dried-up mess. Would he be pleased to see her?

What could she do while she waited? Instead of pacing the room, she went to sit down next to Lewis. Having a cuddle with her son always managed to still her mind. Passing the phone, she noticed that the answerphone light was blinking. The call must have come in while she was unpacking or cooking dinner as she hadn't heard the phone ring. As she went to see who might have telephoned, Toby's van pulled up outside the house.

Nadia's stomach went into free fall. The phone was forgotten. 'Daddy's here,' she told Lewis excitedly.

'Daddy!' He jumped up from the sofa and sprinted to the door. Nadia opened it wide as Toby walked up the path. A look of sheer joy crossed his face and Nadia felt herself sag with relief. He wanted them back.

Lewis jumped into his arms and, obligingly, Toby twirled him round. There were tears of joy in her husband's eyes when he gently lowered the boy to the ground. 'You've come home,' he said.

Nadia wrapped her arms round him, tearful herself. 'We've come home.'

They went inside, reunited, a family again.

'I can't believe it,' Toby said. 'This is more than I could have hoped for. I won't let you down, Nadia. I promise.'

'Ssh,' she said, and kissed him softly.

'I couldn't bear to lose you again.'

'We're not going anywhere,' she told him. 'Why don't you go and tuck this boy in and then have a shower? I'll just check on dinner.' With a smile on her face, she headed towards the kitchen. 'Oh,' she said, 'I almost forgot. There was a call for you. I mustn't have heard the phone.'

When she left the room, Toby pressed the playback button. 'This is a message for Mr Toby Stone,' the voice said. 'This is the Advance Credit Company and we need to speak to you urgently. Please call us on—'

Toby pressed the delete button. Nadia came back into the room, tying an apron round her waist. 'Who was it?'

'No one,' Toby said. 'Wrong number.'

She noticed that tears were still glistening in his eyes. 'Hey,' she said. 'Everything will be fine from now on.'

'It will,' Toby said, his voice choked with emotion. 'You'll see. I'll make sure that it is.'

Chapter Twenty-Nine

Autumn and Addison lay together in the bath. The bathroom was heavy with the scent of a dozen vanilla candles, two glasses of red wine were by their feet. They'd pulled the CD player inside the door and something mellow drifted out. It was Addison's choice of music – her favoured easy listening selection of whale song had been deemed too 'uncool'. She had to agree that this was much more relaxing. Being with Addison was making her loosen up a little. Not everything in life had to be done to save the planet. He might even be improving her musical taste – her pan pipes and African drumming CDs now nestled alongside albums by John Legend, Paolo Nutini and Corinne Bailey Rae. She hummed along with the melody. This was the first time in her life that Autumn felt as if she truly knew what being in love meant. Her head rested on his chest and she twisted in the warm water to gaze at him.

Addison's eyes were closed, but he still said, 'What?'

'I'm happy,' Autumn told him.

'That's good,' he said. 'Add a little more hot water then I'll be happy too.'

Flicking the tap with her foot, she let more hot water gush into the bath. 'Better?'

'Mmm,' Addison purred.

She leaned over and popped a piece of chocolate into his mouth from the dish on the side of the bath.

'Mmm *mmm*.' Her boyfriend smiled at her, opening his gorgeous deep brown eyes. 'Now I *am* in heaven.'

The phone rang. Addison grunted. It rang again.

'Maybe I should get that,' Autumn said, glancing anxiously towards the living room where the phone lay.

'You already know who it is,' Addison pointed out.

'It might not be Richard.' She eased herself halfway out of the bath. 'It could be someone else.'

'He's phoned you constantly for days.'

'I'm worried about him, Addison,' she said. 'He seems to be worse than ever.'

'You have to let go, Autumn. He has to find his own way. You can't be his keeper for ever.'

The phone stopped ringing, but the feeling of anxiety didn't leave her. Addison pulled her down until she was nestled beside him once again. 'I've always looked after him,' she said. 'It's a hard habit to break.'

'Well,' Addison traced his fingers over her breast, 'now you have someone else to look after.' His mouth covered hers and all thoughts of Richard and what he might need went out of her mind.

Hours later, they were lying in bed, arms around each other in sleep, when the phone rang again.

'No,' her boyfriend mumbled, still half-asleep. 'Not again.' His hand reached for hers and missed. 'Leave it, Autumn.'

But before Addison could protest too much, she slid out of the bed, slipped her robe around her and went in search of her phone. It was an unknown number on the display. She peered at the clock through half-closed sleepy eyelids. It was 1.00 a.m. Who could it be at this time?

'Miss Fielding?'

'Yes.' The formality of the voice at the other end shocked her fully awake.

'I'm phoning from the Fulgrave Hospital. We have your brother here.'

She was suddenly wide awake. 'Richard?' Autumn knew that she shouldn't have been as surprised as she was.

'He's had an accident,' the nurse or administrator or whoever this was calling her continued.

'Is he all right?'

There was a pause that went on for a moment too long. 'I'm afraid he's not terribly well.'

'What's the matter? What's wrong with him?'

She didn't hear him come into the room, but she realised that Addison was standing behind her. He slipped his arms round her waist and rested his head on her shoulder. While they were lying there happily making love, something terrible had been happening to Richard.

'It would be better if you could come into the hospital,' the voice at the end of the phone continued.

'Did he ask you to call me?'

'We found your number listed as Mr Fielding's next-of-kin on his mobile phone and you were the last person that he tried to call.'

'I'll be there as soon as I can.' She hung up. 'Richard's in hospital,' she told Addison, tears in her eyes.

Addison kissed her on the forehead. 'Then we'd better both get dressed,' he said.

The ward was darkened, but Autumn could tell which was Richard's bed straight away. In the far corner, a light shone over one area. Nurses bustled back and forth, machines beeped, there was an air of unhurried anxiety. She and Addison approached the nurse at the reception desk. 'We're here to see Richard Fielding.'

The nurse gave her a kind glance. 'You're his sister?'

Autumn nodded.

'We don't know what's happened to your brother,' the nurse explained in hushed tones as they walked to Rich's bed. 'He looks as if he's either been hit by a car or has been very badly beaten up.'

This was surely bad, if they couldn't tell which.

'He was found in an alley by a homeless person who had the good sense to call an ambulance.'

Guilt struck at Autumn's core. If she'd picked up Richard's call, could she have got an ambulance to him earlier?

Her brother was dwarfed by the range of machinery surrounding

117

him. Was that machine helping him to breathe? Was that how close he was between life and death? His heart was beating rhythmically, which was more than she could say for her own. But his face was swollen, virtually unrecognisable – cut, bruised, beaten to pulp. Tears squeezed out of her eyes.

'Rich,' she said. 'It's me. Autumn.' She held her brother's pale, lifeless hand and chafed at it.

'He hasn't spoken yet,' the nurse told her. 'He's still unconscious.'

She hardly dared voice her fears. 'He will get better?'

The nurse placed a hand on her arm. 'We're doing all that we can for him.'

'I didn't do enough for him.' She broke down and wept as Addison held her close. 'I didn't do enough.'

Chapter Thirty

The three of us are sitting in a line in a darkened room in Chantal's private clinic. Our friend is up on the couch, tummy bared.

'Are you sure we're all allowed in here?' I whisper.

'This is the benefit of a private clinic over National Health,' Chantal tells us. 'I can have what I like – so long as I pay for it.'

'I brought chocolate,' I say. 'To help our nerves. Do you think we can eat it without getting told off?'

'If we're quick,' Nadia says. So I furtively pass around a packet of Rolos and we all chew them with a grateful sigh.

I think Chantal is very brave to have us as her birthing partners. I, for one, am sure that I'll pass out when it gets to the crucial moment. Frankly, I've even been known to pass out at the point of conception. Nadia, at least, has been through it before – only once though, which can't mean that she's in a great hurry to repeat the experience. Autumn will be wonderful, because she's useful in every situation. There will, no doubt, be some crystal she can bring along to ease the contractions and she'll be brewing up raspberry tea and chanting and rubbing on aromatherapy oils or whatever until the baby pops out.

We're waiting for the radiologist to come and give Chantal her scan. Just lately, her tummy has grown bigger, while her chocolate consumption has doubled, maybe tripled. Perhaps she's eating for three rather than two?

'Shouldn't Ted be with you for this?' I tentatively suggest.

Chantal stares at the ceiling. 'I haven't been able to tell him yet,' she admits. 'He cried off our theatre trip when I was going to raise the subject and now he's not returning my calls. That's not good. Right?'

We all silently agree that it isn't good.

'Don't you worry about that now,' Nadia says, patting her hand. 'You have all of us to get you through the next few months. You'll be absolutely fine.'

Autumn gives a tired yawn. 'Sorry,' she says. 'I've been up all night.'

'We don't want to know about your wild love-life,' I tell her. 'We'll all be horribly jealous.'

'I've been at the hospital,' she explains wearily. 'A different one. Richard's been beaten up – he's in a bad way.'

'Oh, Autumn.'

'Don't say another word.' She holds her hand up. 'I want this to be a joyous occasion and I might cry if you say anything nice to me.'

'You know that if there's anything we can do, that we will.'

Autumn nods. I quickly give her another comfort Rolo and she takes it gratefully.

The radiologist comes into the room and I hide the rest of the chocolate.

'Have you been selling tickets for this?' she jokes to Chantal.

'These are my best friends,' Chantal tells her. 'I wanted them all to be here.'

'Well, they've got grandstand seats,' she says. 'Let's get started.'

Clear gel is smeared over Chantal's stomach and then suddenly we're the first people to be saying hello to the new life growing inside her.

'Oh,' Chantal says with surprise. 'I hadn't expected it to look so much like a baby.'

Nadia laughs. 'What did you think it would look like?'

'A tadpole,' Chantal says. 'The last time I saw a scan picture it was a fuzzy blob that looked nothing like a baby, but this looks exactly like a kid.' She starts to cry. 'It's got fingers and toes, everything.'

'Looks like you're going to have a little girl,' the radiologist chips in.

Then we're all crying. 'Goddamit,' Chantal says as she looks up at us with red-rimmed eyes. 'I'm really going to have a baby.'

Chapter Thirty-One

Marcus did go straight home after the film. I made absolutely sure about that. Actually, I was quite proud of myself because he was being so kind and loving and it was still raining, and well . . . I sigh out loud and push in another one of my stash of Chocolate Heaven truffles.

Crush slams a file down on my desk. Operation 'Make Crush Friends With Me Again' has not been going well. The coffee I've taken him has remained untouched. The chocolate versions of olive branches have all been rebuffed.

'Sorry to interrupt your reverie,' he says crisply. Instantly, I sit upright and try to appear efficient. 'I'm thinking of organising a team-bonding event.'

I can't help but groan. 'Another one?' I say. 'Haven't we had enough humiliation in this office? I thought the little incident with the broken leg might have put you off team-bonding for life.' That was the result of a disastrous team-bonding, go-karting, me-being-too-competitive-and-too-jealous accident.

'A team that plays together stays together.' There's a very stubborn thrust to his chin.

'I hate this new, grumpy and corporate version of Aiden Holby,' I tell him candidly. 'Can't my old slap-dash boss who let me fiddle my expenses and called me Gorgeous come back? I can beg if you like.'

Aiden ignores my entreaty. 'I thought we'd give paint-balling a try,' he says.

'Great. You don't think I caused enough damage with a go-kart, so now you're giving me a gun? Will you never learn?'

My phone rings and, without thinking, I answer. It's Marcus

and I feel the blood rush to my face. 'Oh hi,' I say. 'I can't talk right now. Yes, I'm in the office.' Marcus tells me he loves me. 'Right. Good. Thanks. Bye,' I say and hang up before I actually found out what – if anything – Marcus wanted.

'Marcus?' Crush is eyeing me critically. 'Will *you* never learn?'

'We're just friends.'

Mr Aiden Holby snorts at me. 'You're an idiot, Lucy,' he tells me. 'And what's worse, you know you're an idiot.'

But before I can summon up a suitable riposte, the office door bursts open and at ear-splitting volume the strains of 'Love Lift Us Up Where We Belong' drift across the room. I stand up and crane my neck to see what's happening. As does everyone else in the office.

In true *An Officer and a Gentleman* style, complete with white dress uniform and matching peaked cap, Marcus marches the length of the entire office towards me, boom box in his white-gloved hand. There's more than a look of the Richard Gere about him. Both Crush and I stand there looking completely amazed.

Marcus puts the boom box down on my desk. With a self-satisfied grin at Crush, my former fiancé skirts round him and comes to stand in front of me.

'Marcus,' I say. 'What are you doing?'

With that, and a small grunt, he sweeps me up into his arms. 'I've come to take you away from your hideous life in this sweat-shop.'

I start to giggle.

Aiden Holby is looking furious – paint-balling adventure long-forgotten.

'Marcus, put me down,' I try, but I'm laughing too much to put up a very effective protest. I wonder if Crush has even seen *An Officer and a Gentleman* – and, if so, exactly who he saw it with.

In the background, Joe Cocker and Jennifer Warnes warble on while my ex-fiancé carries me away from my desk and while I chuckle hysterically. Everyone in the office is smiling and, in the spirit of the film, someone needs to shout, 'Way to go, Lucy!'

– but they don't. Then the staff of Targa's Sales Department are suddenly mobilised and they start to applaud Marcus's audacity as he whisks me away in his arms. Everyone except one person, of course.

Over my shoulder, I can see that Crush isn't very impressed by this at all. His face is stony. I try to recover some decorum. 'I'll be in early tomorrow!' I call out. 'To make up for this!'

But Crush shouts, 'It wouldn't worry me if you never came back at all!'

Chapter Thirty-Two

Marcus has booked us a night at The Ritz. My ex-fiancé has given up carrying me around in his arms. He started to go a bit too red in the face – and panting like an old Labrador is not a good look for a romantic hero. I think he was quite relieved when I told him that I was perfectly capable of walking and that it wouldn't lessen the impact of the gesture by being on my own two feet again. A romantic hero with a thrown back is not great either.

In the lift up to our room, I glance at the man with me. Is that how I see Marcus now? Is he the romantic hero of the piece? I smile at him. He's certainly a lot of fun to be around when he's on form. Is it worth the downside to experience highs like this?

'I'm not sleeping with you just because you booked a room at a posh hotel,' I tell him.

'*The* posh hotel,' he corrects me as he opens the door.

Simply stepping into our suite takes my breath away. 'My God, Marcus,' I gulp, 'this is fabulous. How much did it cost?' What Marcus has paid for tonight's accommodation would cover the rent on my flat for a month – maybe even two.

'It doesn't matter how much it cost.' He takes my hand. 'I wanted this evening to be extra-special.'

Throwing my handbag on the bed, I immediately regret making the place look untidy. The decoration of the room is circa Louis XVI – a voluminous space with acres of thick carpet, heavy drapes, antique paintings and furniture in shades of blue, peach and lemon, all perfectly organised to exhibit unrestrained style. There's champagne chilling in a silver bucket.

'Marcus,' I say with a sigh. 'I don't need all of this.'

He stands close behind me, his hands resting on my arms. 'I want to spoil you,' he tells me, his breath hot against my neck.

'All I ever wanted was for you to be faithful to me.' Moving away from him, I sit down on the bed and try it for bounciness. Perfect. As I knew it would be. They'll probably bring really great chocolates with the turndown service. Not that I'm planning on staying that long. 'I don't need all this high drama. I just want a quiet life with a nice man.'

Marcus sits next to me and takes my hand. 'You'll never find another man like me.'

'I don't want another man like you!'

'Please love me again,' Marcus says. 'I know we've had our ups and downs.'

I want to say, 'Pah!' out loud but nothing will come out of my mouth.

'We can get through this.' His eyes entreat mine. 'These past few months have only served to make our relationship stronger. I really believe that.'

But do I?

Marcus takes off his hat and throws it on the bed behind us. He rakes his blond hair, then he peels off his uniform jacket. Underneath, he's wearing a tight black T-shirt, six-pack very much in evidence. All those hours in the gym haven't been wasted. I kick off my shoes and sink my toes into the plush carpet.

'You look great in uniform,' I tell him. 'You've definitely given Richard Gere a run for his money.'

'And you make a great Debra Winger.' Is that a compliment? I try not to think that she was a down-at-heel factory worker with no future until her Mr Right came along.

'Oh Marcus,' I say. My fingers run over the front of his T-shirt in a distracted manner. 'I could have loved you so much.'

'You still can,' he insists. 'I'm a changed man. I brought you here tonight to plead my case.' He leaps to his feet and pours us both a glass of champagne.

I take one of the flûtes from him. 'So, what are we toasting?'

'Us,' he says earnestly. 'I want us to give this another go, Lucy. I've tried, but I can't live without you.'

As if I haven't had enough surprises for today, Marcus goes down on one knee. 'Say you'll marry me.'

I try to laugh in a light and tinkling fashion but it doesn't come out properly. 'I've already said it once, Marcus, and you blew it. We were engaged and yet I found you with another woman, for heaven's sake. I can't do it again.'

'And you tried to make it work with another guy and you couldn't.' The bare truth of that stings.

There are tears in Marcus's beautiful blue eyes. 'I'll do anything for another chance.'

Now what do I say? My head hurts. It would be nice to have a lie-down on this lovely bed. I wonder, if I asked nicely, would they do the turndown service early?

'Please find it in your heart to forgive me,' Marcus implores.

Isn't that what love is all about? Forgiving the person you love all of their transgressions? I told Crush as much. If I say yes to Marcus, doesn't that prove we can weather any storm? Would that be a good foundation for a marriage? I know Marcus. I know him inside and out. I know how wonderful he can be when he wants to be. And I know just how much of a shit he can be when he doesn't. As he pointed out, I tried to make a relationship with Crush and couldn't. We fell at the first hurdle. My very first transgression has gone unforgiven and Aiden Holby has made it very clear that's pretty much the end of that.

'The wedding venue is still booked, Lucy.'

'You're kidding me!'

'I never cancelled it,' Marcus tells me with an embarrassed shrug. 'I never accepted that it was over between us.'

From his pocket, he produces an enormous solitaire diamond. It sparkles with rainbow colours in the light of the chandelier. I gasp. Oh, this is so much more me than the last engagement ring he chose. 'A new ring for a new start,' he says earnestly, and I wonder briefly what happened to the other one. Did Marcus trade it in for this one, or did he give it to the obliging Joanne for her trouble?

I press the cold glass of champagne to my burning face. I'm finding it hard to think straight without the aid of chocolate. 'Marcus, Marcus,' I sigh. 'I don't know what to say.'

'Say yes,' he urges. 'Say yes, and make me a very happy man.'

I stare deeply into Marcus's eyes and see nothing but sincere love shining back at me. Nevertheless, I wonder if I'm looking at my future ex-husband. Despite that, my brain kicks into another gear, I toss back my champagne to lubricate my bone-dry mouth, then I gaze directly at Marcus and say, 'Yes.'

Chapter Thirty-Three

I had to text all my best girls with a CHOCOLATE EMERGENCY – there was nothing else for it. Now we're in Chocolate Heaven and, once again, I have to fess up. We've all attended to the necessities of chocolate supplies first – Swiss milk chocolate batons, lemon verbena chocolates and an Earl Grey ganache. And now my attentive audience is waiting patiently. It's the first time in my life that the chocolate diet alone isn't hitting the spot and I wish I had a bottle or two of cheap wine to accompany it.

'I have an announcement to make,' I say, rather shakily. 'Clive and Tristan should join us.' The boys are bickering behind the counter. Clearly, all is not well in their world. I wave them over and, abruptly, they break off from their argument and come to join us.

'Is it good news?' Autumn still looks drained. I don't think she could cope with any more bad news.

'I hope so.'

The boys sit down with us. 'Lucy has an announcement,' Chantal tells them. 'But I have one of my own first. I'm having a baby, boys. You're the first people that I've plucked up the courage to tell.'

Clive and Tristan fling themselves onto her and cover her with kisses. 'We'll have to throw a chocolate-themed baby shower,' Clive announces grandly.

When they've calmed down, we hand around Chantal's scan picture again and we all have a coo.

Tristan turns the picture round, trying to work out which way up it is. 'Do you know what sex it is?'

'A girl,' Chantal says. '*My* little girl.' The mother-to-be is bursting with happiness and pride.

'Who's the daddy?' Clive asks with a glorious lack of tact.

'*That*, we're less sure of,' she admits. Chantal tucks her scan picture back into her Anya Hindmarch tote. I wonder, does Ms Hindmarch do baby-changing bags? I smile to myself – our friend has got a lot of lifestyle adjustment ahead of her. 'Sorry to steal your thunder, Lucy,' Chantal says, 'but I bet you can't top that one.'

'Mmm,' I say, sounding sheepish. I've kept my left hand firmly hidden until now, but I produce my ring finger with a rather half-hearted flourish. 'Da-dah!'

Jaws drop all around the table.

'That's one hell of a diamond,' Chantal notes with admiration in her voice. It is, indeed, the sort of ring that would be more at home gracing my friend's elegant fingers.

'Crush?' Nadia says.

'No, no, no.' I bat away his name with impatience. Why do my friends keep trying to fan the flame of hope there, when clearly there is none?

'Not Marcus?' Chantal says with a frown.

'Who else?' Now there are audible gasps around the table. I sound a little snappy when I say, 'Of course it's Marcus.'

My friends exchange bemused glances. 'You promised that your little fling with him at Christmas was just that,' Chantal says.

'Well, I was wrong.'

'Do you want me to do the whole thing with the cake again?' Clive asks, but he sounds unenthusiastic. 'I can go and get one.'

'No, no, no.' This is the reaction I should have expected, but I had hoped for more. 'I just want you to be happy for me.'

No one leaps in to say that they are.

'Look,' I say, 'I really hoped that things would work out with Crush, but they haven't. We hit one little rocky patch and it's all fallen to pieces. Maybe we weren't so perfectly suited after all.'

My friends don't look convinced.

'I know Marcus,' I continue. 'I know him so well.'

'That should make you realise that he isn't great husband material,' Chantal points out.

'I think you're a fine one to talk,' I say crisply. 'Fidelity has never been your strong suit either, but you're expecting Ted to make a go of your marriage. Marcus isn't perfect, but then neither am I.' I think how easily I let Crush down and my shame just won't go away. Am I such a great catch that I can demand nothing less than perfection in a man? 'There's no such thing as Mr Right. Marcus loves me – in his own flawed and imperfect way. And I love him – in my less than adequate way too. We've come through a lot together. Isn't that enough? Our relationship may not be ideal, but it's enduring. How many people can say that these days? I'm not getting any younger. I want to settle down. I want a baby. I want to know who the father is.'

Chantal cringes at my barbed comments, but says nothing.

'I can't throw stones either,' Nadia says. 'I'm married to a gambler, but it doesn't mean that I love him any less. You have to do what feels right, Lucy.'

As I'm wringing my hands, the light is catching my ring. 'I can't waste another five years trying to find someone else who might or might not eventually want to marry me.'

Statistically the odds are against me getting married at all. There are currently not enough men to go around in the UK – we're nearly a million short, ladies. How does that feel? And that's counting *all* men – even the crappy ones with halitosis, pot bellies, comb-overs and a fetish for leopardskin undies – not just decent husband material. Which means that an awful lot of us single women of a certain age simply won't be able to get married unless we jump on a plane and go to Alaska or some place where there's a distinct shortage of girlies. Now I want to burst into tears when I should be feeling deliriously happy.

'I loved Crush,' I tell them. 'But that sometimes isn't enough. We didn't last five minutes. When push came to shove, there was absolutely no substance behind us.'

'Perhaps you're being a little hasty in giving up on him so soon,' Autumn ventures. 'You must have hurt him very badly.'

'I know that.' I feel myself sag. 'But he won't even talk to me,' I remind them. 'He refuses to eat my chocolate.' They, quite rightly,

131

look shocked at that. 'How can I hold out any hope that he might take me back?'

My friends say nothing. So, no one has any smart answer for that question. 'I've made up my mind. I've chosen Marcus's bed and now I'm going to lie in it. That's how it's going to be. All I want is for you to support me in my decision,' I sniff.

The girls are galvanised into action. 'We do support you,' Nadia tells me. 'All of us.' She looks around at the others and they all nod furiously.

'We'll do anything we can to help,' Autumn assures me.

'I want you all to be bridesmaids,' I say tremulously.

They all nod again until their heads are in danger of falling off. 'We'll love that,' Nadia says.

'Even if I pick really crap dresses, you have to promise to wear them.'

'We will,' they say in unison.

'Can I be a bridesmaid and wear a crap dress too?' Clive asks.

We all burst out laughing and that breaks the tension.

'If this is really what you want, Lucy, then you know that we'll give you all the support and love that you can cope with,' Autumn says. We all hold hands around the table.

'Thanks,' I say, really teary now.

'When's the wedding going to be this time?' Autumn asks.

'Same time, same place,' I tell them. 'Marcus never cancelled the wedding. He knew somehow that we'd be together.'

Everyone goes, '*Awhh*.'

'So we're all going back to Trington Manor,' Chantal says with a wry smile.

I know. Trust my wedding to be at the same venue as our brilliant jewellery heist. Is nothing ever straightforward in my life?

'That means that the wedding isn't very far away,' Autumn notes.

'A matter of weeks.' I'm not even going to calculate the exact time as that would scare me far too much.

'You should use a wedding planner,' Chantal says. 'There's so much to do. I can recommend a great one.'

'Thanks.' It even seems too difficult to decide on that at the moment. 'I'll certainly think about it.'

'One word of advice,' Nadia says. 'Please don't buy the dresses until the very last minute. Just in case.'

'That's a horrible thing to say!' We all giggle. But despite what my friends think, this time I really do believe that Marcus and I can make it together.

Chapter Thirty-Four

Nadia lay in Toby's arms. She and her son had been back at home for a week now and she couldn't have been any happier. Lewis had settled into his own room again without any hiccups, thank goodness, and she'd slipped back into her routine as a housewife with a renewed energy. Toby had put his heart and soul into proving that she'd done the right thing, and it certainly felt good to be back in his arms once more.

Her husband glanced at the clock. 'I have to go to work.'

'Mmm.' Nadia stretched out along the length of him. 'Make love to me again.'

But Toby was already flicking back the duvet. 'I'll be late.'

She smiled at him. 'Do you think it's time that we made another baby? I don't want Lewis to be an only child.'

Toby slipped out of the bed. 'This isn't the time to talk about it.'

'I'd love more children,' she said. 'And we're getting ourselves straight now, aren't we?'

'Let's not rush things,' her husband said.

There was sense in that, she knew. Toby might have stopped gambling, but there was a huge backlog of debts to clear – every day the postman seemed to bring yet another stack of bills. The truth of the matter though was that she wasn't getting any younger and there was never a right time to have a child. If you even stopped to consider the expense, then no one would ever be brave or mad enough to have kids. 'Couldn't we at least start to consider it?'

'Sure, sure,' Toby said, but she could tell that he was distracted. He disappeared into the shower while she went downstairs and started to prepare breakfast. In a short while, she'd get Lewis up. It wasn't often that her son stayed in bed longer than they did, so it was nice to enjoy the peace. For the first time in a long while, there was a kernel of contentment at the centre of her being and Nadia sighed happily to herself.

She'd just finished buttering Toby's toast when he came into the kitchen, hair still damp from the shower. He looked more handsome than she'd ever seen him. 'I love you,' she said. 'Have I told you that today?'

Toby hugged her tightly. 'Whatever happens,' he said, 'I want you to know how much I love you too.'

She smiled at him. 'I know that.'

'Please don't ever forget it.' He kissed her hard on the mouth. 'I have to go.'

With that, Toby left for work and Nadia noticed with a strange disquieting feeling that he hadn't even touched his toast.

The nagging feeling of unease didn't leave her all day. She took Lewis to the playground, but while her son played happily in the sandpit, she sat watching him restlessly, staring across the tops of the houses and into the distance, though she didn't know why.

Afterwards, the shopping had been accomplished on autopilot, as had the washing and ironing. Now she was cooking dinner and still the feeling prickled over her like an unscratched itch.

Was it something that Toby had said that was bothering her? Was it something in his demeanour? As always, the spectre of his gambling was close to hand and she wondered if he'd done something stupid.

He was due home at six o'clock, but that came and went. Nothing unusual there – Toby was often delayed if a job didn't go according to plan, which was more often than not.

Nadia gave Lewis his dinner, then she sat on the living-room floor and played a counting game with him, but she struggled to keep her concentration and ended up being pasted by a four year old.

By seven o'clock she was starting to get worried. If Toby was going to be really late, then he'd usually call. She tried his mobile, but it went straight to voicemail. The chicken vindaloo that she'd made was starting to dry up in the oven, so she added some water to the dish in a bid to salvage it. Lewis didn't want to go to bed without saying goodnight to his dad, but with a bit of fuss and a few tears, he'd eventually capitulated.

When eight o'clock had passed and there was still no sign of her husband, Nadia started to pace the floor. The dinner was burned and she'd covered the remnants of it with tinfoil. She was calling Toby's mobile every few minutes, but still it went unanswered by her husband. Eventually, she called his parents in case he'd decided to drop in and see them, but they hadn't heard anything from him either and now she'd worried them too.

On the computer in the office, she looked for the number of the other plumber who worked for him. When she finally found it, she punched Paul's number into the phone. 'Hi, Paul,' she said when he picked up. 'I just wanted to find out what time Toby left tonight. He's not answering his phone.'

'I was about to call him again too,' Paul said. 'He didn't turn up on the job today and I've got a problem that I need to talk to him about.'

'He didn't turn up?'

'No. Usually he calls me, but I've heard nothing. Is anything wrong?'

'I don't know,' Nadia admitted. 'I'll get him to call you as soon as I hear from him.'

She hung up and stared at the computer in front of her. A cold dread gripped her stomach. What on earth had happened to Toby? Instinctively, she went to look at the web history. Where had he been visiting on the internet? Was he back to his old ways already? But there was nothing to show that her husband had been on the gambling sites again. Now what? For lack of any other good ideas, she pulled up his personal filing cabinet and looked at the recent emails he'd received.

The first one that she saw made her feel sick inside. Part of her didn't even want to open it, but she knew that she had to.

Nadia clicked the mouse and the email sprang open in front of her. It was an e-ticket for Virgin Airlines. The seat had been booked only yesterday, yet the flight had left this morning. And it was for a one-way trip in her husband's name to Las Vegas.

Chapter Thirty-Five

Autumn stroked her brother's hand. He still lay in his hospital bed, bruised and unmoving. An array of machines beeped comfortingly around him, monitoring him and miraculously performing functions that Richard couldn't while he was unconscious. She'd slept on a fold-out bed next to him or, more accurately, she'd stayed awake all night staring at her brother and hoping for some signs of recovery.

Richard had got himself into plenty of scrapes before, but there'd never been anything as bad as this. If only he could speak to her and tell her what had happened. Was this simply being in the wrong place at the wrong time, or was it something more sinister? Had someone come after Rich because of the way he was living his life? All she could do was sit here and will her brother to wake up.

Autumn had called her parents, but they were both away on business. Daddy in Geneva, Mummy talking at a Human Rights conference in NewYork.They'd been shocked to hear that Richard was in hospital, but not shocked enough to jump on a plane and rush back to their son's bedside. It was typical of them − they were long on cash and short on compassion. If they could throw money at it, they were the most generous of people. When it came to giving their own children their precious time, then they were positively miserly. It had been the same throughout their lives, so why should she hold out any hope that they would change now? She looked at her brother's washed-out face and it sent a physical pain to her heart. If her parents could see how bad Richard was, surely they wouldn't be able to stay away?

It was lunchtime when Addison appeared at her side. She'd

been given compassionate leave from her job at the Stolford Centre while her brother remained in this condition, but it pained her to think that she wouldn't be there to minister to Fraser and Tasmin and her other students. But she couldn't worry about them now. Richard had to have her full attention.

Her boyfriend slipped into the seat next to her and kissed her cheek. 'How's it going?'

'No change,' she told him wearily. 'The doctors have said that he's comfortable and that's the best we can hope for at the moment.'

'Why don't you go home for a couple of hours?' Addison suggested. 'You look wiped out. Have a nice hot bath and grab a bit of shut-eye. There's nothing you can do for Richard now.'

'I have to be here when he wakes up,' she said.

'They'll call you from the hospital as soon as there's any news,' Addison reassured her. 'He's being well looked after, I'm sure. I'm worried that you're going to make yourself ill.'

'I can't forgive myself for not answering the phone when he was trying to call me,' she said, anguished. 'That's the only time I've not been there for him and look what's happened.' She couldn't get a picture out of her mind of Rich lying in a dirty back alley trying desperately to call her. And she'd ignored the call and had put her own pleasure first. What sort of a sister did that?

'Do you blame me for that?'

She let out a miserable sigh and rubbed her hands over her tired eyes. 'I feel my loyalties are divided at the moment,' she said. 'And right now, Richard needs me more than you do.'

'You can't be your brother's keeper all the time,' he pointed out. 'You're entitled to a life of your own, Autumn.'

'Not now,' she said. 'Richard needs me to be here for him, and nothing will take me away from him.'

She saw Addison's shoulders sag with disappointment. It was easy for him to say that she should put herself before her brother, but it had never been that way and it probably never would be. All of her relationships had foundered when her partner had realised that there would always be two men in her life. Addison too would have to accept that and, if he couldn't, well . . . 'Maybe we should cool things for the time being.'

'I want to be here for you,' her boyfriend said. 'If you'll let me.'

'I can't think of anything but Richard at the moment. He has to be my priority.'

Addison stood up and squeezed her shoulder. 'I'll call you later,' he said sadly. 'See how he is.'

But she wondered, as he walked away, just how long Addison would stay around.

Chapter Thirty-Six

Every time that Crush organises a team-bonding exercise, it involves hideous clothing. For paintballing I'm wearing camouflage combats and a matching jacket that comes down to my knees. I look like a small dirigible balloon that's crashed into a forest. My hands are encased in huge gauntlets which are playing havoc with my nice new manicure and I'm sporting a full face helmet which has flattened my hair to infinity and beyond. I spent hours doing my hair and make-up and not because I wanted Aiden Holby to think that I looked utterly gorgeous, nothing like that. I just like to make an effort in all situations. All to no avail.

I'm not a happy camper. It's only the fact that I'm clinging onto my job at Targa by my fingertips that I'm here at all. Despite the best efforts of my agency – believe that if you will – no other offers of employment have been forthcoming. With all the expense of my forthcoming wedding, there's no way that I can jack it in. So paint-balling I am.

Aiden Holby comes along the line to inspect his troops. The Sales Department always take these things very seriously and some of them have brought their own props so they look like mini-Rambos. Bandanas are much in evidence. God help us. We're up against teams from Human Resources and IT. Not that I'm entering into the spirit of this, but frankly I think we're going to whop their sorry asses. They look like a bunch of lily-livered lightweights.

Crush stands in front of me and I hate to say this, but he looks a little bit fab in his Army get up, all rufty-tufty and macho. What is it about men in uniforms? My knees have come over all unnecessary.

141

He raises my face mask. 'Camouflage paint,' he says crisply. And then, with more enthusiasm than is appropriate, he slaps some brown gloop that looks like mud all over my cheeks. So much for my air-brushed effect foundation. I don't so much look camouflaged but more as if I'm an escapee from *The Black and White Minstrel Show*.

'Is this strictly necessary?'

'I want my team to have the best chance,' he says in the manner of a Sergeant Major or crack SAS person. 'We're going to be the Alpha Males,' he announces to everyone. There is much cheering and hollering.

'But I'm a girl.'

'The token one,' he says dismissively. 'Our first mission is to capture the flag of Team Zero Bravo while defending our own.'

'Is that Human Resources?'

'Yes,' he sighs, as if I don't get this. Which I don't. 'You can stay with me, Lombard.'

Lombard?

'The rest of the team will be deployed on the offensive while we maintain our defence strategy.'

He's going to get right on my nerves if he goes on like this all day.

'Ammo,' he says, and hands me a hopper of paintballs which I cack-handedly clip onto my gun. Crush slams down my face mask and I can hear myself breathing heavily.

News of my forthcoming wedding has done the rounds of gossip at the office, so it must have reached Aiden's ears, but he's said nothing to me. He puts work on my desk at regular intervals, but we're engaging in absolutely no social intercourse at all. I wish he'd shout at me rather than ignore me completely.

There's a bit of a pep-talk from the team leaders stressing fair play and may the best man win, etc. This being Targa we'll be lucky if one of us doesn't lose a limb. And then we're off. It's not raining, but it feels as if it should be.

'Come with me, Lombard.' I long for the days when Crush used to call me Gorgeous even though it annoyed me at the time.

Aiden stomps off ahead of me and I follow him meekly into the woods.

The first paintball shot in anger hits me squarely in the thigh. 'Fucking ouch!' I shout back at my unseen assailant.

Crush grabs my arm and pulls me down on the ground next to him. 'Shut up,' he instructs. 'You'll give our position away.'

'I've already been shot. Doesn't that mean I'm out of the game?'

'We're giving the girls three shots before they're out,' he mutters. 'It sort of evens things out.'

'Great.' One shot would have suited me fine. I'm going to have a whopping bruise there tomorrow. It'll be the size of a dinner plate, at least.

'We'll crawl on our bellies through the undergrowth,' he says.

'I think not.'

Aiden fixes me with a cold stare. 'I thought you were a team player,' he snaps.

I give a big huff which Crush ignores.

My boss holds out his gun in a menacing way. 'Let's see if we can infiltrate their camp.'

'I thought we were the defence?'

'We're a sort of offensive defence,' Crush explains with a shifty look on his face, and then he sets off on his elbows and knees through the ferns and foliage.

I huff again, this time wearily, and trail after him. Dampness seeps through into my knees. I'm already up to my eyeballs in mud. My gun is really heavy and I'm doing a kind of horizontal limp. This is not my idea of fun.

Crush puts his hand on my arm to still me, then he shuffles back until our faces are level – inches apart, in fact. My heartbeat goes into overdrive. 'They've put sentries on the bridge,' he whispers. 'We need to storm it. I can see no other way round.'

'Storm the bridge!' It comes out a decibel or two higher than is preferable in a war situation. I feel as if I'm in the middle of *Apocalypse Now*.

'Hush!' He claps his hand over my mouth and I feel my eyes widen in surprise.

'I'll lead the charge,' he says. 'You stay tucked behind me, covering my back.'

'Right.' I have no idea what he's talking about. But suddenly we're off. Crush runs towards a small wooden bridge across a meandering stream. I puff and pant behind him.

We catch Team Zero Bravo – or the Human Resources Department as I refer to them in real life – on the hop. Crush shoots down two of their men and I keep up a volley of shots to intimidate anyone else who thinks they might like to mess with us. I make a couple of kills of my own – which feels scarily satisfying. We rush across the bridge, scattering our feeble foes, and then dive into the undergrowth where we lie breathing heavily.

'That was brilliant!' I say. 'This gun seriously kicks butt.'

'It's a replica AK-47,' Crush tells me in the way that only boys can. 'Puts out fifteen rounds per second.'

'Wow.' I assume that's a good thing. And when I see Helen the Harridan from Human Resources sneak up to the bridge, I think that it's time to try it out again. When her back is turned, I fire multiple rounds at her prissy little arse. *That's for not telling me that Crush was lost in the Outback, bitch.* Each one hits its intended target and Helen the Harridan clutches her bottom as she falls to the ground, combats covered in a slick of yellow paint that tells me she's out of the game.

'Great shot,' Crush congratulates me.

'I owed her one,' I say seriously. I look at this man and think what might have happened if only his messages had been passed on to me as they should have been. I would never have slept with Marcus. I wouldn't be getting married to him now.

But before I can ponder further on my predicament, I see a swarm of Team Zero Bravo members coming towards us. Crush pulls me down and we roll together into deeper undergrowth. When we stop, Crush just happens to have rolled on top of me. The feet of the other team tramp by us. I'm sure they must be able to hear our breathing. Mine is certainly louder than it should be. Crush pushes his body against mine, heads together, but I daren't move. Actually, it's starting to feel rather too good. I'm sure that everyone in the whole bloody forest can hear me gulp.

'They're gone,' Crush says, but he makes no attempt to get up. He lifts himself on one elbow and smiles at me as he flicks up my face visor. 'Enjoying yourself?'

'I can see the attraction and psychological benefits of mock warfare.'

'I didn't mean that, Gorgeous,' he says.

Oh, my goodness, I'm Gorgeous again! I wriggle beneath him, but that only makes things worse – or better, depending on your viewpoint. It's suddenly gone very warm in this forest. One of his arms is pinning both of mine to the ground. It's very sexy in a submissive sort of way. Oh dear.

'Why is it that I always have so much fun with you, Lucy Lombard?' He sighs and his eyes lock onto mine.

'I don't know,' I say nervously. 'I'm a fun kind of person.'

Then he kisses me, long and hard. And it feels so good. So bloody good. Frankly, I wouldn't mind if he ripped off my camouflage combats and had me here and now in the dirt on the forest floor. I'm getting very hot and bothered. It must be all the adrenaline pumping round my body. Then I remember that I'm an engaged person. I shouldn't be kissing Crush on the forest floor – or anywhere else for that matter. I'm due to be married to Marcus any time now!

Before I can say anything, Crush breaks off from his sexy, tender assault. I can hardly get my breath.

'Can't stay here kissing you, Gorgeous,' he says, and pulls me to my feet, even though I'm still dazed and reeling. 'Much as I'd like to. We've got a war to win.'

He drags me after him, deeper into the woods. We might have a war to win, but somehow I think I might be losing the battle.

Chapter Thirty-Seven

We blow our poxy opponents into the weeds. The Human Resources Department and IT have been decimated. Helen the Harridan is looking particularly cowed. I hope her backside is black and blue, bitch. If I'm lucky there might even be a really painful welt there. The Alpha Males, myself included, are victorious. This is in no small part due to the fact that I am a natural born killer. I blame it on the diet of *Terminator* and *Matrix* movies that Marcus always forced me to watch. Clearly, something has rubbed off.

I've got a fair amount of enormous bruises myself, some of which are forming unsightly lumps – but I'm high on adrenaline and oblivious to my aches and pains. The team has celebrated on cheap champagne and now we're feeling heady with success and an excess of booze. We're chilling out on the edge of the woods and someone's set up a barbecue, so we're all feasting on botulism burgers. The rest of the team are singing bonding songs with obscene lyrics and doing the accompanying gesticulations, when Crush makes his way over and throws his arms round me. He's swaying as if he's on a boat in a force nine gale.

'You were fabulous today,' he slurs. 'Did I tell you that, Gorgeous? Absolutely fabulous.'

'Thanks.' I slur a little myself.

'You're a lean, mean, killing machine.'

'I am,' I say proudly, not attempting to hide my silly grin. Perhaps this would be a good role for me in life – contract assassin – seeing as how I'm a pretty crap temporary secretary. I wonder if there's a job out there anywhere for a hired hitman and chocolate taster combined? Now that's what I call a job.

'I'm sorry I acted so stupidly after you told me about you and Marcus,' Crush says. 'We should have sat down together and talked sensibly. You were right about forgiveness and all that stuff. I can see now that there were extenuating circumstances. I've really missed us being friends.'

Then, before I can formulate a suitable reply, he moves in and kisses me again. My head spins and not just because I've had too much of that cava. His lips are hot and searching and I can feel my knees and my resolve weakening.

But just as it's getting interesting, I pull away. For some reason, I have a moment of stark clarity.

'Let's get out of here,' Crush says, and takes my hand.

'I can't do this,' I tell him shakily.

He looks puzzled. As well he might.

'The thing is,' I say. 'About me and Marcus . . .'

That stops Crush in his tracks. 'You're not still seeing him?'

'We're getting married.'

He suddenly looks more sober than he did a minute ago. 'No.'

Crush sits down on a big tree trunk behind us. Well, more sort of collapses onto it. All the fight, swagger and sway have rushed out of him. He's just a deflated man with traces of mud on his face. 'I thought that was just stupid office gossip. I didn't think for a minute that it could be true.' His expression is bleak when he looks up at me. 'I didn't think you'd fall for all that romantic guff.'

I sit down next to him. 'I did,' I say quietly.

'That ridiculous *Officer and a Gentleman* uniform did it for you?'

'Yes.' How can I begin to explain to him that it's so much more complicated than that? Would Aiden understand that us breaking up so quickly has shaken my faith in me ever managing to make a new relationship? He probably would, but I don't think I'm capable of putting the explanation into words myself. It's not that I was swept away by Marcus's overtly romantic gesture. I know him too well to be fooled by that – really. But there's no denying that I've run for the comfort of something familiar, something that I'm used to rather than face an unknown future alone or deal with the prospect of building another relationship from scratch.

'Wow,' Crush says. 'I wish I'd done that myself now.'

And, for a moment, I wish it was Aiden Holby who had been the one to sweep me in his arms and carry me away. But it wasn't; it was Marcus and now the die is cast.

'I'm such an idiot,' Crush says.

'No. No,' I protest. 'I'm the one that's the bigger idiot.'

Crush grins at me. 'Yes,' he says, 'you are. I guess that's why I love you. *Loved* you,' he corrects.

Already I'm in the past tense. But at least I know that he truly loved me. However briefly. Not that it does me a lot of good now.

'Well,' he says. 'Looks like that's it for you and me.'

'I'm sorry, Aiden. I never meant to hurt you.'

'I guess the timing was all wrong for us.'

I nod in agreement.

Shyly, he takes my hand and fiddles with my fingers. I'm not wearing my great rock of an engagement ring and, for some reason, I'm glad about that. 'We could have been very good together, Gorgeous,' Crush tells me, and I'm not sure that I want to hear that. My throat has closed and there are tears prickling behind my eyes.

'Oh, Lucy.' Crush brushes his thumb over my cheeks. 'Are you sure that you'll be happy with him?'

'I . . . er . . . well . . .' Even if I could be certain of Crush, there is no way now that I can leave Marcus again. Just thinking about it makes my head ache. If I kept doing that, then I'd become the same to Crush as Marcus is to me and that isn't fair on anyone. I've made my decision now and I have to stick with that – for better, for worse. I clear my throat and say, 'Yes.'

'Then that's all I want for you,' Crush tells me.

'I really hope that we can remain friends.'

Aiden laughs, but it's a laugh laced with sadness and regret.

I have to admit, that even to my ears, it sounds like the lamest statement I've ever made in my life.

Chapter Thirty-Eight

Now it's Nadia's turn to have a chocolate emergency and it sounds like it's a pretty serious one to me. She's eating one of Clive's sumptuous fudge brownies while she fills us in on the story, but I can tell that our friend isn't actually tasting one single morsel.

'I've booked a flight for tomorrow morning,' she tells us, glancing anxiously at her watch even though there are hours to go yet. 'That's the first one I could get. I'm out of my mind with worry. Who knows what Toby is doing out there?'

Losing his shirt would be my guess, but I don't voice my opinion. Nadia is only too well aware what her husband is capable of.

'Are you sure you don't mind having Lewis to stay?' Her son will be moving in with Aunty Chantal again.

'Honey, if I can't look after your kid while you're away for a few days, how the hell am I going to manage when I've got one of my own?' Chantal looks down at her bump. 'This will be great training for me.'

'You're an angel, Chantal.'

'I want you to go and do what you have to without worrying about Lewis. He'll be fine. I have four days to turn him into a spoiled brat. I can do that.'

We all clutch at something to laugh at.

'You can't go alone, Nadia,' I say. 'Let one of us come with you.'

'Chantal is looking after Lewis. Autumn has her brother to worry about. And you, in case you've forgotten, have a wedding to organise.'

'That isn't as important as this,' I tell her. To be honest, as much as I care about my friend's welfare, I'm also looking for a reason to dodge all of my responsibilities at the moment. I don't want to be organising a wedding. I don't want to be working at Targa. I don't want to have to face Crush or Marcus or anyone else. A few days in Las Vegas would be a good excuse to skip town, even though it's at the expense of my friend's misfortune. I could escape and be helpful. Multi-tasking. It's what we women do best.

'Do you really think you'll be able to find Toby there?' Autumn wants to know.

'I have to try,' Nadia says with a sigh. 'I've stopped him from using the bank account in the UK, but I can't put a stop on the credit cards that are in his name.'

I think of my own credit card. Perhaps I can't go with Nadia after all, as much as I'd like to. I'm seriously maxed out and can't really afford to fund any rash, philanthropic gestures.

'I want to try to find him before he does too much damage,' Nadia continues. 'If he'd booked for the weekend, then maybe I'd sit it out, but his ticket is one-way only. Does that mean that he isn't planning to come back? Has he left us?' She's struggling not to cry.

'We need more chocolate,' I say, and there are nods all round. Jumping up, I go to the counter to choose our wares.

'How's Nadia?' Clive wants to know.

'Bad. Looks like Toby's hopped it to Vegas and she's going in hot pursuit to try to bring him back.'

Clive shakes his head. I notice that he's pale and there's day-old stubble on his chin, which is a real no-no for someone so image conscious.

'You don't look so hot yourself,' I tell him softly.

He lowers his voice. 'Tristan didn't come home last night.'

'Bummer.' I then realise that's a bad choice of words to use about a gay bloke. 'How terrible,' I try instead.

'I'm not sure if we're going to make it,' he says sadly.

'Not you guys too.' I tut and give Clive a sympathetic smile.

He's too nice a person to be going through this torment. 'Come and join us,' I say. 'You can bitch about him to us.'

'I will when I've got a minute,' he promises. 'If Tristan keeps going missing like this, then I'm going to have to get an assistant.'

'Maybe it won't come to that.'

'I hope you're right.' Clive hands over our plate of chocolates and cakes and I take them back to the table.

'I have to eat these really quickly,' Nadia tells us. 'There's a million things I have to do before my flight.'

And I have to eat them really quickly because my stomach is gnashing away with nausea. The sort of nausea that only chocolate can cure. Is the whole world falling apart? Everyone's relationships seem to be in such a state of flux. What happened to the days when you met someone at a school disco when you were fifteen, got engaged a few years later, then married. By the time you were twenty-one you had two kids and life was sorted. You just had to sit back and wait for the Golden Anniversary cards to arrive. When did all that change? Here we all are in our thirties, bouncing around emotionally like rubber balls. Makes me think that I've done the right thing. I really should grab hold of Marcus with both hands and march him down the aisle while I still have the chance.

Chapter Thirty-Nine

'Bye, bye, Mummy.' Lewis waved his little hand.

Nadia stood sniffing tearfully at the entrance to the departure gate.

'Go,' Chantal said, and made an ushering gesture. 'We'll be fine. Won't we, champ?'

Lewis nodded happily.

'I'll be back as soon as I can,' Nadia promised. 'I love you, Lewis!'

Her son waved again. 'Love you too, Mummy.'

They watched and waved as Nadia had her passport checked and then disappeared into the throng of travellers heading out of Gatwick Airport.

Chantal turned to her small charge and squatted down in front of him. She pulled playfully at one of the toggles on his jacket. 'Now what?'

Lewis smiled and shrugged.

'Wanna take in a movie?'

'Okay.' Lewis slipped his hand in hers. His trust in her made her heart turn over.

'We have a choice of *Cars*, *Over the Hedge*, or *Garfield Two*,' she said, reciting the cinema listings that she'd studied on the internet.

Chantal had taken the precaution of putting a full programme of entertainment in place, just in case Lewis needed distracting from missing his mother. It was the first time Nadia had left him alone and she was worried that he wouldn't cope too well. Chantal hated to admit this, but she'd been rather nervous of having complete control of a child on her own, even though she'd readily volunteered. It was great having Lewis around, but normally Nadia was always there in the background to step up to the plate and make decisions. Now she was flying by the wire for the first time. Chantal wondered whether it would be different with her own child; whether some inbuilt responsibility gene would kick in and you would know instinctively what was best for your offspring. 'Or *Pirates of the Caribbean*. I think that may be a little scary for you.'

'*Garfield*,' Lewis announced happily. 'I like pussycats.'

'Me too.'

They headed back towards the car, Lewis trotting along beside her taking a dozen little steps to one of her long strides. 'What do you want, Maltesers or popcorn?'

'Maltesers,' Lewis said.

Chantal ruffled his hair. 'You make great choices, kiddo.'

It wasn't the kind of film that Chantal would normally have watched, but seeing it with Lewis made it thoroughly enjoyable. He laughed all the way through at the terrible jokes and the preposterous plot, giggling with glee at the cartoon cat. And she came out thinking that maybe it would be cute to get a ginger kitten – a sure sign that she was going soft in her old age.

Chantal glanced at her watch, wondering where Nadia would be now. She would have boarded the plane and be heading out over the Atlantic. She only hoped that the trip would be worthwhile.

'What do say that we hit the park now?' Chantal suggested. 'Then, if you're real good we'll drop by Chocolate Heaven and see how the guys are.'

Lewis nodded enthusiastically. 'I want to go on the swings.'

'That can be arranged,' she told him.

Lewis jumped around wildly. Maybe he was a little hyperactive already on chocolate. She'd have to go easy on that. Rein in her own excesses. Why couldn't chocolate give her the same buzz that it seemed to give to four year olds? She could do with a little of that extra energy.

In the playground, Lewis tried out the climbing-frame first. Then: 'Come on the roundabout with me, Aunty Chantal.'

'I can't do that.'

'You can,' Lewis said. 'It's fun. I'll look after you.'

Chantal checked around them. The playground was empty. No one was here to see her. What the hell. She jumped on beside Lewis and then scooted her foot along the ground to get the roundabout moving. The air whizzed past them, the leaves on the trees blurred and Lewis shrieked with joy. Had she ever been in a kids' playground before? She wasn't sure that she had – not since she was a kid herself, at least. It was great to feel the wind in her hair. She looked down at Lewis's ecstatic face. She could do this. She was sure. She could be a mum – and enjoy it. One day she would bring her own children to this playground. Her hand covered Lewis's.

'Don't be scared,' he said.

And she knew that she wouldn't be.

When he'd made them both thoroughly dizzy on the round-about, he headed for the swings.

'Push me high,' he entreated. 'Push me high!'

Chantal obliged and sent him soaring through the air, making him scream and kick his legs with excitement. She hoped that Nadia would approve of her technique. 'I think that's enough now,' she said, as she slowed the swing down.

When it was moving backwards and forwards gently, Chantal squeezed onto the swing next to Lewis. The seat was more than a little neat on her butt, which was expanding nicely in line with her bump.

'Aunty Chantal,' Lewis said seriously. 'Do you still have a baby in your tummy?'

She turned and grinned at him. 'I sure do.'

Lewis tucked his thumb into his mouth and sucked on it thoughtfully. 'I think you make a very nice mummy,' he said.

'Thank you.' Yes, she could do this. What better approval could she get? A tear came to her eye and she reached over to kiss Lewis on his forehead. 'I think that's the nicest thing anyone's ever said to me.'

Chapter Forty

The taxi whisked Nadia along The Strip. On either side of her, the big flashy hotels brashly advertised their wares. It was like a bonsai version of the world – Egypt, Paris, New York, Venice and Ancient Rome all bound tightly together for the people who, she assumed, couldn't be bothered to travel to the real places. At another time or in different circumstances, Nadia might well have picked up on the tacky buzz of the place, for there was certainly an energy about it – but at the moment, she could only think of the dangers that lurked for her husband behind the glittering signs advertising glamorous shows, dancing girls and cut-price buffets.

Nadia's hotel wasn't on The Strip. It was a few blocks behind it and the atmosphere couldn't have been more different. There was no attempt at even a veneer of glitz here. The budget motel was more than frayed at the edges. Parts of the neon sign proclaiming BUDGET MOTEL looked as if they had long since died and no one, it seemed, had attempted to repair them. That was obviously the attention to detail that you could expect on a budget. Style, cleanliness and charm were optional extras that weren't included. The water in the tiny swimming pool had a green hue and looked like a health hazard – it was clear that the people who came to this flophouse didn't come for the relaxation either. And neither had she.

It was early afternoon when she checked in and the sun was blazing outside, a melting 103 degrees, but even then the darkened hotel lobby was filled with people sitting at the banks of slot machines which were beeping, peeping and flashing away. Pensioners with a measly pot of change clutched in their pigmented hands perched on worn stools and relentlessly fed coins into waiting metal mouths that devoured them and offered nothing in return. Nadia could hardly believe her eyes. It was possibly one of the most depressing places on earth.

Leaving her luggage in the scruffy, soulless room, Nadia headed back to The Strip. Here the atmosphere was glamour all the way. Everything finely tuned to relieve you of as much money as possible. She was sure that she'd find Toby in one of the monster, themed casinos that he'd so raved about after his initial visit to the city – the monster casinos that had triggered his addiction to gambling in the first place. But which one? There were just so many to choose from.

She took a cab to the south end of The Strip and started at the enormous Mandalay Bay resort. Walking briskly past its waterfalls and palm trees and ignoring its indoor shark reef, Nadia headed straight for the casino. Simply to get to your room it was necessary to circumnavigate boulevards filled with opportunities to gamble.

In the casino she was faced by acres and acres of slot machines, crowding her vision to the horizon and beyond, greedily waiting for their next customer. Gaming tables were filled with people playing craps, baccarat, blackjack, roulette and poker – all games that she'd heard of but had never been tempted to try – while cold-eyed croupiers and security staff watched their every move. Perhaps if she knew which was Toby's particular weakness it would make him easier to track down. She had known that this was going to be difficult, but hadn't quite appreciated how much it was going to be like looking for the needle in the proverbial haystack. Where the hell could her husband be in this lot? Not here, it seemed.

Next door was the Luxor resort – an enormous black pyramid that dominated the skyline, complete with its very own Sphinx. Even the lobby resembled a visit to the temples of Ancient Egypt, with towering statues and representations of the gods. But the only god here was gambling and, again, Nadia headed straight for the casino. It looked much the same as the last one and, once inside, it was nigh on impossible to find your way out again. But it was easy to see how these green-baize quicksands could suck the unwary under. Food and drinks were constantly on hand so that there was no need for the dedicated gamblers ever to leave the tables. Climate-controlled rooms ensured their personal comfort – no need to bother with that awful sunshine outside. There was no natural daylight in here, no clocks, no exit signs. Once you were in, you were trapped.

Nadia must have circled the vast room a dozen times, but she could see no sign of Toby. How long was her task going to take her? Casinos like this stretched out along the entire length of The Strip. If there was ever a time that she felt she needed her friends with her then it was now. She missed the other members of The Chocolate Lovers' Club desperately and, despite the bustling crowds of Las Vegas, she'd never experienced such loneliness before.

Hours and hours had passed and her legs were weary from all the walking. Night had fallen and the lights on The Strip were blinking alluringly. She'd been to a medieval castle, a replica of New York complete with indoor rollercoaster, the largest hotel in the world with its thousands of Identikit rooms, and had now landed at a mini-recreation of Paris, including a half-size Eiffel Tower and Arc de Triomphe.

Despite the wide variety of their exterior dressings, inside, all the casinos were the same. Miles and miles of slot machines thinly disguised by a Parisian street scene or a tropical paradise or your very own slice of the Nile. Miles and miles of opportunities to lose vast sums of money. Nadia's mind was whirring with flashing lights, bright colours and endless stimulation. This place certainly earned its title of Disneyland for grown-ups – it was just that the white-knuckle rides here could be so much more costly. But it couldn't just be her who was aware of the dark side of this lavish playground.

Nadia was tired, hungry and losing hope fast. Perhaps she should have let Lucy come with her. She'd so glibly turned down her friend's offer and thought that she could manage alone. Now she wasn't so sure. She seemed to have covered so little ground by herself. It felt like a mammoth task that faced her – even more mammoth than the size of these casinos that were beginning to bear down on her.

Nadia stood under the fine mist that was being sprayed into the street to cool down passers-by and, turning her face to the jets, let the water soothe her. It was a long way from the height of summer, but even at night the temperatures were nudging the mercury to levels that she certainly wasn't used to.

Nadia looked down The Strip. There were miles and miles of casinos still to visit. Toby was here somewhere. He was in one of these gargantuan places, playing the tables or feeding the slots. Losing their money. Losing his sanity. All she had to do was find him.

Chapter Forty-One

Autumn didn't realise that she'd dozed off in the chair until she heard a voice next to her. Immediately, she was wide awake. 'Rich?'

'Hey,' he said. His voice was cracked, barely audible. She moved closer to him.

Taking his hand, she murmured, 'We've been so worried about you. How are you feeling?' She turned and scanned the ward. 'I'll get the nurse. Do you want something to eat? Drink?'

'Water,' he murmured.

Pouring a glass from the jug on his bedside, Autumn noticed that her hand was shaking. She put a straw into the glass and then held it close to her brother's lips. It would have been better to go and get a fresh jug – this water was a day old – but she didn't want to leave him alone for a minute. As he gulped the water gratefully, some dribbled down his chin and Autumn wiped it gently away with a tissue.

'Who did this to you?' she asked.

Richard avoided her eyes. 'The less you know about this the better, believe me.'

'You should go to the police.'

Richard forced a laugh, but it left him wracked with a coughing spasm. 'The police can't protect me from these kind of people.'

'Look what they've done to you,' she said. 'You've got a fractured skull, a broken shoulder, busted ribs and internal bruising. And that's just the top half, Rich.'

'Yeah,' he said, forcing a strained smile. 'Just think what they could have done if they were really trying.'

'The hospital thought that you'd been hit by a car.'

'Baseball bat, more likely.'

Autumn started to cry. 'What will it take to get it through your thick – and fractured – skull, that you're mixing with the wrong people?'

Her brother took her hand. 'This is it,' he said. 'I promise you. As soon as I get out of the hospital, I'll clean up my act.'

Autumn only wished that she could believe it.

'You didn't tell Mater and Pater, did you?'

Autumn nodded. 'They're both away on business.'

Richard snorted faintly. 'Tell me something new,' he said. 'Take it they didn't feel moved to rush back to my sickbed.'

'I didn't tell them how bad you were,' she lied. 'They're very concerned.'

'Of course.' But Richard didn't sound any more convinced than she did. It was just the two of them, as it always had been.

The nurses had tended to Richard and then he'd fallen asleep again. Now there was a faint flush of colour in his cheeks and his breathing was more relaxed. It felt as if her brother was finally out of danger. It was late and she was very, very tired.

Tonight, she'd go back to her own bed. It was about time that she got a good night's sleep. Richard wasn't quite out of the woods yet and there would be weeks of bedside visits yet to come. She was emotionally and physically exhausted. One night at home surely wouldn't hurt.

Autumn had taken a taxi back to her flat and she'd struggled to stay upright in the back of it. It would be so nice to curl up in a ball and let oblivion wash over her. Warm air pumped out from the vents, making her heavy eyes roll. Her lids felt like sandpaper as she tried to blink herself awake.

She paid the driver and let herself into the front door. Normally, the bright security lights were triggered when the door opened, but now the hall remained in darkness and part of her was grateful that she didn't have to deal with the glare of fluorescent tubes.

Fumbling in her voluminous handbag for the keys, Autumn realised she was going to have to put the light on to have any

162

hope of finding them. As she reached out to search for the switch, a hand curled round her wrist and, with one swift movement, wrenched her arm behind her back. Autumn let out a pained gasp and her handbag fell to the floor. She stepped forward and heard the crunching of glass underfoot – the light bulbs had been broken. Her attacker tightened his grip and her wrist burned. Then she felt the press of cold steel against her throat.

'Tell your little brother that we want our gear back,' a gruff voice said against her ear. She could smell whisky, expensive after-shave and recognised a strong East End accent. The guy was tall, thickset, and she could feel his leather jacket pressed against her. 'If not, we'll have to come back and finish the job properly. Get that?'

No words would come out. Autumn tried to nod, but couldn't move either.

The knife nicked against her throat and she felt a warm trickle of blood run down her neck.

'Get it?'

'Yes.' The word squeezed out of her.

'Take this phone and give it to him,' the man said. 'Tell him we'll be in touch.' She felt his grip on her release and he pushed her away from him. Autumn spun round as she heard the front door bang shut, but all she could see was a shadowy figure hurrying away down the street. She felt herself dry retch and touched the blood on her neck again. What did he mean when he said he'd finish the job properly? Was it Richard they were threatening, or was it her they were going to hurt?

On unsteady legs, Autumn made her way up to her flat. The police might not be able to protect Richard from these thugs, but then, it seemed, neither could she.

Chapter Forty-Two

By midnight, Nadia had reached the middle stretch of The Strip. If possible, it was busier now than it had been during the daytime. She'd seen the spectacular fountain and light-show outside the Bellagio Hotel, she'd seen the colourful volcano explode outside The Mirage, shooting flames 100 feet into the air – an event that occurred every fifteen minutes throughout the night. And she'd seen the gondoliers in their authentic striped jerseys singing 'O Sole Mio' on Venice's Grand Canal on the second floor *inside* the Venetian Hotel. She'd watched the cornflower-blue sky overhead complete with its very own fluffy, scudding computer-generated clouds. Only the chill of the air-conditioning reminded you that this was all a pretty illusion.

This whole place was too surreal. It was trying too hard to pretend that it wasn't what it really was – but these fun, family-friendly façades couldn't hide the fact that behind them lurked a place of misery, ruined lives, failed fortunes and a house that *always* won.

Out on the street, the pavements were still burning and her legs had swollen in response. She had the ankles of a baby elephant, making each step painful and slow. Her fingers had blown up to shapeless sausages. Here the hotels were more spread out, the area not quite so salubrious. The police were out in force, patrolling The Strip. Minor skirmishes broke out as she made her way further north – those unlucky at the tables now, perhaps, regretting their rash actions. Haggard, barely dressed women were touting for business; every five minutes a flyer was thrust into her hand for some seedy lapdancing club or another.

It seemed impossible to think that the government at home

was planning to allow a slew of Supercasinos to spring up across the UK, bringing all this misery to British shores. Had anyone actually come here to see the reality? Drunken parties of stags populated the streets and, in the place where Elvis was still very much alive, a couple of dozen guys wearing Elvis masks complete with plastic quiffs lurched past her singing, 'Here we go!' in Home Counties accents, oblivious to anyone else in their drink-soaked joy.

Her phone rang. Perhaps it was Toby. All her calls to him had gone unanswered, but he might have relented and be trying to get in touch with her. There was a drunk passed out on the ground by her feet, his bottle poorly disguised inside a rolled newspaper, as she sank down onto a small wall to answer the phone. She looked at the caller display as she pulled it out of her handbag. Her heart plummeted when she saw it wasn't her husband. It was a text message from Lucy. Not what she expected, but it made Nadia smile tiredly. Even though it must have been the middle of the night, her friend was still thinking about her. It read *STILL NO LUCK?* She texted back *NOT YET.* Lucy came back with: *TAKE CARE, WE ALL LOVE YOU.* Nadia snapped her phone off. It was good to know that she had her friends on her side.

By now, she felt almost delirious with jet lag and lack of food. There was nothing she'd like more than some chocolate – a Toffee Crisp or a cold bar of Dairy Milk. A sugar rush would surely help her concentration. Maybe she should give up for now, grab a hamburger or something, go back to her scabby pit of a hotel and crash out on the bed, get a few hours of much-needed rest. But maybe yards from here, her husband was about to place his next bet. And maybe she could find him just in time to stop him.

Marshalling her last ounces of strength, she pushed on to Treasure Island where the regular pirate shows had long since stopped for the night. By-passing the deserted galleon in front of the hotel, Nadia followed signs to the casino. New York might like to bill itself as the city that never sleeps – but it was Vegas that was the insomniacs' dream come true. It was past 2.00 a.m., but there were still plenty of people seated at the tables and the slots. Toby wasn't among them. Neither was he in Circus, Circus, Riviera or the Sahara.

By now, she could have passed out with exhaustion. It was taking every ounce of her willpower not to lie down on the ground and sleep, but to keep going. She consulted her map. The last hotel on this part of The Strip was the Stratosphere. Its soaring tower reached into the sky above her, and a spectacular light-show danced tantalisingly across the Las Vegas valley. At the very top, 100 storeys high, there were thrill rides – the Big Shot, the X Scream and Insanity. Rides that dangled the truly fearless with death-defying precision over the edge of the tower and 1100 feet above the reclaimed desert below. Nadia shook her head. What on earth would make someone want to do that for fun? She liked to have her feet firmly on the ground.

Once she'd checked out the Stratosphere, she'd have done one full length of The Strip and have taken in more casinos than she cared to remember. Then she could catch a cab back to her hotel and rest. So that tomorrow she could do it all over again. Maybe twice.

The lights were starting to blur before her eyes now and she rubbed them in an effort to keep awake. Then, out of the blue, there was a horrified gasp from the people on the sidewalk just ahead of her and a bolt of cold dread hit her body. As the screaming started, Nadia broke into a run. Pain jolted through her legs, but still she powered on. There was the noise of a siren, shrill and piercing from behind her, and an ambulance screeched to a halt at the kerbside. By the time Nadia reached the tower, legs pulsating with pain, a crowd had gathered.

'There's a jumper,' someone said to her and her heart turned to ice.

A woman in a loud Hawaiian shirt and shorts that were too tight was sobbing hysterically, eyes focused on the top of the tower, while her ineffectual husband tried desperately to comfort her. His head was bald and he was sweating in the heat. Whereas Nadia felt cold, so cold. The paramedics pushed through, trying to clear the rubberneckers away. Against her best instinct, she let her gaze travel upwards where all eyes were fixed on a tiny, barely visible figure at the top of the tower – a pinpoint on the vast blackness of the sky. The man was dangling on the wrong side of the safety barrier, the glare of a spotlight fixed on him and the crowd screamed whenever he made a move. On auto-pilot, she followed the paramedics, taking the path that they'd cleared through the crush of people. Despite the noise of the wailing sirens, she could hear her own breathing.

It didn't matter that she couldn't clearly pick out the man, she knew instinctively who it was. She just hoped that her hunch was completely wrong. Nadia moved forward, easing past the people who'd managed to get prime viewing spots. She touched one of the paramedics on the arm.

'Lady.' He held up a hand. 'Please step back.'

Very calmly, in a voice that Nadia didn't recognise, she said, 'I think that's my husband up there.'

Minutes later, Nadia had been ushered through the crowd and was being whisked up in the elevator. It seemed to take just seconds to reach the pinnacle where she was hustled out onto the observation deck by a burly policeman.

This high up on the top of the tower there was a cool breeze and, for a moment, Nadia thought how pleasant it was to be out of the heat. And then she saw Toby and she wished with all her heart that her instincts had failed her. The area had been cordoned off and there was a policeman, crouched, talking softly to him. Her husband was standing on the outside of the railings, clinging tightly to them. His hair was dishevelled and there was a wild, despairing look in his eyes.

'We have someone here to talk to you,' the policeman said, and Nadia was guided forwards.

'Toby . . .' She had to clear her throat because suddenly it was as dry as the desert beneath them. 'Whatever you've done, we can sort this out.'

'Nadia.' Her husband started to cry. 'I've messed up big time,' he shouted to her. 'I can't see any other way out.'

Her knees had started to shake. 'There's always another way. Think of Lewis. Think of me.'

'I've lost everything,' he wailed. 'I lost ninety thousand pounds online. In less than an hour.' He giggled hysterically. 'Do you know how long it would take me to earn that kind of money?'

Nadia knew only too well. She stood frozen to the spot. Ninety thousand pounds. The floor swayed beneath her and she thought that her legs would surely buckle. *Ninety thousand pounds.* Somehow, she found her voice. 'It doesn't matter,' she said shakily. 'I've come to take you home.'

The policeman indicated to her that she should move forward slowly, so she inched towards her husband.

'I came here to try to win it back,' Toby continued. 'I was going to send you the money, but I lost even more here,' he confessed. 'So much more. There's no way out. I'm so sorry.'

'Just come back inside,' she urged. 'We can talk it through. Do it for me. I love you.'

Toby looked down at the ground. Nadia thought she saw a waver of indecision in his eyes. He moved towards her and she reached out her trembling hands to him.

'I love you too,' he said.

And then she watched as her husband let go of the railings and fell backwards into thin air.

Chapter Forty-Three

M arcus is lying on my couch, feet up, hands behind his head, watching football.

'Marcus,' I say. 'You're not listening to me.'

'I am.'

He's not.

'I am,' he insists and then goes, 'Ooo!' as someone misses a goal on the screen.

'What's your opinion then?' I have my pen poised against my notepad.

My fiancé drags his eyes from the television. 'About what?'

I pick up a cushion and hurl it at him. 'You are *so* not listening!'

He giggles as I start to beat him in frustration. 'It was something about flowers,' he guesses. 'Or dresses.'

I twist his ear. 'Ouch. Ouch. I give in,' he whimpers. 'I might not have been listening.'

'You're not the slightest bit bothered about this wedding,' I say in an accusatory tone as I fold my arms. 'I don't even know why we're doing this.'

Marcus uncrosses my arms, takes my hands and kisses them. 'We're doing it because we love each other.'

'If you loved me then you'd help me. There's so much to do.' I feel as if the pressure is mounting on me and I can't even begin to think about all the stuff I've got to organise.

'Because I love you, I've done something even better,' Marcus tells me smugly. He pulls me to him.

'What?' I'm still pouting to show that I'm not a complete pushover.

'I've organised a wedding planner for us.'

'Oh.'

'I've arranged for you to meet him to go through everything that your heart desires.'

I sit back. 'Him?'

Marcus shrugs.

'He's not gay, is he?'

'I don't know,' Marcus admits. 'Does it matter?'

'He might want to put me in a big pink meringue of a dress.' I know what Clive and Tristan are like. Their sartorial taste doesn't run to understated. I'll end up wearing some hideous monstrosity and probably fairy wings to boot. It would make Jordan's nuptials look low-key.

'The guy's just organised a wedding for someone at work. They said he was the business. It was the wedding of the century, just as ours will be. Gay or not, he comes very highly recommended.'

'And he sorts everything out?'

'Yes.' Marcus curls his fingers through mine. 'I want you to enjoy this, not to be stressed out. We're never going to do this again, Lucy. I want it to be perfect for you.'

'I bet he's hideously expensive.'

Marcus sighs. 'Will you let me worry about all that,' he says. 'I just had a great bonus and I want to blow it. This is a day that you'll remember for the rest of your life. It should be special.'

'Okay.' I hug him, as I surreptitiously reach for the remote control and turn off the football.

'I can deny you nothing.' Marcus smiles at me indulgently. 'Can you meet him tomorrow? I know that time's getting tight.'

'Sure.' It will give me a great excuse to phone in sick, thus avoiding having to see Aiden Holby's sad face in the office. 'Thank you, Marcus. That's a really lovely thought.' I plant a kiss on his lips.

'Come here, sexy,' Marcus growls and pulls me down on top of him.

'Ouch!' I complain.

'Oh, sorry,' he says, as he lifts the hem of my skirt. 'How was the paintballing?'

170

'Painful,' I tell him. For more reasons than I could ever explain.

'Ooo.' My fiancé's eyes widen when he sees the black and blue blotches that cover my legs. 'Those are pretty heinous bruises.'

'Yeah.' I admire my war wounds – which, frankly, hurt like stink. 'You should see the others.'

Marcus laughs. 'I bet you gave them all hell.'

I laugh too and then my arrogant demeanour fails. What Marcus doesn't need to know is that I put one of my colleagues through more hell than the others. To my shame, once again I've left Aiden Holby with a great big bruise – and it wasn't anything to do with my skill with a gun.

Chapter Forty-Four

Chantal takes my hand and pulls me forward. 'I don't want to be here,' I say.

'Do you think I do?' she replies. 'You're the one getting married here in a few short weeks. Maybe you should get used to the idea.'

She yanks again, more forcefully this time, and I fly up the steps and into the Reception of Trington Manor.

'I didn't know that Marcus had set up the meeting here,' I sulk, 'otherwise I would have refused to come.'

'Why?' Chantal wants to know. 'This is your wedding venue. You can't avoid it for ever.'

I tut heavily.

'You're behaving like a four year old.' Lewis, the four year old who's holding her other hand, smiles angelically at me. If I was behaving like him, all would be well. It seems strange to see Chantal with a kid in tow, but it doesn't seem to be phasing her. 'It's not often I agree with what Marcus does, but this is a really great idea.'

'I'd just prefer it if Marcus and I went away somewhere quiet and did the dirty deed,' I say, referring to our forthcoming nuptials. 'I don't want a big fuss.'

'Looks like you're getting a fuss whether you like it or not,' Chantal reminds me. 'Besides, this is your big day. Relax and enjoy it, honey. Marcus has said no expense is to be spared.'

'That's why I'm having a wedding planner.'

'There's no way you can organise everything by yourself,' my friend tells me crisply. 'Not at such short notice. You need help. And Marcus, like most guys, won't be anywhere in sight when there's anything practical to be done.' Chantal releases her death grip and links her arm through mine instead. 'Who are we meeting?'

I look at the business card that Marcus gave me. *Elysian Occasions.* Very posh. Giggling nervously, I say, 'It's a bloke. What kind of bloke wants to be a wedding planner? I'm worried that he's going to be gay.'

'No,' Chantal says cagily. 'He's definitely not gay.'

'Are you speaking from experience?' I joke.

Then I notice that she's gone slightly pale and turn to follow her gaze. The smile is wiped off my face, for standing in front of me is Jacob, Jazz or whatever incarnation this is of him. Chantal does indeed have personal carnal knowledge of him. And we both know that he's not gay. This is my ex-boyfriend who was the male escort with whom my friend Chantal enjoyed several lusty liaisons.

'Hi, Lucy,' Jacob says shyly.

He's looking as gorgeous as he ever did and my panic button is hit right on the nose. 'Oh no,' I say, backing away. 'I can't do this.'

'Lucy—' he says.

Turning to Chantal, I say, 'You knew about this!'

'I didn't,' she swears. 'Jacob is the very person I would have recommended for you, but I had no idea that Marcus had contacted him. Please do this, Lucy. I still think it's a fabulous idea.'

'No!'

'Come on,' Chantal urges. 'This is Jacob's new career and he's really great at it.'

'I heard that he was pretty good at his last career,' I say snippily, as we talk about Jacob as if he isn't there.

Chantal laughs – which I have to say I think is inappropriate. 'Let bygones be bygones,' she tells me. 'Isn't that what you guys say?'

'I have some great ideas,' Jacob offers.

'Yeah? Well, *shagging* one of my best friends wasn't one of them.' I lower my voice because of Lewis.

'Marcus has organised this especially for you,' Chantal points out. 'What would you tell him if you cancelled?'

'I don't know,' I say. 'And what's more, I don't care.'

'Be sensible, Lucy,' she counters. 'You need help. You know Jacob. You can trust him.'

You know, I really don't think my friend is being ironic.

'Please,' she says. 'Just listen to what he has to say.'

'I've booked a table in the restaurant,' my wedding planner says. 'We can try the food, look at menus. They have great chocolate desserts here.'

They do? Maybe things are looking up.

'And we need to choose a theme,' Jacob adds.

'A theme?' That sounds truly terrifying. How can I begin to explain to Jacob that I've actually had trouble settling on a bloody groom?

'Say you'll do it,' Chantal pleads.

My brain is having its usual quandary and is knocking round uselessly in my skull, while my mouth says, 'Okay.' I hold up my hands in resignation. 'I'll give it a go.'

Jacob and Chantal smile at each other.

'But if I ever find out that the two of you cooked this up between you then you are no longer my friend, Chantal Hamilton.'

'I want you to do this because I love you,' Chantal says, 'and I'm worried about you. I know that Jacob will take good care of you.'

I'm not even going to ask how she can be so sure of that.

'Now I'm going to leave you two alone so that you can get down to business,' my friend says. 'I'll take Lewis out into the garden to run off some energy. He'll be bored otherwise. But I want to be filled in on every single detail when I get back.'

With that, she leaves us standing there together and before I can consider the wisdom of my decision, Jacob says, 'Well.'

'Quite,' I reply.

He offers me his arm which I take, then with his usual impeccable manners he escorts me through to the restaurant. Nerves have twisted my stomach into a knot and it's not just the thought of getting married very shortly.

174

We're seated at a table in the corner before we speak again.

'I want to offer you my congratulations,' Jacob says. He's wearing a smart charcoal-grey suit that flatters his beautiful, baby-blue eyes. His teeth are perfect, his smile just the right side of utterly charming. I can see why he was so successful as a high-class hooker. I can still see why he was a great boyfriend. 'But I also want to apologise to you.'

'There's no need,' I say dismissively.

'There is,' he insists. 'I'm really sorry for the way things turned out between us.'

'It's all water under the bridge,' I say airily, but I'm surprised that I can still feel something burning up inside me.

I liked Jacob. I *really* liked him. And I wonder if Chantal has encouraged me to use him as my wedding planner with the hope that it might actually reignite something between us and snooker my marriage to Marcus. I wouldn't put it past her – she can be a very sneaky American person when she wants to be. Well, she's wrong. There's no one for me now but Marcus.

'Thanks for agreeing to work with me, Lucy,' Jacob says. 'You won't regret it, I promise. I'll make sure that you have a great wedding.'

It's not a great wedding that I'm worried about. I'm more concerned that I'll have a great marriage to go with it.

Chapter Forty-Five

'Come on, slowcoach.' Marcus comes up behind me, lifts my hair and kisses me on the neck. 'We're going to be late.'

It would be true to say that I am dragging my heels somewhat. Tonight, we're having dinner with Marcus's parents and, frankly, I'd rather have my teeth pulled. All of them. Without the benefit of modern anaesthetics.

'How did the meeting go with the wedding planner yesterday?'

'Oh, fine,' I say. There's no way I'm going to tell him that our wedding planner is an ex-call boy and my ex-boyfriend to boot.

'Was he any good?' Marcus says. 'I only want the best for my girl.'

'I think the wedding will be wonderful,' I say evasively. Even I have to admit that Jacob came up with some great ideas – a chocolate fountain for the evening reception being among the best of them.

'I've booked a table at Alfonso's,' Marcus continues. 'Your favourite.' It's not really my favourite, Marcus just thinks it is. I wonder what else he thinks about me that simply isn't true?

'Lovely,' I say, but I make it sound as if it's anything but lovely.

'I know that you find seeing my parents an ordeal, but they *adore* you,' Marcus tells me.

They don't *adore* me. Marcus's mother, Hilary, barely tolerates me. She makes it abundantly clear that she thinks I'm stealing her only baby away from her when, patently, I'm not worthy. The more I talk, the more she glares at me, so I talk less and then she glares at me as if I'm a moron. Can't win.

His father, David, is a bit better, but I always try to sit as far away from him as possible. This might be a terrible slur on his good name, but he looks like one of those old Lothario types who'd be happy running a hand up your thigh under the table-cloth. Know what I mean? You might say like father, like son – but I don't want to go there.

I've seen them barely a handful of times in the five years that I've been with Marcus and that, I would say, is rather too many. I'm sure they'd agree.

Finally, I'm ready. Or as ready as I'll ever be.

'You look fabulous,' Marcus tells me. He lets his hands travel over my body. 'I think I'd like to make love to you right now.'

I ease away from him. 'Then we'd be even more late.' And your mother would know, she'd just *know*, exactly what we'd been up to.

'Later then, you sexy bitch,' he growls playfully, and squeezes a handful of my bottom.

Even in the cab Marcus can't keep his hands off me and I wonder what's making him feel so damn frisky. He's been like this since we got back together. To be honest, I'm having more sex than I can comfortably cope with. I've been taken over the back of the sofa more times than I care to count. I don't know if this is Marcus trying to show just how much he loves me. Or whether it's the fact that he hasn't got another woman on the go for once that I'm being rogered senseless every five minutes. We can't continue at this pace. It's not human.

It's sort of flattering that Marcus wants me so much, but as his finger slips inside my bra and toys with my nipple, out of the corner of my eye, I can see the cab driver looking in his mirror. Not only is he getting an eyeful, but I bet he's thinking, Slut! Has Marcus been taking Viagra, I wonder.

I manage to get to the restaurant without being ravished in public, but I'm feeling flustered and flushed. While Marcus, of course, is as cool as a cucumber. His parents are already there, which knocks off points for me straight away.

David hugs me warmly, but I feel his hand slide over my back as if he's checking out whether I'm wearing a bra. Hilary keeps a safe distance while she pecks at both of my cheeks, clearly hoping that I'm not riddled with some infectious disease. We sit down and, of course, I end up sandwiched between David and Marcus.

'Let's have champagne,' David says magnanimously. 'We've not yet had a chance to celebrate your engagement.'

Hilary makes no comment.

The champagne comes and the obligatory toasts are completed. Marcus turns to his father and starts to talk about golf, leaving me to deal with Hilary.

'This is all rather short notice,' she says crisply.

'Well,' I say, 'we've been together for five years. I guess it was going to happen sometime.'

Marcus's mother looks as if she rather wishes that it hadn't. 'People who we *desperately* want to be there are struggling to be able to accept their invitations.'

There are about two thousand people coming to this damn wedding, all of them invited by Hilary and none of them ever heard of by me. Even Marcus is clueless about most of them. They're Golf Club, Cricket Club and Bridge Club cronies, I think and, personally, I don't give two hoots whether they're there or not.

Hilary continues in the same vein and I try to blank her out while giving Marcus the evil eye which says, 'Rescue me!' He's so engrossed in recounting the intricacies of his last round, that he completely fails to acknowledge me. I scan the restaurant, hoping that I can see succour arriving in the name of food.

Then my eyes alight on a table in the corner. A very romantic nook of a corner, as it happens. Crush is sitting there. And he's not alone.

Chapter Forty-Six

A luscious brunette with catwalk model looks is sitting opposite Mr Aiden Holby. They're chatting away, laughing lightly.
A nasty green thing flares inside of me. Not five minutes ago he
was trying to snog me in his combat gear, face covered in crap.
Now look at him! I've spent all day in the office with him and
he didn't mention a thing about having a date. Then again, why
should he? I didn't tell him that I was coming here with my
future in-laws either.

As if he realises that he's being watched – or maybe I should
have turned down my death-ray glare – Crush turns to look at
me. He recoils slightly and I'm not sure if it's in surprise or terror.

He lifts his hand and gives me a friendly wave. I grit my teeth
and wave back. He's wearing a black shirt and looks fucking
gorgeous. Inconsiderate bastard.

'An admirer?' Hilary asks, as if she's amazed that I have one.

'My boss,' I tell her, unable to keep the note of misery out of
my voice.

Why am I suddenly so depressed that Crush is here with
another woman? I'm here celebrating my engagement and forthcoming wedding. Why should it matter what Aiden I've-Got-A-
New-Girlfriend Holby is up to? I bet she's useless with a replica
AK-47 fully automatic paintball machine gun. She looks the sort
who'd be happier having a manicure than crawling through the
dirt on her knees. Come to think of it, so am I.

We get through dinner somehow. Hilary whines on in my ear
and David keeps giving me very funny looks. Course after course
arrives and I keep having to check out Crush's table and it seems
they're eating at exactly the same pace as us. I had hoped that

they'd rush through a couple of dishes and clear off, but no such luck. But then if they had cleared off early, I'd only be wondering what they were up to. Bollocky-bollocks.

Finally, thankfully, dessert arrives: molten chocolate cake with vanilla cream. Oh yes, oh yes. I risk a glance at Crush's table and he's being served exactly the same thing. Marcus has chosen summer pudding which has no chocolate in it at all. How can that be classed as a real dessert? I wonder how much I really have in common with my future husband. How can anyone sane choose flipping fruit when there is delicious chocolate on the menu?

Crush spoons a mouthful of his chocolate cake into Miss Catwalk Model's mouth. He's only doing it because I'm watching. How childish. I won't look over there again just to spite him.

Then, just as I'm tucking into my chocolate cake, I feel a hand slip up my thigh. Freezing, I clamp my knees together – which does nothing more than force the hand higher. I look over at Marcus, but he seems completely oblivious. I look at David, and he's grinning widely at me. Ohmigod. I'm being sexually assaulted under the table by my fiancé's father!

Yes, there it goes again. Another over-familiar squeeze.

'Excuse me.' I abandon my dessert. 'I must visit the ladies' room.'

Dashing across the restaurant, I take refuge in the loo. It's very chic in here, all hardwood with cherry-red highlights of colour. I splash water on my face even though it'll ruin my make-up and then I run my wrists under the tap. While I'm contemplating my next move, there's a tentative knock on the door and I hear Crush's voice call, 'Lucy? Are you in there, Lucy?'

I've nowhere to hide. There's no rear exit. I'm cornered. Aiden Holby pushes the door ajar. 'Are you all right?'

'I'm fine,' I say, sounding half-strangled. For some reason, I lower my voice to a stage whisper. 'What are you doing here?'

'In here?' Crush says. 'Or in the restaurant generally?'

'Both!'

'I'm in the restaurant because I have a lovely date. I'm in here because I've come to see if you're okay. You looked very distressed when you shot across the restaurant like a scalded cat.'

'I *am* distressed.'

'Want to talk about it?'

'In here?'

He pulls me into the cubicle at the end of the row and closes the door behind him. I put the lid down on the loo and sit. Crush leans against the wall. 'Is it anything to do with me?'

I fold my arms and try to look haughty. 'Why do you think my whole life revolves around you?'

He grins at me. 'You looked pretty pissed off when you saw me with another woman.'

'I was not!'

'I've had a few dates with her,' Crush tells me, even though I'm not the slightest bit interested. 'That's all. She's Italian. A catwalk model over here on assignment.'

Oh, no! Not only does she look like a catwalk model, but she bloody well *is* one! Life is *so* fucking unfair. She's probably one of those bitches who's 'not *so keen* on chocolate', as well. I despise the very ground she walks on.

'You look like you're having a great time.' I try not to sound bitter and twisted.

'You, on the other hand, look thoroughly miserable.'

I say nothing to incriminate myself.

'Who's the scary old bat with the Botox and hairspray over-dose?'

'That's Hilary,' I say. 'Marcus's mother.'

'Ooo,' Crush says. '*That's* going to be your mother-in-law for the next twenty-five years or whatever.'

I sag on the loo. 'Don't remind me.' I shake my head, trying to get the image of David's hand creeping up my leg out of my mind. 'That's not the worst of it. I'll kill you if you breathe a word of this to anyone else.' I give him a look that says I mean it. 'I've just been groped by Marcus's dad.'

Crush laughs out loud.

'Don't laugh,' I moan. 'It's not funny.'

181

Then I hear the door open, so I shush Aiden. A moment later, Hilary's voice trills out. 'Lucy? Lucy? Are you all right? You've been gone ever such a long time. Marcus has sent me to look for you.'

'I'm fine, Hilary,' I say.

Crush scooshes me backwards and silently climbs onto the loo in front of me. What's he doing? I give him a look and he puts his finger to his lips to quieten me, then he points to the gap at the bottom of the cubicle door. I have to hold onto his thighs to stop him wobbling. His groin is perilously close to my mouth. My heart is banging in my chest and it's only partly because Hilary the Hun is prowling just outside the door.

Marcus's mother's head does, indeed, appear at floor-level. Bloody hell, she is actually trying to peep under the loo door. What does she think – that I've got a man in here! Oh. But then I have.

'Are you sure there's nothing wrong?' she says under the door.

'Slightly dodgy tummy,' I tell her quickly.

'Must be all the excitement,' she replies.

Must be because your husband's trying to cop a feel of my growler.

'I'll be out in just a minute,' I say. 'Don't wait for me. Tell Marcus that I'm okay.'

Then she leaves and you don't know how relieved I am that she didn't decide to pay a visit to the facilities while she was here. I don't think I could have coped. No one should be forced to listen to their future mother-in-law having a wee.

When the door closes behind her, Crush jumps down from the loo seat. I am almost faint with relief.

'That was fun,' he says. 'In a pervy sort of way.'

'How did you know that she'd look under the door?'

'Those sort of women always do,' Crush tells me – though quite where he has gleaned this knowledge from, I have no idea.

'Buggeration.' I hold my head in my hands. 'What sort of a family am I marrying into?'

'I have to be going,' Crush says. And even though we're in a toilet, Aiden Holby kisses me quickly and firmly on the mouth. 'Enjoy the rest of your evening,' he says with a grin as he breezes out of the cubicle.

But he knows damn well that I won't.

Chapter Forty-Seven

Nowe of us know what to say. We're sitting in Chocolate Heaven, but even a plate of Clive's finest champagne truffles is failing to soothe us. Our mood is sombre in sympathy with our friend's terrible tragedy.

Nadia is dressed in black. Her face is pale and drawn. She's picking at a chocolate without enthusiasm. Eventually, she gives up and pushes the plate away from her. 'Toby's body is due to arrive back later today,' she says into the silence. 'Could one of you come with me?'

'We'll all come,' I say. 'We should never have let you go to Las Vegas alone. This is just awful for you.'

'I don't think it's really hit me yet,' Nadia admits. 'And I don't know what I would have done without you all.'

I can't take much credit myself, but Chantal has been absolutely wonderful. She's stepped into the breach once again, looking after Lewis and helping Nadia with the organisation of the funeral. Why is it, at a time when all you want to do is fall to pieces, there's so much paperwork to complete? This has all been a living nightmare for Nadia, but she's coping incredibly with it. I don't know that I'd have been so stoic in her situation.

'Does this mean that Toby's debts are cleared?' I venture. Not a nice question, but I know that we all want to ask it. I hate to think that Nadia will still be struggling with financial problems on top of everything else.

'I wish.' Nadia sighs. 'I went to see the solicitor this morning. The bank could chase me for all of Toby's debts if they want to play hardball. She's going to try to negotiate for me just to pay off a proportion of it.'

'How can the banks be so heartless?' Autumn wants to know.

'It's business,' Nadia says with a weary shrug. 'The trouble is, if they come after the estate, there's nothing there. The house is mortgaged up to the hilt, we owe money everywhere – including to Chantal. Even Toby's work van is financed. He'd managed to rack up ninety thousand pounds' worth of debt on twelve different credit cards – all on internet gambling sites. *Ninety thousand pounds*,' she stresses. 'How could he do that? He blew another forty grand in Vegas trying to claw something back.' Her expression is bleak. 'Needless to say, it didn't work. If the banks choose to pursue me, they could make us homeless.'

'You'll always have a place with me,' Chantal says.

'Thanks.' Nadia tries a wan smile, but tears are quick to follow it. 'I just keep wondering if there was something more that I could have done. Was there something I could have said to stop him?'

'Nadia,' I tell her as I clasp her hand in mine. 'You know that you did everything possible. Please don't beat yourself up over this.'

'Part of me is grieving for the loss of him,' she says. 'Part of me hates him for leaving me and Lewis in such a mess. And part of me is simply relieved that he won't be able to gamble any more. I don't know which emotion to deal with first.' Nadia rubs her hands over her face. 'My brain feels as if it's about to explode.'

'We'll help you through it,' Autumn promises. 'That's what we're here for.'

'I had to get out of the house today,' Nadia continues. 'It just feels so empty without Toby there. I keep expecting him to come through the door.'

'It's going to take a long time for that feeling to stop,' Autumn tells her. 'Just keep talking to us about it, don't bottle it up. You know we'll do all we can. I'll make you a blend of aromatherapy oils to help you sleep.'

'I have full-hit Temazepam sleeping tablets helped down with a slug of cooking brandy which seems to be doing the job.'

Autumn nibbles at her nails anxiously, then she touches the plaster at her throat.

'Looks like you've got some troubles of your own, honey,' Chantal says softly to her. 'Cut yourself shaving?'

Autumn shakes her head. 'Threatened by one of my dear brother's business associates.'

Another worried glance does the rounds. 'This sounds as if it's getting pretty heavy, Autumn,' I tell her.

She nods in agreement. 'I think this time, Rich is way out of his depth.'

'And you're getting dragged into it.'

She nods again. 'There was some thug waiting for me when I got home from the hospital last night. Wanted me to pass on a message to Richard.'

'So, how is he?'

'Better,' she says with a weary sigh. 'I'm going to see him later.' She fingers the plaster again, subconsciously. 'Pass on his message.'

I sink back into my chair and pick another chocolate. 'We could do with some good news.'

'Well,' Chantal says with a smile as she pats her tummy protectively, 'I felt baby Hamilton move for the first time this morning. It was great. I think I'm finally getting used to this baby lark.'

'How are things with you, Lucy?' asks Autumn.

'Same old, same old,' I say dismissively. 'I spent half of last night in a loo in an Italian restaurant after being groped by Marcus's dad with Crush's testicles an inch away from my mouth while Marcus's mother tried to look under the door.'

Is it a measure of my tortured life that my friends accept this garbled tale without question? 'Now I've got to phone both of my parents and their chosen life-partners and invite them to the wedding. God, I hope they're too busy to come. Would it be wrong to wait until a few days beforehand to ask them?'

'Lucy, you are silly,' Autumn chides. 'What prior commitments would possibly stop them from coming to their daughter's wedding?'

'Golf, bridge, tennis. All of these could be factors. If it's the club championship for any of them, then I'm onto a dead cert. Even my mother having a long-standing hairdressing appointment could make her think twice.' Come to think of it, they'll get on brilliantly with Hilary and Dave. 'My mum and dad haven't been in a room together since their divorce. I can see blood up the walls. We'll be lucky if they survive the day without killing each other.' Then I feel bad about mentioning anything to do with killing, with Nadia so recently bereaved.

'At least we've got something to look forward to,' Nadia says, thankfully ignoring my gaffe. 'It's only the thought of your wedding that's keeping me going.'

'I'm dreading it,' I say – for reasons that are too varied and complex for me to even start thinking about.

'It will all work out perfectly,' Chantal says. 'You wait and see.'

Nadia is also quick to reassure me. 'You'll make a beautiful bride.'

'I do hope so.' I swallow a champagne truffle for comfort. 'With my luck, the universe will conspire against me getting down that aisle at all.'

Chapter Forty-Eight

'He said that you'd got something that belonged to them.' Autumn had just finished telling Richard the story of her encounter with the late-night knifeman. Her brother had gone paler by the minute.

'He held a knife to my throat.' She pointed, unnecessarily, at the plaster covering her wound. Then she realised that this was probably the same man who'd given her brother this beating and she wondered whether, this time, she'd got off rather lightly.

'I'm sorry, sis. I never meant for this to happen.'

'Is it true what he said? Have you got something that belongs to them?'

Richard tried to shift slightly in his hospital bed, holding his ribs in pain. He looked away from her.

'So, that's a yes?'

'I'll sort it as soon as I get out of here.'

'Will they be prepared to wait that long?'

'They'll have to.'

It was bold talk, maybe foolhardy. But, at least she reckoned Richard would be safer in here than anywhere else. Autumn folded her arms, hugging them round her body. She was missing Addison. She was missing being held. Since Richard had been in here, she'd hardly seen him. Now it was time to rectify that.

'What is it that you're hiding? Money? Drugs?'

'The less you know about it the better, Autumn,' he said. 'But I promise you. I'll fix it, once and for all. You didn't go to the police?'

'No,' she said. 'Stupidly, I didn't.'

'Good girl,' Richard said with a sigh of relief.

Her brother seemed to be out of danger now, even though he was still very weak. He was pale and sweating, and there was a tremor to his hands whenever he reached for his glass of water. Autumn wondered how much of it was to do with his injuries or whether he was suffering from the sudden withdrawal from his drugs. To be honest, she didn't really want to go into details with him. He was suffering and that was all she needed to know. She'd had enough of sitting by his bedside. Addison was right, there was only so much she could do to protect him. The rest had to come from Richard himself, otherwise she was going to worry herself into an early grave on his behalf.

Autumn stood up. 'Sleep,' she said. 'That's the best thing you can do. Sleep. Get strong and get out of here.'

'Don't go,' her brother begged. 'Stay here. I feel better when you're around.'

'I have to leave,' she told him as she kissed him goodbye. 'I'm due at work shortly. You're not the only person in my life, Richard. There are other people who need me.'

Her brother didn't look very enamoured of that statement, but he'd have to live with the knowledge – just as she had to live with the knowledge that whatever she did for him, it was never going to be enough.

It was good to get back to some kind of normality. Having a knife put to her throat had shaken Autumn more than she cared to admit. Back in the sanctuary of her workshop, she toyed with a piece of peacock-blue stained glass; the depth of the colour reminded her of a tropical ocean, soothing her troubled spirit.

Fraser looked up at her. 'Penny for them, miss.'

'Sorry, Fraser,' she said, with a smile at one of her favourite clients. 'I was miles away.'

'It's good to have you back.'

'And it's good to be back. How's that suncatcher coming along?' Her student held up his work proudly. All his months of attending here with the sole object of chatting up Tasmin hadn't been entirely wasted. An unexpected by-product was that, at long last, he was starting to become quite a reasonable artist with his stained-glass creations. Well, they didn't instantly fall to bits any more, which Autumn took as progress. 'That's great, Fraser. Really great.'

The young man glowed with pride. So often these kids were just lacking a little praise and encouragement in their dark lives. Finding one simple thing that they were good at could, in a few lucky cases, open the floodgates and turn their lives around.

Out of the corner of her eye, she spotted Addison standing in the doorway watching her. 'Hi, there,' she said.

His eyes went to the plaster on her neck, but he said nothing. 'Did Fraser tell you that we've got him fixed up with a job?'

'No.' Autumn beamed with delight.

'Engineering apprenticeship,' their client said, puffing his chest out. 'Start next week.'

'And you're going to be there on time every morning and stay there all day,' Addison said with a warning note in his voice.

'Sure thing!' Fraser frowned. 'D'ye think I'm a wee idiot?'

'I'm going to call you every morning,' Addison promised. 'Just to make sure that you're up on time.'

'Tasmin can give me a nudge in the ribs. That always wakes me up.'

Ah, Autumn thought. So progress has been made on that front too. Romance had clearly blossomed while she'd been away and, suddenly, it felt as if she'd been away for months, not weeks.

Tasmin came over to join them. She was wearing bright pink eye-shadow that matched her lipstick and her slashed T-shirt. Her jet black hair hung over her deathly white face and yet another new stud had been added to the collection on her lips. The girl leaned against Fraser with a casual disdain. She held out a bracelet for Autumn. 'I made this for you, miss.'

The silver wires twined delicately round tiny pieces of polished kiln glass in pastel shades. 'That's fantastic,' she said. 'Is it really for me?'

Tasmin sniffed to hide her embarrassment. 'We've kinda missed ya,' she admitted grudgingly.

'Isn't this wonderful?' Autumn said to Addison as she slipped the bracelet onto her wrist and admired it. The glass sparkled as it caught the light.

Her boyfriend certainly looked impressed and she let her hand rest on his, wanting to feel closer to him as they both admired Tasmin's artistry. Addison acknowledged her touch with a warm smile which made Autumn's tummy flip over.

'Have you thought about setting up your own stall to sell this stuff?' he asked the girl. 'It's good enough.'

Tasmin shook her head.

'Somewhere like Camden Market would be perfect.'

'That's a great idea,' Autumn enthused.

'Would you be interested?'

Tasmin shrugged.

'Leave it with me,' he said, taking her off-handed response as approval. 'Let me see if I can get some more information and maybe some funding from somewhere.'

An uncertain smile briefly crossed Tasmin's face, which they all knew meant that she was deliriously happy.

Autumn and Addison walked to the other end of the work-shop. 'I'm sorry I've not been around much,' Autumn said. 'I plan to make up for it.'

'I'm glad to hear it. You didn't think that you'd get rid of me that easily, did you?' Addison replied. 'If it means that I have to share you with your brother, then so be it.'

He brushed her chin with his thumb and threw a glance at her throat. 'What happened here?'

'I took a message for Richard.'

A frown darkened Addison's brow.

'I'm frightened,' she admitted. 'They came after me at my flat.'

'I'm moving in with you,' Addison said flatly. 'From tonight. It isn't safe for you to be there alone. I won't hear any arguments.'

She hadn't intended to offer any. It might not have been the most romantic discussion about the possibilities of co-habitation, but it worked for her.

'Thank you.' Autumn stood on tiptoe and kissed her gorgeous, thoughtful man on the lips.

Chapter Forty-Nine

Jacob has accompanied us all on a visit to the bridal department of one of London's most famous stores. This man is proving to be an excellent wedding planner – not that I have anything to compare him to, but you know what I mean. He even went as far as checking our hands for chocolate-y residue after our trip to Chocolate Heaven on the way here. We simply *had* to fortify ourselves for the long haul ahead. Something so important needs a good solid foundation of chocolate on which to work, I think you'll agree.

I'm already on my seventeenth dress. To be honest I've felt pretty indifferent to all of them, but Jacob has hated them with a vengeance. This one is sparkly – but not *too* sparkly. Despite our recent visit to Chocolate Heaven, my chocolate levels are, I think, dropping dangerously low. My mind is wandering to thoughts of Cadbury's Fruit and Nut far too often. Back to the job in hand, the assistant zips me up and I emerge from the changing room, once again. My friends are sitting in a row, waiting patiently and I give them a twirl.

'No,' Jacob says, stroking his chin.

'I quite like it,' Autumn pipes up. Perhaps their patience *is* wearing thin.

'Me too,' Nadia agrees. We are still managing to drag our friend to all of our assignations despite her grief and despite her protestations that she's thoroughly miserable company. There's no way that we're going to let her sit at home on her own and brood.

'Absolutely not.' Jacob seems to be morphing into Stella McCartney.

Chantal purses her lips. 'I'm with Jacob.'

'The problem is,' I say, admiring myself in the full-length mirror, 'that I really envisaged myself on a beach at sunset, barefoot, in a shift of gossamer white fabric, clutching an orchid or two.' Not that anyone seems overly interested in my opinion.

'This is certainly a long way from that,' Chantal says.

I sigh at my reflection.

'It's not too late to back out,' she adds.

'I don't want to back out,' I tell her. 'But all of this . . .' I lift up the billowing skirt. 'It isn't exactly me. I hate fuss. I'd rather have a very simple, low-key ceremony with just my best friends attending. I don't even know half of the people who are coming. They're all friends of Marcus's mum.'

'That's why you have to look your very best,' Jacob says. He hands the assistant another dress. 'This is it. Last one.'

I shuffle off into the changing room and, with much disgruntled huffing and puffing, I cast off the previous one and wriggle into this one. And because I can't risking touching any chocolate in this dress, I get out my emergency bar of Galaxy and slowly lick the wrapper all over, gaining the benefits of chocolate consumption by osmosis or something. Out I go again.

This time, my friends gasp.

Now they're making me very nervous. 'What?'

'Oh, Lucy,' Nadia says. Her eyes have filled with tears. But then, Nadia is understandably a bit over-emotional at the moment.

I look at myself in the mirror and I gasp too. 'Is that vision of loveliness really me?'

We all giggle. Then Nadia takes out a tissue and sobs noisily into it. Autumn puts an arm round her to comfort her.

'Perfect,' Jacob announces.

And he's right, it is perfect. I look fabulous. Truly the blushing bride. The dress is a sheath of shot silk in a rich shade of white chocolate. It gives me curves where I'm supposed to have curves and has gentle pleating to hide those little areas that show a life-long friendship with chocolate. I never knew that a simple dress could imbue this degree of sophistication on a person who has previously been so lacking.

'We'll take it,' Jacob says.

Then I look at the price tag and gasp again. 'I can't possibly pay this for a wedding dress!'

'Feel the pain and bend the plastic anyway,' Chantal says.

'I can't.'

'Marcus will love it,' Nadia says, sniffing her tears away.

'But if I buy this, then we'll have to get your bridesmaids' dresses from Primark. You'll be wearing something cheap and nasty in lime green.'

'It's paid for,' Jacob says. He avoids meeting my eyes and there are two high spots of pink on his cheeks. It makes him look very cute. 'It's my wedding present to you.'

'Don't be ridiculous.'

'You're very special to me, Lucy,' he says. 'I'd like you to accept it.'

'You can't do that, Jacob. It's far too much.' I look round for someone to back me up. 'I couldn't possibly accept.'

Chantal nods to me that I should. Clearly she thinks that Jacob can afford it. I have no idea what it costs to hire his services, but maybe his new profession is even more lucrative than his last one.

'And I'll pay for the bridesmaids' dresses,' Autumn says. 'Just so long as they're not something that clashes with my hair.'

Now I'm crying my eyes out too. Nadia is back on the tissues as well and she hands one to me. My friends all come to hug me. Even Jacob joins in.

'Thank you,' I tell him gratefully through my sobs. 'Thank you, Autumn.'

Everyone is being so kind to me. Despite the nagging doubts that are still assailing me, perhaps my wedding day will turn out to be the most wonderful day of my life.

Chapter Fifty

Toby's family were Catholics. The funeral service had been arranged in their local church as Nadia knew that it would please them. She could hardly bear to look at Toby's weeping mother. Although there were no accusations in her tearful glances, somehow Nadia thought she would have felt better if there were. His mother viewed her son's suicide as the ultimate sin. Nadia thought the biggest sin was for him to leave his own son at such a tender age. Toby had never gone to Mass, neither had she, but Nadia knew that it mattered to his mother and she wanted to offer what comfort she could to the red-eyed grieving woman.

Had Toby meant to let go of the rails at the top of the Stratosphere Tower, or had he been intending to climb back to safety, to her? There was a moment, the briefest of moments when she felt she'd connected with him again, seen the old Toby, but then she'd watched him drop backwards into oblivion. Perhaps it had been a figment of her imagination, a fantasy born out of false hope rather than reality. It was something that she could never be certain about.

What would she be feeling now, if Toby had stepped back over those railings and into her arms? She'd still have a husband who was addicted to gambling, still have a mountain of debts, still have a future just as uncertain as her current circumstances. Would she have hated him, or would she still have been able to cling on to her love for him? It was an unanswerable question. The maelstrom of conflicting emotions refused to be calmed no matter how hard she tried. Even the cocktail of potent drugs she was taking to blunt her senses were only helping so much.

The service was entirely alien to her. There were flowers everywhere and, it was a truly bizarre thought, but she considered the expense that such a lavish funeral was piling on top of everything else. There were prayers she couldn't recite. Hymns that she didn't know the words to. Ritual chanting that meant nothing to her. There was much standing up and kneeling down and Nadia followed it all with robotic movements. It felt as if the whole thing was happening to someone else. She was dry-eyed and hideously detached. There was no way she was even able to picture her husband lying, his body horribly broken, in the oak casket adorned with lilies that had been placed by the altar. Toby was gone. He wasn't here. It might as well be empty for all she cared. Perhaps she'd done all her crying for Toby when he was alive. Was some part of her glad that he'd taken this way out and had given them some form of relief from his destructive addiction? Only time would tell. Even though she'd laid the unhappy soul of her husband to rest, the spectre of his debts would continue to haunt her. All she could do was try to get through each day without breaking down, for Lewis's sake.

What would she have done without her friends? Lucy and Autumn had been fabulous – they stood along the row from her now. But Chantal had really come through for her, once again; she had been a complete brick. Chantal had chosen the flowers, Nadia's outfit, and they were all going back to Nadia's house after the service to eat food and drink wine that Chantal had organised. Her friend clutched her hand. Somehow it felt good to be close to Chantal now, Nadia thought, as if the life growing inside her was a kind of compensation for the life that had been so prematurely lost.

Lewis stood next to her on the other side. It was his first outing in a man's suit and her heart squeezed painfully. How would he cope without his father? Had he any concept that Toby would never be coming back? She'd told her son about the whole heaven scenario – even though she wasn't sure if she believed in any of it herself. If there was a God, why had He made her husband with such a tragic and fatal flaw? She hadn't told her son of the fall through the air of a wonderful husband who couldn't live any longer with his terrible addiction. One day she would – when he was much, much older and could understand. She sincerely hoped that gambling wasn't an hereditary condition.

At the end of the service, Nadia was glad to be out in the fresh air again, leaving the cloying scent of the incense behind. Chantal looked fabulous in her smart black suit and was attracting the attention of one of Toby's more rotund and red-nosed uncles. Nadia smiled to herself. Chantal was sure to be loving that.

Now she was busy shaking the hands of a line of damp-eyed people whom she didn't even know. Toby's death had made all of the red-top national papers, run alongside articles about the increasing dangers of online gambling and the imminent intro-duction of Vegas-style Supercasinos into Britain. Nadia had turned down all the invitations to give interviews to the press. Her family must have read all about it, yet she hadn't had so much as a phone call from them. In her case, it wasn't true that blood was thicker than water. She'd been cut off from her family because of Toby, and even his untimely demise hadn't brought any kind of sympathy or softening of their attitude.

A mobile phone rang nearby and she saw Autumn reach into her handbag to answer it. A moment later, her friend's hand touched her arm.

'Nadia,' she said, 'I have to leave. I've just had a call from the hospital. Richard's taken a turn for the worse. I have to go to him.'

Nadia nodded.

'It was a lovely service,' Autumn said.

'Thanks. I'll catch up with you later.' As she squeezed the hands of more strangers, Nadia watched her friend as she ran down the road, searching for a cab. Autumn had to go to Richard. She was needed elsewhere. And Nadia realised that there was only Lewis who needed her now. She pulled her son to her side and hugged him. This four-year-old boy was going to be her reason for living. From now on, she was going to have to face everything alone.

Chapter Fifty-One

R ichard's lung had collapsed, the hospital staff told her. An array of expensive equipment was keeping him alive. More seemed to have been added every time she visited. It beeped, hissed, sighed and functioned where her brother's body couldn't. A tube drained fluid out of the side of his chest and into a container which bubbled as Richard laboured to breathe. The nurse fussed around, taking Rich's blood pressure, changing the dressing around the canula in the back of his hand and smoothing down his sheets. Frowning, she took his temperature. He'd developed a fever and his brow was damp with sweat.

'Comfortable?' the nurse asked.

'Never better,' he said sarcastically, and Autumn wondered why her brother couldn't be more gracious to those who were trying to help him.

The nurse bristled and stomped away. When she'd gone, Richard turned to his sister. 'This is a very bad development,' he said softly, wheezing noises accompanying every word. His voice was dry with dehydration and Autumn wondered why the heating was always so high in here. It was absolutely sweltering. How much did hospitals contribute to global warming? It was just as well she hadn't brought him a box of chocolates, otherwise they'd be a sticky puddle on the floor.

'It's just a setback,' she reassured him. The collapse in his lung had been caused by his chest injuries, the doctors had told her, probably aided and abetted by his weakened immune system due to his drug abuse. In the end it always came back to that. 'If you rest, I'm sure it will only delay you going home by a couple of weeks.'

Richard reached out and gripped her wrist. 'I don't *have* a couple of weeks.'

'There's nowhere else you need to be,' she told him. Autumn didn't want to rub it in, but there was no job or girlfriend or family waiting for him to rush back to.

'The men . . .' Richard said, and faltered. With a dry tongue, he tried to moisten his cracked lips. 'The men who came after you, who did this to me, they won't wait that long.'

She shrugged with a nonchalance she didn't feel. 'They'll have to.'

A wave of irritation crossed her brother's face and his eyes flashed with frustration. 'There's no "have to" with people like that,' he said. Despite how ill he was, there was a barb of menace in his tone that she didn't care for. 'I owe them, Autumn. And you won't be safe until they've got what they want.'

'Thanks for that,' she said flatly. 'That's really what I needed to hear.'

'You'll have to do the drop for me.'

'*The drop?*' Autumn couldn't suppress her laugh. 'What drop? You're talking as if you're in a Hollywood movie.'

'This isn't funny,' he said baldly. 'My life could depend on it. Yours too.'

That certainly stopped her laughter in its tracks. Autumn shook her head sadly. 'Is this legal?'

Richard's answering laugh was hollow and it sparked a coughing fit. She waited while it abated, pouring him a glass of water and matching her breathing to her brother's as if that would urge him along.

When he stopped coughing, she handed him the water and he took a welcome sip. His darkly shadowed eyes met Autumn's as he handed back the glass. 'When has anything I've ever done been on the right side of the law, darling sister?'

'Why involve me? Isn't there one of your drugged-up cronies who'll do it for you?'

He sighed and his body sounded as if it was filled with air. 'There's no honour among thieves, these days. You have to help me, Autumn. There's no one else I can trust.'

She thought of the times throughout their lives when she'd fought Richard's fights for him. Without fail, she'd been there watching his back. She didn't want to be involved in this, he must know that. But how could she let him down now, when he needed her most of all?

'I'll do it,' she said with a heavy heart.

Her brother smiled faintly. 'Good girl.'

'But this is it, Richard. I swear. After this, you're on your own.'

'You need to call this number.'

'They gave me a phone to pass on to you.'

'You keep it,' he instructed. 'Use it to call them. If we show willing then things might not turn out so bad.'

It was clear that her brother was still talking more from bravado than bare fact. She pulled a piece of paper from her tote bag and rummaged around until she found a pen. Richard reeled off the number which had clearly been committed to memory and she duly wrote it down.

'Ring them as soon as you get out of here and they'll tell you what to do.'

'Who are these people?' she asked.

'They're your worst nightmare. Don't mess this up, Autumn. Everything they tell you to do, do it right or we'll both suffer.'

'You're trying to tell me that I could end up in the bed next to you.'

'I hope it won't come to that.'

She wondered what the hell Addison would say when she told him exactly what her brother had cooked up this time. Or maybe, for the sake of harmonious relations, it would be better if she withheld this particular piece of information.

'There's a false bottom in the wardrobe in my room at home.'

'You haven't brought Mummy and Daddy into this too?'

Richard shook his head. 'They know nothing, Autumn.' He shot her a warning look. 'And they don't need to either.'

She said nothing.

Her brother continued, 'There's a holdall hidden there. Don't even look in it. Just take it as it is to *wherever* they tell you and *whenever* they tell you. Do all that. Walk away and everything will be just fine.'

Autumn held her head in her hands. 'I can't believe I'm agreeing to do this.'

'You're my sister,' Richard said. 'We're in this together. Don't forget that.'

How could she? Autumn suppressed the shiver of fear that she felt, despite the stifling heat. It was true, what they said about not being able to choose your own relatives.

Chapter Fifty-Two

Chantal stayed with Nadia for the rest of the day, but by early evening most of Toby's relatives had gone home and it was clear that her friend was exhausted. Like the church, the house also looked like a florist's shop, with floral tributes filling every possible receptacle they'd been able to find. Chantal wasn't sure why people would send them. Her friend needed money – didn't they realise that? There was enough about their dire financial situation in the newspapers. Cold hard cash would have been a lot more useful than a few chrysanthemums that would be dead by the end of the week. She didn't voice that opinion to her friend. Nadia, red-eyed and listless, was fussing with the tidying up and Chantal's heart went out to her.

Taking away the glasses that Nadia was clutching in her fingers, Chantal said, 'Leave this. I'll clear the worst of it away.' She steered her friend to the nearest comfy chair. 'You need to sit with your feet up and have some fine chocolate.' From her handbag, Chantal produced a bar of Clive's single Madagascar that she'd bought earlier in preparation for this moment.

Nadia gave an appreciative sigh. 'You're a lifesaver.' She snapped off a piece and then savoured it in her mouth. 'Fabulous,' was her assessment. Then she passed the bar back to Chantal, who did the same.

'Thank goodness that chocolate isn't on the list of banned foods during pregnancy,' Chantal observed. 'I'd never make it.'

Lewis was playing with his Thomas & Friends train set on the floor and Nadia opened her arms, beckoning him to her. 'Come and sit next to Mummy.'

The boy went over and squeezed onto the chair next to her.

His legs, permanently bruised from robust play, were soon slung across his mum's. Nadia stroked the blue-black marks and felt the tears that were never far away prickle behind her eyes. 'Who's going to rough and tumble with you now?'

'Aunty Chantal,' Lewis said innocently.

They both laughed at that.

Taking his chance, Lewis asked, 'Can I have some chocolate, please?'

'This is chocolate just for grown-ups,' Nadia said. 'You wouldn't like it.' She gave Chantal a wry glance that said, Surely as a mother I'm entitled to employ the age-old lie every now and then? Her friend smiled at her.

'You can have a chocolate biscuit and some milk before bed,' Nadia countered. 'But only if you promise to clean your teeth really, really properly.'

'I will,' Lewis vowed solemnly.

'I'll get it for him,' Chantal offered. 'Then I'll finish up in the kitchen.' She slipped out of the room.

The wreckage wasn't too bad, Chantal thought as she cleared away the last few glasses and plates. Nadia could keep herself busy in the morning tidying up the rest.

The funeral today had gone as well as could be expected in the circumstances, even though she had been sure that some of Nadia's relatives would have crawled out of the woodwork to be there to support her. But watching Nadia and Lewis coping stoically with their loss had left her feeling more alone than ever. Her own relationship was going far from smoothly. She and Ted were still on very shaky ground. They hadn't spoken to each other since he'd stood her up for their date at the theatre. Not that she hadn't tried to contact him, but all of her calls went unanswered. She stroked her growing bump. Life was what happened when you were busy making plans. What if anything happened to Ted? What if a drunk driver hit his car? What if one little artery decided to clog up? We all assume that we have our tomorrows to look forward to, but we never truly know what's waiting just around the corner. Seeing Nadia cope with the premature loss of her own husband had put all of this into perspective for her. What if she was never able to tell Ted that she might well be carrying his baby? She could hardly bear to think about it and Chantal knew that she had to put things right with him before it was too late.

Glancing at the clock, she noted that the night was pressing on and it was time that she made herself scarce. She collected a glass of milk and two chocolate digestives for Lewis and then went back into the living room. Both mother and son were dozing in the armchair, but Nadia roused as she went across to her. Speaking softly to her exhausted friend, Chantal said, 'As soon as you've put Lewis to bed, you need to take a long, hot bath and get an early night.'

'Don't you worry,' Nadia assured her with a yawn. 'That's *exactly* what I'm going to be doing.'

Kissing her friend warmly, Chantal said, 'I'll see you tomorrow.'

'Thanks for everything, Chantal.' Nadia squeezed her hands. 'I really appreciate it.'

'You stay where you are,' Chantal said. 'I'll see myself out.' Closing the door behind her, she stepped out into the street and took a deep breath. It was time to go and see Ted.

Chapter Fifty-Three

E ven though Chantal still had a key to the house, she somehow felt uncomfortable about letting herself into her own home. She'd been away from the place she'd formerly called home for quite some time now and she was starting to feel like a stranger here. Maybe even an unwelcome one.

Their house was darkened and there was no sign that Ted was home yet. As a result she'd decided to wait outside until he came back from the office. It might not get them off on the right footing, if Ted came home to find her installed in the lounge with her feet up, watching television with a glass of his mineral water in her hand. So, Chantal had parked at the end of the street so that she'd have a good view of her front door and could see when Ted arrived home. It was getting late and, hopefully, he shouldn't be long now. Rummaging through the glove box for her stash of chocolate, she settled down with a bar of Valrhona Grand Cru to pass the time. The rich milk chocolate with a hint of strawberries and cream melted on her tongue. Expensive chocolate was always helpful in difficult situations. A bit of Il Divo on the CD-player helped too. A slow and sultry Italian version of 'Unbreak My Heart' washed over her as she savoured each creamy square.

Half an hour later, when her back was just starting to go numb and all her chocolate had gone, a cab pulled up outside the house and Ted jumped out. Chantal watched his fluid movements as he let himself into the house and then waited for a few minutes before she got out of her own car. Her stomach was churning as she stood at the front door. Junior was doing backflips too. Smoothing her hands over her small, tight bump, she wondered if her husband would notice instantly that she was pregnant –

which would mean that they could avoid the speech that she'd so carefully rehearsed. Taking a deep breath, she rang the bell.

Before she could dwell on it further, Ted flung open the door. He was clearly surprised to see her.

'Hey,' she said softly. 'Got time for a visitor?'

Ted glanced quickly at his watch, which made her hackles rise. 'I'm going out,' he told her. 'This is a quick turnaround for me.'

She hadn't come all this way to see him only to be fobbed off now. 'It won't take a minute.'

Her husband held the door open, while she squeezed past him. Then they went through into the kitchen and stood regarding each other awkwardly. The house looked exactly the same as when she'd last been here. But then, why shouldn't it? There were no bachelor-esque piles of dishes to be seen. No heaps of crumpled clothes in need of an iron. Nothing in the domestic arena was Ted's responsibility. They had a very reliable cleaner, Maya, who came in every day to see to that side of things. Her husband was perfectly capable of knocking together a quick and nutritious meal for himself – his pasta and pancetta was legendary. And, as she wasn't required to perform any wifely duties in the bedroom, Chantal wondered whether he had actually missed her at all.

'You haven't returned any of my calls,' she said, trying not to sound too accusatory.

'I know.' Ted spread his hands in a what-can-I-do? gesture. 'Work has been manic.' He frowned. 'Was that what you wanted to talk about?'

'No. No.' She shook her head and then leaned heavily against their oak dresser.

'Then shoot.'

'Er . . . I, er . . .' Suddenly, her nerve deserted her. Her mouth went dry. Her heart pounded unevenly. The carefully rehearsed announcement of her 'condition' went straight out of her head. 'Lucy's getting married.'

Ted looked puzzled. 'Lucy?'

'Ted,' she chided. 'You know who I mean. My friend from The Chocolate Lovers' Club.'

'Oh,' he said. '*That* Lucy. I hope she'll be very happy.'

Ignoring his lack of interest, she ploughed on. 'I know that we've never really spent time with the other members of The Chocolate Lovers' Club,' she babbled. 'But I thought this could be a great opportunity for you to meet them all. I hoped that you might like to come to the wedding with me.'

'I hate weddings,' Ted said.

She swallowed the needle of irritation that pricked at her. 'This one will be nice.'

Her husband shrugged. 'Okay. Let me know when and where, and I'll see if I'm free.'

So that was how it was going to be. This was going to be harder work than she'd imagined. 'I should leave.'

As she went towards the door, Ted said, 'You just got here.'

'And you said you had other arrangements,' she reminded him.

'I have a few minutes.' Ted capitulated with a sheepish glance. 'Want a quick glass of wine?'

Chantal took another deep breath. 'I'm not drinking at the moment.'

'Dieting?' Ted helped himself to a bottle of white that was chilling in the fridge. Chantal felt as if she could commit murder for a single sip. 'I could get you a soft drink.'

'No.' She shook her head. 'Nothing. Thanks.'

'You look like you've put a little weight on.' Her husband smiled. 'I know that's not a great thing to say to a woman, but you look good. Curvy. It kinda suits you.'

'Ted . . .' Chantal cleared her throat. 'There's something I need to tell you.'

Ted chewed his lip nervously. 'There's something I need to tell you too.' He took a hearty swig of his wine, then blurted out, 'I'm seeing someone else.'

That wasn't quite what she'd expected.

'Sit down. Sit down,' Ted instructed.

Chantal sank into the nearest chair, steadying her hands on the table.

Her husband paced the kitchen floor, avoiding her eyes. 'I could come to this wedding with you, if you need company. But I want you to know that there's someone else on the scene.' He glanced back at her for a reaction.

Chantal sat there calmly while she absorbed this news. She'd lost her husband to someone else. Ted was clearly hoping that she'd ask him more about it, but she couldn't. Her brain simply couldn't take in any more. 'I see,' she said finally.

Ted laughed uncomfortably. 'I'm glad that's out in the open,' he said. 'We are separated, but, well . . . I didn't like to feel that I was sneaking around.'

She wondered if it was a barbed comment aimed at her, but decided to let it go. 'I can understand that.'

'I'm sorry,' Ted said. He busied himself looking at his watch again and draining his glass. 'But now I really do have to be going. I have a reservation at Hakkasan.'

It was the ultra-smart Chinese restaurant across town that had been their favourite hang-out for Oriental food.

'Nice,' she said. It was a table for two, no doubt.

'What was it that you wanted to tell me?'

Her brain froze over. She couldn't even find the words to begin to tell Ted about the baby. Not now. Not at this moment. Ted stood waiting while the cogs inside her head slowly tried to work together. Eventually something clicked.

'The wedding,' she said. 'Lucy's wedding. You'll probably need to wear your morning suit.'

Chapter Fifty-Four

M y desk is covered in cards bearing cheery wedding greet-
ings and there's a beautiful bouquet of white lilies perched
on the corner. Even the harridans from Human Resources have
signed a card for me. I leaf through them again. Crush hasn't. My
lips purse together sadly.

Still, no use crying over spilt milk, as they say. It's nearly seven
o'clock and everyone else has left the office for the night, so I
take my holdall that normally holds my gym gear and head into
the ladies' loos to make my preparations for the evening's entertainment ahead.

It's my hen night and the members of The Chocolate Lovers'
Club are going out on the town. Clive and Tristan are coming
with us too as, basically, they're honorary girls. I'm not sure if
this form of ritual humiliation is supposed to be fun, but I'm
going along with it because my friends insist that they've organised a great night out. They're all meeting me outside, at the
front of Targa's office in about ten minutes, so I'd better get a
move on.

As part of the 'fun', I've been given a joke wedding dress to
wear. I think my friends must have bought it from a sex shop.
It's minuscule and extraordinarily tarty. If you wore this sort of
thing as a real bride, then the vicar would pass out. I so don't
have the legs for this – or the heart. Nevertheless, I elbow my
way into a cubicle clutching my compulsory outfit and, with a
complaining sigh, peel off my work suit and wriggle into this
ridiculous confection.

There's a corset that laces tightly up the front, forcing my bust
to spill out over the top, making me look vaguely reminiscent of

Nell Gwynn. The excuse of a skirt froths out from my cinched-in waist and stops rather abruptly below my bottom, about twelve inches short of decent. There's a red 'L' plate stitched to the back. I've got white stockings to wear and matching white Essex girl shoes. A cheap net train about ten feet long comes from a sparkly tiara that I jam onto my head.

Out by the sinks again, I check myself in the mirror. It's worse than I imagined. I look like some sort of *Playboy* wedding fetish model. There's no way I can go out in public looking like the slut bride from hell. My phone rings.

'Get a move on,' Chantal says. 'We're all waiting downstairs. The festivities are soon to begin.'

'And you've got costumes on too?'

'Oh yes,' Chantal says. 'We're all suitably attired. Come on, we're wasting valuable drinking time.'

'You don't drink any more.'

'I'm sure there's a mineral water somewhere with my name on it,' she counters.

Right. Vodka, I think, will be my tipple of choice. I have no intention of being sober in this outfit for very long.

'Shake a leg,' Chantal says, showing that she can remember appropriately stupid English phrases.

'If I shake anything else, it will all fall out.'

'That's the spirit,' she says with a laugh, and hangs up.

Scanning the mirror again, I realise that I have no option but to go out looking like this. I resign myself to the fact that, at least, no one I know will see me.

I tiptoe out into the office and, rather furtively, head for the door. Just then, it opens and Aiden Bloody Holby swings in.

'Whoaw!' he says when he sees me, and pulls up sharply. His eyes pop out on stalks.

'What are you doing here?' I have a bouquet of loud fake flowers in clashing colours which I hold against my hip in an aggressive pose.

'I forgot my laptop,' he explains, still wide-eyed. Then, in a rather leisurely manner, he takes in my skimpy outfit. A smirk settles on his lips. 'I'm glad that I did.'

'Don't you dare tell anyone else in the office about this,' I threaten him. I even wag my finger in his face. 'Or you'll never get your hands on any of my chocolate ever again.'

Crush starts to laugh. His eyes are travelling between my boobs which are spilling out of my dress and my stocking-tops – which probably have my thighs spilling out of them. As always in the presence of Aiden Holby, I turn beetroot-coloured. He tries to organise his face into some semblance of seriousness when he says, 'I take it that's not your real wedding dress.'

'Don't be ridiculous.'

'*I'm* the one who's being ridiculous?' He smiles at me. 'Actually, you look kind of sexy, Gorgeous.'

'It's my hen night,' I tell him. Which, as we know, is an excuse for all kinds of appalling behaviour.

'Funny, but I'd sort of gathered that.' We stand and look at each other uncomfortably. 'Where are you going?'

'Mistress Jay's.'

'The drag club?'

I nod in confirmation. Clive and Tristan have set this up – even though Clive insists that female impersonators are now considered a hideously outmoded and politically incorrect form of entertainment. Maybe it's Tristan who goes for men in sling-backs and thigh-slit gowns. I have no idea. Frankly, I have enough trouble sorting out my own *raison d'être* without worrying about theirs.

For some stupid reason, I'd like to ask Crush to come along with us, but my mouth won't form the words.

'You'll have a blast,' Aiden says.

'I intend to be very drunk, very soon,' I tell him.

Then his eyes lock onto mine and they look so terribly sad. His voice softens. 'So you're really going through with this wedding lark?'

I nod. A lump comes to my throat. 'Yes.'

'Do you love Marcus?'

I make myself nod again.

'Then I wish you all the luck in the world,' Crush says.

'I'd really like you to be at the wedding,' I blurt out.

'So would I,' he says. 'But only if I can be the groom.' Then he turns and leaves.

And, as I look after him, utterly speechless with shock, I notice that he's forgotten his laptop once again. He's going to be really annoyed when he realises what he's done.

Chapter Fifty-Five

Nadia and Autumn are also both dressed as slut bridesmaids, which makes me feel much better. They're wearing stockings too, ankle-turning high-heels and dresses that leave little to the imagination. How Chantal has managed to persuade Nadia out of her widow's weeds and into this outrageous outfit, I've no idea. But I'm very glad that she has. Actually, Autumn looks fantastic too. She should think of becoming a shameless tart rather than an eco-warrior as the look really suits her.

Chantal is dressed as a three-tiered wedding cake after arguing that a woman in a pregnant condition shouldn't be required to bare her body in an unseemly way, though it doesn't stop most of the celebs these days. The guys are also in fancy-dress costume. Tristan is a rather red-faced priest complete with that frilly white garment they all wear, and Clive is clearly supposed to be my betrothed, but he's wearing an oversized, joke morning suit. His usual immaculate spiky hair has been given a centre parting and is greased down.

My heart lightens as we totter down the street, giggling like a bunch of schoolkids, and the horribly sad look on Aiden Holby's face starts to fade away. Or, at least, I pretend it does.

I look over at Nadia and take in her appearance properly. She's lost weight – the pounds are literally dropping off her, but other than that she's bearing up remarkably well and I hope that a night on the town will help to keep her that way. Autumn's boyfriend Addison is babysitting Lewis. I can tell that she's anxious about leaving him so soon after Toby's death, but she has agreed to do it for my sake and I love her for it. So much so, that I don't hold it against her that she was the one who helped Chantal choose my slut bride look.

'You look great,' I tell her as I slip my arm round her and give her a squeeze.

'I look terrible,' she says, 'and we both know it.'

'I don't even know how you're managing to be upright,' I tell her, 'let alone go through this.'

'I'm existing on a divine blend of denial and prescription drugs.' She gives me a tired smile. 'I'm hoping that adding strong drink to the equation will make oblivion come more quickly. I've spent every night since Toby died just staring at his empty armchair willing him to reappear. Going out dressed like a hooker is welcome relief. Your getting married is very timely; if I hadn't come out tonight I think I would have gone quietly mad.'

'Oh Nadia,' I say, feeling my friend's pain. 'You'll be fine. Just fine. We'll all make sure that you are.'

'Well,' she sighs, 'I know for certain that I couldn't do it without you.'

'No more sitting alone at nights, for one thing,' I tell her. 'I'll be round just as often as you like with a box of chocs and a crappy film.'

She kisses me on the cheek and I put my arm round her and we huddle together.

'Come on.' I force a spring into my step. 'Let's go celebrate my last night of freedom.'

At Mistress Jay's club, we're escorted to our table in a crescent-shaped booth by a beefy guy who's over six foot five dressed in a hot pink basque, a thong and vertiginous black patent leather heels. For a moment, I feel slightly overdressed. His blonde wig tumbles to his waist and, as he seats us, he pouts his collagen-enhanced lips at Tristan.

The theme here is very burlesque – all red velvet and gold embellishments. Even this early in the evening, the place is crowded, mainly by hen parties, and mainly inebriated ones. Our overpriced champagne, too, is quick to arrive and we make a brave stab at catching up with our rivals – except for Chantal who, much to her disgust, is drinking nothing stronger than Perrier water.

215

'I hope this young lady realises all the sacrifices that I'm making for her,' she complains, patting her stomach fondly.

I raise my champagne glass, feeling ridiculously emotional. 'To us,' I say. 'To The Chocolate Lovers' Club.'

'To us,' my friends echo, and we clink glasses together.

'And to your forthcoming wedding.' Chantal hoists her glass of water again.

The others join in. 'To Lucy's wedding.'

'To my wedding!' I say, but my voice sounds over-bright and forced. I slug back my champagne, feeling ridiculous and wanting to cry.

The cabaret begins. High-kicking male showgirls – who were probably builders and computer programmers in a former life – strut their stuff across the stage. All the favourite hen-party standards are reeled out: 'It's Raining Men', Aretha's 'Respect' and 'Sisters Are Doin' It For Themselves', 'One Night in Heaven', 'I'm Every Woman' – the oldie but goldie hits keep on coming. And the audience go wild.

Between acts, the compère called Raunchy Roberta takes the floor. He or she is another six-footer but this time sporting a red curly wig and a sparkly white dress slit to the thigh. Roberta tours the audience and insults everyone in close proximity. Our food comes and so does more champagne. Lots and lots of it. The main star of the cabaret takes the stage. He's dressed as Marilyn Monroe in full-length gold lamé and matching gloves. Marilyn machine-guns out round after round of blue jokes that, if I hadn't had so much to drink, would make my ears want to curl up.

We drink more and then we all lurch onto the dance floor and sing loudly to more songs that are mainly about what bastards men are – Clive and Tristan, for some reason, singing the loudest. Why are gay men always good dancers? Does the gay gene and the good-dancing gene go hand-in-hand? Is this why all straight men *can't* dance? The boys put us to shame, strutting their stuff, while we girlies try to do coordinated dance steps, but are generally thwarted. After a few songs, it proves too much for us so, giggling, we all head back to our table.

I flop gratefully into my seat just as our dessert arrives. 'Ohmigod!'

'Just for you, Lucy,' Clive and Tristan say proudly.

They've made a special chocolate mini-wedding cake which they must have had delivered to the club for me. A bouquet of sparklers is fizzing at the top and the chocolate fudge icing looks an inch thick. It's utterly fabulous. I get envious glances from the other hen parties. Ha. Hands off!

'You guys!' I say, all teary, and I do a mock cutting of the cake. Everyone cheers and then we tuck in. I give myself a megaslice – yum. Just to be polite, you understand. Mind you, if I eat too much of this, I'm never going to be able to get into my wedding dress. I'll have to live on fresh air for the next few days to make up for it. I feel drunk, light-headed and very slightly disorientated. Can this really be happening to me?

Then, as I look up, I see Crush standing in front of me and I know that I have entered a more hallucinatory realm. My fork stalls on its way to my lips.

'Don't do this,' he says bleakly.

I can't think of anything to say. My mouth opens but nothing comes out.

'Don't get married.'

When I look round, I see that the forks of all of my friends have also stalled.

Then, with impeccable timing, Raunchy Roberta, the red-wigged compère, breezes up to our table.

'Oh – hello, love.' His immaculately manicured fingers latch onto Aiden's arm and he pulls him into a robust cuddle, theatrically squeezing his biceps. The spotlight swings onto our table. The rest of the drunken hen-party audience 'ooo' their appreciation. I want to die. Crush blinks against the harsh light and I want to stand up and stop this, but I can't. My brain can't make my legs work, or my mouth, or anything vaguely useful. 'You're a handsome young thing.'

Crush looks perplexed and desperately uncomfortable with the glare of attention.

217

'Are you the lucky groom?'

'No,' he says flatly.

'You look like you wish that you were.' The audience cheer. Crush says nothing.

Chantal whispers in my ear, 'For an old drag queen, this guy is remarkably perceptive.'

'Take her home and give her a good shagging,' the compère advises. 'It might be your last chance!' And then he moves on to the next table which is hosted by a bride who looks at least six months' pregnant as her bump's twice as big as Chantal's. Still he hasn't finished with Aiden, as he shouts over his shoulder, 'If she won't have you, then maybe you can give me a go!'

Chantal takes my fork from me and returns it to my plate. 'You should both get out of here,' she says to me and to Crush. 'It seems as if you've got a lot to talk about.'

My friend somehow pushes me to my feet and my legs remember how to do the walking thing. Crush takes my hand and leads me out of the club. And it just goes to show what a state I'm in, since not only have I abandoned my friends at my own hen night, but I have left chocolate cake unfinished and I don't even think about it until much, much later.

Chapter Fifty-Six

Crush and I find a 'late-nite' coffee shop somewhere in the depths of Soho. It's possibly the scruffiest place on earth. The flooring is all cracked and dirty. The windows look like they haven't seen soapy water in many a year. Spent coffee cups and the remnants of muffins and biscuits litter the tops of the tables. We find one by the window that's relatively clean and I slide into my seat.

There are a few dossers in here and a couple of lads in hoodies. They all take in my outfit. The hoodies don't try to disguise their smirks. If I had the strength I'd tell them all to fuck off, but I don't.

'Do you want coffee?'

I nod. It's the first thing that Aiden has said to me since we left the club. He slips off his jacket and puts it round my shoulders. I hug it to me. It smells of his aftershave. Then he goes to the counter and waits while the order is prepared by a surly Polish girl who clearly would rather be anywhere else than here. Part of me knows how she feels.

My heart is racing with adrenaline and there's a warm buzz inside me. My head is spinning, but it's nothing to do with the amount of champagne that I've sunk. Aiden came after me. He came and found me at my hen night and plighted his troth – possibly. But part of me doesn't want to be having this conversation at all. I'm marrying Marcus the day after tomorrow and I want to be deliriously happy about that. Part of me is. But part of me is filled with sheer terror. Is that the right thing for a soon-to-be-bride to feel?

Crush brings our coffee back. Two lattes. Most of it is slopped into the saucers, but it's not Aiden's fault. 'I brought us a couple of chocolate muffins too,' he says.

Despite the scabby appearance of the café, the muffins look great. Homemade. Chocolate chip. And I can't eat a bite. This is a dire situation. Crush makes a half-hearted attempt to pick at his.

The coffee's passable too. Although I did tip three packets of sugar into it. I need the energy lift is my excuse. It's hot and I like the burning feeling in my hands as I nurse my cup. Pulling off my headdress and veil, without thinking, I set them down on the table next to me in a puddle of coffee.

'So what are we going to do?' I ask.

'I don't want you to make a mistake, Gorgeous,' Crush says eventually.

'And you think that's what I'm doing?'

'Don't you?'

'Until a few minutes ago, I would probably have said you were wrong.'

'And now?'

I shake my head. 'And now I don't know.'

'Marcus isn't right for you,' Crush tells me.

I hazard a smile. 'And you are?'

'I think so.'

'We tried it, Aiden, but it didn't work out.'

'I think we were too hasty,' he says. '*I* was too hasty.' He reaches across the grubby table and finds my hand. 'What we had was very special.'

'And I blew it.'

'We shouldn't have split up. I was too hurt, too hasty.'

'That was exactly my excuse.'

He shakes his head. 'I know.' He tries a smile. 'It was an excellent excuse.'

'So?' I realise that I'm fiddling with my engagement ring and stop. 'Are you asking me to marry you?'

'No,' Crush says. 'I just think we should give our relationship another go.'

'You want me to call off my wedding with two days to go on the strength of the fact that we might have a hope of being able to forge a decent relationship?'

'It's more than that,' he says. 'You know it is.' He rubs over the back of my hand with his thumb. 'I know that I'm asking a lot, Lucy.'

'Too right you are.' I aim for flippant and miss.

Distractedly, I mop up the coffee with my veil as I think of the chic, sophisticated number that's hanging on the back of my bedroom door. Should I cancel the wedding on the off-chance that I can make a go of a relationship with Aiden 'Crush' Holby, who I seem to be unable to get out of my system? Or shall I stay with Marcus, who is a long way from perfect, but who wants me as his wife?

Chapter Fifty-Seven

As is the tradition of all good hen nights, I have a stupendous hangover. I'm slumped on a sofa in the corner of Chocolate Heaven surrounded by my best girls. They have hangovers too. Except Chantal – who looks so awful that she should have a hangover.

I'm clutching my head and my stomach. I don't know which is hurting most. I am bravely eating my way though a slice of chocolate banoffee cheesecake with the aim of restoring my equilibrium. Chocolate is a well-known cure for a hangover – as well as the common cold, PMT, nosebleeds and possibly verrucas. In fact, the only afflictions it doesn't cure are, unfortunately, acne and obesity. Bananas are loaded with protein too, which is good for you – so this, effectively, is medicine.

'What are you going to do?' Nadia asks. She is prostrate on the sofa next to me. Her voice replicates the gravel-soaked tones of Bonnie Tyler.

'It's good to see that, even though I abandoned you, my dear friends, during the prime of my hen night, you were able to continue the party quite successfully without me.'

'We thought you might come back,' Autumn says.

'We didn't know if we were celebrating for you or drowning our sorrows,' Nadia chips in. 'So we did both.'

I hang my head. 'What am I going to do?'

The girls glance at me nervously and Chantal acts as spokesperson. 'That's what we want to know, honey.'

'Crush has asked me to cancel the wedding.'

Nadia puts her hand on my arm. 'And is that what you want?'

'I don't know.'

'You have one day to make up your mind,' she points out.

Don't I know it. Right after our hastily convened meeting here, I'm setting off to Trington Manor. Marcus has organised a car to pick me up and transport all my stuff there. He's joining me later as are my parents – my dad and his bimbo hairdresser; my mum and her balding millionaire. Already, I feel faint at the thought of it.

'You can't cancel a wedding with one day to go before it,' I say wearily. 'Just think of the expense. This has cost Marcus thousands. Thousands and thousands.'

'You can't get married when you've got so many doubts, Lucy.' Trust Autumn to spot that one.

'I do love Marcus,' I insist. 'It's just that . . .'

'You love Crush more.'

'I don't,' I say. 'It was simply an infatuation. It's just that he's so very persuasive.' I think of him sitting in the café last night with his big brown puppy-dog eyes and I could quite easily believe that anything was possible. I could cancel the wedding, let Marcus down lightly with no hard feelings and sail off into the sunset with Crush, knowing that despite our shaky start, we'd be deliriously happy in the end. Then I realise that I've been watching far too many romantic films. Richard Gere and Debra Winger have a lot to answer for. This sort of thing only happens in Hollywood. I have to remember that. In real life, everyone will be really upset and no one will ever speak to me again. I'll lose Marcus and then Crush and I will break up and I'll be left alone with no one to love me. People don't cancel weddings at the eleventh hour. It isn't the done thing. How could I cause so much pain? I shake my head sadly. 'I'll phone Crush and tell him that I got carried away with the moment, but that it would be a big mistake for me to cancel my wedding.'

My friends nod at me – Nadia and Autumn trying not to move their heads too much – but they don't look convinced.

'I want you all at the hotel bright and early,' I say, trying to sound upbeat. 'Darren is coming out to do our hair first thing and he's bringing an assistant to do the make-up.'

Marcus has booked us separate rooms for tonight – call us superstitious, but he didn't want to risk any bad luck. Which means a bit of a lie-in and a cooked breakfast for me. Yay!

Clive comes over. 'How are my best customers today?'

'Sssh,' I say. 'Don't shout.'

He lowers his voice. 'Hangovers?'

We all risk a nod again. Clive throws a business card on the coffee-table in front of us. It says: *Raunchy Roberta – Female Impersonator.*

'One of the drag queens?' I want to know.

'Yes,' he confirms. Then he sighs unhappily. 'I found this in Tristan's pocket. Why would he have it there? He's seeing other men, I'm sure of it.'

Does he mean men or women? I don't like to ask.

'I think the writing is on the wall for our relationship,' he continues. 'He's been making secretive phone calls all morning and now he's disappeared out to who knows where.'

'There may be a perfectly plausible explanation,' Autumn suggests.

'Maybe Tris is making a booking with Raunchy Roberta to jump out of my wedding cake,' I put in.

'That would have to be one *fucking* big cake,' Clive says and, despite his misery, we all burst out laughing together.

'I'm going to have to get myself a reliable assistant,' he continues when the giggles have subsided. 'I don't know how long I can depend on Tristan being around. Let me know if there are any of your friends who'd be interested.'

'I wouldn't mind doing some shifts,' I say. What I think is that I'm never ever going to be able to go back to Targa and face Crush as Mrs Marcus Canning. That chapter of my life has to remain resolutely closed. Aiden Holby has to be firmly beyond the reach of temptation. 'When all the fuss from the wedding has calmed down, of course.'

'No way. You'd eat all my profits,' Clive quips.

I fold my arms huffily. 'That's gratitude for you.'

We all laugh again. Clive moves away. 'Let me know if you need anything else,' he says over his shoulder.

'I need to be making tracks.' I squeeze in the last mouthful of my chocolate banoffee cheesecake. This could be my last chocolate fix as a single woman. The thought makes me shiver. 'I can't eat another thing,' I say, feeling thoroughly podged. I smooth my hands over my stomach. It's currently rounder than Chantal's and she's pregnant! 'You're all going to have to shoehorn me into that damn dress. How can I lose two stone by tomorrow?'

'Have both of your legs amputated,' is Nadia's helpful suggestion.

'That would make walking down the aisle interesting.'

'I didn't say it was the perfect solution,' my friend tells me. Then she glances round the group, seeking approval. 'I'll ask one last time, Lucy,' Nadia says. 'Are you sure that you're doing the right thing?'

'Yes.' I stand up and tug my handbag over my shoulder. 'The wedding will go ahead tomorrow.' I sound extraordinarily decisive, even though my stomach lurches in terror. 'Marcus and I will be married and we'll be very happy together.'

Chapter Fifty-Eight

Autumn and Richard's respective bedrooms at their parents' house had barely changed since they were teenagers. In Autumn's case, there were no pop posters on her wall, since she'd been listening to folk music when everyone else was into Madonna or Queen or whoever. Her rosettes from her Pony Club prizes, still plastered around the dressing-table mirror, held a fine layer of dust. Downstairs, the house had been revamped and redecorated a dozen times, but going up three flights of stairs to the top floor took you into a time-warp.

Opening Richard's door, the familiar smell of old wood and boys' shoes hit her. Apart from a brief visit on their disastrous Christmas Day, it was years since she'd spent any time up here. Years since she'd needed to. Autumn remembered barefoot pillow fights, bouncing on her brother's creaking bed, too far up in the house to be heard by their parents – if they were even there. Work had always been their first priority and, thankfully, they were both still out of the country until the end of the week, so no need to explain away her impromptu visit. She didn't want to start lying to them about what she was doing in Richard's bedroom. Although she still did have a door key for emergencies, Jenkinson had let her in, but she knew that she could trust him not to mention her visit to her mother and father. Their old butler had often been more of a father figure to her than her own parent.

Autumn whisked the curtains open. This was definitely a boys' room. It was tidier now, but the bookcase still held Richard's copies of *The Outsiders*, *Lord of the Flies*, *Catcher in the Rye* and a copy of *The Complete Works of Shakespeare* stolen from the school library. A row of shakily constructed Airfix models graced the top, including a Harrier jump jet which her brother had spent hours making at the time when he had longed to become an RAF fighter pilot. She ran her hand over the model and wondered what had happened to his dreams. How could someone who had so much potential have messed up so spectacularly?

Alongside was his battered collection of *Star Wars* figures – toys that he'd had as little more than a toddler. Autumn examined them, picking up Han Solo, R2-D2 and Chewbacca in turn, handling them as you would fine porcelain. She was amazed that they'd survived the ritual indignities that Richard had put them through, including regularly blasting them into space tied to the back of a firework. Godness knows why their parents kept all of this stuff. It wasn't as if they were ever sentimental about anything that their offspring did. More than likely, it was a lack of interest and never having a need to use the rooms for anything else. Even though Richard's collection was hideously dated, there must be disadvantaged kids out there who would appreciate these toys.

Autumn lay down on the bed and stared up at the ceiling, somehow hoping to connect to the boy that her brother had once been. But try as she might, it was hard to reconcile the man Rich had become with the boy who had spent so many years being formed in this room. That boy, with his passion for *Star Wars*, good books and a yearning to fly for his Queen and country, was long gone.

In the corner of the room stood Richard's heavy mahogany wardrobe. How different from today's teenagers' rooms – there was no flat-screen television, no PlayStation, iPod or computer. She hauled herself from the bed and went over to the wardrobe, prising open the doors. His old school blazer still hung inside with a few other bits and pieces of clothing, but there was precious little else in the wardrobe. Autumn had brought a screwdriver and a hammer with her in her handbag in case she needed some brute force to complete the task in hand, but she needn't have worried. There was a digit-sized hole in the wood at the bottom of the wardrobe and she slotted her index finger inside. The false bottom lifted easily away. Squashed inside was a soft black Puma holdall and Autumn lifted it out. Richard had specifically told her not to look inside the bag and she'd promised not to. Frankly, the less she knew, the better. She'd phoned the number that Richard had given her, but the person who answered simply told her to wait until they got in touch with her. Now all she could do was sit tight with her illicit stash of whatever it was. Hoisting the bag onto her shoulder, she took one last look at the room and closed the door behind her.

'What have you got there?' Autumn was taken aback. Addison was already waiting for her in the workshop when she arrived at the Centre. He nodded at the holdall in her hand. 'Are you doing a runner?'

Autumn felt her face fire up. 'This is just some stuff that Richard asked me to collect from our parents' house.' She hadn't wanted to risk leaving the holdall – or, more importantly, its contents – at her apartment. For some reason, she thought it might be safer if she hid it somewhere at the Centre until she had the call to say where the drop would be. Autumn was beginning to think now that it was a rather stupid idea.

'Why didn't you tell me this morning? I could have come with you.' He kissed her cheek and laughed. 'I came to tell you that I've got some great news.'

She couldn't find her voice.

'Looks like I might have some funding in place, so Tasmin could well have her stall on Camden Market. I can get her a grant, so she'll have enough materials to make her stock, and there are several spaces available so she should be able to get a regular pitch.'

'Wow,' Autumn managed, but she knew that it didn't convey the degree of enthusiasm she actually felt.

'I thought you'd be dancing round the room with joy.' Addison cocked his head on one side, puzzled. 'What's wrong? You're looking very guilty.'

'No, no,' she said.

His eyes travelled to the holdall again. 'Anything to do with this?'

'This?'

Her boyfriend nodded.

'It's just some clothes and bits, I think . . . I'm not sure.'

Addison's brow creased in a frown. 'I've been working for too long with clients who don't necessarily stay on the straight and narrow, Autumn,' he said. 'I can tell someone who's being shifty from a mile away.'

'It's nothing. Really.'

'Let me look at what's in the bag,' he said steadily. And she didn't resist when Addison reached for the zip.

Her boyfriend held up a teddy bear. It was cute, honey-coloured and wore a bow tie and a very stupid grin. There were dozens of identical ones packed in side by side. 'Soft toys?'

Autumn shrugged and tried a careless laugh. It came out miserably. 'You know Rich!'

'Too well,' Addison said, and taking a craft-knife from the workbench next to him, he slit the teddy bear's stomach.

Autumn gasped. Little packets of white power were pushed inside the bear.

Addison lifted one out and rolled it between his fingers. 'You know what this is?'

'No,' she said, 'not exactly. But I know that it's not good.' She'd always been a useless liar. Her shoulders sagged and she dropped heavily to sit on the nearest stool. 'I've agreed to deliver this holdall for Richard,' she confessed.

Addison looked even less happy. 'To who?'

She took a deep breath. It was time to be straight with him. 'To some very dodgy blokes.'

'You have to go to the police with it.'

'I can't. Richard could be in big trouble.'

'He's in big trouble anyway, Autumn.'

'Me shopping him is hardly going to help,' she pleaded. 'I've always been the one to get Richard out of the shit. But no more, I promise. I have to do this one last thing for him and then that's it. He's on his own.'

'You've brought this into a drug rehab centre,' he said tightly.

'Risking your job and our reputation just to save your brother's skin?'

'Yes,' she said quietly. It was the first time she'd seen it in quite that light.

Addison handed her the teddy bear. From deep inside it came a fearsome growl. 'I can't deal with you any more, Autumn. I'm sorry. Your brother's completely fucked up and he's dragging you down to his level. Don't mess up your own life by getting involved in this.'

'What else can I do?' she cried. But by then, Addison was already slamming the door behind him.

Chapter Fifty-Nine

M arcus takes me in his arms and holds me tightly. 'This is it, babe,' he says. He never calls me babe.

We're at Trington Manor. I've been ensconced here for a couple of hours already. Doing nothing much more than panicking, really. I'm glad that Marcus has finally bowled up as I'm sure that will make me relax more.

It seems as if I've hardly seen my fiancé for weeks. There's been so much to do, so much to organise, despite Jacob's wonderful input. It's been so frantic that I haven't even had the chance to move out of my flat and into his apartment. Yet, already, the wedding is upon us. 'Feeling nervous?' I ask.

Marcus shakes his head. 'Not a bit. I'm really looking forward to this,' he tells me softly. 'Lucy Lombard's going to be my lawfully wedded wife. That makes me the luckiest man alive. Why should I be nervous about that?' He tightens his arms around me and gazes lovingly into my eyes. 'Are you nervous?'

'No. No,' I say. Not nervous. Shit scared would sum it up better.

As well as living separately, we've also booked separate bedrooms for tonight. Marcus is hideously superstitious and doesn't want to see me before I get to the church. I agree. It doesn't take much for bad luck to rain down on my head, and I'm not keen to tempt fate.

'My parents have arrived,' I tell him as I wrinkle my nose.

'That will make you feel better,' he says. Actually, that will make me feel like picking up a pump-action shotgun and killing people indiscriminately.

'I've booked a table for dinner at seven o'clock.' This will be fun as it's the first time my parents will have been in a room

231

together since their rather acrimonious divorce. Perhaps time will
have mellowed them all, water under the bridge, etc., and my
mum won't feel like clawing out The Hairdresser's eyes and my
dad won't be tempted to deck The Millionaire. Perhaps, also,
Victoria Beckham will cut back on her spending and the polar
ice caps will stop melting.

Marcus rubs his chin thoughtfully. 'I haven't seen your parents
since . . .'

'Since they were married to each other,' I remind him. 'I've
barely seen them myself since then either.' My father now resides
in connubial bliss on the South Coast of England with a woman
half his age, while my mother has opted for sex-filled siestas in
Spain with a man who looks twice hers.

'Sneaking away to a Bahamian beach by ourselves is suddenly
very appealing,' I say.

'The wedding will be fabulous,' Marcus promises me as he
kisses my lips tenderly. 'Everyone will remember it for years.'

First we have to get through dinner. Marcus is at the head of the
table. I'm at the foot. My warring parents are facing each other.
You try doing a table-plan for people who you know will all
detest each other. Three biros ran dry in the process. This could
well be the longest evening of my life and I suddenly wish that
Crush and I could be hiding out in the ladies' loo together again
to liven it all up. Then, summoning all my strength, I push any
images of Aiden Holby to the back of my mind and smile widely
at my assembled guests.

Despite my mother's mahogany tan, I know that her face is
white and tight beneath it. My dad is looking exhausted and I
don't think it's because he plays too many rounds of golf. The
Hairdresser – Myleen – has come dressed as a hooker. She has
on a white plunge-neck top that is barely skimming her nipples.
Those things *cannot* be her real tits, surely? She'd be impossible
to drown, that's for certain. The Millionaire is transfixed by her.
He's laughing very loudly at every single thing that she says –
which isn't much. Every now and again The Millionaire winces,

which must be when my mum's foot connects with his shin. My dad is glowering darkly at my mum across the perfect arrangement of white roses.

This is fabulous, I sigh to myself. And we're only on the starters. How in hell's name are we going to get as far as the dessert? Believe me, we are sticking it out that long. I'm not going to go through all this angst without the lure of chocolate at the end. This could well be my *very* last chance to eat chocolate as a single woman and I have to seize it.

Marcus is doing his best to be the congenial host. 'Did you both have good journeys?'

'Wonderful,' my dad says. 'Always get a good ride in a top-of-the-range Bentley.'

I assume he's talking about the roads, but I can't be sure these days.

My mum toys with her champagne glass. 'Howard chartered a private jet,' she says coolly.

My dad splutters into his fizz. I'd say that a private jet trumps a top-of-the-range car – even a Bentley. One nil to Mum.

Marcus tries harder. 'This is a great hotel, isn't it? Are your rooms nice?'

'We're in the Honeymoon Suite,' my dad tells us without taking his eyes off my mother.

'Presidential Suite,' my mother slaps down. 'Enormous.'

Hmm. Not sure about that one. The Honeymoon Suite implies that you're still having loads of sex, but the Presidential Suite smacks of having loads of money, but possibly needing Viagra. Think that one might go to Dad. My mum must think so too as she necks her champagne in a very aggressive manner.

This is a nightmare. I almost wish that we'd invited Marcus's parents along too. At least, I'd have had the distraction of fending off being fondled by Dave the Groper, and Hilary the Hun is more than a match for my mum. No doubt, they'd have started a hat war or something.

My fiancé glances at me in a tortured manner. I return his gaze with a sympathetic smile. I'm so cross with my parents – here's

Marcus trying really hard to make us have a nice evening and they're all being so rude. Why is it that weddings and funerals bring out the very worst in people? They've only got to be civil to each other for a few hours and then we needn't see them again until their first grandchild is born. That's how it works these days, isn't it? I look round the table at the folded arms and the scowling faces and my heart sinks. There's a lot of effort and expense going into this wedding; all I can hope is that they behave themselves long enough for us to have a truly memorable day.

Chapter Sixty

Marcus sees me to my bedroom door. He pins me up against the wall, presses himself against me and kisses me long and hard. 'Mmm,' he murmurs in my ear. 'Is it bad luck to shag the bride senseless the night before the wedding?'

'Quite probably.'

'Want to risk it?' he says as his hand caresses my bottom. His kiss deepens. 'I wanted to run my hand up your thighs in the restaurant, like I did that night at Alfonso's.'

I break away from his embrace. 'That was *you*?'

Marcus laughs. 'Who did you think it was?'

I can't really say, 'your dad', can I? If I'd thought it was Marcus caressing my cellulite then I wouldn't have legged it to the ladies' loo and I wouldn't have ended up kissing Aiden 'Crush' Holby. A headache starts behind my eyes and I can feel a chocolate crisis coming on. 'We have to be up really early,' I tell him. 'I should go straight to bed.'

'That's what I'm suggesting,' Marcus says with a twinkle in his eye.

'Tomorrow,' I promise, kissing him. But now the mood is broken. 'Let's save it until we're husband and wife. It will be more exciting then.'

'Will it? Isn't that the end of our sex-life, when we get married?'

I shrug. 'Doesn't seem to be that way for my parents.'

Marcus pulls away. 'Yes, but they've both remarried,' he points out. 'Were they like that when they were married?'

'Of course not!'

Marcus lets go of my hands. 'That's what I'm saying.'

'They were normal,' I tell him. 'They rowed. They sulked. They

235

probably had sex once in a blue moon. But most of the time, while they were married, they rubbed along pretty well together.'

My fiancé suddenly looks very serious. 'Is that what you want for us? To rub along nicely?'

'No,' I tell him. 'I want more than that. I want you to be my husband and my best friend. I want you to be my lover and a great dad to our kids.'

'I want all that too.'

I smile at him. 'Then we'll be very happy.'

Marcus fiddles with my watch, rubbing his thumb over it distractedly. 'So why did your folks split?'

'I think they got divorced more out of boredom than anything else,' I say. I've never really talked to either of them about the nitty-gritty. Well, you don't, do you? My mum would more than likely launch into a vivid description of my father's shortcomings in the bedroom department and, frankly, that's more information than I need. I love my parents and all that, but I don't want to know *too* much about them. I settle for, 'They were going through a bad patch.'

Ironically, my mum was fed up with my dad looking like an eighties throwback and persuaded him to update his image. He happened to try a new barbers where Myleen The Hairdresser gave him a bit more of a makeover than he'd bargained for. Quite what she saw in his greying comb-over I'll never know. But then you can never really see your own parents as sex objects, can you? 'Then Dad met someone else. Not to be outdone, so did my mother.'

My fiancé looks very worried about this revelation. Perhaps he's thinking back to his own indiscretions.

'It doesn't have to be the same for us.' I give his hand a reassuring squeeze. 'But we'll have to work at it, Marcus. Good marriages don't happen by accident.'

'You're right,' Marcus says, but I can tell that something has switched off in his eyes. He laces his fingers through my hair and kisses me for the last time but his lips aren't on fire any more. 'We should get an early night.'

Then he walks off down the corridor and I watch him go. 'See you at the church,' he shouts over his shoulder.

'I love you,' I call out, but I don't think that he hears me.

Chapter Sixty-One

I'm lying awake on the bed staring at the ceiling. I've eaten the chocolate that was on my pillow. Not bad. Not great. A fairly poor quality chocolate, in fact, considering that it could *absolutely* be my last chocolate as a single woman. I should have brought a stash from Chocolate Heaven to keep me going. That's a severe oversight on my part and it makes me wonder what else I've forgotten. Perhaps I had too much coffee too at dinner, because now I'm feeling wide-eyed and wired.

Down the corridor, Marcus is probably sleeping soundly. In the Honeymoon Suite, my dad and The Hairdresser are probably hard at it, as will be my mum and The Millionaire in the Presidential Suite – even though the latter coupling might need a little chemical enhancement. If it's unpleasant enough to imagine your parents shagging, it's even worse to think of them shagging other people – and *enjoying* it! Yuk. I try not to dwell on it. Yet all over the world people are in the same situation – sleeping, making love, lying awake worrying.

I slip onto my side and try to get more comfortable. My mobile phone is lying on the bedside table. It winks at me tantalisingly. I wonder what Crush is doing now. Is he sleeping soundly too? Is there someone else in his bed? Is there any chance he could be lying awake thinking of me?

Picking up the phone, I fiddle with it. Despite my promises, I didn't contact him after our discussion in the dodgy café. I had every intention of calling him to explain my feelings but, to be perfectly honest, I had no idea what to say to him. So I would have um-ed and ah-ed and generally fucked it up. Crush deserves more than that.

It's three o'clock in the morning. This is the time of night when more people die, the time of night when drunken people phone up their exes and beg to get back together, the time of night when all manner of stupidity occurs. I know all that. So, before I can think better of it, I find Crush's number. Hopefully, it will go straight to voicemail and I can leave a nice message explaining what a pillock I am, and that I hope he'll be happy, and that I'll miss him. Dreadfully. That kind of thing.

After three short rings, Crush picks up.

'Hi, Gorgeous.' He sounds very sleepy. So he still has my number in his phone.

'I didn't mean to wake you up,' I say.

There's a pause. 'It's three in the morning.' I hear him suppress a yawn and it makes me smile. I've never been in bed with Crush – more's the pity – but it doesn't take a great feat of imagination to picture every inch of his body beneath the covers, the curve of his spine, his strong legs, how he'll be propping himself up on one of his broad shoulders. I can see him as if he were here, lying right next to me. My legs are restless and searching in the bed. 'What did you think I'd be doing?'

'I can't sleep,' I tell him.

'Big day tomorrow.'

'Yeah.' I curl up in the duvet. 'I shouldn't be phoning you.'

'Maybe not,' Crush says. 'But I'm glad that you did.'

'Now I don't know what to say.'

'Tell me what you're wearing,' Crush says. 'Are you naked?'

I giggle. 'You're a sick fuck, Aiden Holby.'

'That's better,' he says with a laugh. 'That sounds more like the Lucy I know and love.'

A gulp travels down my throat and my stomach lurches. 'I'm wearing Winnie the Pooh pyjamas.'

'Sexy,' he murmurs. 'I wish I could see them.'

'This will probably be the last time that I contact you,' I say. 'I can't ring you any more – it's not fair on Marcus. We should both take each other's numbers out of our contact lists.'

'If that's what you really want,' Crush says.

'I think it's for the best.'

Aiden lets out a long, sad sigh. 'So now what happens, Gorgeous?'

'I hang up and that's that. Tomorrow I get married.' Why on earth have I started to cry? I sob quietly into the phone. 'I just wanted you to know that I did love you very much.'

'And I still love you, Lucy.'

'I'd better go now.' I wipe my tears on the arm of my Pooh pyjamas. 'Goodnight. Sleep tight.'

'Goodbye, Gorgeous. Have a nice life.' And with that Crush hangs up.

Chapter Sixty-Two

Darren's assistant has already applied a pound and a half of make-up to my pale, tired face. Lancôme's *Flash Retouche* has been out in force trying to disguise the dark shadows beneath my eyes and she's making a fine job of turning me into a blushing bride. I'm sitting in my underwear, complete with stockings and suspenders, with Darren piling my hair up on my head, when the members of The Chocolate Lovers' Club arrive in force. They burst through the door, all smiles and giggling – and instantly my spirits lift. Darren is brushed aside as my friends all come over and kiss me.

'How's the bride-to-be?' Nadia asks as she hugs me warmly.

'Terrified.' It's not yet ten o'clock and my hands are shaking. My emotions are a whirling maelstrom. There's a tremor in my knees that isn't showing any imminent signs of abating. I think it's best that I don't tell them about my late-night call to Crush.

'You have a right to be,' Nadia states. 'Getting married is a big deal. But you'll be fine. Absolutely fine.'

'I will. I will,' I chant robotically. 'I will.'

'We brought supplies,' Chantal says. 'Open wide.'

I do and she pops a truffle straight into my mouth.

'Oh,' I sigh. The wonderful taste of Madagascar single plantation chocolate melts on my tongue. Oh, yes. Oh, yes. 'Mmm. That certainly helps.' This could be my very, very, *very* last chocolate as a single woman. I'd better enjoy it.

Marcus called me first thing this morning and told me that he loved me. I've been welling up ever since. Finally, a lone tear creeps out of my eye.

'No crying on your make-up,' Chantal instructs, whipping a

241

tissue to the offending water with the alacrity of a speeding bullet. 'Sniff it up. Sniff it up. You can only cry *after* you've said "I do".'

I sniff it up. Heartily.

'Sure you're okay?' Nadia asks.

My lip wobbles. Nothing much gets past that girl, so I might as well come clean. 'I called Crush last night,' I confess. What's that thing about going to your execution with a clear conscience? Maybe it's the same for a wedding. 'He told me that he still loves me.'

The members of The Chocolate Lovers' Club exchange worried glances.

'It's cool,' I say, holding up my hands. 'It's cool. You still need to get me to the church on time. We got things straight between us.' My voice cracks very slightly. 'We agreed that we wouldn't see each other or speak to each other again. It's only fair.' At which point I burst into tears. I don't give a flying fuck about my make-up. I just feel so miserable.

'It's nerves,' Nadia says briskly. 'You sit down and eat chocolate. Don't get it on your underwear.' She wraps me in a fluffy towel and leads me to the edge of the bed, patting it as I sit down. I feel terrible that she's had so much to cope with and she's done it all so bravely and here's me, turned into a complete jelly at the thought of marrying the man I've been professing to love for the last five years or more.

'I'll get tea sent up.' Chantal heads to the phone. 'And vodka.'

'You are my best girls,' I wail.

'Darren can start on us,' Nadia says. 'You just take half an hour to calm down. What you need is something to distract you.'

I've had a good cry, two shots of vodka, three cups of tea and four chocolate croissants – which *definitely* has to be the last chocolate I eat as a single woman otherwise they won't be able to zip up my blessed dress. Suffice to say, I'm feeling much, much better.

Jacob pops his head around the door of my room. 'Are you all decent?'

'That's a matter of opinion,' Nadia says. 'But we're all clothed.'

He comes inside, taking in the scene. 'Wow!' He gives us a beaming smile. 'Don't you all look great.'

The girls have all had their hair and make-up done now and are resplendent in tight silk numbers. Autumn's dress is the colour of chewy caramels, Nadia's wearing a rich shade of coffee and Chantal has on a dark, bitter chocolate. Jacob has gone for a chocolate theme – what else? My dress is white chocolate and, collectively, we look like a box of handmade delights. The man really is an angel and I have long forgiven him his dodgy past. The bouquets have arrived – glorious confections of cream flowers, interlaced with chocolate-coloured ribbons.

I'm currently having my make-up repaired and am still in my underwear. I don't care if Jacob gets an eyeful – actually, I puff out my chest and cross my legs seductively, hoping it makes them look slimmer. It might make him realise what he missed. But then I remember that he has seen lots of women in their underwear in a professional capacity and that this is just a different profession for him, so I give up with the vamp pose.

Flopping down on a chair next to me, Jacob asks, 'Everything okay?'

I nod. I really think that it will all be fine. My histrionics were just a temporary blip, nothing more. If I don't think about Crush – even in a friendly way – then everything will be tickety-boo.

'The dining room is looking splendid,' he assures me. 'You'll be bowled over. The florists are just finishing in the church and that looks amazing too. This is going to be one *hell* of a wedding.'

'I hope you're right, Jacob.' I give him a brave smile. 'Thanks for all your help. There's no way I could have done this without you.'

'I wouldn't have wanted you to.' He kisses me tenderly on the cheek.

'Don't smudge the make-up,' I warn.

'See you later,' he says. 'I'll be there all the way making sure that everything is just perfect.'

*   *   *

We're all ready and raring to go, yet there are more than three hours left to wait. Darren and his assistant have finished their work here, so they've gone off to do my mother's hair and make-up, leaving us alone.

I'm swinging my legs, kicking my cream silk shoes against the fluffy carpet.

'What do we do now?' I say. It seems as if Jacob has been a bit over-zealous with his timetable. 'We've got at least two hours to kill before the photographer arrives.'

'We could give you a pep talk about marriage,' Chantal suggests. 'I've got a few tips on how *not* to go about it.'

'No,' I say. 'That will only start me off all over again. Besides, Marcus and I had a little heart-to-heart last night. We both know that we've got to work hard at keeping on track, and we're both prepared to do that. I know that the wedding day is all very symbolic and stuff, but I really do feel that this is the start of a new, more mature era in our relationship.'

My friend smiles at me. 'I'm sure it is, honey.'

The clock in my room ticks loudly. I kick my heels a bit more and puff out a breath. 'We could have had a lie-in.'

'I guess Jacob's left plenty of time for unexpected emergencies,' Chantal says. 'There's not a wedding day that doesn't have some little drama crop up.'

'I should have brought some of Lewis's board games,' Nadia says. 'Snakes and ladders would have kept us amused.'

'I spy with my little eye something beginning with "C".' My eyes light on the remains of the box of Chocolate Heaven goodies.

'No more chocolate, Lucy,' Chantal tells me. 'You'll make yourself sick.'

'As if!'

'You'll get it on your dress,' Nadia adds.

'I need something to do,' I whine. 'I'm just getting more nervous again, sitting here waiting.'

Then a mobile phone rings and we all jump sky high – Autumn more than any of us. She scuttles across the room to her handbag to find it. 'Hello,' she says, turning away from us into the corner.

We all crane to hear what she's saying as we've nothing else to do. Then we pretend that we weren't when she hangs up and comes back towards us.

'I've just had some bad news,' she says. Autumn turns to me, her eyes brimming with tears.

'Don't mess up your make-up,' I warn. Chantal sweeps in with a tissue again. 'The chance of any of us getting down that aisle without mascara tracks is looking slim.'

'It might not matter,' Autumn says. 'I don't think I'm going to be able to be your bridesmaid after all.'

Chapter Sixty-Three

'**Y**ou've got a delivery to make? What kind of delivery? I want to know.'

Autumn drags a holdall out of the corner of the room. 'This kind.'

Nadia, Chantal and I all look as blank as each other.

'The guy that attacked me the other night – that's what it was all about,' Autumn goes on. 'This bag belongs to them. My dear brother had it.'

'What's in it?'

'Soft toys.' Autumn unzips the holdall and lifts out a fluffy teddy bear. 'With a street value of a million pounds or more.'

My eyes feel like popping out. 'You're wearing a bridesmaid's dress and you have a bag of Class A drugs?'

'That's about the sum of it,' Autumn confirms.

'Why did you bring it here?'

'I couldn't very well leave it at my flat. They might have broken in and ransacked it. I thought it would be safer here. Plus I'd been told to expect them to call me and let me know when the drop would be.' She sighs heavily. 'Well, they just called. I have to make the drop now.'

'Now?'

'It's this side of London,' she says, 'but it'll be tight for me to get back in time. That's if everything goes according to plan.'

'Can't it wait?' I say. 'Tell them you're at a wedding and that you'll do the drop tomorrow.'

'These aren't the type of people who you tell to wait, Lucy. You know how much your wedding means to me,' she says, 'but I can't let Richard down. He says they'll kill him if they don't get this back.'

'And he's letting you go out and face them alone?'

'What else can I do?'

'Does Addison know about this?' Nadia asks.

Autumn nods. 'I didn't want to say anything to spoil your day, but I haven't heard from Addison since he found out what I was planning to do. He packed his stuff and went back to his own place. He was so angry with me for agreeing to do this.'

Can't say I'm surprised.

'I don't blame him if he wants nothing more to do with me.' Autumn's eyes fill with tears again and her voice wavers. 'Quite rightly, he's sick of me putting Richard first. But this is the last thing I do for my brother, the *very* last thing. I swear.'

I want to rake my hands through my hair, but can't because I'll dislodge my bloody tiara. 'You can't do this,' I say. 'Not alone.'

Autumn, Nadia and Chantal do another exchange of worried glances.

'We are top heistmasters,' I remind them. 'Operation Liberate Chantal's Jewellery was a textbook scam. We're women who are experienced in the ways of the dubious underbelly of society.' Already the latent criminal part of my mind has kicked into gear. 'We can do this together.'

Chantal sits heavily on the bed.

'We can blat back to town. Chantal, you're an ace getaway driver.' I don't volunteer to drive, as last time I did, I crashed a van. 'Do you reckon that you could get us there and back in two hours?'

'That butts us right up against the photographer,' she points out with a worried chew of her lip.

'So we have a few less bouquet shots.' I shrug. 'That's plenty of time.'

'You can't do this,' Autumn says with a vigorous shake of her curls. 'You can't even consider it.'

'This is our "little drama",' I remind them. 'It's fate that Jacob allowed us just the right amount of extra time. We've got nothing else to do.' For some reason there's a note of excitement creeping into my voice.

'It's dangerous,' Autumn tells us starkly.

'All the more reason for us to come along too,' I insist. 'There's no way you can do this by yourself. Am I right?'

Nadia and Chantal nod reluctantly.

'Then let's go,' I say. 'We're wasting valuable time talking about it.'

'I have to make one more call,' Autumn says, and she moves away from the group.

'We should take everything with us,' Chantal says. 'Just in case we are tight for time and can't get back to the rooms.' She hands us all our bouquets and then gives us all the once-over. 'Jeez, we are looking fabulous.'

'Right.' I smooth my hands over my wedding dress. 'Have you got the holdall, Autumn?'

Our friend lifts it up.

'We ought to tell someone that we're going out,' Nadia says.

'No. We can't.' I shake my head, and am glad to note that my tiara doesn't even think about wobbling.

'You should tell Marcus.'

'No,' I say again. 'He'll only try to stop us. The less that people know about this, the better. This has to be our secret. Besides,' I say, 'we'll be back before anyone realises we're missing.'

Chapter Sixty-Four

Purposefully, we all stride out of Trington Manor and head for Chantal's black four-wheel drive Chelsea Tractor. The sun is shining and, even though it's February, there's a modicum of warmth to it. A fine day for a wedding, you might say. A perfect day.

Our friend slides into the driving seat while my two other bridesmaids help me to feed my dress and veil into the front passenger seat. When I'm settled, Nadia hands me my bouquet.

'You look lovely,' she says.

'Just the thing for a drugs drop?'

We all manage a nervous laugh, and while I smooth down my skirt so that it doesn't crease too much, Nadia and Autumn hop into the back.

Chantal puts on her shades. She looks very mean. Ideal for a getaway driver. Except for the bridesmaid's dress, of course. 'Ready?'

'Ready,' we all agree and she fires the ignition.

Nothing happens.

Chantal swears under her breath and pumps her foot on the accelerator in a very aggressive manner. Still nothing.

'It might have pre-wedding nerves too,' I suggest with an ill-advised chew at my newly manicured nails.

'Fucking heap of shit,' Chantal mutters, even though her car is brand new and is something ferociously expensive. That matters not, as despite numerous attempts to get the beast to move, it steadfastly refuses.

Autumn checks her watch anxiously.

'Don't panic,' I say. 'Don't panic. We just need to implement Plan B.'

'We need to get another frigging vehicle,' Chantal complains as she hits the heel of her hand against the steering-wheel. For someone who wasn't keen to go in the first place, she seems very disappointed that we're not shooting out of the gravel drive, wheels spinning.

I give my friends a knowing smile. 'We have an alternative vehicle.'

They all turn to look at me. Chantal frowns. 'We do?'

My dad's Bentley has been volunteered to be the wedding car. The small church that Marcus and I are getting married in is in the grounds of the hotel, but it's a long walk – particularly in silk heels – and my father has kindly offered me the use of his very posh car so that I can travel the short distance in style. Jacob has had both the interior and the exterior of the car decorated with chocolate and cream ribbons. It looks absolutely great. Excessively bridal. Now we, the good members of The Chocolate Lovers' Club, are all standing staring at it, bouquets in hand.

'We could take this,' I suggest. 'It might even save us a bit of time as we could then drive straight to the church.'

'We're going on a drugs drop in bridal outfits,' Chantal reminds me. 'We don't want to attract any more attention to ourselves.'

'Right. Good thought.' I purse my lips. We all stay silent. 'We don't actually have any other options though.'

Plan C steadfastly fails to materialise. We all sigh as we consider the Bentley.

Eventually, Nadia says, 'Looks like we need to get the keys to the wedding car.'

'Wait here.' I hitch up my dress. 'I'll be back in five minutes.'

As fast as I can in silk pumps, I sprint up the steps and back into Reception. Breathless already – must do more aerobics – I pant, 'Could you please call Mr Lombard's room for me?'

The receptionist, not appreciating the desperate hurry, slowly checks the room number and then, in an equally leisurely manner, dials it. An interminable wait ensues. I tap my foot and want to gnaw all the flowers out of my bouquet.

'There's no reply,' she tells me after a few moments.

'There must be,' I say. Where the hell else could he be? It's the morning of my wedding. My dad is walking me down the aisle. He should be getting ready.

'Perhaps you could try the spa,' the receptionist suggests.

Spa, my arse. He'll be holed up in the Honeymoon Suite playing bouncy cuddles with The Hairdresser and too damn busy to answer the phone – that's *exactly* where he'll be.

I shoot over to the lift, more foot-tapping and gnashing of teeth while I wait for it to come. When I'm finally inside I try to think pleasant, relaxing thoughts and enjoy the inane Musak filling the space. I must not want to kill my father. I must not want to kill my father.

Finding the Honeymoon Suite, I bang on the door. 'Dad. Dad! Open up. I need to talk to you.' Nothing. I don't want to put my ear to the door in case I hear things that I'd rather not be party to. I know that my dad and his new wife get down to it on an alarmingly regular basis – they could barely keep their hands off each other over dinner – but it doesn't mean that I have to be happy about that knowledge. I bang again. 'Dad. *Dad!*'

The door opens and my father stands there in nothing but a towel. A small towel. His hair is standing on end, his face is flushed. But the dead giveaway is The Hairdresser lying legs akimbo on the bed behind him. 'Where's the fire?' he says with a smile that fails to hide the fact that he's disgruntled at having his coitus interrupted.

'In your underpants,' might be a good rejoinder, but this *is* my dad. 'I need to borrow your car keys,' I say.

His red face pales slightly. 'The Bentley?'

'The same.'

'Why?'

'I have a little errand to run.'

'You're getting married soon,' he reminds me pointlessly.

'I haven't forgotten,' I say. 'I'm ready.' I indicate my outfit. 'It's just something I've forgotten to do. Something tiny and unimportant. I won't be long.'

'It's my pride and joy,' Dad says weakly.

'I'm your daughter and it's my wedding day,' I say. 'I ask very little of you.'

My dad looks shame-faced, but still he doesn't move.

'Have I been a good daughter?'

A tear springs to his eye. 'You've been a wonderful daughter.'

'Then give me the car keys.'

With a very grumpy sigh, he wanders away from the door and then comes back with his car keys, which he hands over with the utmost reluctance. I kiss him on the cheek. 'I love you,' I say as I swing them round my finger and start to run back towards the lift. I call over my shoulder, 'Now you can get back to your shag. But make it quick because I'm getting married soon and I don't want you to be late!'

My dad slams the bedroom door. I smile to myself. We have no respect for our parents these days, but then they so rarely deserve it.

Chapter Sixty-Five

The members of The Chocolate Lovers' Club all pile into my father's Bentley. 'I'd better drive,' I say nervously. 'If we crash, I wouldn't want anyone else to be responsible for it.'

'You've been drinking,' Autumn reminds me.

'Two vodkas,' I say. 'Still within the limit.' Frankly, I could be blind drunk and it would do nothing to make my driving skills any worse. I'm hoping that the four chocolate croissants will have mopped up any alcohol in my bloodstream.

My friends help me as I slip into the driving seat, then fold my dress around my legs, so that I can use the pedals. Chantal is riding shotgun. Like a good bridesmaid, she takes my bouquet.

Checking that my bridesmaids are ready, I say, 'Let's go!'

Spinning the wheels in the gravel of Trington Manor's sweeping drive, we head back to The Smoke. Taking in a couple of flowerbeds on the way, we speed away from my parents, Marcus and my wedding. The chocolate-themed ribbons on the car flutter in the breeze. I feel we should have some rousing hymns playing, but all my father has is Celine Dion CDs. 'My Heart Will Go On' booms out.

I glance over my shoulder. 'You sure you know where we're going, Autumn?'

'Yes,' she nods solemnly. 'I'm sure. Girls . . . I can't thank you enough for this.'

'Enough with the grovelling,' I chide her. 'We're doing this because we're like The Three Musketeers – "All for one and one for all".'

'All for one and one for all,' Nadia and Chantal chant.

Come to think of it, there were four of them too, even though they were, confusingly, called The Three Musketeers. I look to Autumn again. 'All you need to do is tell me which way to go.'

An hour later and we're driving through a very seedy part of North London. A part more seedy than I ever knew North London possessed – and I've known some pretty seedy parts, believe me. Even the sun has scuttled back behind grey clouds. Everything is bleak and monotone, and the area looks as if it's been recently bombed out. Dubious-looking lock-up garages line the roads. Businesses offer quick tyre changes, paint jobs and repairs, and you can tell the sort of car owners that they'll be having as customers. I'm surprised that they don't offer blood removal and dead body disposal. I somehow don't think there'll be too many mums here in their Ford Fiestas getting a little dent knocked out that they've picked up on the school run.

My dad's shiny vehicle complete with wedding decorations looks far too conspicuous and it makes me realise that this really is a dangerous thing that we're doing – not to mention illegal. Marcus would kill me if he could see me now. I hope that his Best Man is managing to keep him distracted in a rather less robust way. A few drinks in the bar might be preferable. What on earth was I thinking about when I said we should do this?

We seem to be driving deeper and deeper into the arse end of nowhere. I've no idea where we are, but I know that I don't like it much.

'Bloody hell, Autumn,' I say with an anxious exhalation. 'Are we nearly there yet?'

My friends turn and glare at me.

'What?'

Autumn takes a map out of the top of the holdall. 'Yes. We're nearly there. Turn right at this next junction, Lucy.'

We turn into the street. The buildings have all had their windows punched out, giving the road a nice coating of broken glass.

'The drop-off point should be around here somewhere,' Autumn says. 'We're looking for a disused piece of ground in between two derelict factories.'

'Sounds charming.'

We carry on down the road, and the mood in the Bentley becomes very sober as we crawl along, keeping our eyes peeled for the rendezvous location.

'That looks like it,' Autumn says. She points to a ragged bit of ground enclosed by the high walls of the falling-down factories, turning it into a vast, scruffy courtyard with only one entrance. It's private, away from prying eyes and – if I was a drug dealer – would look like the perfect place for a meet.

'Let's do it,' I say and, taking a deep breath, I swing the Bentley onto the rough ground.

'We're to park at the far end,' Autumn says. 'With the front of the car facing the entrance.'

I do as I'm told and we take up our position. 'Where have you got to drop the stuff?'

'We're to wait here until they come.'

We all spin round and look at Autumn. 'They're coming *here*? *Now*?'

She looks taken aback. 'Yes. I thought you knew that.'

'I thought we'd just drop the stuff and clear off,' I say. 'Then they'd swing by a bit later and collect it.'

'I don't think it works like that,' Autumn says nervously. 'I suppose they need to check that everything's legitimate.'

'I think that you mean the gear's sound,' Nadia corrects.

For a borderline member of the criminal fraternity, Autumn is missing a certain amount of gangsta speech from her vocabulary. She still talks like the totally optimistic, red-haired social worker that she is. Bless.

'Bloody hell,' I say, glancing at the clock in the Bentley. 'I hope they're punctual criminals as time's getting a bit tight.' I want to get back to Trington Manor as soon as we can, maybe have time to relax a little, eat my final chocolate as a single woman.

'It will be fine,' Nadia says. 'I'm sure.' But her voice is wobbling underneath the confident words.

'I've got some Rolos in the holdall,' Autumn says. 'For emergencies.'

'I think this could be classed as an emergency.'

'We'll be up to the eyeballs in chocolate,' Nadia reminds us.

'It's worth the risk.' Autumn searches in the bag of Class A drugs to find our chocolate stash and then duly hands round the Rolos. As I pop one into my mouth, trying not to get melted chocolate on my fingers, or dribble on to my dress, I say with a sigh, 'This could well be my last chocolate as a single woman.'

I settle back in my seat. All we can do now is wait.

Chapter Sixty-Six

When we've chewed our way anxiously through the whole packet of Rolos, a big black car with big, blacked-out windows turns into the derelict ground in front of us. It trundles across the weeds, dirt and broken concrete towards us, kicking up dust with an insouciant air.

I swallow down the last of the creamy caramel from my Rolo with a nervous gulp. 'Looks like it's showtime.'

In the back seat, Autumn has gone pale with fear.

'What do we do now?'

As I ask the question, Autumn's mobile phone rings. She answers it, eyes wide with anxiety. We can hear someone talking at the other end, but can't tell what they're saying.

'Yes,' she says timidly. Then she hangs up. 'I'm to get out of the car alone and walk towards them with the holdall held at arm's length.'

'Sod that,' I say. Sometimes I wonder where all this bravado comes from. 'You're not going anywhere by yourself. We haven't come all this way to let you go into the lions' den alone. I'm going with you.'

Then we see two men get out of the other car. Rather alarmingly, they're holding sawn-off shotguns.

'Fuck,' Chantal says.

'Fuck indeed,' I echo.

'I can't move,' Autumn says.

'Yes, you can. Come on.' I'm out of my seat and opening the back door to help Autumn out. 'Give me my bouquet,' I say to Chantal.

'What?'

'My bouquet.' I hold out my hand for it and Chantal obliges. 'I'm hoping that like hitting a man wearing glasses, they won't shoot a bride with a bouquet.'

Autumn lugs the holdall out of the footwell of the Bentley and holds it out. We exchange a nervous glance. 'Easy does it,' I say. 'I don't want my wedding photographs blood-spattered.' Although I now realise that I'm going to have to drive like a bat out of hell to have any hope of getting back in time for pre-wedding photographs. The idea of me relaxing with appropriate chocolate treats and a glass or two of wine has long gone.

Slowly, Autumn and I make our way across the uneven ground of the courtyard. I'm aware that the two terrified faces of our friends are watching our progress, but I'm too frightened myself to worry about their fears.

The men stand with their shotguns pointed at the ground, which I'm tempted to view as a good thing. As we approach them, I see that they are also slightly open-mouthed. In the manner of all good criminal scenarios, the villains of the piece are dressed in black leather jackets, black jeans, sturdy black boots. They're wearing black sunglasses too, even thought it's quite cloudy, and have black baseball caps pulled down over their eyes. Perhaps they hadn't expected to see a group of four women sporting colour co-ordinated bridalwear. We totter forward in our heels.

When we get within speaking distance, one of the men says to Autumn, 'You were told to come alone.'

'I'm her bodyguard,' I say. I thought they might laugh, break the tension, but they don't.

He nods at me. 'What's with the outfit?'

'I'm getting married,' I tell him in a voice that sounds stronger than I feel. 'And I'm going to be late if we don't get a move on.'

'Throw the bag to the floor,' he tells Autumn. 'By my feet.'

Autumn gives the bag a swing and it sails through the air, landing with remarkable accuracy right at the guy's feet in a little shower of dust. 'I'm going to check it,' he says. 'Then you'll get your bag.'

Our bag? I risk a sideways glance at Autumn. She's looking blank too.

One of the guys kneels next to the holdall and unzips it. He takes out a very cute teddy bear. There's a slit in his tummy. 'This one's been opened.'

'I had to check the merchandise,' Autumn says calmly. 'It's all there.'

'It had better be,' the guy growls. He slits one of the packets and tastes the contents with his finger. Then he smiles. 'Your brother is a very good boy.'

'That's a matter of opinion,' Autumn says.

'Don't move,' the guy instructs us as he and his accomplice move towards the back of their car. A moment later they emerge with a very similar-looking holdall which they throw at Autumn's feet. She stands there frozen.

'You should check it,' he tells her.

'We trust you.'

They both laugh at that, which I think is a bad sign.

'I'll check it,' I say. I give my bridesmaid my bouquet and step forward. My heart is pounding loudly. I bend down, trying not to get my wedding dress dirty, and unzip the bag. My eyes widen in shock, surprise, I don't know what. I turn to Autumn, let my veil drop over my face and whisper, 'This bag is full of money.'

'I don't want it,' she says.

'We have to take it. Otherwise it might look suspicious.'

My friend has a moment of indecision. 'Okay,' she says.

'That seems to be in order,' I say to the hoods and I pick up the bag. Which is bloody heavy. Who'd have thought that paper would weigh that much – but then there's an awful lot of paper in here.

'That concludes our business then, ladies,' one of the guys says.

'That's our cue to get out of here, girl.' I take Autumn's hand and hurry her back towards the car.

Behind us, the guys start to laugh. 'Congratulations on your forthcoming wedding,' one shouts. 'I'm sure you're going to make someone a lovely wife!'

Yes, very hilarious. If I wasn't about to poop myself then I might be able to think of a witty retort. As it is, I feel that if we don't get a move on, I'm not going to be making anyone any kind of wife at all.

Chapter Sixty-Seven

Autumn and I get back into Dad's Bentley wedding limousine/getaway vehicle combo. My knees are shaking and I suspect Autumn's are doing exactly the same thing.

I hand Chantal the holdall stuffed with money. 'Okay?' she says.

Letting out a long, shuddering sigh, I say, 'We're home and dry.'

'Good girls,' Nadia says. She's holding Autumn's hand and also reaches across to squeeze my shoulder.

We sit there for a moment and, while I try to get my surging adrenaline under control, we all watch as the drug dealers slam their car into reverse and start to back out of the disused ground.

'If I really flatten my foot to the floor, then we should just make it back in time,' I say. I wonder what the top speed of a Bentley is?

'I can't thank you enough for this,' Autumn says again. 'I never meant to mess up your wedding day.'

'It isn't messed up,' I assure her. 'We can still do this. We'll be back in the nick of time and no one will be any the wiser. This has all gone *very* smoothly.' I allow myself a congratulatory smile. 'Now. If we're all sitting comfortably, let's hit the road.'

Then the car bearing the drug dealers screeches back into the yard in front of us and, slewing sideways, comes to a halt. Following it, rather rapidly, are three big four-wheel-drive vehicles.

'Oh, no.' I duck down behind my bouquet. 'This is not good. Not good at all.'

'Who do you think this lot are?'

The hoods jump out of their car and are immediately pounced on by a mass of other black-clad men who, similarly, have jumped out of their cars. We watch, transfixed, as a scuffle ensues, but eventually the second lot come out on top and they bundle the hoods into the backs of their cars. The last drug dealer turns towards us and shouts, 'It was those bitches,' he spits. 'They're the ones you want!'

The men turn and now become aware of our Bentley sitting harmlessly at the far side of the land.

'Do you think they're after the money?' Autumn says.

'I don't know,' I answer. 'But they're more than welcome to it.'

Two of the men head slowly, but purposefully, towards us. My heart is pounding. 'Now what?'

'We are armed police officers,' they shout as they near the Bentley. Badges are flashed at us. 'Stay exactly where you are. Put your hands on your head.'

'They're police,' I say with a relieved sigh. 'Thank goodness. I thought they were more thugs.'

I drop my bouquet into my lap and put my hands on the sides of my head. There's no way I'm spoiling my hairdo.

'We've just done a drugs drop,' Nadia points out. 'And we've got a bag stuffed full of money. Couldn't that be classed as incriminating evidence?'

'Oh, shit.'

The policemen still walk towards us. Now in a very determined way.

'Bad,' I say. 'This is bad. Give me the money,' I hiss at Chantal. 'Quickly.'

She hands it over and I fluff out the skirt of my wedding dress and put the holdall between my legs, hiding it with a swathe of silk. The policemen come towards the driver's window and I wind it down. 'Play dumb,' I whisper to my friends/accomplices/bridesmaids. It's something I do rather too well.

'Hello, Officers,' I say cheerily. 'I wonder if you can help us? We seem to be terribly lost.'

They eye the beribboned Bentley suspiciously.

'We're on the way to my wedding.' Sometimes our police force are criticised for not being overly bright, but I'm sure that even they can tell that I'm kitted out in a bridal fashion.

262

'You're a bit off the beaten track,' one policeman observes.

'Yes. We seem to have taken a wrong turn.' They smile smugly between them, clearly commenting silently on the navigational skills of women.

I call on all my drama skills, think of dying kittens, terrible hunger and cold, a life without chocolate, and conjure up a tear to my eye. 'We're going to be very late. Could you possibly just direct us to the motorway? We're in a terrible hurry.'

They cast a glance over the Bentley again. 'Would you like to step out of the vehicle, ladies,' one of them says. 'I'm afraid that you're going nowhere fast.'

Chapter Sixty-Eight

The policeman kicks the Bentley's tyre. 'Puncture,' he says.

It must have been the broken glass we had to drive over on the way here. Now I'm tempted to cry for real.

The policeman folds his arms and regards me coolly. 'You didn't see anything while you were sitting there?'

'No,' I say, looking to the girls for confirmation. They all nod vigorously. 'We realised we'd missed our turning and simply came into this disused ground to swing round. While we were doing it, the other car came in. It looked as if they were up to no good, Officer, so we backed away to the far end.'

'Very sensible,' he says. 'You don't want to be messing with those kind of men.'

I try to smile, but my cheeks are locked into an expression of terror as I think of the bag of dirty money in the front footwell of the Bentley, barely covered by a rather nice arrangement of Singapore orchids, tiny white roses and other floral-type stuff.

'Was there another car?'

'No.' We all shake our heads as hard as we can.

The policemen look puzzled.

Then tears, real tears, come to my eye. I can see my big moment sliding away from me. Marcus will be frantic with worry. Everyone will be sitting in the church waiting for me and I won't be there. I'll be banged up in a cell in some dingy police station with my bridesmaids while they contemplate throwing away the key. I try to swallow, but it comes out as a sob. 'I'm going to be terribly, terribly late.'

The policemen exchange a glance. 'Well then, we'd better get this tyre changed for you,' one of the coppers says in a kindly manner. 'Then you can be on your way. Do you know where the jack is?'

'Jack?' We all look blankly at him, encouraging him to exchange another smirk with his colleague – this time to do with women's inability to change car tyres.

'It's my dad's car,' I inform the policeman, lips quivering. 'This is the first time I've driven it.' I don't tell him that I had to prise the keys out of my darling father under the utmost duress – and that I might not even be insured to drive this thing, come to think of it. I'm going pale at the thought.

'Don't worry, love,' the policeman says in reassuring tones. 'We'll find it.'

He strides to the driver's door and yanks it open. Chantal and I exchange a terrified glance. 'The boot release must be under here somewhere.'

Yes, along with the bag of ill-gotten drugs money. I'm very close to hyperventilating. If we manage to get out of this without criminal convictions then I'm going to lie in a dark room completely surrounded by chocolate and eat my way slowly through it. He leans on the bag to get a better look under the dashboard. If only he knew what was in there. My heart nearly stops.

'Ah.' The policeman pulls the catch and the boot pops open. He goes round to the back of the car and moments later has reappeared, brandishing a jack. Treating us to a winning smile, he says proudly, 'You can't hide anything from a policeman.'

I think it's at this point that I faint.

The tyre is changed, I'm back in the land of the living and the police still haven't discovered our starring role in their drugs bust.

We're all sitting in the Bentley. The policeman pats the roof. 'Take care, ladies,' he says. 'I hope we don't see you on our patch again.'

'No,' I agree. 'Thank you, Officer. You've been very, very helpful.'

'All in the line of duty,' he says, like *Dixon of Dock Green*. 'Are you sure that we can't escort you to the motorway?'

'No. No. No.' I try to keep the panic out of my voice. 'You've already done enough for us.'

'Enjoy your wedding,' the policeman says. 'I hope that you and your future husband will be very happy together.'

'So do I,' I say as I slam the car into gear and we pull away, waving madly, smiles fixed in place.

'Dear God,' Nadia says as we turn out of the yard. She gives a relieved huff of breath. 'That was a very close call.'

'I can't believe it,' I say. 'We were so lucky not to get busted.' See how criminal words slip so easily into my vocabulary? 'I wonder how they knew that this drugs drop was going down?'

Now I'm sounding like a bad-assed ho'.

Autumn coughs gently and we all turn to look at her. Well, I eyeball her in the rearview mirror. 'I told them,' she says quietly.

'What!' I say less quietly.

'I had no idea that there was money involved,' she explains. 'Rich just told me that we were making a delivery. I didn't think that we'd be incriminated in any way if the police turned up.'

'That was a very risky strategy, if you don't mind me saying.' I grip the steering-wheel tightly and head back towards the motorway as fast as the Bentley will take us. 'I could have been spending my wedding day in a prison cell.'

'I know,' Autumn says. 'I'm sorry.'

'As it is, I'm going to be ferociously late.'

'Not if you put your foot flat to the floor,' Chantal says. I press harder on the accelerator.

'Just don't get nicked for speeding,' Nadia warns. 'We've seen enough of the boys in blue today.'

'I need to call Marcus,' I say. 'Tell him that we're probably going to be late.'

'I'll call him.' Chantal takes my mobile phone from the console. 'We don't want you getting nicked for using your phone while driving either.'

'Suddenly everyone's concerned about me not becoming a criminal. Shame you didn't think about that a little while ago,' I point out.

We all burst into fits of giggles.

'This is terrible,' I say. 'Autumn, we have a bagful of dodgy money in the footwell. What are you planning to do with it?'

'Technically, it belongs to Richard, I suppose. I should give it to him.'

'He doesn't seem too deserving to me,' Chantal remarks.

'You're right,' Autumn agrees. 'After he's put us in so much danger, I think he owes me one. Maybe I should find one of my good causes to donate it to.'

'Perhaps it should go to the drugs rehab programme,' Nadia suggests. 'There seems a certain sort of irony in that.'

'Good idea.'

Chantal finds Marcus's phone number, presses dial and holds my mobile to her ear. 'It's going straight to voicemail,' she tells me. 'Do you want me to leave a message?'

'Perhaps it's better if we don't,' I say. 'He'll never expect me to be on time, anyway. Isn't it a bride's prerogative to be hideously late?' We're on the motorway now and we're speeding along. It won't be too long before we're back. So long as there are no more technical hitches, of course.

The chocolate and cream ribbons are flutteringly wildly in the breeze. Celine's still warbling on.

'Marcus will understand,' I say. I grit my teeth, press my foot down hard and hope to goodness that I'm right.

Chapter Sixty-Nine

'Twenty minutes,' I say, looking at my watch. 'Twenty minutes late isn't so bad, is it?'

My bridesmaids look nervously at me. After customising a few more of Trington Manor's flowerbeds on the way back, we've now slowed our pace to sedate rather than breakneck. And, while it might be unusual for a bride to be driving her own wedding car, nothing else looks untoward. Even my hair is miraculously untrammelled by its adventures.

The church is picture-perfect. Set in the grounds of the Manor, it hails from the year dot. Medieval, I'd guess. The brickwork is all worn and mellow. A little gravel path winds its way towards the door through immaculately tended lawns. There's an arch of brilliant white roses around the door just for me. It's the perfect setting for a fairytale wedding. A fairytale wedding that's going to be mine. My heart sets up a shaky and uneven beat.

I can see the photographer hovering at the entrance to the church – and rather a lot of the guests too. Perhaps they're waiting to take snaps of me as I arrive. Although, I admit, I had sort of expected them to be sitting in the church, anxiously nibbling their nails at my tardiness by now.

'This has been fun,' I say to my friends. 'How on earth we've managed get through all that unscathed, I don't know. But we have. Miraculously. 'Now the serious stuff starts. Are we ready?' My best girls nod at me.

'You're absolutely sure about this, Lucy?' Nadia asks, hand on my arm.

A flutter of nerves grips my stomach and I can't speak to answer her. This is it. This is really *it*. Perhaps it's due to the excitement and stress of the last few hours, but I feel weird. I feel as if this isn't really happening to me at all. In a very short time, I'm going to be Marcus's wife.

I slow the Bentley to a dignified halt right outside the church. My dad wrenches open the passenger door. 'Where the hell have you been?' he barks. My parent is red in the face and, I have to say, it's not the typical address for a father to give his daughter on her wedding day, I would have thought.

I can't really answer, 'To North London on a drugs drop,' so I say, 'We had to pop out. You knew that. I went in your car.'

He's too apoplectic to speak.

Chantal comes round and helps me out of the car. I fluff my skirt, check that my bouquet has survived its trials unscathed – which it has – and, serenely, we head for the church gates.

'It's all right now,' I say calmly to my father. A mist of numbness has settled on me. I don't know where my emotions have gone, but they're not here at this moment. I'm centred, grounded, positively Zen. 'We're here now. The proceedings can begin.'

I might have thought that the organ would have been playing to entertain the congregation, but there's no hint of music in the air. Everything's very quiet. I see Clive and Tristan lurking by a particularly fine yew tree – their faces are drawn and I hope that they've not been fighting again. I want this to be a day of love and joy. Jacob is there as well, and when he sees me, he starts towards me, his face wracked with anguish. All the hairs on the back of my neck stand up. Something's definitely not right. I wonder if we've turned up on the wrong day.

Then I hear my mother wail like a banshee. She's heading for me too, blubbing her eyes out. 'Oh, Lucy. Oh, Lucy!'

'What?' I say. There are a lot of embarrassed faces staring at me. Dave the Groper and Hilary the Hun are there. Hilary, too, is sniffing into her handkerchief. 'What's happened?'

'Marcus,' my mother says dramatically, along with a sob.

My blood runs cold. 'What about Marcus?'

'He's gone.'

Chapter Seventy

I wrench the church doors open, thinking that this must be some kind of sick joke. There's a gasp from the few people who are sitting chatting in their pews. Any conversation grinds to a halt and they all stare at me.

The organist, clearly shocked into action, starts up with a robust version of the 'Wedding March'. Checking out the altar, I see that it's remarkably groom-free. The vicar is there. He's frantically waving his arms to try to shut the organist up. The church is decorated beautifully – Jacob has done a great job. Fabulous arrangements of lilies and roses and orchids perfume the cool air. The space where Marcus and his Best Man should be is empty. It's true. Marcus has run out on me.

'Where is he?' I say to no one in particular as I wheel round. 'Where's that bloody bastard gone?'

That stops the organist in his tracks. The 'Wedding March' grinds to an abrupt halt. Our guests fidget furtively in their seats.

My mother is at my side. 'He was here on time,' she sniffles. 'He looked so lovely.' More tears.

I'm sure he did. Marcus always suited morning dress. Just looks as if he was allergic to wearing it at his own wedding.

'Then when you were late,' my mother continues, 'he suddenly announced that he couldn't go through with it and left.'

'What a tosser!'

She tries to take my hand. 'Don't upset yourself, Lucy.'

'I'm not upset,' I cry, snatching my hand away. 'I'm fucking *furious*! He couldn't wait twenty minutes? We were supposed to spend the rest of our lives together and he couldn't wait for twenty frigging minutes!' I gesticulate at the church, at the wonderfulness of it. 'All this – and he couldn't wait for me?'

'How could he do this to us?' Mum sobs. 'I can't believe it.'

Unfortunately, in a dark part of my heart, I can believe it. I *can* believe that Marcus could do this.

My mum is at a loss for words; she melts into the background and I'm suddenly surrounded by my best girls. They form a huddle around me. None of us speak, we just hold each other.

'Fuck,' Chantal says eventually. 'It's been a hell of a morning.'

I feel a smile form on my face at the same time as the tears flow. A giggle chokes up into my throat. They all join in. 'That wanker,' I say through my tears. 'How could he leave me in the lurch like this?'

Autumn wraps her arm around me. 'This is all my fault,' she says miserably. 'I feel so terrible.'

'Nonsense,' I say crisply. 'This isn't down to you. For goodness' sake, I could have had a wardrobe malfunction with my bra or my shoes or my hair – anything – and that would have made me twenty minutes late. It doesn't matter one jot what caused the delay.' Although I realise we are quite lucky not to be in the nick looking forward to porridge for breakfast. 'If Marcus can change his mind in that short space of time, then he doesn't deserve me anyway.'

'Good girl,' Nadia says. 'That's the spirit. Now you've got to face this lot. Stiff upper lip. We can help you through it. There'll be time for tears later.'

I brush my eyes with the back of my hand. 'I'm not going to cry over Marcus,' I say steadily. 'This wedding is going to go ahead,' I laugh again – a bit on the hysterical side. 'We're just going to have to skip the church part.'

The girls look at me, bemused.

'Are you absolutely sure?' Nadia asks. 'No one will expect you to stay around. We can go off quietly somewhere.'

'There's a chocolate fountain waiting in that hotel,' I say, pointing in the general direction of where the reception is to be held. 'There's no way I'm going to miss that.' In fact, I intend to make myself heartily sick with it. 'I want everyone to come. Everyone.

271

Even Marcus's bunch.' Most of the guests are Marcus's family, anyway. Currently, they're trying to sneak out of the pews without me spotting them. I don't hold any of this against them. Marcus might be related to them, but I'm damn sure that none of them are feeling any particular familial warmth towards him at the moment.

'Some of these people have come a long way.' Some of them will have bought new frocks. I feel a pang of anger at Marcus for putting them through this. For putting *me* through this! I would have walked through fire for that man, and this is how he's repaid me.

Dragging myself back to my present crisis, I say, 'They can't go home without being fed.' There's a mountain of food waiting for us up at the Manor House and there's no way they're going to give Marcus a refund on it. Though his relatives better not hog the chocolate fountain or there will be trouble.

'You must go out and tell them for me.' I grasp Chantal and Nadia's hands. 'The rest of my wedding is going ahead, come hell or high water. We are all going to go and have a great time. At Marcus's expense. It's a shame he won't be here to enjoy it.' I take a deep shuddering breath. 'With or without Marcus, life goes on.'

And, at this moment, I truly believe that.

Chapter Seventy-One

'You're being very brave.' Jacob slides into the chair next to me. He takes my hand and squeezes it.

'This is a lovely wedding, Jacob,' I tell him truthfully. 'You've surpassed yourself. I hope that you'll double your bill when you send it to Marcus.'

He laughs gently. 'You're a lovely lady,' he says. 'Marcus must be mad.'

'Yadda, yadda,' I say. If too many more people tell me how lovely I am or how mad Marcus must be, then I will be bawling my head off very soon. As it is, I'm extremely pissed and that seems to be helping to numb the pain. 'You promised me a wedding that no one would forget. Well, I've certainly had that.'

'I didn't mean it quite this way.'

'I'm enjoying it anyway,' I tell him. And, bizarrely, I am. I even opted to stay in my wedding dress, complete with beautiful, sparkly tiara and veil. I have to face it, this might be my only chance to wear a dress like this so I may as well make the best of it.

The room looks beautiful. Each table is decorated with lavish arrangements of white flowers, and a bunch of helium balloons anchored by chocolate-coloured ribbons stretches towards the ceiling, bobbing gently in the warm air.

Most of Marcus's relations have come along to the reception. One or two cried off, but most people have girded their loins and come along to the 'celebration'. Some of them look like they want to keep an eye on what's happening to their presents and I guess that I'll have to work out how to make sure everyone gets their gifts back in due course.

Marcus's parents looked wracked with anxiety, but other than that everyone seems to be having a good time. Jacob quickly reorganised the seating plan so that the absence of a groom on the top table was less noticeable. My parents and Marcus's parents have been relegated to lower tables and now the members of The Chocolate Lovers' Club are flanking me on either side and I know that I wouldn't have been able to get through this without them. As always, they have been there just when I needed them.

We're halfway through the wedding breakfast, and I'd like to be able to say that I haven't managed to eat a thing or that I picked delicately at my food while looking wan. But, frankly, after all the excitement and trauma, I'm as hungry as a horse and I've woofed everything down in sight and have thoroughly enjoyed it all. Very little puts me off my food. The smoked salmon mousse was divine, the chicken – exquisite. I've eaten my way through more chocolate desserts than I care to count, even though there is still the chocolate fountain to come this evening, and now the calories are straining manfully against the confines of my dress. Wonderful!

I glance at my best girls and they're all looking happy. Like me, they have had an awful lot of champagne. Except Chantal, of course. Though I'm not sure how she's managing this day without the aid of strong drink. Secretly, I think they're relieved that I haven't married Marcus even though the circumstances are quite traumatic. I'm also pleased to see that Addison has turned up at the wedding, much to Autumn's delight. I hope everything will work out for them as they make such a great couple. Ted's here too – though he's looking a little tense. I've asked Jacob to make sure that everyone's glass remains permanently topped up. I don't want anyone sober enough to remember that this isn't really a wedding at all. Most of all me. So I knock back some more champagne.

We're going to skip the speeches – which my dad is heartily relieved about. It seems almost worth his daughter being stood up at the altar to avoid that particular embarrassment, and I wonder why we go through these terrible rituals that none of us enjoy in the name of tradition. Maybe if Marcus and I had sneaked away somewhere quiet by ourselves to get married then he might not have freaked out at the last minute. I always knew, in my heart of hearts, that a grand bash like this was a really bad idea.

My mobile phone vibrates, making my little silk purse hop about the table. I pick it up. There's a text message waiting for me. It's from Marcus, and all it says is SORRY.

'From Marcus,' I say to Jacob and I hand him the phone.

He reads the message. 'Prat,' he says with feeling. 'Where do you think he's gone?'

'Not very far.' Then a thought goes through my mind. I take my napkin from my lap and put it on the table. 'Excuse me, Jacob,' I say. 'I'll be back in just a moment.'

Chapter Seventy-Two

I don't know why I didn't think of this before. Taking the lift up to the fourth floor, I find Marcus's room and knock on the door.

'Hello.' Sure enough, Marcus's voice comes from inside. It was only when Jacob asked me where Marcus might be, that I realised he could still well be in the hotel, holed up in his room, hiding.

'It's me,' I say. 'Can I come in?'

There's silence and then a moment later, Marcus opens the door. His eyes are red from crying. 'My God,' he says flatly. 'You look fabulous.'

Then I realise that he hasn't yet seen me in my wedding dress. 'Thanks.'

He moves aside as I step past him in my beautiful silk slippers. Marcus is still wearing his morning dress, though his cravat and morning coat are abandoned on the bed. His suitcase is there too.

Marcus studies me intently, and his eyes fill with tears again. 'I seriously messed up this time.'

'Yes,' I agree. 'You did.'

He rakes his hands through his hair. 'How could I do this?'

I sit down on the edge of Marcus's bed near his case. 'It's a question that a lot of our guests are asking.'

'Lucy, Lucy, Lucy,' he says. 'How much have I hurt you this time?'

'Quite a lot,' I tell him.

'You'll never forgive me. Will you?'

'Oh Marcus,' I sigh. 'I always forgive you. I always have a list of excuses ready to explain away your bad behaviour.'

'But not this time?'

'This time, it would be fair to say that I'm struggling a little.'

'I panicked,' Marcus admits.

'At the thought of spending the rest of your life with me?'

'No. No.' He rubs his hands over his face. 'Well, maybe that was part of it. Christ, I saw everyone standing there waiting, waiting. There was so much expectation in their faces. They were waiting for me to do this momentous thing. I thought about what it might be like to be married and I couldn't do it. I just couldn't, Lucy. I don't know why. It was the thought of ending up like our parents, like the divorced guys in my office. Half of the bloody congregation sitting there were on second, even third marriages. I didn't think that I could be a husband, after all. It was all too much.'

'You could have waited for me outside the church and we could have talked about it,' I say quietly.

He hangs his head. 'That would have been the mature and sensible thing to do.'

'Yes.' It doesn't occur to Marcus that I might have been having my own doubts and insecurities. Perhaps if I hadn't had the distraction of a drugs drop with my best girls then I would have had more time to reflect on whether *I* actually wanted to go through with our marriage or not.

Marcus comes to kneel at my feet. 'I can make this up to you.'

'I don't think so,' I say firmly.

'I love you.' His expression is bleak. 'This isn't because I don't love you. Don't think that. *Please* don't think that.'

'If you really love me, Marcus, then you'll pick up all the bills for today's fiasco and you'll let me move on.'

'It's the least I can do,' he says. 'The bills, I mean. But you . . . how do I get you back? I don't want to live my life without you.' He runs his hands over my legs, taking in the silkiness of my dress. 'Tell me what to do.'

'Look.' I let out a shuddering exhalation. 'There's a great party going on downstairs. You're paying for it all. Come and join us.'

'I can't.'

'No one will blame you.' Well, my mother might. 'They'll get over it. You can't hide from them for ever.'

'I can't. I can't face anyone.' I don't remind him that by rights it should be me who's hiding away, weeping and wailing, but I can't find any more tears for Marcus.

'Then you should finish packing your bags and leave,' I say. 'Take the tickets for the honeymoon and go on it, otherwise you'll lose the money for that too. See if you can find someone to go with you.'

I'm thinking along the lines of his Best Man, but I wonder if Marcus is already mentally scanning the contents of his little black BlackBerry.

There's a spark of hope in his eyes. 'We could go together. I've booked the most fabulous place in Mauritius.'

Mauritius. I've always wanted to go there.

'We have a bungalow over the water, our own hot tub. We're flying first-class and I've organised champagne and chocolates for the plane.'

Mmm. Champagne and chocolates on a first-class flight. How tempting does that sound?

'It will be fabulous,' he entreats.

'It does sound wonderful,' I have to agree.

A faint smile lights up his tear-stained face.

'There's just one snag, Marcus,' I say, as I stand up. 'I don't want to be with you.'

Marcus looks as if I've slapped him. With a deep breath, I reorganise my train and head for the door. 'Be happy, Marcus.'

My ex-boyfriend, ex-fiancé and my ever-so-nearly husband folds to the floor. 'What have I done?' Marcus cries after me in anguish. 'What have I done?'

'You fucked up big time,' I tell him, and I close the door behind me.

Chapter Seventy-Three

The tables were being cleared and the disco had already started up. Chantal had certainly eaten enough of the delicious chocolate desserts for two – maybe even three or four. She hoped that being a chocoholic was hereditary as she wouldn't want to deny her daughter this pleasure. Leaning against Ted, she smiled up at him. 'Wanna take me on a tour of the dance floor?'

Ted toyed with his champagne flûte. 'Are they playing our tune?'

'I'm not sure what our tune is,' she said. 'Did we ever have one?' Perhaps that had been a fault in their relationship – not enough sharing. Weren't couples supposed to share their hopes, their dreams? With luck, she'd have the opportunity to correct that.

Ted might be seeing someone else, but Chantal viewed it as a good sign that her husband had chosen to come along to Lucy's wedding today. Even though, technically, it couldn't be classed as a wedding any more. Chantal thought that Lucy had coped wonderfully and she wondered whether she would have been so strong in the same situation.

Jacob came and rested his hands on the back of their chairs and spoke to Chantal. 'Everything okay?'

'Wedding or not,' she said, as she turned round and smiled at him, 'this is a great party.'

'Yeah,' he replied. 'I hope that Lucy will consider me for her next wedding.'

'Next time that girl tells me she's going to get married, I'm going to knock her flat.'

Jacob grinned. 'I can't say that I blame you.'

Next to her, she was aware that Ted was fidgeting uncomfortably. 'This is my husband, Ted,' she said to Jacob. 'Ted, this is Jacob, the wedding planner.'

Ted shook his hand.

'Nice to meet you, Ted.'

Her husband didn't reciprocate the greeting.

'Catch you later,' Jacob said. As he was moving away, he winked at her. 'Save a dance for me.'

Ted's frown deepened as he watched Jacob cross the room. 'You know that guy?'

'A little,' Chantal said, not meeting his eyes. This wasn't the time to confess that she'd been intimately involved with Jacob. And had paid handsomely for the privilege. Though, even with the fallout, she still considered it money well spent. 'We've done some business together.'

'Really? What kind of business?'

'Come on.' Avoiding the question, Chantal took her husband by the hand. 'I don't want to talk about work right now. You can show me some of your moves instead.' She led him to the dance floor, strutting her stuff in front of him as she led the way. It was amazing that he still hadn't noticed how well she was filling out her bridesmaid's dress. Maybe that was down to Jacob's excellent choice of a flattering style, or maybe it was still down to the fact that her husband didn't look at her too closely these days.

She couldn't say that she felt the same indifference. Ted looked great today. He was wearing a charcoal-grey suit with a crisp white shirt – she thought that he'd look much better out of it. She'd booked a double room for them tonight, hoping against hope that he might stay over with her. Were pregnant women supposed to still want to seduce their husbands? She didn't know.

Obligingly, the music was slow, a tune she didn't recognise, and she wrapped her arms around Ted. Surely now, her husband would realise that her bump wasn't just down to an excess of chocolate brownies.

They did a couple of turns round the dance floor and Ted

started to relax; his arms loosened around her. The music grew sexier.

'This is nice,' Ted said. 'Why did we stop doing this?' He pulled her closer. It was her now or never moment.

'Ted,' Chantal said softly. 'I've got something to tell you.'

'Mmm,' he said against her hair.

'You're going to be a daddy.'

He recoiled in horror. 'How did you know?'

They both stood stock still on the dance floor and dropped their arms from each other. Other couples brushed by them.

'The usual way,' she said with a nervous laugh. 'I got the results of the pregnancy test.'

Her husband blanched. 'From Stacey?'

'From me!' Chantal took a step back and gave him a bewildered look. 'Who the heck's Stacey?'

Chapter Seventy-Four

'I'm so glad that you came,' Autumn said, tracing a finger over Addison's cheek.

Her boyfriend held her tighter as they circled the dance floor. 'I couldn't stay angry with you,' he said. 'I know how difficult it is for you to say no to your brother. It was wrong of me to leave you alone after I'd promised to look out for you. I had to make sure that you were okay.'

'That's it,' she assured him. 'No more of Rich's dirty work. It could have all gone so terribly wrong. There's no way I should have done that delivery today. It was madness.'

'At least you had the foresight and the conscience to tip off the police.'

'I had no idea how bad it might be. I feel so stupid and naïve. I put myself at risk. I put my friends at risk.' She bit down on her lip. 'It may well have been my fault that Lucy's wedding didn't take place.'

'Sounds like you've done her a favour,' Addison said.

'None of us wanted her to marry Marcus,' Autumn admitted. 'But none of us wanted it to turn out like this for her either.'

'She seems to be coping very well.'

'I haven't seen her for a while.' Autumn scanned the room. 'I should go and look for her, make sure she's all right.'

'I love the fact that you care so much for other people,' Addison said. 'But don't forget me sometimes.'

'From now on, you're going to be my top priority. I promise.' She kissed Addison on the lips. 'I told Richard that once I'd completed this business he was on his own. And I mean it. There's just one last thing . . .' Her boyfriend didn't look surprised. 'They gave me a huge bag of money, Addison. I have no idea how much is in there.'

'Where is it?'

'It's upstairs in my room, squashed into the safe. I don't know what to do with it. Technically, I suppose it belongs to Richard, but I don't want to give it to him. If he's got a bag full of cash then that will only start him on the same route again. I have to think very carefully about where it goes.'

Addison put a finger to her lips. 'Don't worry about that today. I'm sure you'll think of something. We should just be glad that you're safe and that it's over. And we should help Lucy to celebrate her non-wedding and have a great time.'

'It's so much better with you here,' she said.

Her boyfriend took in her caramel-coloured bridesmaid's dress. 'This kind of get-up suits you.'

'You think so?'

'Hmm.' He smiled at her. 'Do you think my family would get used to me marrying a rich, white, older, upper-class woman?'

Autumn laughed. 'Do you think my parents would get used to me marrying a poor, black, younger, youth worker?'

'I guess if we gave them enough notice they'd both learn to live with it.'

She looked up at him. 'Is that a proposal, Addison Deacon?'

'I think it might well be,' he said. 'Just promise me one thing. If we get married . . .'

'*When* we get married,' she corrected.

'. . . please don't organise to do a drugs run for your brother just before we're due to tie the knot.'

'*That*, I can very safely promise you,' she said.

Chapter Seventy-Five

Nadia didn't know whether she was upset for herself, upset for her friend or upset for all the miserable, terrible, traumatic things that happened in life in general. All she knew was that she'd been hiding away in the ladies' loos now for the best part of fifteen minutes crying her heart out. She'd managed to get through most of the day without resorting to painkillers, antidepressants or – with the exception of a few glasses of champagne – a surfeit of booze. Now it all seemed a bit too much for her. Every damn slushy song that the DJ played reminded her of Toby and the happier times they'd had together. Mind you, her wedding day hadn't been quite as glamorous as Lucy's, but at least the groom had turned up. Her heart went out to her friend. Life was, most of the time, so bloody unfair. Nadia sat on the loo seat and ripped another handful of paper from the dispenser to sob into.

A minute later, she heard the door burst open and a familiar voice shout, 'Mummy!' Lewis's small, determined footsteps crossed the tiles. 'Mummy, are you in here?'

She sniffed into the tissue. 'Yes, darling. In here. I won't be a minute.'

'I didn't know where you'd gone,' her son said crossly.

Nadia flushed the loo, pointlessly, and then opened the door. She forced a smile onto her face. 'Here I am. I left you with Aunty Autumn. What are you doing in here?'

'She was dancing with Addison, so I sneaked away to look for you,' he confessed.

She knelt in front of her son and smoothed his mad hair from his forehead. 'You shouldn't do that,' she told him. 'But I'm glad that you found me.'

'This is a nice party. I've had lots of chocolate.'

Like mother, like son. He'd probably be bouncing off the walls later from all that sugar. They were sharing a room and it looked unlikely that she'd get any sleep tonight. Still, it wouldn't hurt for once. Nadia laughed despite her concerns. 'Yes, it's very nice.'

Lewis tugged at the neck of his smart shirt. He looked quite the little man dressed up like that. 'If it's nice, why are you crying?'

She was about to tell Lewis that she wasn't crying, but her red eyes and blotchy cheeks would be a dead giveaway. Her son might only be four, but he was as cute as they come. Even at his tender age, he'd know that she was lying. Yet how could she begin to explain to Lewis that she was feeling raw with pain at the loss of her husband, her love? This was the first function she'd had to attend without her partner by her side and, though she wouldn't have missed it for the world, it had been difficult to hold it all together – particularly when the day hadn't quite gone according to plan.

She wondered what was going on in her son's head. Was he missing his dad as much as she was? Lewis was coping incredibly well since Toby died, but she was sure that inside, he was hurting. He'd hardly cried at all and rarely mentioned his father – surely that wasn't good for him? How did a child assimilate such a devastating emotion as grief? If only she knew what her son was thinking, perhaps she could help him through this. 'Mummy's just a bit sad.'

'Because Daddy isn't here?'

Nadia nodded. 'I miss your daddy very much, every day.'

'Daddy isn't coming back from heaven, is he?'

'No, sweetheart.' She gave him a comforting squeeze. 'It's just me and you now.'

'We'll be all right together, Mummy.' Her son leaned against her and slipped his thumb into his mouth, something she hadn't see him do for a long time. 'I'll look after you.'

'Then I've nothing to be sad about.' Nadia hugged him to her.

'Daddy would have liked all the chocolate today.'

'Yes,' Nadia agreed. 'He would have.' Looking at her son's anxious

285

little face, she knew that she had to stay strong for him. Nadia ran a thumb gently over his cheek. 'You know we can talk about Daddy anytime that you want to. Whenever you're missing him, we just have to say things about him – things that he would have liked, things he would have done and that'll make us feel better.'

'Okay.' Lewis shrugged. It seemed a simple enough solution to her son. Perhaps it was. 'Can we go back to the party?'

'Will you dance with Mummy?'

'Do you think the man will play "Bob the Builder"?'

'Maybe not,' Nadia said. 'I was hoping for some George Michael myself.'

'Who?' Lewis said, looking disgusted.

Chapter Seventy-Six

The party is in full swing by the time I come down from Marcus's room. I try not to think of him packing his bag alone, going on our honeymoon without me. The music is pumping out, the dance floor is full, people are getting leery – to all intents and purposes it looks just like a regular wedding. With one notable exception, of course.

My mum and dad are dancing together – which is something of a miracle as they never danced together when they were married. They're strutting their stuff to 'I Will Survive' – a good wedding stalwart – and my mother is singing the words rather too enthusiastically. The Millionaire and The Hairdresser are nowhere to be seen. Clive and Tristan sweep up to me. They both look resplendent and screamingly gay in matching cream linen suits and chocolate brown shirts. They are the Elton John and David Furnish of the chocolate world. I wonder if all this wedding lark is making them think about tying the knot. 'Darling,' Clive says, 'how are you bearing up?'

'I'm doing okay,' I tell them with a considered nod.

'Don't suppose that you'll want to cut our fabulous cake?'

'Why not? Am I likely to miss out on the opportunity for chocolate cake?' I give a shrug. I'll probably skip the tossing of the bouquet, but I'm game for everything else.

Clive grins gratefully. Frankly, I could do with a sugar rush after all this trauma. Plus, my dear friends and chocolatiers have created a five-tier monster of a cake for me as my wedding present – chocolate, of course, and decorated with white chocolate leaves and crystallised kumquats. How can I not cut it? 'Find me a sharp knife, make sure Marcus is kept well out of the way of it and let's do it.'

Clive gives me a hug. 'That's the spirit.'

Five minutes later and Jacob comes to find me. He has the sharp knife. His brow is lined with concern. 'Are you sure this is a good idea?'

'It will make Clive and Tris very happy,' I tell him. 'Besides, I'd hate to see this beautiful cake go to waste. Our guests might as well enjoy it.'

'I could have it quietly taken away and cut up,' he suggests.

'No. Let's make a bit of a fuss. Clive has gone to a lot of trouble to make it. It feels wrong to sneak it out and for him to miss his moment of glory.'

'If you're sure,' he says.

I nod.

'Then I'll make the announcement.' Jacob goes to take the microphone. 'Ladies and gentlemen,' he says. 'Please gather round for the cutting of the cake.'

Only when I'm safely ensconced next to the cake does Jacob hand me the knife. The photographer has been dispensed with, so there's no posing for ridiculous photographs. 'Clive.' I beckon my friend towards me. 'Come and do this with me.'

My friend folds his fingers over mine and, teasingly, looks into my eyes as if he loves me. I only get a momentary pang of what might have been, if Marcus had been here cutting the cake with me. We push the knife into the glorious icing and soft sponge and earn an uncertain cheer from our guests. Then, out of the corner of my eye, I see a sight that makes my blood run cold.

'Oh no,' I say. Clive looks up and follows my gaze. He gasps out loud. As do all the guests still standing in a circle after the cake cutting.

Coming into the room, wearing a pink satin basque, flowing skirt and killer heels is Raunchy Roberta – six statuesque feet of drag queen, here at my wedding. I recognise him/her as the compère from Mistress Jay's nightclub even though his wig is a different colour.

Raunchy Roberta goes up to Tristan and flings his arms around him. Tristan looks more than a little surprised as Roberta gives him a long, slobbering kiss.

'Euuw!' I turn to Clive, whose face has gone very dark. He's clutching the knife menacingly. I take it from him gingerly.

'Excuse me, Lucy,' Clive says tightly and he marches over to where Tristan and Roberta are taking a breather from their embrace.

'What's she, *he* doing here?' Clive hisses at Tristan. Hisses loud enough for everyone to hear.

'I didn't want you to find out like this,' Tristan says dramatically.

'Don't you think that I'd guessed?' Clive wants to know. 'All those clandestine disappearances – do you think I'm a fool?'

'Yes,' Raunchy Roberta says in a remarkably gruff voice. 'Now clear off.'

'Make me,' Clive, rather unwisely, says.

Raunchy Roberta, it has to be said, has a mean right hook. He punches Clive on the jaw and my friend staggers backwards, looking rather shocked and heading towards the cake. The table on which it's standing wobbles alarmingly. Jacob and I exchange a worried look. One of the legs holding up the tiers shakes too much and then collapses. The tier slides graciously out of line and then knocks against the tier below until they're all unstable. Jacob and I make a valiant dive to save the cake and fail. The tiers cascade to the floor in a shower of crystallised kumquats, chocolate leaves and chunks of featherlight sponge.

I pick a lump of chocolate icing from the tablecloth. 'Mmm. This is very good,' I tell Jacob as I lick my fingers.

Tristan leaps forward and dashes to Clive's aid. 'Are you hurt? Are you hurt?'

'Of course I'm *fucking* hurt!' Clive shouts. 'I've never been so hurt. That's it. You can get out. Get out of my chocolate shop. Get out of my life. Get out and take that big butch bastard with you.' With that, he bends down, picks up the top tier of my lovely chocolatey wedding cake which has fallen next to his feet and then he smashes it into Tristan's face, rubbing the crumbs in firmly for extra effect. My assembled guests gasp again with horror.

As Raunchy Roberta lurches forward and lunges again for Clive, he slips on the mess of chocolate cake on the floor, twists his ankle in his deadly stiletto heels, one of them snaps and Roberta goes arse over tit. With a hefty thump, the drag queen extraordinaire ends up sprawled on his back with his pink basque askew, his falsies popped out and his wig lopsided. It's not a pretty sight. I can't, at this moment, appreciate what Tristan sees in him. Then Clive bursts into tears.

Jacob and I look at each other again. 'Perhaps cutting the wedding cake wasn't such a great idea,' I say.

Chapter Seventy-Seven

After the eventful cutting of the cake, Chantal and Ted found a quiet corner away from the fray in which to talk. Despite being pregnant, Chantal was longing for a glass of champagne or any form of alcohol. There are some conversations that shouldn't be faced on mineral water alone.

They now sat on a Chesterfield in a small private lounge which was relatively peaceful. Finally, they were alone and the music from the disco had faded to an irritating background thrum, competing with some twinkly piano music from the hotel sound system. Ted swigged at his champagne and avoided her eyes. 'So how long have you known you were pregnant?'

'A month or more,' Chantal said.

'And you didn't tell me?'

'I tried,' she said, 'but I could never find the right moment. And you did spend a lot of time avoiding me.'

Ted hung his head.

'How long have you known that there was another baby on the way?'

'Around the same amount of time.' He finished his champagne and topped up the glass from a bottle he'd purloined. 'I told you that I'd had a fling,' he said. 'Well, it was one or two.'

'Anyone I know?'

Her husband shook his head. 'Mainly women from work. One more serious than the others.'

'Stacey?'

'Stacey,' he confirmed. 'She's very nice.'

'If she's going to be the mother of your child, I'm glad to hear it.'

'The thing is,' Ted said, 'we're no longer in a relationship. She's a fine young woman, but too needy. She wanted me to be everything to her and I hadn't realised how much I liked the fact that you were so independent.'

'Maybe a little *too* independent.'

'I wanted to sleep with other women,' Ted confessed. 'I wanted to see how it felt. Level the playing-field. It was a mistake. It didn't make me feel better about myself. All the time that I was with them, no matter how hard I tried, I just realised that I wanted to be with you.' He shrugged. 'And now there's a baby on the way.'

'Actually, there are two.'

'Two babies.' Ted gave a snort. 'What is it the Brits say? They're like buses – first you can't get one and then two come along at once.'

'Do you know for sure that Stacey's child is yours?'

'Christ,' Ted said. 'I think so. How do you know these days? She could have three other guys on the go and I'd be none the wiser.'

Chantal decided to keep quiet.

'I have to ask this, Chantal.' Ted turned towards her. 'Is *your* baby mine?'

'Truthfully?'

'It's usually the best way,' her husband advised. Chantal had found that it wasn't always so.

'I don't know,' she said. 'I believe it is. We can only find out for certain after the birth.' If there was any way of willing this child into being the fruit of Ted's loins then she damn well would. 'I'll get a DNA test as soon as possible. It carries more risks to the baby to have one before it's born and I don't want to do anything that might harm it.' She folded her hands protectively over her stomach. 'The baby's a little girl. A daughter.'

Tears filled her husband's eyes. 'This is all I ever wanted, Chantal.'

'I wish you'd said earlier,' she said with a tired laugh. 'Maybe we could have saved ourselves a whole heap of trouble. Now it looks like you're gonna get a double helping, Daddy.'

'I have one other question,' Ted said. 'That guy, the wedding planner. Did you have an affair with him?'

Chantal felt a flush come to her cheeks.

'There's a chemistry between you. A chemistry that only comes with being intimate with someone. I see that in his eyes.'

Jeez, if only her husband was always so observant. He couldn't spot that she was four months' pregnant, yet he could tell that there was a spark between her and Jacob.

'Could it be his child?'

'It's unlikely,' Chantal said. 'He knows nothing about this. We had a very brief liaison.'

'And you're just friends now?'

'Just friends,' she confirmed. There was no need to tell Ted that she'd thoroughly enjoyed her time with Jacob – even though the cost, in more ways than one, had been astronomically high.

'I'd like us to stay friends too,' he said.

'I'm still hoping that we can get back together,' Chantal said.

'Even after everything that's happened?'

She patted her stomach. '*Especially* after everything that's happened.'

Chapter Seventy-Eight

'Bloody hell,' I say with a hearty sigh. 'I needed to get away from that lot.' I've abandoned the frantic atmosphere of the disco and have come in search of sanctuary and five minutes' peace. I don't know quite how I managed to get through this day, but I'm at the point where I think I might like it to end. Marcus's relatives – having decided to stick it out – are now showing no signs of wanting to go home.

'Come and join us, Lucy.' Chantal pats a chair next to her.

Gratefully, I flop down in the chair next to Chantal, who I've found hiding away in a little lounge with her hubby.

'I was just going. I'll leave you ladies to it,' Ted says, rising. He kisses me on the cheek. 'Great wedding, Lucy.'

'Thanks.'

Ted, as promised, leaves us to it. With a moan of pleasure, Chantal kicks off her shoes and lets her head fall back, then stretches out, so that her feet rest on the seat opposite her. 'All this emotion is taking its toll,' she tells me.

'Tell me about it.' I, too, kick off my shoes and, rearranging my wedding dress, curl my legs under me. 'Let's text the others. See if we can all steal a few minutes alone. I'm missing my girls.' I punch CHOCOLATE EMERGENCY into my phone and the name of the lounge that we're in.

Minutes later, Nadia and Autumn have tracked us down. 'Look what I've found,' Nadia announces as she comes in. She's bearing a tray loaded with the remnants of my wedding cake.

'You didn't pick it up off the floor?' I want to know.

'No,' she says. 'But we'd still eat it anyway, right?'

We all nod our agreement. A little bit of carpet fluff wouldn't detract from the superb taste of chocolate, would it? Autumn is bearing a bottle of champagne and some glasses. She hands out the flûtes, pops the cork and pours. Even Chantal takes one. 'This kid can cope with a few sips,' she says. 'After the discussion I've just had with Ted, I need it.'

'I didn't interrupt anything important, did I?' Come to think of it, they did look very cosy when I found them and, of course, I just blundered on in.

She shakes her head. 'He'd just finished telling me that he's going to be a daddy.'

We all look at her, puzzled. 'We know that.'

'By a woman other than my good self.'

'We didn't know that!' we all say.

'Well,' Chantal says, 'it was news to me too.'

'How do you feel about it, Chantal?' Autumn asks.

'Surprisingly calm,' she admits. 'I took his announcement well. He took mine well.' She shrugs her shoulders. 'Though quite where we go from here is anyone's guess.'

'This is definitely, *definitely* a chocolate cake moment,' I say. And, duly, we all tuck in.

'How's Clive?' Chantal asks.

'Crying in the toilets,' I tell her. 'The *ladies*' toilets. Marcus's mum is currently wiping his tears.'

'Poor Clive,' Nadia says.

'Poor Tristan, more like,' I chip in. 'Looks to me like that Raunchy Roberta will make mincemeat of him.'

We all laugh. Chantal shakes her head. 'Last I saw of them, Roberta was manhandling Tris out of the front door.'

'This has been a very interesting wedding,' I say, noting that Marcus hasn't really been missed that much. 'I can't wait for the next one.'

Then Autumn, who with her red curls and her freckles would never have the right complexion for a poker player, goes bright red.

We all wait expectantly. Our friend squirms in her seat and blushes a bit more. 'I think Addison might have asked me to marry him.'

'You *think* he did?'

She nods. 'And I think I said yes.'

'Yeeeeeees!' We all let out a cheer.

'I have to check with him,' she said. 'When we're both sober. It was a very casual proposal.'

'Casual or not, we're damn well toasting it!' I tell her.

Nadia sploshes some more champagne in all of our glasses and we raise them to Autumn.

'To Autumn and Addison,' Chantal proposes. 'May your wedding be less "interesting" than Lucy's!'

'To Autumn and Addison,' we all echo. More wedding cake is consumed.

'If you do it quickly,' Nadia suggests, 'we could all wear the same bridesmaid's dresses.'

'I'm not going to fit into mine for much longer,' Chantal reminds us.

Me neither. My diet starts tomorrow. In earnest. No more chocolate . . . Ye gods! What am I saying! How could I manage without chocolate – particularly in my current emotional state? Chocolate is all that I have. Maybe I'll just give up all other food-stuffs instead. There must be a chocolate lovers' diet out there? Surely you could lose weight on just three, or perhaps four, Mars Bars a day?

While I'm still trying to work out my calorific requirements to survive, Nadia takes my hand. 'You've done so well today, Lucy,' she tells me. 'We're all very proud of you.'

'Life goes on,' I say. 'I might not have Marcus, but I have my friends and I have chocolate.'

'To friends and to chocolate,' Chantal says, and we all raise our glasses again.

'And you have Crush,' Autumn says.

Crush. My heart lets out a sigh. The day has been so manic that I've barely had time to allow my thoughts to go there. Letting my mind drift, I wonder where Mr Aiden Holby is right now. I should call him and tell him about the wedding that never was. He probably won't want to hear from me, but I owe him that much.

'You should call him,' Nadia says, echoing my thoughts.

'Later,' I tell her. I need time to work out what I'm going to say to him and my brain's far too whirry now – not to mention a little drunker than is appropriate for rational thought. 'Now I should be getting back to my guests.'

Nadia makes to stand up. 'I should be going too. I've left Lewis with Jacob. He's a really nice guy.'

None of us can argue with that. 'You're coping really well too, Nadia,' I say.

'I am,' she says proudly. 'I'm going to be okay.'

'We'll make sure that you are,' Chantal adds.

'What a truly resilient bunch we are,' I note.

'I'll drink to that,' Nadia says, and we all clink our glasses together again.

For good measure I steal another piece of chocolate cake and cram it in on top of the rest. Sod the diet. Curves will eventually come back into fashion.

'Come on then,' I say, jumping from my chair. 'We've got a sugar high to dance off. Let's hit that party.'

Chapter Seventy-Nine

We're all in the corridor, holding hands, giggling and heading back to the action. There's a man in a smart dark suit striding purposefully towards us, head down. We ease to one side as he gets near to us and he looks up to say thanks.

Then he does a double-take. 'You!' he shouts out as he recognises us. He stands back to get a better view and, waving his finger at us all, he shouts again: *'You!'*

Ohmigod. This is what I'd feared most for my wedding day – the thought that Marcus might abandon me had never crossed my mind, but I always dreaded bumping into this man.

Last time I was at Trington Manor with the members of The Chocolate Lovers' Club we were committing a cunning heist – retrieving Chantal's jewellery from a charming conman who'd shagged her and then stolen all her stuff. That same man – he of the awful alias, Mr John Smith, Gentleman Thief, is standing in front of us.

We all gasp out loud. I knew it was a really, really bad idea to hold the reception here.

The man takes in our wedding garb. His face has gone an unattractive shade of thundercloud. 'You robbed me, you bitches,' he yells. 'You drugged me. You destroyed my car.'

I'd forgotten about that bit. We found all of Chantal's belongings in the boot of his Merc and then, well, we pushed it into the lake. It seemed like a really, really good idea at the time.

'I think that I'd call it quits,' Chantal informs him coldly. 'You had it coming to you.' She's sounding like a gangsta – mean and moody, particularly for a pregnant person.

He's advancing on us, menacingly.

'Quick,' Nadia says, and she grabs him. I throw my little silk bag to the floor and join in. Chantal and Autumn do the same. Seconds later, after a bit of impromptu wrestling, the four of us have his arms pinned behind his back and he's struggling ferociously.

'What now?' Autumn says.

'In here.' Next to us is some sort of cupboard and I nod towards it. Chantal flings open the door. It's a small space stacked with towels and cleaning equipment with just enough extra room to store a conman. He's screaming and shouting abuse at us as we bundle him inside and close the door behind us all.

Chantal searches on the shelves and finds something that looks like a clothes-line. 'This will do nicely,' she says triumphantly. She must have been a Girl Scout in her formative years as she makes an excellent job of tying Mr Smith's hands and feet together.

Autumn finds a small towel with *Trington Manor* embroidered in the corner. She stuffs the bulk of it into Mr Smith's mouth and then ties the loose ends at the back of his head.

'Mtherfthin cnth,' he mutters darkly.

I think, transcribed, that would come out as a really rude statement.

Chantal puts a hand against the shelves and leans over our captive in a very threatening manner. 'Remember this,' she says tightly. 'I have all your details, Mr Felix Lavare.'

I'd forgotten that was his real name and that we actually knew it.

'When you get out of here, my advice is to leave this hotel straight away. Hightail it right outta here and don't look back. Give us any trouble and I'll go straight to the police. Understand?'

He stops struggling and there's a muffled, 'Eth,' from the depths of the towel.

'Now calm down like a good boy,' she tells him, 'and someone will let you out real soon.' Chantal gives his bonds the once-over again. Looking good.

Checking that the coast is clear, we all exit the cupboard. As a finishing touch, Autumn holds up a sign that says NOT IN

USE. 'Found this,' she says, speaking in a stage whisper. 'Thought it might come in useful.'

Our friend hangs it on the door knob at a jaunty angle. Tiptoeing away from the cupboard, we all huddle together. Nadia rubs her hands together in the manner of a job well done. 'Do you think that will hold him until we're out of here?'

'I hope so,' Chantal replies. 'Let's pray that the housekeeping staff don't need any fresh towels until the morning.'

'It's a quiet corridor, so not many people are likely to come this way,' I point out. 'I just hope there's no one waiting in his room for him.'

'The thought of it makes me shudder,' Chantal says.

'I just had a horrible thought too,' I say to my friend. 'That man could be the father of your child.'

'Don't remind me.' Chantal shivers. 'I hope to God that it's *anyone* but him.'

'Bloody hell,' I say. 'This is too much excitement for one day. My heart's still banging in my chest.'

'Mine too,' Chantal adds with a weary exhalation.

'My knees have turned to jelly,' Nadia says.

'Do you think he'll cause trouble for us?' Autumn, out of all of us, looks the most concerned.

Chantal shakes her head. 'Not if he knows what's good for him.'

'Collectively, we've had three run-ins with him so far. The score is two to the members of The Chocolate Lovers' Club and only one to the handsome criminal. I think he should realise that he's no match for us.'

We all enjoy a good laugh to relieve the pressure. 'I have to go back to the party,' I say. 'See what else has gone wrong in my absence. Come on.'

'You go on,' Chantal says. 'We'll be right behind you.'

'Don't be long,' I tell them. 'There's still a chocolate fountain for us to decimate.'

As I leave, I don't see my good friend bend down to pick up my little silk bag that I dropped in the struggle with Mr Smith.

300

The girls wait until I'm out of sight, then Chantal pulls my mobile phone out of it and brandishes it, gleefully, at the others.

'If Lucy won't phone Crush,' she says to Nadia and Autumn as she flicks through the list of numbers, 'then I think it's about time that we did.'

Chapter Eighty

'Thanks for looking after Lewis,' Nadia said to Jacob. Her son was on the dance floor, strutting his funky stuff with Jacob who was holding carefully onto his small charge's hands. One of them, she noted, had a very cute, wiggly bottom – and it wasn't necessarily her son. The sounds of Madonna's 'Like a Virgin' pumped out. The way her son was dancing, he didn't seem unduly worried that it wasn't 'Bob the Builder'.

'No worries,' Jacob said, slightly breathlessly.

'Come and sit down, Lewis,' Nadia said.

'Don't go yet,' Jacob urged. 'Let's all dance together.'

She shrugged her shoulders and smiled. 'Okay.' So she joined Jacob and her son, taking hold of one of Lewis's hands and not objecting when Jacob reached out and took her other one. They danced in a cosy circle to Britney Spears, Beyoncé and the Black-Eyed Peas. Laughing, Nadia felt freer than she'd done in months. Yes, she was grieving – but there was a release in there too after the stress of trying to deal with Toby's gambling. All that was finished. She had no need to worry now.

When the music slowed to Robbie Williams's 'Angels', Jacob pulled them both in close. He hoisted Lewis up to his shoulder and they huddled tightly together, both embracing her son as they moved slowly in time to the music. Jacob's hand rested lightly on her shoulder but Nadia could feel the heat from it. It felt so good to be touched by a man again. He wasn't coming on to her – there was nothing salacious in his touch, just warmth, caring and concern. She'd missed Toby so much today, but she'd managed to get through it all relatively unscathed. There would be hard days to come, no doubt, but she knew that she'd be able to cope. A tear came to her eye and she squeezed her son. She noticed that both of his arms were around Jacob's neck. Perhaps Lewis would miss a man in his life even more than she would.

Jacob ran his thumb tenderly under her jaw. 'Chin up,' he said softly. 'You'll both be fine.'

'We will,' she answered. 'It'll just take time.'

'If you ever need anything,' he said, 'you only have to ask. I know that you have all of your friends – and they're great. But there are some things for which you need a man.'

Nadia gave him a sideways glance. Maybe he was thinking of making a pass at her, after all.

'That came out wrong.' Jacob laughed. His eyes were sparkly, sincere. Nadia could see why Chantal had been tempted to pay handsomely for his services. She should ask her friend one day whether he was good value. 'I've definitely given up my old profession. What I meant to say was that I'm pretty handy with a hammer and a drill. I can lift heavy objects too.'

Nadia relaxed and laughed too. 'Always an attractive attribute in a man.'

'Just call me,' he said, 'if you ever need any help. As a friend – nothing more. No strings. I mean it.'

'I'll remember that,' she replied. He spun them both round again. Lewis shrieked with laughter. 'Thanks, Jacob.' Nadia reached up and kissed him lightly on the cheek. 'You're a really great guy.'

The tempo had been upped again and the dance floor was full. Now they were bopping again to Kylie's 'Can't Get You Out of My Head'. Nadia was la-la-la-ing along quite happily. She didn't think she'd danced like this for years. She was really getting into her stride, remembering long-forgotten moves when suddenly a fist came out of nowhere and cannoned straight into Jacob's jaw.

Ted stood over him. 'That's for having an affair with my wife,' he shouted at him above the thump of the disco. 'And for possibly being the father of my child.'

With that, Ted marched away.

Jacob lay on the dance floor, stunned, rubbing at his jaw.

303

'Cool,' Lewis said, jumping up and down with excitement.

Nadia bent to help him sit up. 'Are you okay?' It was a stupid question, she realised. The guy had just been knocked flat.

'What was that all about?'

'Sounds like the game might be up,' Nadia said. 'Ted suspected that you and Chantal might have had something going. I don't think he knows *all* the details though.' Jacob's hourly rate was probably still a secret. And the fact that he once *had* an hourly rate.

Jacob was still looking dazed. That Ted packed a mean punch. 'What did he say about a child?'

Nadia pursed her lips. 'Maybe you need to talk to Chantal about that,' she advised.

Chapter Eighty-One

I'm deliciously, gloriously and thoroughly pissed. Hurrah. And I'm hogging the chocolate fountain. Lovely, scrummy chocolate is cascading before my eyes, filling my vision, and I'm gorging myself with strawberries, marshmallows and fudge slathered with the stuff. Yum. I let the molten chocolate drizzle over my tongue. Yum. Yum. Yum. I'm sure I have a ring of chocolate right round my mouth in the style of a messy five year old.

I cast one slightly squiffy eye back to the proceedings on the dance floor. My parents are flirting outrageously as they gyrate to 'He Wasn't Man Enough' – which, again, my mum is singing along with *way* too enthusiastically. She's waggling her bosoms at my father in a manner that's not altogether seemly for a wedding. Perhaps she's working on the theory that this, technically, isn't one and so has thrown caution to the wind. I can't see The Millionaire anywhere in sight. He seems, probably wisely, to have disappeared into the night. My dad's other half, The Hairdresser, is currently rubbing herself up and down against Marcus's dad – giving Dave the Groper every chance to live up to his nickname, even though it seems he acquired it somewhat unfairly. My absent groom's mother, Hilary the Hun, is currently wrapped around Clive like one of those creepers that try to squeeze the life out of hapless trees. She appears to be in the process of trying to convince him that he isn't really gay. What's happening to everyone? Have they all been drinking too deeply at the chocolate fountain and are all loved-up inappropriately on its aphrodisiac qualities?

Clive looks over Hilary the Hun's shoulder and mouths to me, 'Help!'

I smile and decline to rescue him. Being manhandled by a forceful woman might well take his mind off Tristan's ill-timed departure with the beefy drag queen, Raunchy Roberta. When everything gets back to normal, I'll introduce Clive to my hairdresser, Darren, as I'm sure they'd have a lot in common or, at least, Clive might be able to get free haircuts for a while. New haircut, new man – that usually works out well. It's probably the same for both sexes.

Out of the corner of my eye, in the car park, I see Marcus trudging across the gravel. I've never seen anyone look quite so alone. The morning suit has gone and he's wearing jeans and a shirt that I bought for him. He seems like a man who has the weight of the world on his shoulders – as well he might. In his hand is his small suitcase and I watch as he loads it into the boot of his car. I wonder, will he go on our honeymoon by himself; or will he take Joanne or some other woman with him? I try to feel jealous or angry, but I only feel sadness.

Marcus walks round to the driver's door, opens it and then takes a good long look back at Trington Manor. Can he see that his dreams have gone up in smoke, like mine have?

It would be so easy to go out there – right now. If I ran straight away, I could stop him before he drove off. I could tell him that I've changed my mind and that despite his betrayals and his abandonment that I will give him yet another chance. My stomach is gripped with a feeling of panic. I know that I'm watching Marcus walk out of my life for ever. My heart is thudding erratically. If I want to stop him, if I have any desire to keep him in my life, then my brain needs to do something to make my feet move.

My ex-lover, ex-fiancé, ex-everything gives one last rueful glance at the hotel and then he sees me watching him through the window. He raises his hand in an uncertain wave. I hold my fingertips up against the glass. Marcus blows me a long and lingering kiss. If I could move, I might reciprocate, but I don't. I stay frozen like a statue. His mouth moves and I think he's saying, 'I love you,' but I can't hear him any more.

With that, Marcus lowers his eyes and turns away. He slides

into his car and closes the door. I can't hear his car start either, but I imagine him putting the key in the ignition and firing the engine. I'm still standing in the same spot as I see Marcus steer his way smoothly round the curve of the drive, missing all the flowerbeds, and out of the ornate gates. A tear squeezes out of my eye, rolling slowly over my cheek as I watch him until he's out of sight, a tiny speck of darkness in the distance.

Good grief, I need more to drink. I think you'll agree that it's been quite a day. Grabbing another glass of champagne, I swig some down. Taking another one of the dear little cocktail sticks provided, I spear a strawberry and dip it into the flowing chocolate. Then I decide 'to hell with it' and ditch the cocktail sticks and the strawberries and simply stick my tongue into the delicious stream. Chocolate fills my mouth, running over my chin and splashing all over my wedding dress. I think some ricochets into my hair. I want to be drunk on chocolate. To feel it inside and out of me. The sensation is wonderfully decadent and, frankly, I'd like to strip off all my clothes and stand naked under it. Perhaps that would be the perfect ending to the proceedings – though it might shock the vicar.

'Hello, Little Miss Plastered,' a voice behind me says. A voice I know so well.

I spin round. A bit unsteadily. *'Crush?'*

Are my eyes deceiving me? There, grinning widely and standing right in front of me, taking in my chocolate-y mouth, my chocolate-y wedding dress and my chocolate-y hair is, indeed, Mr Aiden Holby.

Chapter Eighty-Two

'Ohmigod! It's you! What are *you* doing here?' I babble. 'How did you get here?'

'Your friends called me and invited me,' Crush says. 'And I drove here.' He smiles tenderly at me. 'You look a little worse for wear, Gorgeous.'

I burst into tears. 'I've had a very terrible day.'

Crush grabs hold of a napkin from next to the chocolate fountain. He gently brushes my tears away and then traces round my mouth with a corner of the fabric, wiping away all the traces of chocolate. I cry a bit more at his tenderness.

Then he takes me into his strong arms. 'Ssh, ssh. I'm here to make it better,' he says softly. I blub some more. Crush holds me tightly even though I'm probably putting chocolate all over his lovely, lovely suit. He starts to circle us slowly in time to Toni Braxton's 'Unbreak My Heart' which happens to be playing. I think of making a token protest, but by now, most of my guests are so drunk that they don't even bat an eyelid that I'm smooching with another man.

'Marcus stood me up at the altar,' I snuffle.

'I know. I know.' Crush smooths my hair from my face. 'I'm so sorry, Lucy.'

'*I'm* not,' I sniff. 'I'm glad really. It would have been the wrong thing to do.'

'It would,' he agrees. 'Actually, I'm not sorry at all. I'm deliriously happy. I couldn't stand the thought of you being married to Marcus, and although I wouldn't have wished this on you, I'm pleased that the wedding didn't go ahead. I couldn't wait to get down here when Chantal phoned me. Good job you never took my name out of your contacts list.'

I smile. 'Isn't it.'

'I probably could have flown here without the aid of a plane, I was so high on joy.'

'You don't think I'm horrible and unlovable?'

'No,' he says. 'I think you're gorgeous. I always have.'

'I thought I'd blown it with you. I thought that we wouldn't be able to make it.'

'Ssh.' He puts a finger to my now chocolate-free lips. 'That's all in the past.'

'I'm sorry for all the stupid things I've ever done.'

Aiden laughs. 'That's why I love you.'

'You love me?'

'I do,' he says.

'I do too.' I've gone all moony. 'Love *you*, I mean.'

By now, the guests are moving off the dance floor until Crush and I are the only ones left. The DJ puts the spotlight on us. Then he plays 'If I Ain't Got You' by Alicia Keys. Crush and I grin stupidly at the soppy lyrics. This is going to be our song.

'Shame that the vicar is passed out drunk in the corner,' Crush murmurs.

'I think it's been very stressful for him. He's probably only used to a drop of Communion wine.'

'When we get married I'd like both the vicar and *you* to be sober.'

Giving Crush a sideways glance, I say, 'Is that a proposal?'

'Not yet,' he answers. 'But I'm dropping not-so-subtle hints so that we both start to get used to the idea.'

I hug him as if I never want to let him go. 'Sounds good to me.'

At the edge of the floor, I see my fellow members of The Chocolate Lovers' Club linking arms, swaying in unison. They all stick their thumbs up at me and I feel a laugh gurgle in my throat.

Crush whispers in my ear, 'Shall we get out of here, Gorgeous?'

'I have a room booked for tonight,' I say. 'It's not the Honeymoon Suite.' I glance across the dance floor – my mum and dad are still entwined around each other like teenagers. Yuk. I do hope they're not going to get down to it later. I'd hate to think that I was responsible for *that*. I try to block the image as I say, 'Somehow, I think my parents might be sharing that.'

The music comes to a halt and all the guests applaud us – even Marcus's mum and dad, although they're at opposite ends of the room and are glaring at each other with unbridled hostility. Aiden and I take a bow.

'Let's split,' he says.

'I have one last task to perform,' I tell him. 'Wait here.' I scurry off towards the chocolate fountain where I've dumped my bouquet. I wasn't going to do this, but what the hell? Grabbing the slightly wilted flowers, I risk one last fingerful of warm chocolate to fortify myself. There's nothing quite like chocolate to mend a broken heart. Crush winks at me as I glance back at him. Chocolate and a fabulous man telling you that he loves you, of course.

I go back to the centre of the dance floor and strike a bouquet-tossing pose. The DJ, obligingly, puts on some bouquet-tossing music. I'm trying to aim this squarely at Autumn so that fate might formalise Addison's vague proposal.

'Ready?' I nod in her direction

My friend nods back. Then I turn away.

On the count of three, I swing the bouquet and throw it gently in the air. It sails over my head and I spin round to see whether it's going towards its intended target. Autumn has her eyes turned to the ceiling, hands held out, following the bouquet's trajectory. I purse my lips. Looks like it's falling a bit short to me.

'Go for it!' Chantal and Nadia shout in unison and they give Autumn a helping push forwards.

Perhaps too much of a helping push. She stumbles forward, arms aloft. I think she's going to fall, so I rush forward to try to catch her. Ohmigod! Now it looks as if the bouquet is going to clonk her right on the head. That bouquet is bloody heavy. I can't let that happen. Jumping up, I reach out and snatch my bouquet from the air, saving my friend from a severe headache.

My guests let out a cheer. 'What?' I say. 'What?' Then I realise that I've caught *my own* bouquet. How did that happen?

'Looks like you're going to be the next single girl to get married,' Crush says. 'Congratulations.'

He kisses me to the sound of more raucous cheers and applause. I let the bouquet fall to the floor and sink into his embrace. Maybe today isn't turning out too bad after all.

Chapter Eighty-Three

'Your husband punched me on the chin,' Jacob said, clearly affronted.

'He did?' Chantal frowned.

Rubbing at his jaw, Jacob asked, 'Does Ted know the exact nature of our friendship?'

She shook her head. 'He knows that we've been intimate, that's all. Our relationship is on such shaky ground that I'd rather not come clean about everything.' Chantal gave him a wry smile. 'I'd like to keep secret the fact that our liaison started out as a business arrangement.'

Jacob had come to find her and had hustled her into the small, tucked-away lounge that had come in so useful once again. They were sitting on a sofa which was too floral to be tasteful. Jacob turned to face her. There was an angry red mark and a burgeoning bruise where, she assumed, the blow had connected. Even now, after all that had happened, there was still the temptation to kiss it better.

'He said something about a baby, Chantal.' Jacob fixed his eyes on hers, holding her with his steady gaze. 'He said something about it being mine.'

Chantal sighed. 'I didn't want you to find out like this.'

Her friend looked taken aback. 'Is it true?'

Spreading her hands across her stomach, she smiled. 'This isn't just down to an excess of chocolate, Jacob. I'm pregnant.'

'I could tell that you'd put a little weight on,' he said, 'when we were doing the fittings for the bridesmaids' dresses. But I thought it was down to . . .'

'Chocolate,' she said with a wry grin.

Jacob laughed. 'You guys do eat quite a lot of it.'

It had been a long day. Her legs and her head ached. All she wanted to do now was go to her room and sink into the tub.

'And is it mine?' he said. 'I thought we were . . . careful.'

'We were,' she assured him. They'd used condoms every time they'd arranged to meet – a requirement of Jacob's job, she guessed – but sometimes rather hurriedly, and those things were never 100 per cent foolproof. Until she knew for sure, there'd always be an element of doubt. 'I really want this baby to be Ted's. I hope that we can get back together and raise this baby as a family. But the truth is, I don't know, Jacob. I won't know until after the baby's born.'

'I'd be a great dad,' he told her. 'The thought of this doesn't phase me at all, Chantal.'

'Well, it does me,' she said.

'If it is my baby, I'd like to be closely involved in bringing the child up.'

'And I'd like that too,' Chantal said, giving his hand a squeeze. 'You've been such a good friend to me, Jacob. You came along at a time when I was feeling very low and unloved. In a strange way, our time together really helped me to put things in perspective.'

Jacob smiled. 'I knew I was more than just a cheap shag to you.'

Chantal laughed. 'You were never, ever a *cheap* shag, Jacob.'

'We could make a go of a relationship together, Chantal. We have fun together, there's certainly chemistry. And you've helped me to turn my life around. I'll always be grateful for that.'

'Oh, Jacob,' she said. 'You'd be a very easy person to love. But, despite all of my stupid behaviour in the past, I still love my husband very much and I'm praying that fate will give me a decent break for once and prove that my Ted is the father of this child – and that he'll want the baby and that he'll want me. I'm hoping against hope that we'll be able to get back together.'

'If that's what you really want, then I hope that you do too,' Jacob said.

All she had to do was convince her husband that he felt the same.

Chapter Eighty-Four

Autumn rinsed the soap from her face and regarded herself in the mirror. The entire afternoon and evening had passed and she'd hardly thought about her brother at all until now. True, she'd had other distractions to keep her occupied – but it had to be viewed as a step in the right direction. Perhaps she should have called Richard and let him know how the drugs drop had gone, but she felt like letting him stew. He hadn't thought twice about putting her in danger and she'd stupidly agreed to it. No, she wouldn't phone him until tomorrow. Let him worry about *her* for once.

She hung up her bridesmaid's dress and pulled on the filmy slip of a nightdress that she'd bought for tonight. It was nice to have someone she could dress up and be sexy for. That had been missing from her life for far too long. She'd been so relieved when Addison had turned up today as she'd feared that it was all over between them – and she wouldn't have blamed him if he had walked away. Her focus had been all wrong, but now that would change.

With one thing and another, it had been an exhausting day and now she was looking forward to nothing more than curling up against her boyfriend. Autumn fluffed up her hair and, smiling to herself, went back into the bedroom.

Addison was sitting on the sofa. His eyes were closed and his head was resting back. He looked all in too. He'd taken his jacket off. The neck of his shirt had been loosened and the cuffs turned back. His lips were full and luscious. His black skin flawless. He had eyelashes that most women would kill for. She thought he was the most handsome man she'd ever seen. There was no way she was going to let this one slip through her fingers.

'You didn't need to wait for me,' she said softly. 'You should have got undressed and slid into bed.'

'I have something to do first,' he replied. Then she noticed that there were two glasses of champagne bubbling away in front of him on the coffee-table. Autumn didn't think she'd ever drunk so much in one single day – it was a miracle that she was still standing. She supposed one last glass wouldn't hurt. Tomorrow was soon enough to go back onto the herbal tea.

'Come and sit down next to me.' Addison patted the sofa beside him.

When she sat down, he turned and faced her. 'I think I may have left you in some doubt about my intentions towards you earlier,' he said.

Autumn gave him a puzzled look, but before she could say anything further, her boyfriend had slipped off the sofa and was down on one knee in front of her.

'Autumn Fielding,' he said, 'would you do me the very great honour of marrying me?' He opened his hand and there was an enormous solitaire diamond ring in his palm.

Autumn was sure she recognised it. 'Addison?'

Her boyfriend shrugged. 'Lucy loaned it to me,' he confessed. 'We can go out and buy one of your own choosing just as soon as you say yes.'

Tears sprang to her eyes. 'Yes.'

Addison slipped Lucy's engagement ring onto her finger. 'That means it's official,' he told her. 'No wriggling out of it now, no matter what reaction we get from parents, relations, *brothers.*'

'Absolutely not,' she agreed. 'From now on, what you and I both want is the most important thing.'

Addison came and sat next to her again. He handed her a glass of champagne. 'To us,' he said.

He clinked his glass against hers.

'To us,' Autumn said. '*Just* us.'

Chapter Eighty-Five

Chantal had searched the hotel looking for Ted and she wondered, for a moment, whether he'd had enough and high-tailed it back to Richmond for the night. She was just about to give up and retire to her room when she spotted her husband sitting outside on the stone steps overlooking the moonlit Manor gardens.

Wishing she had a warm coat with her, Chantal stepped out into the cold night air. Lucy's wedding was all but over now. Looking back through the windows, she could see the last few stragglers staggering round the dance floor as the hackneyed strains of Bryan Adams singing 'I Do It For You' drifted out to her. On the terrace, Chantal picked her way slowly across the uneven paving, trying not to turn her ankle. Stopping herself from shivering in the process was proving more difficult. She was right behind Ted before he heard her approaching.

'Hi,' he said flatly, as he glanced over his shoulder at her.

'Lost in thought?'

'Something like that,' Ted said, and resumed staring out into the blackness.

Chantal sat down next to him, heedless of the fact that the soft green and yellow lichens covering the steps might well stain her bridesmaid's dress. The day was done, she'd have no more use for it now. Her struggle not to shiver gave out and a chill ran through her. 'It's cold.'

'You came out without a coat,' Ted noted. Then he sighed and slipped his jacket off and draped it round her shoulders.

'Thanks,' she said. 'Now you'll be cold.' So she scooted along the step and snuggled up next to him.

After a moment's hesitation, Ted slipped his arm round her shoulders. The weight and warmth of him against her felt good.

A fitful breeze buffeted wisps of cloud across the moon. The tips of the bare branches of the trees glistened with silvery light.

'Thank you for coming today,' Chantal said. 'It meant a lot to me.'

Her husband laughed, but without humour. 'That was some wedding,' he said with a forced chuckle.

'Lucy will be okay,' she said. 'She's remarkably resilient. I'm sure she'll be able to move on.'

'Looks as if she already has,' Ted observed. 'Last I saw of her, she was entwined round some other man on the dance floor.'

'That's her boss,' Chantal explained. 'Long story.'

'Do all of you guys have an entourage of men waiting in the wings?'

'It's not like that.'

'I don't know if I can ever stop thinking about the other men that you've been with, Chantal,' her husband admitted frankly. 'How many more of them am I just going to "bump into" like I did today?'

'There'll be no one else, I'm sure,' she promised. 'I'm a one-guy woman from now on. If you'll give me another chance.'

'And what about the women I've seen?'

'I can forgive you for that,' she assured him. 'I can see your reasons.'

'What about Stacey? She's going to be the mother of my child. I can't simply abandon her. If you and I stay together, she'll inevitably be a part of our lives. Could you handle that?'

'I could try. I could try my hardest.'

Ted shrugged his broad shoulders. 'Do you think we could make it?'

'I hope so, Ted,' she said. 'If we split now, what would we do? Try to make a go of things alone, or maybe try our luck with new partners. All we'd do is swap one set of difficulties for another. We have such a lot going for us, we have history and we have a better foundation than most people.' Even though they'd recently

317

given that foundation a good shaking, she was sure it would hold fast, given the chance. 'Let's not waste that. Besides, I still love you. I always have.'

'And I love you.' Her husband pulled her close and her head nestled into the warm curve of his neck. 'So where do we go from here?'

'I need to go to my room,' Chantal said wearily. 'I'm pooped and I need to hit the sack.'

'Is there space in your room for an overnight guest?'

'There sure is.'

Ted turned to her and covered her mouth with hot, searching kisses. 'You're looking very sexy,' he whispered. 'Very womanly. Can you make love when you're pregnant?'

'I have no idea,' Chantal answered honestly. 'I've been deliberately avoiding all of the pregnancy "How To" books.' The less information she had about the technicalities of childbirth, the happier she was. 'But I guess there's nothing to stop us giving it a try.' She smiled hesitantly. 'If that's what you want.'

'Maybe we should do just that,' her husband said, and he helped her to her feet. 'I want to look after you now. Will you let me?'

She nodded, suddenly feeling quite tearful. Perhaps it was her erratic hormones. All that she ever wanted was for her husband to love her, and it looked as if she'd finally got what she most desired.

Chapter Eighty-Six

'I should carry you over the threshold, Gorgeous,' Crush says as we approach my room hand-in-hand.

'I know it's my wedding day,' I say. 'But I'm not *actually* married.'

'Indulge me,' he says with a grin. Before I can respond, he sweeps me up into his strong arms. I lace my fingers around his neck and he kisses me deeply. My head spins and it gives me a better rush than all the champagne I've knocked back today. This is as romantic as I always hoped it would be – even if the circumstances aren't quite as I envisaged.

Crush dips while I put the keycard in and then, very manfully, kicks the door open. I'm glad I tidied up this morning as at least the room now looks presentable – even if it isn't the Honeymoon Suite.

Aiden sets me down on my feet. 'I think we should get you out of those chocolate-coated clothes right away,' he says with a twinkle in his eye. 'Before you catch your death of cold.'

'You don't catch a cold from chocolate,' I remind him. 'In fact, it's a well-known cure for the common cold.' With the amount I've eaten today, I probably won't catch a cold for another five years or more.

'Is that right?' There's a hunger in his expression that I can't wait to sate. 'Maybe we ought to err on the side of caution. Just in case.'

He starts with my tiara, taking it from my head and placing it carefully on the dressing-table. Then he sets to work on my veil, carefully teasing out all of the clips and pins which Darren the hairdresser has rammed into my head to hold it there. I think it would have been quicker to spot-weld it in place. Either way, this thing wasn't going to move, even in a force nine gale. Darren clearly imagined that all of my troubles today would be weather-related. Crush is unphased by my hairdresser's over-engineering. He meticulously and tenderly unpins me as if he has all the time in the world. I know this sounds a bit sad, but I'm getting turned on already. Just as I'm about ready to risk losing parts of my scalp and rip the thing off my head, Crush takes out the last pin. He carefully lays the veil over a conveniently-placed chair. I wonder if he's had much experience of undressing brides as he's making an expert job of it.

'I could do this myself,' I tell him, meaning, 'I'm in a bit of a rush to jump your bones, so get a move on!'

'I've waited a long time to do this, Gorgeous. I'm going to enjoy it.' He takes the pins out of my hair too, until it's free once more. Then I do that porn-Librarian move and shake it loose. I never really bought into that cheesy old stereotype thing, but believe me, it feels very horny. Aiden smiles his appreciation. 'You are one sexy lady, Lucy Lombard.'

Then Crush moves behind me. He covers the back of my neck and shoulders with hot kisses, slipping the straps from my gown – my gown that looks as if Jackson Pollock has had a chocolate frenzy on the front. Maybe if I was an artist I could use it as a statement about the consumerism associated with the modern wedding – something like that. Instead, I'm a woman in love and I can't wait to get the damn thing off me.

There are hundreds of tiny buttons all down the back and, I kid you not, he takes about ten minutes to undo each one as he kisses and nibbles every part of my back as it is bared. I've gone past the point of being aroused and am now in a state of complete torture. I want to grab him, throw him to the bed and have my wicked way with him. I've no idea how he's showing such restraint.

When Mr Aiden Holby finally lets my dress fall to the floor, at this point I'm really glad that I invested in some knockout underwear. His hands skim over my basque, my suspenders, my stockings. Now we're both breathing heavily, but slowly he unhooks my stockings. I slip off my shoes and inch by inch, he rolls the silky fabric down my legs, stroking them as he does so. When he unhooks my basque and I'm finally standing naked before him, I don't feel in the slightest bit shy. I feel empowered, wanton and more than a little hot.

My new love drinks me in. 'You're so beautiful,' Crush says.

This is the point where, usually, someone would crash through the door with bad news, or the ceiling would fall in or I'd trip over an inopportunely placed pouffe, breaking a limb, or a water main in the hotel would burst and a million gallons of water would come pouring down on my head. But I realise that my luck has changed as nothing happens. I take a deep breath. Nothing whatsoever. And I know that all is going to be well from now on.

I wiggle my eyebrows at Crush. 'Now it's your turn.'

And I'd really like to say that I go for the slow burn too, but I don't. I throw myself onto Aiden who starts to kick off his shoes and tug at his socks all at once – which I'm pleased about because you don't want the first image of your lover to be him standing there in nothing but his shoes and socks. While he does that, he tries to shrug out of his jacket at the same time. I tear at the buttons of his shirt and yank at the buckle of his belt. My disrobing of him might not be as seductive, but it sure is fun.

My boyfriend would make a great quick-change artist as, within seconds, he's naked with a pile of crumpled clothes at his feet. I might not be a great judge of people, but taking in the picture before me, I'd certainly say that Crush is as ready for this as I am.

He lifts me into his arms again and, both of us giggling like loons, spins me round wildly until I'm shrieking for mercy. Then he makes a dive for the bed and we crash-land all tangled together. Crush pins my arms above my head, just as he did that day on the forest floor at the paintballing extravaganza, the day that I started to wonder how I was going to live without him.

'I love you, Gorgeous,' he says.

I don't think of my wedding that never was, of the pain of Marcus jilting me, nor that my parents are getting down to it right now in the room that I should have been sharing with my husband as I started out on my married life. I think of none of that. I bask in the here and now, looking up at the wonderful man above me, and know what it is to feel true happiness. Instead of trying to express all that, I simply smile and say, 'I love you too.'

Chapter Eighty-Seven

So. Life is back to normal. We're all gathered in Chocolate Heaven. We've bagged our favourite spot on the comfy sofas and have dug in for the afternoon. We have plates of chocolate brownies and chocolate chip cookies – already half-devoured – in front of us. I have some of Clive's extra-special single Madagascar truffles working their magic. There are blissed-out smiles on all of our faces. I'm exhausted by all the excitement I've been through in the last few days, but I do feel – at last! – as if I've stepped off the emotional rollercoaster and am once more cruising aimlessly down life's highway. I put my feet up on the coffee-table and lay back my head. This is what it all should be about.

The only person that's struggling in here is Clive. Tristan has officially departed with Raunchy Roberta, the drag queen – sorry, female impersonator – and our dear friend is having to manage Chocolate Heaven alone. The queue at the counter is getting steadily longer and Clive has an harassed flush to his cheeks. He's managed to fix himself up with a date with Darren the hairdresser tonight – as they were both checking out of Trington Manor, they were checking out each other too. So it seems my skill as a matchmaker wasn't required after all. I was worried that it might take Clive a long time to get over Tristan, but perhaps this *is* a long time in the gay world. I don't know. But I do hope that he manages to shut up shop in time.

Things are going well for me too. Crush has just texted me to say that he loves me, leaving me with a silly grin on my face. I haven't seen my best girls for just a few days but, already, we've got heaps of stuff to catch up on. Aiden's moving in tomorrow – the prospect of having a new roommate is filling me with nothing but joy and excitement. Frankly, I can hardly contain myself. I'm going to take home one of Clive's sublime chocolate tortes to mark the occasion. Though whether it will last in the fridge overnight is a moot point. We might have to celebrate early.

'I brought your ring back, Lucy,' Autumn says. 'Addison and I are going to pick up mine this afternoon. Thank you so much for the loan of it.' No doubt Autumn has chosen something more ethnic, made by someone in the 'developing world' with a material that's easy to recycle. But I don't care what her engagement ring looks like, so long as she's happy. And, patently, she is.

I take back the huge rock that until so recently graced my finger. 'What am I going to do with this now?'

'Bank it,' Chantal says. 'One day you might need the money and you can sell it.'

'I couldn't do that.'

'Believe me, honey, one day it will cease to have any sentimental value and it will be just an asset that you can dispose of if you want to. Marcus isn't likely to want it back.'

She's probably right; he's hardly going to pass it onto the next person he decides to get engaged to. I slip it into my handbag and think that I'll figure out what to do with it later.

'Have you set a date for the wedding yet?' Nadia wants to know.

Autumn shakes her head. 'We don't seem to have had a minute to discuss things. But one thing's for certain – it's going to be a very quiet affair.'

'Hear, hear to that,' I chip in.

'To quiet weddings,' Nadia says, and we all raise our mugs of hot chocolate in a toast.

Then I pull Nadia to me. 'You and Lewis both got through the wedding day brilliantly,' I tell her. 'I'm so proud of you.'

'You did a good job yourself, kid,' she says.

'I did,' I agree with a small flush of pride. 'It was certainly a wedding to remember.'

'I have a lot to thank Lucy for,' Chantal says. 'Ted and I decided to try to make a go of things. I'm giving up my apartment and I'm moving home again.'

'This is after Ted punched out Jacob's lights?' I query.

Chantal acknowledges it with a rueful smile.

'Well, I'm pleased to hear that some good came of it.'

'None of us wanted you to marry Marcus,' Nadia says. 'You're better off without him.'

'I know.' I nod sagely. 'You all tried to warn me.'

'Any more news from the fall-out after your non-wedding?' Chantal asks.

'My mother's moving back in with Dad,' I say with a sigh. 'She's gone back to Spain to bring all her stuff over.' That should tie up an entire fleet of removal lorries for the foreseeable future.

'You don't sound too pleased.'

'I can't see it lasting and then we'll have to go through the upset of them splitting up all over again.' I'm actually very worried about the possibility of my mother ending up on my couch. She's not the easiest of people to live with and my dad seems to have forgotten all that in the heady rush brought on by a few cheesy songs and a few glasses of champagne too many. Let's see how long their rediscovered love lasts when my mother is back in the cold, windswept fields of Blighty on my dad's unnecessarily tight budget. He might have plenty of cash but he doesn't like to splash it about – particularly where my mother's concerned. Another reason why they split up in the first place. I can see that flush of love fading quicker than her tan when she's not lounging by the pool at her eight-bedroom villa in the year-round Spanish sun with a limitless charge account and a doting Millionaire to cater for her every whim. Hmm.

And I hope they don't decide to have another wedding as I just don't think I could stand the strain. With a bit of luck they'll slink away to a desert island together and all I'll have to do is send a card. From now on, I'm going to be permanently traumatised every time I hear the 'Wedding March'.

'The Millionaire doesn't seem to be unduly concerned about my mother's departure,' I tell my friends. 'Neither he nor Marcus's mother have been seen since the reception.' I wonder if Marcus's mum got fed up with trying to convince Clive that he wasn't gay and set her sights on the balding playboy instead. Maybe they've flown off somewhere wonderful in his private jet to start a new life together.

They all laugh. 'It's not funny!'

'I wonder how Marcus's dad is taking it?' Autumn worries about everyone. Frankly, I think Dave the Groper had it coming to him. Last I saw of him, he was still wrapped round The Hairdresser. Perhaps his lust will wane when he discovers she's incapable of having a conversation that doesn't involve straightening irons or volumising shampoo.

'You haven't heard from Marcus?' Nadia asks.

'No.' I shake my head sadly. 'It seems strange not to have heard anything at all from him. I don't know where he is or who he's with. I was going to give him a call, just to make sure he's okay . . .'

'Lucy!' they all chorus.

'But I didn't!' I hold up my hands. 'I didn't. Okay?' But it's hard to get my last image of Marcus walking away all alone out of my head. I know my friends would kill me if I even mentioned it . . . and who could blame them?

Then the door opens and we all watch as Tristan walks in. Despite the fact that Clive has a great long queue, his former boyfriend goes straight to the front and announces, 'I've come to collect my things.'

'Fine,' Clive says tightly over the heads of his customers. 'Don't let me stop you.'

Tristan looks tired and pale, his normal ebullience missing. I wonder if it's Raunchy Roberta who's responsible for the downturn in his appearance. That's got to be a whole lot of man/woman to handle. 'I don't have to go,' Tristan says.

'Is that your way of saying you made a mistake by running off with that . . . that . . . *gorilla*?' Clive's goatee is trembling with rage and his customers have stepped away from the counter, jaws falling open. He doesn't wait for Tristan's answer. 'Don't

326

do me any favours. Go on, get out. Pack your bags and get out.'

Clive reaches for a cappuccino fairy cake and hurls it, missile-like, over the counter. His customers duck for cover. Even the members of The Chocolate Lovers' Club who, after my non-wedding, are more used to these displays, stop with their own chocolate cakes halfway to their mouths. Tristan covers his head with his hands as the fairy cake bounces off his brow. You can never fault the lightness of Clive's sponge.

'Ohmigod,' I say.

'I've learned all that I need to know about unfaithful men from Lucy,' Clive shouts.

Gee, I think. Glad to be of service.

'I am *so* not going there.'

I'm out of my seat. 'I have to stop this before Clive ruins his business,' I mutter to the girls.

When I get to the counter, I put myself between Tristan and the fairy-cake grenades. 'Now, boys,' I say like a strict school-teacher. 'Perhaps you should go upstairs to the flat and continue this discussion in private.'

I walk Tris to the end of the counter, still providing a human shield, and then I pick up an apron. 'Clive, I'll take over here for the time being. Go and sort this out once and for all.'

Clive, now cowed, obeys. Digging out a scrunchy from my pocket, I pull back my hair with it. I tie on the apron and give my hands a good wash. The boys disappear towards the staircase that leads to their first-floor apartment, giving each other a wide berth.

I clap my hands together in the manner of someone who's in command of the situation. Clive's customers shuffle forward, jostling to regain their previous positions in the queue. This is the first time I've been on this side of the chocolates, brownies, cakes and cookies. The view from here looks pretty good too.

'Right,' I say to the first customer. 'How can I help you?'

327

Chapter Eighty-Eight

'I kinda like this one,' Ted said. He scanned the sales literature. 'It has "true off-road capabilities. Ideal for both city and rugged landscapes, the new XRS will make light work of whatever the terrain throws at it".' He looked suitably impressed. 'Sounds good, right?'

'It sounds great,' Chantal agreed.

'This thing has a heap more features than my Mercedes.' Ted looked at it with something approaching awe as he checked out the meaty tyres and its sleek bodywork. 'Locking swivel wheels, gate-style opening bumper, fully adjustable suspension.'

Chantal smiled to herself. Who'd ever have thought that she and Ted would be looking at strollers together. Yet here they were in an upscale department store browsing through their range of Out and About products – or prams, pushchairs, buggies and strollers to the uninitiated.

'It has a buzz box,' he told her.

'What's that?'

'I have no idea. But it sounds great.' Her husband circled the stroller once more. 'There's a portable shopping assistant too.'

'Really?'

'I think that's the deep basket contraption at the bottom.' He rubbed his chin, taking in all the features. She had had no idea that her husband would take this so seriously, and she loved him all the more for it. If this baby could be willed into being Ted's daughter then it certainly would be. She hoped that eventually the DNA tests would prove what her heart was already sure of. 'We can get an add-on Climate Control Pack.'

'And that would be?'

He checked the notes. 'A multi-position raincover and hi-tech sun canopy.'

'Essential.'

'It says here that this is no ordinary Infant Transport System. Apparently, the minimalist design brings the pushchair back to its very essence while incorporating contemporary and classic features.'

'Wow. Then we really can't argue with that,' she said with a smile. 'Does it have wipe-clean upholstery?' She was sure to pass on her chocoholic genes to her daughter, so as the next five years or more were likely to be spent sponging chocolate-y fingerprints off stuff, it was better to be safe than sorry.

'Yes. And we can have it in Lulu Guinness fabric complete with colour coordinated changing bag, mat and fleece-lined foot-muff.'

Chantal shrugged happily. 'That's sold it to me.'

'Let's order it then.' He turned to head toward the tills.

She put her hand on Ted's arm. 'Are you sure you want to do this?'

'You mean you like the TSi RockBaby better?'

Laughing, she said, 'No, I like this pushchair just fine. I meant, are you sure that you want to bring up this baby together no matter the outcome?'

Ted slipped his arm round her and pulled her close. 'I want us to be back together, to be husband and wife again. If that means bringing up someone else's child then I think I can live with that.'

'Thank you.' Chantal kissed him tenderly. 'I love you so much.'

Ted grinned. 'Then let's buy this buggie. Only the best for Baby Hamilton.'

'There's just one other thing. Shouldn't we be ordering two of these?' she asked, gently reminding him that there was another Hamilton baby on the way other than her own.

Her husband sighed. 'This situation sure is complicated.'

'We can all handle it like adults,' she assured him. 'We *are* doing so. Our arrangements may not be conventional, but I guess they're not so unusual these days. I think I should meet Stacey, sooner rather than later. If this child and her child are going to be half-brothers or sisters then we should all make an effort to get along.'

'The strange thing is,' Ted said, 'I think that you'll really like her.'

She linked her arm through his and steered him toward the pay-point. 'Then there should be no problems at all.'

Chapter Eighty-Nine

They were being jolted along on the bus, heading to see Richard at the hospital. Autumn's head rested on Addison's shoulder and she stared at the beautiful ring on her engagement finger. Addison had taken her shopping for something more suitable for her. They'd settled on a young, up-coming designer who created engagement rings that suited her rather Bohemian tastes – a traditional, solitaire rock just wasn't her. The members of The Chocolate Lovers' Club would love it instantly and she couldn't wait to show it to them.

She smiled as the last of the weak winter sunlight came through the grimy window and caught the diamond in her ring. It was a small, tasteful stone bounded by delicate petals of amethyst, pink sapphire and aquamarine in a flower design, set in white gold. It was soft, gentle, unique and sparkled just for her. Toying with it on her finger, she tried to get used to the newness of its comforting presence.

'A penny for them,' Autumn said when she realised that her fiancé was deep in thought.

Addison roused from his reverie. 'Oh, nothing much,' he said.

'Come on.' She nudged him gently. 'I can tell a worried frown when I see one. Is it because of Richard?' They were on their way not only to see if her brother was improving, but to tell him of their commitment to each other. They also needed to discuss the thorny subject of what was going to happen to the bag of money that was now safely paid into Autumn's bank account rather than stashed under her bed.

'No. No.' Addison shook his head. He turned to her with a tired smile. 'But I bet you're worried about him.'

'I called his consultant earlier. Apparently, he's not improving as he should.'

'His immune system is probably shot to pieces after all those drugs,' Addison observed rather succinctly. 'It will take him longer to heal than the average Joe.'

'And he only has himself to blame for that.' Autumn sighed. Sometimes she found it difficult to cope with the frustration and the futility of it all. 'If it's not my dear brother, what is it?'

'I wasn't going to bother you with it today,' Addison said. 'I know that you've got more than enough on your plate.'

'A trouble shared is a trouble halved,' she quoted.

'I thought I'd got some funding in place to help Tasmin set up a jewellery stall at Camden Market.' He tutted to himself. 'It looks like that may not happen now. The sponsor pulled out at the last minute. I'm not sure where else to go.'

Autumn rooted in her handbag and pulled out a bar of Fairtrade organic dark chocolate. 'Here.' She snapped off a couple of squares. 'This will make you feel better.'

Addison laughed. 'Is chocolate your answer to everything?'

'Sometimes.'

The bus halted at their stop and they stood up to make their way to the doors.

'Don't worry about Tasmin's situation just yet.' Autumn winked at Addison. 'Maybe all is not lost.'

Outside, the dusk was gathering quickly to blend into night. In Richard's ward it was perpetual daylight. As well as turning down the heating in these hospitals, Autumn thought, maybe they should consider shutting off some of the dozens and dozens of bulbs that blazed all day long. That would go a long way to helping the National Health funding crisis.

Her brother lay in his bed, still hooked up to as many machines as the day he'd been admitted. Surely, if he was on the road to recovery, there'd be a reduction in the amount of technology needed to keep him alive by now? He looked thin and wasted, almost skeletal. Autumn wondered if he was managing to eat properly. Since Lucy's non-wedding she hadn't been in here at all. More than a week had gone by before she felt able to face Richard and confront him about the drugs drop he'd duped her into doing. Anger was an emotion that she didn't like to embrace, but Autumn didn't think she'd ever been as angry with anyone in her life as she was with Richard.

But, one look at him and the fire went out of her and she felt nothing but sorrow. He made a pathetic sight. The cheeky, charming cad that he'd once been was long gone. His skin was pale, mottled, his hair greasy. With every heaving breath, his lungs rattled and complained. Each one sounded like it might be his last. She wondered if some of the kids from the KICK IT! programme would mend their ways if they could see how low Richard's love of recreational drugs had brought him. His story was certainly a salutary one against drug use in any form.

Autumn slid her hand into Addison's and he squeezed it tightly. As they approached Richard's bed, her brother opened his eyes. It looked as if he was struggling to focus. The eyes that had once shone so brightly, had been so full of mischief and confidence, now sat dully in deep, dark sockets. It was terrible to see him this way.

'Sis,' he croaked. 'Thought you'd forgotten about me.' It wasn't a bitter comment, it was just incredibly sad and needy. It made Autumn feel terrible for staying away.

'I needed time to come to terms with some stuff,' she said as honestly as she could, as she sat down on the plastic seat next to his bed.

'All right, mate?' Addison said, as he sat down beside her.

'Never better,' Richard said, but there was no venom in it.

'You look well,' Autumn lied.

'That's bullshit,' he murmured. 'We both know it.'

She didn't have the strength to deny it. 'We have some news for you,' she said, with forced brightness as she turned to Addison for support.

'Don't tell me,' he said. 'You and Addison are getting married.'

Autumn laughed. 'How did you know that?'

'Because I've never before seen you look so very happy.' He

tried to lift his head from his pillow and failed. 'I'm pleased for you. For you both.'

'I was worried how you'd take it,' Autumn confessed.

'Am I such a bastard?' Richard wanted to know. Then, in answer to his own question, 'Yes, I probably am.'

'We haven't set a date for the wedding yet.'

'It had better be quick, otherwise I might not be around to see it.'

'Don't talk like that,' she admonished. 'You'll be absolutely fine. It will just take time.'

'Time is the one thing that I don't think I have any more, sis.' A tear slid from beneath her brother's eyelashes. 'Now that you're soulmates, I suppose you've told Addison about the favour you did for me?'

'He knows everything,' she admits. 'There are no secrets between us.' Autumn looked lovingly at her boyfriend.

'Do you want to discuss this alone?' Addison asked. 'I can always nip out and get a cup of putrid hospital coffee.'

Richard slowly shook his head. 'Stay. You're family now.'

Addison settled in his chair again.

Her brother said, 'I take it it all went smoothly?'

'Yes,' she answered. 'There were no problems with the drop at all. But I did call the police and they were all arrested straight afterwards.'

Richard tried to shrug, but didn't manage it. 'It doesn't matter now,' he told her. 'They're not going to come after me in here.'

'They gave me a bag of cash.'

Now her brother looked surprised. 'They did?'

'It's a lot of money, Rich.'

'I never thought that they'd pay up.'

'So it is your money?'

'Yes,' he admitted. 'My ill-gotten gains.'

'I'm not going to give it to you,' Autumn said. 'When you come out of here, I want you to clean up your act. I want you to be legit. No more drugs. No more running with the bad guys. I'll help you all that I can. You know that.'

Richard reached for her hand and she clasped his. 'You always have done.'

'I want to use the money to help the kids at the Centre,' she said.

Her brother's machinery hissed, beeped and gurgled again. 'Let's face it, I'm not going to be coming out of here,' he said. His tired, opaque eyes took in his cold, clinical surroundings. 'Use the money for whatever you want. I'd like to think that something positive could come out of this. Do some good with it.'

Autumn started to cry. 'Thank you, Rich.' She kissed him on his cheek. His skin smelled of acetone, of illness, of death.

'See?' he said with a faint laugh that wracked his body with painful spasms. 'I'm not such a bastard after all.'

'Believe me,' she said, 'you're going to change the life of at least one young woman.' Autumn turned to Addison with a beaming smile. 'Now Tasmin can have her jewellery stall.'

Chapter Ninety

The letter was lying on the doormat when she got home from the supermarket. It was from their insurance company and it was a letter that she'd been dreading for weeks.

Nadia picked it up and carried it, along with her carrier bags full of groceries, through to the kitchen. After dumping the shopping on the work surface, she took a good long look at the envelope. She didn't think that she could bear any more bad news. Avoiding this wasn't going to make it any easier, though.

Lewis was at nursery school until noon, so she was alone for the next hour or so before she had to collect him. Taking time to make herself a cup of coffee and carefully lay out three chocolate-coated Hob-Nobs on a plate, she delayed the moment of truth for a few minutes longer.

Nadia had a sip of the coffee and a bite of one of the Hob-Nobs while she stared at the envelope which was propped up in front of her against the jar of Nescafé. Then, when she couldn't stand the suspense any longer, she slit the letter open with a knife. It started with *We are pleased to inform you* . . . Surely that had to be good? Nadia scanned the rest of the letter as quickly as she could. The paper shook as her trembling hands struggled to hold it still.

It looked as if the US Coroner would be recording a verdict of Accidental Death, it said. Three of the policemen who were in attendance at the top of the Stratosphere Tower on that fateful night had witnessed her husband's death. All three of them had been unsure whether Toby had deliberately let go of the safety railings or whether he was intending to climb back and accidentally slipped to his death. As there was inconclusive evidence to prove suicide, Toby was to be given the benefit of the doubt by the authorities.

Nadia felt her insides turn to water. Could she give her husband the benefit of the doubt too? If she closed her eyes she could still feel the warm desert air on her skin, see the terror on Toby's face as he tumbled backwards, falling away from her to his death. Had he really meant to let go, or had there been a moment when he'd considered climbing back over those rails, hoping that they could put things right, knowing that they still had a marriage? She wondered what had been going through his mind. Had he really been determined to end his life, or was it nothing more than a pitiful cry for help? The fact that she'd never really know the truth would haunt her for the rest of her life.

The letter continued that if this was, indeed, the case and the Coroner's expected verdict was confirmed, then she would be entitled to receive a pay-out from Toby's life insurance policy. A sum of nearly one hundred thousand pounds. *One hundred thousand pounds.* The words blurred together, the figure banging against her brain as relief flooded through her. She felt it was about time that something went her way. Nadia rubbed her hands over her face, trying to let the details sink in. She could only hope that the insurance company's initial assessment was correct. Surely they wouldn't commit their findings to paper unless they were certain of the outcome? They wouldn't raise her hopes only to dash them again? With a hundred thousand pounds in the bank, she could pay off the loan she'd taken from Chantal and maybe even reduce the mortgage to a level that she could manage by herself – assuming, of course, that someone was willing to employ a woman like her, who'd been a stay-at-home mum for the last four years. Her business skills might be rusty and her suits a little tight around the waistband, but with a little luck, someone would be able to see that she still had a lot to offer.

The credit-card company was still hounding her over the debts that Toby had run up via the online casino sites and in the real deal in Vegas. The sum amounted to over one hundred and thirty thousands pounds, with interest accruing every month. Her lawyer was still convinced that they could come to a settlement where Nadia would only pay back a fraction of the outstanding amount, or that some of the credit-card companies would discover that they had a heart of gold after all and would cancel the debt completely. The national newspapers were keeping a close eye on developments, which might well help her cause. The credit-card companies might be reluctant to look bad in print.

She needed to make sure that she could provide a stable home environment for Lewis, who had been through too much recently. All she wanted for him was a happy life and she'd do her very best to give him that.

Autumn was going to look after her son while Nadia went to a job interview this afternoon. Her stomach became a mass of nerves just thinking about it. The job was a good one – selling advertising for a local online television station that had just started up. She could do it – she knew she could. All she needed was the chance to prove it.

Nadia broke the last of the Hob-Nobs in two and ate it, enjoying the chocolate-y sensation. She crossed her arms, wrapping them round her body, and gave herself a big hug. Whatever happened, it was time to look to the future.

Chapter Ninety-One

'If you could put down your chocolate for long enough, you could help me with one of these boxes,' Crush says.

'Oh, yeah. Sure.' I was just having a celebratory Mars Bar – you know how it is.

Watching Aiden struggle with a load of CDs and DVDs, I can't help but smile to myself – not because he's struggling, but because he's here at all. I've never had a permanent roommate before – not one that I was intimately involved with, anyway – and I feel a thrill of joy rush through me when I think that he's really moving in with me. Really, *really* moving in with me. 'Better still,' I say, 'why don't you put that box down, I'll flick the kettle on and we can share this chocolate?'

He dumps the box immediately and flops down onto my rug. 'You're a very hard woman to say no to.'

I stroke his face. 'You look all in.'

'Well, I have been humping and dumping boxes since first light,' he informs me as if I didn't know. His friend has loaned him a van to move his stuff and he has to return it by four this afternoon. Crush grins at me. 'This is hard work. Very soon I might have to lie down and take all my clothes off.'

'You stay right there.' Planting a kiss on Crush's nose, I then wade through the sea of boxes that's washed up in my living room to make my way to the kitchen. I never knew that guys had so much stuff. There are clothes, magazines, gadgets galore, and I'll swear that Aiden Holby has more cosmetics than I do. I love the thought of fighting for face space in the bathroom mirror with him every morning. Though I hope that he doesn't hog the shower like Marcus did. When my ex-boyfriend finally emerged, there was never any hot water left for me. Says a lot about our relationship, I think. Crush would never leave me with lukewarm leftovers.

The thought of Marcus pokes a pin into my happy bubble. This morning I received a postcard from him. It was posted in Mauritius and shows a beautiful tropical paradise – ideal for loved-up honeymoon couples. All it says on the back, in Marcus's spidery writing, is *Wish you were here*. And there are two forlorn kisses on the bottom. It makes my heart ache for him and I wonder if Marcus is there alone. If he is, then he has no one to blame but himself. It makes me sigh, anyway.

'Where's that tea, Gorgeous?' Crush shouts from the lounge. 'I thought you might rush back to join me on the rug.'

Smiling, I shout back, 'Coming!'

I look at the postcard once again and very deliberately and very carefully tear it into tiny little shreds before throwing it into my wastepaper bin.

'What's that?' Crush asks from the doorway behind me.

'Nothing important,' I tell him.

'Do you know how much I love you?' he says.

'Yes.' And it's true. For the first time in my life I know what it feels like to love and be loved honestly and openly in return.

'You're not going to go all complicated on me now that you've moved in?' I want to know.

'No.' He slips his arm around my shoulders and pulls me towards him. 'As long as you keep me supplied with plenty of chocolate and tea then everything should be just fine, Gorgeous.'

Chapter Ninety-Two

'When are we going to start our diets then?' I currently have a muffin top of a midriff flourishing over the top of my trousers. It's not a good look.

'I'm still eating for two,' Chantal reminds me. 'The only craving I've had is for more and more chocolate.' She grins stupidly. 'How fabulous is that?'

When I get pregnant it would be just my luck to become suddenly repulsed by chocolate and crave nothing but coal dipped in olive oil or cold custard with Gorgonzola cheese on top. That's a scary thought. Maybe my life plan should be to remain child-free.

'I'm going to worry about regaining my figure long after this baby has dropped.' Chantal massages her tummy affectionately. 'In the meantime, bring on the calories!' To prove a point she eats yet another praline with gusto.

Pregnant women are so smug. I wish I was having a baby too then I could eat like a pig too. A chocolate-eating pig.

'I don't need to diet as I haven't actually put on an ounce,' Autumn says piously.

I could begin to despise vegetarians too.

'I've actually lost weight,' Nadia points out.

'Oh.' My spirit sags as I lose my last possible ally. So, looks like it's just me on the fat-free salad from now on. Oh well. One final blast of chocolate before the pain starts won't hurt, will it? No. Of course not. It's actually bad for you to deny the body the things that it most desires. It's scientifically proven. I'm sure I read that somewhere. And my body frequently desires chocolate. Clive's chocolate-chip muffins are currently getting the Lucy Lombard treatment.

'What would you rather give up?' I ask no one in particular. 'Food or chocolate?'

'Food,' Nadia answers without giving it much thought. 'The day I can have an orgasm while eating lettuce, I might change my mind.'

I am *so* with that girl. 'Then would you rather give up sex or chocolate?'

'I've gone off sex,' Chantal admits, and we all recoil slightly. 'Yes, very funny,' she says at our reaction. 'Ted, on the other hand, is mad for it. There's irony in that, right?' She strokes her belly lovingly. 'I don't know what to do with this. Where am I supposed to put it? Yet Ted seems to find the figure of a pregnant woman incredibly sexy.'

'Some men do,' Nadia informs us as the only woman among us who has been there and done that. 'Toby loved it when I was pregnant.' And then her eyes momentarily fill with tears.

'I guess the problems start when you have the figure of a pregnant woman, but you're not.' I stroke my own belly and the moment of sadness is broken by our laughter, once again. 'Very few people find that attractive.' Although I'm sure there are plenty of websites dedicated to those that do.

'I'm just starting to get into sex,' Autumn confesses, a beetroot blush colouring her cheeks. 'I can't believe that it's taken me so long. Addison is a fabulous lover.'

'That's what's commonly known as "too much information", my friend,' I tell her. Addison is having a great influence on Autumn – she's even turned up wearing Lycra today instead of head-to-toe cheesecloth. Surely an improvement? Watch this space – very soon she'll be tucking into bacon sandwiches, wearing leather shoes and voting Tory, you mark my words.

'Sex or chocolate, Nadia?'

'Sex,' Nadia says through lips pursed in deep thought – obviously a trickier one. 'Chocolate. Sex. Chocolate. Definitely sex. No. Chocolate.' She nods her head decisively while munching on some chocolate-coated peanut brittle which Clive is road-testing on us. 'I'll stick with chocolate at the moment, though I'd love to have the choice.'

342

'Maybe if Jacob comes round to lift heavy weights for you as he's promised, then you might not have to wait too long,' I tease. Looking pointedly at Chantal, I add, 'I've heard he's good.'

'He's *great*,' Chantal says, unabashed. 'And I'm the only one here who knows that.'

'You're the only one who could afford him,' I remind her.

'Seriously,' she says, 'there are worse guys around, Nadia. If Jacob wants to come and play power tools at your house then I wouldn't be in a hurry to say no.'

'He's a nice person,' Nadia agrees, 'but it's way too soon for me to be thinking along those lines. It's going to be a long time before I can even look at another man.'

'Stick to chocolate,' I mumble through a mouthful of the stuff. 'You know it makes sense.'

'What would you give up, Lucy?' Nadia asks me in an effort to sway the conversation away from her. 'Crush or chocolate?'

'Chocolate,' I say firmly as if there's no contest.

'Now we know that this is true love!' she replies and Autumn and Chantal laugh.

'Absolutely.' I couldn't have put it better myself. There are some things in life that you might not want to live without – take chocolate, for example – but you know that when push comes to shove, you could. Other things are as necessary to life as breath. I smile to myself. Mr Aiden Holby counts among the necessary. Though I'd prefer it if I could still have chocolate too.

The café is quiet today and some mellow jazz wafts out of the speakers, soothing our souls. When there's a lull in customers, Clive whips off his apron and comes over to join us, settling into the sofa next to Nadia.

'How are my best girls today?'

'Good,' we tell him collectively.

'How are things with you guys?' I ask him.

'Not bad,' he says tentatively. 'We're holding hands again. Playing nicely. Talking things through.'

'I'm glad.' Looks like Clive won't be getting free haircuts and Darren will miss out on some great chocolate. Such is life.

'We have something we both want to ask you.' On cue, Tristan comes out of the back and he's bearing a bottle of chocolate vodka and some shot glasses.

'Oh, yes,' Nadia says enthusiastically as she spies them.

'Isn't this a bit early for vodka? I don't think the sun is over the yardarm yet,' I tell the boys.

'There's no sun because it's February,' Clive points out, 'and I have no idea what a yardarm is.'

'We hope that we're going to be drinking a toast,' Tristan chips in.

I'm intrigued. 'That's vodka all round then,' I say.

Chantal holds up a hand. 'Not for me. Pregnant woman pouring cold water on drinking party.'

'I'll get you some chocolate milk instead,' Tristan says, and heads back to the counter to pour her a glass.

'And some more of that chocolate-covered peanut brittle,' Nadia calls after him.

When he returns, Clive says, 'We're thinking of going to France.' He looks tenderly at Tristan. 'We haven't had a proper holiday since we set up this place. Although it's fun to run, we're both exhausted and now we feel that we need some time for us.'

'Splendid idea,' I say. 'I'll drink to that.' I hold up one of the shot glasses expectantly.

Clive, obligingly, fills it. I knock it back. Then he does the same for the others, before topping up my glass again. He and Tristan exchange an uneasy glance. 'The thing is, Lucy,' he says. 'You know how much we adore you . . .'

'Of course.' I grin stupidly. The drink is starting to talk already.

'We're hoping to go away for a month, maybe longer.'

I shrug happily. 'Sounds fabulous.'

He gives me more vodka. 'And we were hoping that you'd look after Chocolate Heaven for us while we're away.'

'Me?'

'We know how much you love it here and we thought you'd like the challenge.'

344

It would be a challenge. 'I don't know anything about chocolate,' I remind them. 'Except how to eat it in great quantities.'

'We'll give you a crash course before we go,' Clive promises.

A crash course. 'Using the word "crash" in relation to me is
not a good thing,' I warn them.

'You'll be wonderful,' Tristan urges. 'The customers will love
you. We couldn't leave our business in safer hands.'

'I don't know,' I say hesitantly. 'Last time I offered to help out
you were worried that I'd eat my way through your business.'

'We've had a change of heart,' Clive assures me. 'You can do
it. We know you can.'

So they're desperate. But what if I do scoff all of their profits
and they have no business left by the time they return? It's a
distinct possibility.

'Do it,' Chantal urges. 'What have you got to lose?'

'Go on,' Nadia says. 'This is your dream job.'

It is really, isn't it? This could have been what I've been waiting
for all of my life.

'You're a natural,' Autumn adds.

I realise that Clive and Tristan are both holding their breath.

'Guys, this is going to seriously sabotage my diet.'

They both gasp and Clive asks, 'Does that mean you'll do it?'

My face breaks into a grin. 'I guess it does.'

Clive punches the air. 'Yeeessss!' The boys hug each other joyfully.
Then they hug me and cover me with kisses. Let's hope they still
feel like this in a few months' time. Already I need more vodka.

The door opens and Crush walks in just as Clive and Tristan
are detaching themselves from me. 'Thought I'd find you here,
Gorgeous.'

'I have a new job,' I announce brightly.

'Oh?' he says. 'And how are the management at Targa going
to cope without you?'

'Quite well, I should imagine,' I tell him.

'I'll be the judge of that,' he says, as he slips his arms around
me and kisses me warmly.

'Don't you want to know what my fabulous new job is?'

'So now it's a *fabulous* job?'

'It is.' I smile happily at Clive and Tristan. We haven't discussed terms, conditions, pay or anything yet — although I already know what the perks will be. But whatever the deal, I know that I'll be in my element doing this. And I can do it. I can rise to the challenge. How hard can it be? 'I'm going to be running this place while Clive and Tristan are away.'

'That sounds like a match made in heaven.'

'Chocolate Heaven,' I add. 'It's a match made in *Chocolate Heaven*.'

Tristan finds Crush a glass and splashes in some chocolate vodka.

'To Lucy,' Clive says.

My friends and my lover echo, 'To Lucy!'

A lump comes to my throat. What would I do without these people who love me so much? I'm so grateful that I have all the finest things that life has to offer. I lift my glass, 'To good friends, a gorgeous man and great chocolate.'

What more could I possibly want?